AMBUSH

People got off the bus, and others got on. Serena moved to a seat by the exit door, but she could not escape the man staring at her. He changed seats to stay where he could see her.

Red, resentful anger snarled to life in the dark at the back of her mind. She put a leash and muzzle on it, and she got off the bus at the next stop. The peeper stayed on board, but gray anxiety came out of the dark mental den, to bump at her ankles and make her hurry along the sidewalk.

The bus hummed away, and footsteps scuffed somewhere nearby in the thick fog. The small visible patches of empty sidewalk led Serena to the corner, where a streetlamp's hazy cone of light barely reached the ground.

She told herself to stop being paranoid and pulled out her handset to let Naomi know she was going to be late.

Then the phone was dropping from her hand, and the ground came up fast and bounced against her shoulder. A long, disjointed moment later she connected those events to a fiery pain in her lower back. The booted feet and black-clad legs of her attacker were in front of her nose. She looked up. The stun wand in his hand rose again.

Serena let the red, snarling anger off the leash, then crawled into the darkness of her mind to hide while her defender snapped and bit and wreaked bloody havoc on everything it could reach.

FLIGHT PLAN

A STORY OF THE RESTORATION

K. M. HERKES

DAWNRIGGER
Publishing

Electronic Format:

ISBN-10: 1-945745-05-3

ISBN-13: 978-1-945745-05-8

Print Format:

ISBN: 1945745045

ISBN-13: 978-1-945745-041

Second Edition 2016

Dawnrigger Publishing, Illinois USA

Cover art by Nicole Grandinetti using CC0 licensed images from Pixabay users tealyea, ckirner and dschmunis.

Title logo by Niina Cord

Series logo & decorations designed by Rachel Bostwick

DEDICATIONS

Paul, without you I would be only a dreamer, not an author. Your steadfast support made this happen. No dedication, no acknowledgement, no words will ever be sufficient to express my gratitude and love.

Berni, Blynn, Cathy, Dan, Deb, Doug, Emily, Hugh, John, Lisa, Lynn, Susan, Tess—you are all awesome, and I want the world to know it. At various points in the gestation of this novel, each of you offered critical feedback, monumental editing help, necessary encouragement, or pivotal plotting solutions.
Thank you all.

BOOKS BY K. M. HERKES

FLIGHT PLAN

CHAPTER ONE

2 DAYS BEFORE RESTORATION WEEK BEGINS

N AOMI KWAN ARRIVED at work breathless from running the whole block from the bus stop to the clinic. She crossed her fingers and hoped her disastrous lunch hour would remain her little secret. The odds were in her favor for once. The hot sauce stains on her blouse would rinse off, and her first afternoon client wasn't due for another half hour. The tardiness would only be an issue if the clinic receptionist noticed, and Sleepy Susan always took a noon nap when business was slow. The day before the Restoration holiday, everything was running slow, including the buses.

Naomi's spirits sank when she reached the glass front doors of the clinic. Susan wasn't working the front counter. Sourpuss Lucy Ayala was. The clinic director's watery eyes missed nothing, her ability to hold a grudge was unsurpassed, and her soul was as shriveled as her wrinkled face. Naomi lived in fear of accidentally calling her *Sourpuss Lucy* out loud someday.

Right now Lucy's full and doting attention was focused on two men standing with their backs to the door, and Naomi's spirits lifted again, just a little. She had dubbed the pair Wow Guy and

Wired Guy on first meeting them, and their presence might sweeten Lucy's mood enough to prevent disaster.

They were brothers, Carl and Parker Harris respectively, and lean, twitchy Parker was Naomi's client. Carl was big and blond, with hair down to his shoulders in a Viking-wannabe style. His default setting was "charming," and he had a voice as rich and promising as butter melting on a hot griddle. Parker had brown buzzed hair, bright hazel eyes, and a whip-thin body that was always in motion. Both men favored work boots and cotton twill in neutral colors no matter whether San Francisco's fickle weather turned foul or fair, and they looked as out of place in the chrome and pastel clinic as wolves in a tea shop. Lucy was fawning over them. Everyone did.

Naomi was tempted to sneak off and call in sick, but with Restoration break around the corner, Parker wouldn't get another session for a full week. She couldn't let him down, so she scraped up determination and stepped into the reception area.

"Hi, Parker, sorry I'm late," she said. Mustering up a real smile didn't take much effort. "I see you brought your morale officer today. Nervous about your evaluation?"

Parker grinned as he shook his head. Naomi stifled the urge to grin back like a lovesick teenager. Professionalism demanded that she maintain a pleasant but disinterested front with her clients, but Parker made that difficult. A grueling series of surgeries that would have physically wrecked most people had only scraped him down to chiseled essentials, and physical therapy was literally a hands-on job. She stifled her usual reaction to him and said, "Go ahead to my workroom. I'll catch up."

Parker snapped his fingers and headed across the gym with a bounce in his step. He was lucky to have fingers at all. He'd undergone complete replacement of both bones in both forearms, as well as a partial rebuild of left elbow and right wrist. Finger-snapping had been a major milestone.

In eight weeks he'd said fifteen words: seven "Thank you's" and a "Thanks."

Naomi looked up at Carl. "You haven't tagged along like this for a long time. Does he have new questions he wants you to ask for him?"

"No." Carl broke into a wide grin, the kind of smile that made a woman feel like the center of the universe. "Today the issue is transportation rather than communication. We're heading straight from here to the station to grab the up-coast zip train. You weren't late, by the way. We were early."

Naomi was warmed by the reassurance. Carl was one of the nicest people she had ever met. His admiration wasn't sexual, which was a relief. He never commented on her race, remarked on her tiny feet, or stared at her braided, blue-black hair, even though it was long enough to swing at her waist. He also bestowed exactly the same stunning smiles on Lucy. Naomi suspected *charming* was simply his default setting. The kindness felt as impersonal as a crow's attraction to shiny baubles.

As soon as Carl was out of earshot, Lucy hissed, "You *were* late. Why can't you eat lunch in an hour?"

Naomi always swore to herself that she wouldn't make excuses, but she always broke the promise. "I'm sorry, Mams had another meltdown about the stove, plus I had to get a surcharge reversed when I picked up her meds because she's on Subsistence even if I'm not now, and then the first two buses were full."

Lucy pursed her lips in the expression that had inspired her nickname. "There's always a sob story with you. If you want to get ahead, you have to juggle your personal problems on your own time. I needed you here."

One glance at the empty gym floor disproved that claim. The Friday before Restoration was always slow. Patients shifted schedules to clear extra days around the holiday week. There were only three appointments all afternoon, and they were all Naomi's clients.

She bit her tongue. Insubordination would be another black mark she didn't need. "I'm here now."

"Yes, finally. I'm putting the door on buzzer and trusting you to check in your own clients. Don't screw it up." Lucy reached under the counter and came up with an intern's jacket in one hand. "Put this on. Your shirt is filthy. Can't you even eat like a civilized person?"

Naomi held her breath until she had spots in her vision. Then she let it out in a rush. There was no shame in wearing a Subsistence uniform, but she'd paid for the right to *not* wear it, paid with six years of back-breaking labor and six more as an indentured apprentice.

"I will work naked first," she said before she could stop herself. "Fire me if you want, but I will never wear Sub-issue again." Her heart thumped fast in her chest. She needed this job, but there were some indignities she could not endure.

Lucy only made her Sourpuss face again and folded the jacket away. "Don't get snippy with me. I was trying to be nice. If you'd rather look like a pig, that's your business."

"I'm—I'm sorry." Naomi choked on the apology. "I can't."

"You should be sorry. Make it up to me." Lucy tapped the workstation screen. "Certify Parker Harris as 'ready to resume.' I checked his chart. He has good muscle tone, decent rotation, and adequate grip strength. Pronation and supination are almost up to par. Move him on. I expected you to drop him the second week."

"I know you did. That isn't the point." Naomi kept her tone even. Admitting her anger and frustration would only give Lucy ammunition to use against her.

Parker had gone through five therapists in three clinics before landing in Naomi's hands. She had been given a potentially disastrous assignment for the same reason she got the worst schedule and received reprimands for every minor transgression: the clinic couldn't bring in a new Subsistence intern until a job opened up. She had been set up to fail, but she had succeeded instead.

Working with Parker was challenging on a professional level and satisfying on a personal one, and she wasn't about to give him up without a fight.

"The point," she said, "is that he isn't ready to resume normal routine. I know you've seen the commando tats across his shoulders when he works with weights. Good, adequate, and almost are not his normal. There's a reason we have a progressive skills list."

"Naomi, he isn't safe." Lucy glanced around as if afraid of being overheard. "He has no service record to go with those Combined Forces tattoos, which means his file was sealed, which means black ops. They are both dangerous, mark my words. We don't need their kind of trouble following them in here. Write him off. Please."

The plea stunned Naomi speechless. Parker's permanent ink collection also included a discharge date nearly a decade old. He'd been assaulted or lost a fight, nothing more exotic or mysterious than that. He and Carl were electrical contractors, and construction could be a rough business off the worksites as well as on them.

Naomi saw no diplomatic way to tell Lucy that she sounded paranoid, so she said, "Let's see how I feel about the idea after the evaluation."

"Did I ask you how you felt? If you won't step up, then I'll do it myself when I get back from Restoration break. Send his eval to me with a priority flag. And don't even think about sneaking out early. I'll check the time code."

Two full minutes passed after her departure before Naomi's hands stopped shaking. She rubbed her left wrist to ease the tense, aching muscles and went to tend to her patient.

PARKER WAS PERCHED on the worktable in the center of the room, swinging his feet while he did fingertip touches. Carl sat in the visitor's chair stationed inside the open door, next to Naomi's desk. He was slouched back with his arms folded across his chest, and he delivered a warm smile as Naomi came in. She stepped over his outstretched legs and stopped. Doubts bubbled up.

Carl had a stiff manner that made even slumped shoulders and casual clothes look formal. He also had scars under those tightly buttoned cuffs and that high shirt collar. Naomi had seen them on occasion. Careless gestures sometimes revealed thin lines of skin paler than the rest.

"Lucy has a loud voice," Carl said. "And the door was open. I can guess what you're wondering."

Naomi shifted her gaze from his sleeves to his face. The smile was gone, replaced by an irritated scowl. Embarrassment heated Naomi's cheeks. "I'm sorry. I guess paranoia is contagious. Should I be worried?"

"You're in no danger from us." Carl's voice was as flat as his face was expressive.

She sighed. "Not what I meant. Should I be worried about you two? Someone tried to cripple Parker. Are they going to try again? Was that how you got hurt? If you got sucked into something illegal, I might be able—"

"No, we're in no danger." Carl extended one arm so that his wrist showed clearly, displaying pale slashes that were older and more numerous than Naomi had realized. "There was trouble, but it's over and done. These are from a work accident ages ago. Unrelated."

His smile came back. For once it looked sincere. "Thank you, though, for caring enough to ask. Compassion is a precious commodity, and you're generous with yours."

"The more you give away, the more there is to go around." Naomi moved to Parker and patted his leg in the usual signal for getting started. The man growled at her. Like an angry tomcat or a dog in a fight, he *growled*. The sound sent prickles up Naomi's spine and raised the hair on her arms.

She kept her hand on Parker's leg and pondered the antagonism. The gist of it was *why bother?* Evaluation hurt if done right, and he'd overheard Lucy's plan to cut short his rehab.

"Trust me," Naomi said.

Parker scowled at her sidelong, then snorted before he lifted one shoulder. Naomi responded by tugging at his collar. He shrugged out of the shirt. After a pause for aesthetic appreciation, Naomi focused on her job.

Nearly an hour later, she hopped onto the worktable beside Parker and entered her notations into a datapad so he could watch. Small steady gains were recorded. Orders were issued to continue sessions on the same schedule, with a new evaluation in two weeks.

The report went straight to the federal database under Naomi's ID and biometric seal. She waited for confirmation from the clinic, and then she savored the possibility of Lucy suffering a stroke when she saw it. The director kept forgetting that Naomi had a full license now. Once again, being overlooked would work to her benefit.

Parker's breath puffed out in a satisfied little chuckle, and he sat with his eyes shut and shoulders drooping while cold packs and wraps were applied. Naomi encouraged him to lie flat on the table. Ten minutes later he'd dozed off during a basic cool-down massage.

Naomi collected Carl with a glance and followed him out to the gym.

"I will never get used to that," Carl said once the workroom door was shut. "You barely ever say a word, and he relaxes enough to fall asleep in an unsecured location. He never does that."

"Silence is restful for a lot of people. Could you tag along for his next appointment too? The continuance is guaranteed, but Lucy may assign him to another therapist. They might need a go-between, the way I did at first."

"Monday after next, one o'clock, right? I'll be there." Carl tipped his head to one side, and the smile turned wry. "He can talk perfectly well, you know, when he thinks it's worth the effort. You won't lose him. He won't allow it."

A bell chimed loudly several times in quick succession. Naomi jumped, Carl ducked slightly, and a second later the door to the workroom banged open. At one side of the opening, Parker stood shirtless and unencumbered by cold packs. He flexed his right hand and made a fist.

"What the fuck?" he asked.

That made eighteen words, now. Naomi struggled to keep her smile from showing. "It's only my next client. My sessions overlap today. Finish your rest interval. I'll open the toy box for you as soon as I get him settled."

She unlocked the glass entrance door, and Amar Hussein made his way inside, still awkward on the replacement for the foot he'd lost to infected ulcers. He frowned at the empty gym, and his white moustache bristled at the sight of Carl and Parker.

"Who are they?" he asked in a loud voice he thought was a whisper. "The door was locked. Are you in trouble?"

Amar liked to distract himself from the rigors of adapting to his new prosthetic by telling Naomi what he called "old man stories." Every week she heard a new adventure about pre-Restoration militia actions. Now he pulled his hunched spine straight and stepped in front of her like a grizzled guard dog.

Naomi tucked her arm through his. "No trouble, Amar. They're my clients too, just like you are. Honest workmen and brothers."

"They don't look alike."

"Lots of people don't." There was no mystery to the lack of resemblance. Parker's medical file held an adoption flag just like Naomi's did. She led Amar into the gym area. "Come on, Colonel. Let's get to work."

He laughed at the nickname, as he always did, and a few minutes of effort saw him walking on the treadmill with a mirror program that helped him adjust his stride. Naomi kept an eye on Parker's occupational exercises while she coached Amar. Carl played with a phone handset and offered mockery and encouragement to his brother in equal measures. It ended up being a pleasant hour.

"Your old friend has a point about security," Carl said after Amar left, while Parker was cleaning up. "Transit goes to the holiday schedule at five. How late are you working? Can we offer you a ride home? We have a car for business."

"I won't finish here until nearly six." People with enough money to own automobiles did not give free rides to people like her. She gave him a polite escape. "That's a long time to wait. What about your train?"

"We can catch a later one. It's the least we can do to show our gratitude. Please, don't say no."

That smile was hard to resist. Parker's puppy-dog stare was even more persuasive. Then he added four whole words. "Want you home safe," he said.

Naomi satisfied pride by making them drop her off at the edge of the housing complex. Caution made her watch her surroundings once they drove off. The usual loiterers and loungers were out, but no one accosted her or even jeered at her for getting a ride from rich men.

A thin woman in a worn yellow bathrobe was toddling unsteadily along the sidewalk outside Naomi's apartment building. Naomi's heart skipped a beat. She sprinted the last fifty meters and grabbed the woman by the shoulders. "Mams, what are you doing outside?"

"There's my selfish daughter." Her mother's cheeks crinkled up around a smile. "You bad girl. You ran away from chores and lessons again. I heard you playing outside."

The woman's ratty hair was still black and thick, but the disease that was killing her seemed to add years to her skin even as it stole her vitality and destroyed her mind. Brown shriveled hands softly patted Naomi's arms. "Ah, but I found you. So happy. Now I'm tired."

She sat down on the dirty curb and started rocking. Naomi knelt and embraced her mother's fragile body. "Oh, Mams. I'm so sorry." There was no telling what the woman had heard. Dozens of children lived in their building. "I never should've left you alone. I'll find someone to sit with you full-time from now on. Let's go inside now."

"No. I want to sit. My feet hurt." She grew agitated, plucking at Naomi's shirt and hair. Naomi undid the lower half of her braid to make stroking it easier. Some things couldn't be rushed. Mams was one of them.

Tires crunched over debris on the street, and doors slammed. Naomi spun to her feet and turned, braced for the worst. Only people with money had cars. Nice people with money didn't visit this neighborhood.

Carl stepped back, hands raised, and nearly stepped on Parker behind him. "Hey, sorry. I didn't mean to frighten you. It's only us again. You took off like a rabbit. What's wrong?"

"Nothing."

"Nothing," Carl repeated, eyebrows raised. "Nothing looks a lot like a homeless woman holding you by the hair. Are you sure you don't need help?"

Naomi gave up on the hope of getting away without introduction. "This is my mother. Mams, meet Carl and Parker Harris. Carl, Parker, meet Hong Mei."

Mams stopped petting Naomi's hair and subjected Carl to a disapproving examination. "Big round-eye, isn't he?"

Parker edged into view behind his brother, and Mams clambered to her feet. "Are you stupid, Naomi? Why are you with two big bully-boys? Come inside safe."

"Yes, Mams." Naomi gave Carl an apologetic look as she was tugged along the sidewalk. "I'm so sorry. She doesn't mean it. It's dementia. We're fine, thank you. She needs supper, that's all. I have a friend coming to help."

Carl didn't take the hint to leave. He held open the door, and Parker offered his arm to Mams. To Naomi's shock, she accepted it. Both men came up the elevator, and Parker helped Mams make her slow, awkward way to their tiny apartment, while she babbled nonsense at him. Naomi wondered what they would do if she sat down on the floor and burst into tears. Humiliation warred with gratitude.

"She doesn't look well," Carl said quietly, watching Parker seat Mams at the table. "Dementia, you said?"

Mams demanded her mah-jongg tiles, and Parker set them out according to her querulous instructions. Naomi sank down on the couch where she slept and pushed aside the blankets she never had the energy to fold.

"She's dying." The bitter words spilled out. Her mother was only sixty-three, and she was dying. "She fell and cut herself, and something got into the scrape. A battlefield bug, not a plague, thankfully."

Microscopic weapons from the years of chaos before Restoration still lurked in pockets of disaster all over the world. The original version of this mutated monster would have killed in hours or days. Mams was still clinging to life after three years. "We still have some good days together. It could've been worse. It could've been another Omaha."

When the doctors had delivered their diagnosis, after two days of quarantined terror, Mams had wept with relief that the death toll would stop at one. Naomi had bawled herself sick from less complicated grief. She didn't care about strangers. She cared about losing Mams.

Public Health cared. Omaha had lost half a million people to a war-plague outbreak. After Mams' diagnosis, quarantine crews incinerated everything within ten meters of where she had fallen, rebuilt the affected building wall and trucked in sterilized soil. People planted flowers there now, some seasons.

After a long pause, Carl said, "A thousand deaths or one, it's equally tragic. I'm sorry."

Mams spoke up. "I like the quiet one, Naomi. He's polite."

"He really isn't," Carl said, but he smiled. "Stop flirting, brother mine. Time to go."

Parker kissed Mams' hand, which made her giggle, and then he shoved his way past Carl at the door, knocking the taller man off balance. Carl laughed and followed him out.

Naomi closed her eyes to hold in a drowning tide of emotions that she could not allow herself to feel. When she looked into the hall, they were gone and the stairwell door was swinging shut.

She went to get supper ready.

CARL SLOUCHED DOWN behind the steering column of the rental car, but it was not a comfortable fit, no matter how tightly he tucked his elbows and knees. "It's getting late," he said. "At this point we won't hit Seattle until Sunday night. If we end up missing Alison and Justin's big Remembrance party, I'm blaming you. Are you ready to face the consequences of disappointing Alison?"

Parker continued watching the street. They knew from their taps on Naomi's phone that she was expecting her friend Serena, and Parker didn't want to leave until the woman was safely settled in. Carl said, "Ask nicely with words."

"Wait, please? Bad neighborhood."

"Watching won't change that." Carl squirmed. His elbow cracked into the door. "Too bad we can't escort Serena to Naomi's door. Have I mentioned how much I hate lying to people for a living?"

"Yes." Parker sighed. "Please, Carl."

"Fine." Carl killed time checking the data downloads he'd

collected earlier while Parker worked with Naomi. He soon found good news. "The illegal funds transfer is hidden in the clinic's monthly balance sheets again. When we go back for your first session after break I'll pull the recorders and alert the Bureau so they can make the arrests."

"Jail's too damned good for Lucy Ayala," Parker said.

"And that attitude is exactly why we're spending Restoration break a thousand klicks from temptation, where you can do nothing to jeopardize a nice, legal arrest that will get us paid."

Parker wanted blood. In his eyes, smuggling drugs and framing an innocent to cover her own crimes were the least of their target's crimes. Watching week after week of harassment was wearing down his limited patience. Naomi had first gotten through to him therapeutically, but she'd gotten under his skin personally too.

Carl said, "Don't expect tearful gratitude when you break cover. She's a forgiving soul, but she might never trust you, after this."

Parker's sigh was a worried plea for advice. After a moment's thought, Carl said, "You're on the right track with her mother. Be useful to the people she does trust, and be patient. This environment doesn't reward risk takers."

The ranked blocks of high-rise apartments were not as depressing as some Subsistence zones Carl had visited. Rooftop gardens looked green and thriving, and piled debris from demolition on older buildings had been cleared for community space. Children were shrieking and playing outside in the foggy gloom. The predatory inhabitants of the area lurked in doorways and down alleys, posing and preening for each other while they eyed passersby for weakness that would mark potential prey.

Parker sat up straight in his seat as a tall, brunette woman in skimpy shorts and a torn shirt hopped down from an arriving bus. Serena Nguyen had arrived. She made it past the loitering crowd with a minimum of confrontation, but she was visibly agitated when she reached Naomi's apartment. Carl switched on the surveillance bugs he and Parker had placed there two months earlier.

Serena cried herself hoarse and pounded on a perfectly innocent wall until her knuckles were bloodied. A long hug and a shoulder rub from Naomi reduced her to quiet sobs and mumbled apologies. Given that the woman had been discharged from the Combined Armed Forces for episodes of "intermittent explosive disorder," the only surprise was how quickly she calmed under Naomi's care.

Parker growled, watching the scenario unfold. He hated retreating when he felt needed.

Carl said, "You can't help anyone tonight without compromising the case. We can still make the 2 a.m. train. That gets us into Seattle early Sunday evening. We'll miss the speeches at Justin's party, but we might escape Alison's wrath. That's my advice. It's your call. Stay or go."

"Go," Parker said after a surly pause.

Carl headed for the train station.

REMEMBRANCE

RESTORATION DAY 1

Begin by remembering we destroyed ourselves. Remember how pride, selfishness, and anger threw this country and all the world into chaos. Remember and honor those who gave the last full measure of devotion to the resurrection of this great nation. Remember those who came before you. They made Restoration happen. You will make it succeed. Each of us must be steadfast in our loyalty if our new union is to long survive

—A Young Citizen's Guide to Restoration Week

CHAPTER TWO

L ATE ON THE FIRST day of Restoration Week, Serena Nguyen's datapad screen flashed to an image of children smiling up at a boldly colored banner of the words, "Your Citizenship Calendar!" She blinked and wondered how long she'd been staring. Her eyes felt gritty.

The happy children and the clock display glowed in the evening gloom. Six-fourteen. Serena set aside the device to turn on a light. Guilt flared up. She had planned to confirm her end-of-month bill payments first thing in the morning, but bad old memories had crowded up when she saw the date, and then she'd noticed the dead plants on her windowsill.

That made her cry because she knew she would only screw up the other chores the way she'd bungled caring for them. She'd cried until she ran out of tears, and then she'd buried herself in stories and lessons from long-gone happy times when the world made sense. Now it was six in the evening, she'd missed the bank payment cutoff time, and she'd done nothing useful to balance out that miserable failure.

A howling void yawned open in her mind, ready to suck her down. If she burned down the building, no one would care about the unpaid bills. If she sat there until she died of thirst, her shame about the plants and all her other problems would wither away.

"Remembrance," she recited desperately. "Duty. Courage. Sacrifice. Faith. Commitment. Hope. Hold the principles celebrated on these days close to your heart, and you will never fail."

The litany pushed aside the chaos, and a new emotion crept out to gnaw gently at her thoughts. The apathy growled like a big black dog eager for playtime and cuddling. Serena gave it a mental hug and burrowed deeper into the couch with it. Numbness was a comfortable, reliable defense against the deeper darkness. When nothing mattered, there was no need to lash out.

She could be strong. Life had thrown her plenty of horrible twists, and she had coped with all of them. She tried to remember that, when the world overwhelmed her and she had to scream and howl until the pressure eased. She had failed at the only career she ever wanted, her family had rejected her, and then in a crowning blow from fate she'd been buried alive after the biggest earthquake in a century. She had been strong enough to survive all that, in the four months before her twenty-second birthday. Life couldn't be as hard as it felt.

Rude food servers and assholes who groped her tits on the street shouldn't leave her shaking with rage. She'd made peace with far worse indignities. A broken door handle or a missed bus shouldn't reduce her to helpless fits of sobbing. She hadn't cried once, lying trapped and alone under a pile of rubble. She should be stronger, but on bad days the tears and the boiling anger were stronger.

Sometimes bad days turned into bad weeks. Sometimes her strength ebbed, and the hard, noisy brightness of life hurt so much that she had to hide herself away from it all.

She'd been hiding a lot lately. The floor was covered in garbage and dirty clothes. Serena kicked things aside and took a wander through the apartment. The kitchen was filthy. The bathroom was unspeakable. She'd insisted that she could take care of herself without help, but she was failing yet again. She couldn't even pay her own bills without confusing herself.

Her mood growled at the rising darkness again. She didn't care about the accounts. They could wait. Everything could wait. Nothing mattered.

Serena growled back at the apathy. *Not this time*, she told it. She was in charge, not her bleak, destructive emotions. She pictured herself buckling the black dog into a harness with spikes and a studded leather collar and tied it up inside her skull. Determination ran along her spine on shivery little feet, and she shook herself into action. Enough was enough. One step at a time. Later was now. She would cope. She could be strong again.

First she deleted all the unanswered messages and calls waiting in her account. Then she opened the windows to let in fresh air. Fog was rolling off San Francisco Bay, and the damp breeze smelled amazing and fresh. She took one deep breath, and another, and then the phone chimed.

The sound jarred her nerves. She froze. The call forwarded from the broken wall unit to the handset buried under junk on the table, then to the nearby datapad. The chime sounded like an accusation. By the time Serena worked up the nerve to face it, the noise had stopped, and a message flag lit the screen. She braced herself and hit playback. One call. She could handle one call.

Naomi Kwan's face popped up: round cheeks, pointed chin, and shiny black eyes that scrunched up into happy commas when she laughed. She laughed a lot, despite having a job that meant working every day with patients who had suffered horrible injuries. Helping people heal made her happy, she said, as if a little happiness made up for a boss who undermined her and barely earning enough money to keep off Subsistence. Serena wasn't in a position to judge anyone else's choices, though, so she could hardly argue.

Naomi's image didn't look happy today. Her message said, "Hey, Serena Ballerina. You're late. I'm leaving for Fiorello's without you. Like it or not, we're partying. That was the whole point of getting fresh STI vaccines and prophylactics. Our whole Service Unit gang is at the restaurant. Meet us in an hour, or brace yourself for a hostile incursion. Intervention. Whatever. Life blows. Suck it up. I've given you a month of independent living. You were a mess Friday. If you can't hold yourself together, you'll have to move back with me and Mams."

The message ended, and Naomi's grumpy face went still. The image-freeze caught her in the act of petting her absurdly long hair. Serena rubbed a thumb across the screen to pet it. Naomi was right as always. This was no night to stay home. It was the start of party week. She could do it for Naomi's sake.

The bathroom was too filthy to face taking a shower. A splash in the kitchen sink took care of essentials. Serena admired the new medical tattoos she'd already forgotten she and Naomi had gone to get on Friday, and she dressed in the cleanest clothes she could find. Then she was ready to head out, ready to visit with old friends and make new ones.

She should've known it wouldn't work out.

As night fell, the weather took a turn towards awful. The fog off the Bay grew from drifting veils to a thick soupy mass that stuck to her lungs and skin, and the bus was late. When she finally climbed aboard and dropped into her seat, she was sopping wet and miserable, and the black-dog mood was getting powerful enough to make her hands numb. She stared at the misty window glass. Her image stared blankly back: dark eyes set at a slant in an oval shadow of face, mouth a thin line, hair a clinging mop of wet black strands. She looked like the big miserable lump she was.

The black dog was not visible in her reflection, but she could feel it inside. It was as real as anything else in her mind, and that intrigued her. She had suffered bouts of depression all her life, and the last five years had been hellish, but she'd never had an apathy dog until now. For all she knew, she might have a whole kennel in her head.

Caring for her own private pack of metaphors might be fun. She could take them on walks and scare the neighbors. The thought made her reflection smile.

People got on the bus, and others left. One man kept staring at Serena. She switched to the seat by the exit door. He changed seats to stay where he could see her. And Serena discovered that Black Dog had at least one pack mate. Red, resentful anger snarled to life inside her skull and stalked forward. Red Dog grumbled and growled about blood, and it begged to snap and bite and cause damage. Serena muzzled it and got off the bus at the next stop. Gray anxiety came out of the dark next, to bump at her ankles and make her hurry along.

The peeper stayed on board. Serena watched him and struggled to keep her grip on both the gray hyperactive wariness and its more vicious red friend. Black Dog retreated, giving her space to think.

The bus hummed away. Footsteps scuffed in the thick darkness down the block. Serena looked all around at the lights of passing traffic and her small visible patch of empty sidewalk. The corner streetlamp's hazy cone of light barely reached the ground.

She saw no one. Nothing.

Depressed *and* paranoid now. "Fabulous," she said, and bit her lip because talking to herself was not a sign of sanity. Whiny self-pity was a tiny useless yappy thing that had been dyed blue and belonged in a purse. Serena laughed at it as she stuffed it away into its den and felt better about herself for some obscure reason.

The names on the street sign were unfamiliar. She pulled out her handset to find out how close she was to the restaurant and called to warn Naomi that she was going to be late. "Hey, Bao-bao. I'm lost, but I'm coming, I swear. I'm at the corner—"

Then the phone was dropping from her hand, and the ground came up fast and bounced against her shoulder. A long, disjointed moment later she connected those events to a fiery pain in her lower back. Her eyes focused on the booted feet and the black-clad legs of her attacker. She could see the stun wand in his hand, rising up for another strike.

She let Red Dog off the leash and hid in the dark while it wreaked snarling havoc. The dark was warm and safe. She only came out of hiding when Red Dog snuffled at her and nudged her out of the way because it was tired and ready to rest.

She was on her knees in an alley between two buildings, and her hands were slick with blood and water. She took a breath, and sore muscles pinched. Her right foot hurt. The shoe sat three meters away, lying next to her fallen opponent. A second man was sprawled motionless a few steps further into the foggy shadows.

Serena crawled to where her phone lay in a puddle, leaned against a wet brick wall and called Naomi with fingers that left red smears on the screen. No one answered.

No one answered, and no one answered, and when the black dog whined, Serena unclipped its leash and let it lay itself warm and loving across her lap.

CHAPTER THREE

ALISON GREGORIO WAS JUST beginning to relax and enjoy the biggest must-attend Remembrance event in Seattle when her boss decided to climb onto the buffet table.

The big chandelier lights had recently dimmed from admire-the-expensive-food to flatter-the-inebriated, and most people had abandoned their assigned tables to socialize in standing groups. The party was large enough to fill a huge room decorated in bland coordinating colors, and conversations drowned out a low sound-track of recorded music. Servers scrambled to keep coffee cups and wine glasses filled, and the buffet showed the depredations of a pleased and satiated crowd.

Justin Wyatt, one of the richest people in the world before his retirement at the ripe age of thirty-five, got to his feet between the remains of a cheese plate and a big silver salad bowl and beckoned to Alison. She offered up the glass of beer Justin had handed to her earlier, and she gave him a meaningful look that said *Why can't you stick to the plan?*

Justin answered with a tipsy smile. *Plans change.*

He was scheduled to make official announcements in half an hour, before the band arrived and the dancing began. The podium was being set up on the dais in front of the long VIP table where they had recently finished their meal.

Alison could have brought up those points, but she saved her breath. Justin had made up his mind to give his speech standing on the buffet, and there would be no talking him out of it. She stood back and let him do his thing.

More and more of the elegantly dressed guests began watching their host sway in place while he inspected the clarity of his beer. He was not very tall and not very stable on his bad leg, and his chosen attire of tan cargo pants and a black flannel shirt stood out in a room filled with tuxedos and gowns.

Over the course of the evening, Alison had taken more snapshots of the contrast between him and other guests than was strictly polite. He had agreed to a haircut and a late shave, so his dark wavy hair was neat and his face smooth, but the best that could be said about his outfit was that it was clean.

At least Justin's partner had dressed up for the occasion. Tyler Burke was unusually well-groomed and looked sharp in his charcoal-gray formal wear. He bent down to whisper in Alison's ear, "Nice dramatic touch, but he'll ruin the whole effect if he falls off the table and lands on his face."

"This isn't my idea, surfer-boy." Alison had to resist the urge to comb Tyler's sandy blond hair out of the way so she could see the twinkle in those sky-blue eyes better. "You're younger and bigger than me. You stop him."

Tyler snorted. "No, thanks. He might hit me with those fists of steel, and that might kill me. Besides, I know why he's clocking out early. I saw Carl and Parker before he did. I'm not standing between them and Justin. They shoot people. Well, Parker does. And they're both bigger than me."

He waved to the pair of tall men standing near the door to the ballroom. Parker offered a lazy salute in return. His cropped brown hair and alert demeanor set him apart from the other guests as much as the tan utilitarian clothes he wore, and his companion made an even more memorable impression.

Carl was a head taller than most of the guests swirling around him, and his crisp black shirt and slacks made a sharp contrast against pale skin and shaggy blond hair. He nodded back to Tyler before returning his attention to Justin.

Justin had finished the beer and was watching foam slide down the sides of the glass while he waited for more people to notice him. One by one, conversations hushed to whispers.

"He's making me nervous," Alison admitted.

"It's one of his many talents," Tyler said. "What are we all going to do if he tells everyone that he's leaving on a journey and disappears at the end of the speech?"

Alison laughed and put her arm around Tyler's waist. "Count on you to see that possibility. He would never do that. He's impatient, not cruel. Besides, it isn't his birthday."

Tyler beamed at her for catching the reference to one of his many fiction-based obsessions, and Alison tightened her grip on him. No one who put the job title of "Loyal Sidekick" on his tax forms and listed his office as a "SuperSecret Science Facility" could ever be taken seriously, but Tyler did add zest to life.

Once the room quieted to his satisfaction, Justin lifted his empty glass and bestowed the tipsy smile on the room at large. "It's customary to toast the excuse for this party before anyone passes out," he announced in a soft, hoarse voice. "And I won't last much longer. Here's to the forty-fourth birthday of this incarnation of these United States, and may the current edition last longer than the original. Restoration Week, Day One, everyone!"

He waited out the applause until the crowd went back to watching him, then said, "Speeches bore me, so I'll skip to the punch line: the Dawnstar Foundation thanks you for your generosity. Enjoy chatting with the tame scientists the board invited tonight. You'll see where the money goes. That's it. No, wait. There was one other thing …"

He smiled down at Tyler and Alison, but she saw the hint of fear under the joking mask. "Biovitel," she prompted him in a whisper, hoping it was enough.

Seconds slid past. Alison was reaching into her purse for Justin's notes when he raised his hand again. "Ah, yes. You'll all be pleased to hear that Biovitel Innovations' first patents passed their Fed certification before the Restoration break."

The room went dead silent. Justin gave everyone a grin. "None of you have heard of them? Well, Biovitel's chief research officer is here tonight, along with their team leaders, so get acquainted. They took a shot at chip-rot resistance from the biotech side and hit a solid bulls-eye. Dawnstar has been their exclusive sponsor for over a decade, but with the approvals they can start courting investors and bring forty years of cybernetic stagnation to an end."

The applause this time was deafening. Justin soaked it up with that wide smile holding firm the whole time. He had founded Dawnstar specifically to underwrite quixotic research with low success probabilities, and Biovitel's mission qualified. The self-sustaining nanoweapon called chip-rot was generally considered to be as unbeatable as it was pervasive.

The first pandemic had nearly destroyed every industry that relied on electronics, and regional epidemics still came and went every few years. The elusive contagion was mutable, degrading specific compounds in one outbreak, sequestering rare earth elements in another, eating critical alloys in the next. Developers continually countered its effects with new designs and materials, but resistance wasn't immunity, and the cost of maintaining basic services had crippled innovation.

Excitement wasn't the unanimous reaction to Justin's announcement. Alison saw several people cast glances at the biohazard sensors prominently mounted next to smoke and radiation detectors, and someone muttered, "As long as the cure isn't worse than the disease."

Prejudice would be one of several major challenges still facing

Biovitel. Genetic manipulation had caused far more horrific biological disasters than chip-rot during the decades of chaos that preceded Restoration. All but a few lines of genetic research were banned on a global scale, and even fewer projects were allowed practical application. Federal production approval was an epic endorsement.

The noise fell to a murmur yet again, and Justin's smile sobered to a look of quiet pride. "Your contributions do change the world. Remember that. That's why we saved the announcement for tonight. What better time than Restoration to announce a new Renaissance? Enjoy the rest of the evening, everyone."

His dismount was performed to a patter of claps and a rising mutter of excitement. It wasn't graceful, but he didn't fall on his face, and Tyler and Alison retreated with him to one of the unoccupied tables.

Justin groaned as he sat down. "That was grueling. Next time Manny Bannerjee needs a favor, say no. Put it on the list with Helen whining for an escort when her other ex backs out of social obligations. I'm going to show my new toys to Carl and Parker now."

"Not until you say hello to the rest of the people who want to meet you." Alison squeezed his hand. "I turned down a third plea from Helen about her Hope Night event this Saturday, but Manny does a great job managing Dawnstar for you. A public appearance was hardly too much to ask."

"Fantastic. I am officially a circus act. 'Meet Justin Wyatt, infamously reclusive inventor! Pay a jillion dollars a plate to hear him say Important Things!' " Justin slumped in his chair. "Imagine their reaction to the real freaky stuff. Should I climb back onto the table and go invisible for them? Get it out once and for all?"

Tyler choked on the drink he'd been sipping. Justin looked at him sidelong. "Relax, boy genius, I'm joking. I wouldn't steal Gina's thunder like that. She gave me a Biovitel prototype to play with."

Gina was Gina Hiyabusa, Biovitel's CEO and driving force behind the start-up's success. Alison said, "Gina and Manny will both be at the big Bootstrap Fund event on Saturday too. Are you sure I can't convince you to attend? It would give you a chance to push Biovitel to most of the West Coast corporate top tier, and it would throw Helen a bone. You are contractually obligated to give her two public events a year."

"Not that one. Too risky." Justin put his arm over Alison's shoulder, stroking bare skin with his thumb. "I would ask someone how they justify donating to a charity when they never promote anyone off Subsistence, and Helen would stab me. That would make great headline. 'Reclusive Inventor Stabbed To Death By Ex-Wife.' No, thank you." He coiled Alison's hair around one finger. "I'll escort her to a premiere or something neutral. Those are fine. I get a kick out of watching people fumble over me. Tonight I learned 'That's quite a tan' means 'I didn't recognize you.' "

Alison moved his hand to more neutral territory. "I hope you didn't deny it was sun exposure. You're still eight kilos under your pre-crash weight. If you say it's a skin condition they'll think you're dying."

Justin gave his glass a guilty frown, which meant that Alison would be getting a worried call from someone soon. She said, "And you need to take this seriously. The networking is important. Attending parties like this keeps people from bothering you the rest of the time. You pay me to be your business manager. I do know what I'm doing."

Justin pulled away from her and tossed back the rest of his beer. "You're my life manager," he said, slurring the words. "And to prove how much I appreciate you, I'll finish the dancing bear routine before I make my escape. First, I should rescue Parker before someone gets hurt."

He nodded at one of the tables near the entrance, where a redhead in a gold outfit had cornered Parker. The conversation was one-sided. "That does look dangerous," Alison said. "What happened to Carl?"

"He got a call while I was being pompous. It looked urgent." Justin stood up. "Here I go. Wish me luck."

He meandered through conversations towards Parker, leaving laughter and shaking heads in his wake. Alison smiled at Tyler. "See? He won't run away from us. He's impatient, that's all."

Tyler rattled the ice in his empty glass. "He isn't really sloshed, is he? It's a bluff to keep people from noticing when his brain hiccups."

"Right. Even when he doesn't go blank he still loses track of details and names and gets panicky. Intoxication is a good cover."

"I should've known. He never gets drunk."

"Yes, he does. You should've seen him this time last year. He was unconscious by sundown."

"I spent Restoration break in Alaska last year, remember? Visiting my cousins plus trying to find our crash site and the rest of that experimental crap that got into his leg wound. Plus, you know, the bodies. For burying." Tyler ran aground there and pushed off with, "So, he gets drunk on Remembrance?"

"No, it's the date, not the day. Last year, Remembrance was a devastating hangover. Forewarned is forearmed, so this year I didn't leave him enough free time today for him to crawl into a bottle."

"What date? Oh." Tyler's blue eyes went wide. "Damn, I'm dense. The Clooney & Associates thing was two years ago, wasn't it? When Justin's second wife and your lawyer friends blew up? There was a story this morning. A news thing. A couple of them. I'm sorry."

"Me too." Alison reined in the impulse to critique the clumsiest expression of sympathy ever. Tyler was fairly well socialized for someone who spent most of his waking hours buried in math equations. The problem was that he spent the rest of those hours in the woods or in front of an entertainment screen and looked more like a ski bum than a physicist.

Alison restarted the conversation. "I thought you'd figured it out already. You teased Justin about the puffy eyes when we got here. He and I went to the memorial this afternoon."

Tyler shrugged. "I notice he's glum, I yank his chain, he smiles. He's cranky most days. I didn't make the connection. Teasing is our default mode."

"Well, all the guilt piled onto political chatter makes him extra cranky, and he'll get worse as the week goes on. Do not get him started on cutting back the Civilian Security Bureau budget or splitting the Combined Armed Forces. Don't even *think* about using the phrases 'New Senate' or 'Constitutional Referendum' around him."

"I already told him no politics and no work until we start a new project next week. I'm finally getting a handle on the architecture of those power cells of his, you know. It's sort of like a pumped storage system for electromagnetism, if that makes sense."

"Not a bit, but artistic composition bewilders you, so we're even. Let's not talk too much work." Alison leaned over to give him a peck on the cheek. "He relies on us. Be extra there for him for a while, that's all I'm asking. Please?"

"Sure, Allie. Of course I will. I'd hand you my beating heart if you asked for it like that."

The statement came out on a tremor of raw emotion, not a dry sarcastic twist to be heard. He'd meant that, and not as a joke. Alison composed her face to hide her surprise. "That has to be the sweetest and the grossest thing anyone's ever said to me, all in one sentence."

Tyler looked away, blushing. "Look at that," he said a moment later. "Dancing bear to the rescue. Is the surprise visit from the dynamic duo part of your cheer-up-Justin plan?"

Justin had rescued Parker from the clutches of the redhead

and pulled him into a corner. They looked alike in many ways. Justin's wiry body was a darker, smaller version of the other man's athletic build, and both of them had guarded expressions, sharp eyes, and hands that never stopped moving. When Justin began to mingle again, he brought Parker along like an aggressive accessory, and the average duration of his chats dropped precipitously.

Alison took a snapshot to add to her collection before answering Tyler. "Of course I organized it. I organize everything. They have to spend the break somewhere. Why not with friends? They'll be in town all week."

"Nice. How did you track them down? I haven't heard from them since they dropped off the face of the earth around New Year's."

"They took a job running an undercover thing for the Bureau. They're security contractors. That's what they do. And Parker likes writing letters, which helped me keep in touch."

"I cannot even imagine him writing letters. Oh, hey." Tyler stood and waved. "Hey, Carl. Over here."

Carl made his way to them through the throng. The assorted VIPs parted before him like water for Moses without consciously realizing they'd moved. He looked lost in thought as he approached, and he looked startled when Alison pushed out Justin's chair for him.

Tyler shook his hand before they both sat down. "Long time no see, big man. Even Justin noticed you were gone."

"Has it been that long?" Carl's voice reminded Alison of a good whiskey, rich and smooth with a dry edge. Tonight he sounded distracted. "I guess it has. We're plugging leaks in Rydder Institute's pharma supply for the CSB, and it's slow work."

"Is that new?" Alison asked. "Parker said you were shutting down Ghost dealers." The drug was one of the latest designer pharmaceuticals to seep into the mainstream, and it was burning out thousands of lives along the way. News reports were declaring it an epidemic all along the West Coast.

That caught Carl's attention. "We are, but only as a means to an end. Ghost has a psychogenic base identical to a Rydder Institute proprietary drug. The CSB's investigations from the Institute end came up dry, so they've put us to tracking distribution back from the street, one outlet at a time." Carl combed the length of his pale hair behind his ears. "It's dull work and I'm tired of lying, but at least Eddie got a decent physical therapist out of the deal."

"Naomi, right? From what Parker's told me, she's a sweetheart and tougher than nails all at once. He's positively gaga over her, you know."

Carl's smile eased into a genuine grin. "He is. And he's thrilled that you're such a good pen pal. You know he goes by 'Eddie' with friends and family, right?"

"I know, but I met him as Parker. That's what he'll always be to me. And getting Justin to remember 'Parker' is hard enough, thank you. I'm glad you could get away for the week."

"As it turns out, it's especially lucky we came north. I've just been handed a live grenade of a problem right here in Seattle."

Alison poked him in the ribs. "Don't joke about grenades. What's wrong?"

"Eddie was stuck here so long for the primary repairs on his arms that buying a house made more sense—" Carl broke off and glanced over his shoulder.

Justin and Parker were approaching. When they arrived, Parker held out a phone handset. Carl waved it away. "I heard. Did Pete call you too? He says he's sitting on my damned porch in Ballard. Is that what's been making you so jittery about—"

"Pete? No. Not Pete. Naomi." Parker thrust the phone at Carl and then sat down in the chair on Alison's other side. He laced his fingers together over the top of his head and pulled in his arms tight. When he bent forward and made a low keening noise, fear sent prickles along Alison's skin. She looked up and met Justin's worried eyes.

Justin said, "Carl, should we be bolting for an exit? I only saw him act like that once, but it was memorable. Isn't that his early warning system on overload?"

"It is, but not for anything here." Carl stared at the phone. "He's been climbing walls all day, couldn't pin down a reason. When I got that call from Pete I thought…"

He frowned. Tyler said, "There's a grenade problem?"

Carl didn't seem to hear. "First one of Rydder Institute's neopsychs lands on my doorstep unannounced, and now this in San Fran…" His throat worked as he swallowed hard. "Pete has to be priority one: he's delusional or under duress. So, I need to check the house, but if Eddie's reacting like this, then Naomi must —but without Pete we can't—"

He fell silent, looking dazed. Alison took the handset from him and read the screen while Tyler and Justin looked over her shoulders and Parker rocked at her side.

Two years fell away in a heartbeat, and she was shaking and numb again, stunned by news of destruction. This time the headline read: "Explosion Destroys Subsistence Housing Block During Day One Celebrations: 132 Dead Hundreds Missing."

She rode out the shock and focused on practicalities. Someone Carl and Parker cared about was dead, missing, or homeless. That was the important point. "How can we help?" she asked. "Do you have a car? Did you fly in?"

"Train from San Fran, tram here," Carl said after a delay. "I have a van at home. Home. We need to get to my house. First we have to—dammit, I can't think. I need to go."

He stood, staggering as he rose.

"Whoa, Carl. Wait a minute. Wait for us." Justin wiggled his fingers. "Plane. Allie, can you call the charter guy? Tell him to start flight prep. Tyler, call Whosits, your Bureau buddy. See if he can forward preliminary local reports."

Tyler nodded and stepped away. Carl mouthed the word "charter" and shook his head.

"Don't argue," Justin said. "There's a car for you to borrow, too, and I'll stick with you until you straighten out whatever's at your house and get safely on a plane to San Francisco." He turned to Alison then, and his eyes were full of apologies he would never put in words.

She stood up to kiss him good-bye. "Go. I'll take care of everything else. Taking care of things is what I do."

CHAPTER FOUR

HOURS AGO, SOMEONE HAD brought Naomi a cup of bad coffee. It was cold now, and the black oily liquid was eating through the paper cup. The room was gray and dank, the wide wall mirror was dirty, and the yellow light on the camera above it was blinking.

Her body ached, and her ears were still ringing. Her eyes burned with fatigue. The soft-voiced man across the table from her said, "One more time, Ms. Kwan. Please talk me through the evening from five o'clock on."

He was patient and kind and sympathetic, and Naomi thought of him as Nice Cop. He'd broken the bad news first thing: very sorry, no one on her floor had survived. Very few residents in the whole wing escaped. Then he encouraged Naomi to tell him what had happened.

She'd lost her only remaining family and her every earthly possession, and if it had been any other night of the year, she would be dead too. That was what had happened. She wanted to curl up in a ball and wail. Instead she was being a cooperative citizen and walking Nice Cop through her evening for the fourth time.

"Again? Why?" For a moment she felt her mother's thin hand patting her cheek, heard the thin voice mumbling, "Why do you try my patience? You are such a good girl when you try."

She had kissed Mams on the forehead and thanked Mrs. Wong from 705, who was always happy to trade a few hours of mama-sitting for help with her sciatica. The old lady had gifted Naomi with a rare and indulgent smile, told her to go be young for once, and closed the door. And now Naomi would never ever see either of them again. Angry, frustrated tears stung her eyes.

"I've told you everything." She pushed away the coffee and pressed her hands to the table to stop the shakes. She pushed away all the anger and the pain too, pushed it down and away into a dark, cold corner of her heart where it couldn't burn her alive inside.

Nice Cop remained silent. Naomi's aching heart sank, and alarm bells belatedly rang in her mind. This kind, patient man was treating her like a suspect, not a witness.

"One more time," she said. "And then I walk, or you explain what's going on, or you charge me, although for what, I'm sure I don't know. I put my mother to bed at eight with a sleepy-shot because all the partying was getting her worked up. I had plans with friends." She recited their names, the restaurant name, and the reservation time. Again. "I went downstairs to catch the bus—"

"Six flights."

"Seven flights, I *told* you, and I was between floors when everything heaved up, and there was a roar, and then it was dark and I couldn't move my legs, and I was coughing, and my head hurt."

Adrenaline trickled into her blood, made her heart race and her fists clench. "Everything was black. I smelled smoke and felt with my hands. I was under the stairs at the bottom. There was a gap, I squeezed out, and I kicked open the fire door, which was stuck.

There were people and lights and fire, and someone brought me here."

She crossed her arms and lifted one eyebrow the way she'd practiced for hours in front of a mirror when she was nine. The look said, "Do your worst. I can take it."

It was a lie, but Nice Cop didn't challenge it. No one ever did. He said, "So you were meeting with Serena Nguyen as part of a larger get-together?"

The alarm bells in Naomi's head started ringing louder. "Tonight, yes. We did our government service in the same work unit. The whole group gets together to celebrate Restoration. The whole eat, drink, and be merry thing."

The reunion was Naomi's once-a-year indulgence. To hear her coworkers talk, other people her age got intoxicated and negotiated no-commitment sex every weekend, but she didn't. She had responsibilities. Other people had social lives and romantic relationships.

She had Serena and her mother.

Now her mother was gone. Naomi's eyes filled with tears as she saw the direction this conversation was going. "Was Serena— oh, please no. She wasn't at my place, was she? I called, when she was late, but that was earlier. Please say she wasn't caught in the explosion."

"No." The word came out on a startled note, as if its emergence surprised Nice Cop as much as it relieved Naomi's fears. "No, she wasn't there. I was hoping you could tell me more about her, that's all."

Another man came into the room, and they held a whispered conversation. Lots of vehement sibilants were exchanged before the new arrival turned to Naomi and said, "Here's the situation."

He stood with his hands on his hips, voice loud and hard: Mean Cop to balance Nice Cop. Naomi looked down to hide the smile they wouldn't appreciate.

"Serena Nguyen is in custody for the murder of two patrol officers," Mean Cop said. "She's incoherent, but she asks for you by name, and she was calling you right before that explosion. Your apartment—the one you'd left moments earlier—was ground zero according to the arson investigators. Help us connect the dots."

"What dots? I thought it was a gas explosion. We didn't even have gas. First I turned it off because Mams kept leaving on the stove when no one was there—the dementia, you know—and then Pacific Power turned it off at the valve years ago because Mams kept calling—and—and—none of that matters." Naomi forced herself to stop babbling. She was angry now, not exhausted or hurting. Not miserable and confused. *Angry*, because Serena needed her and no one had told Naomi until now.

It felt so good to shove all the other feelings to the side. She took a deep breath. "What do you mean *Serena's in custody*? What do you mean, *murder*? What happened?"

"That's not relevant," Mean Cop said.

"Yes, it is." Naomi shoved her seat back and stood up. Metal screeched as the chair legs scraped across the floor. "Serena is asking for me because I'm her legal guardian. You should've contacted me and our attorney of record as soon as you arrested her. You obviously didn't, and that is going to cost you. Get me our lawyer, and take me to her. Now."

The room went deathly quiet, and Naomi looked at herself in the mirrored observation window. Her face was smeared with soot, and her hair had sprung loose from its braid in waving tendrils. Her thin, sparkly party dress had never been practical, only pretty. Now it was torn, and her leggings were ripped and filthy.

Her fists thumped the tabletop, and she leaned across it. "Lawyer. What is your problem?"

Mean Cop moved back a step. Nice Cop squirmed in his seat and kept reading his datapad screen. Nice Cop spoke first. "Our problem is that this is Day One," he said. "Six more to go. Six more opportunities for catastrophe."

He glanced up. "You're being held on suspicion of domestic terrorism, Naomi. So is Serena Nguyen. That puts you under CSB Central detention rules. No lawyers. No rights at all, frankly. We're only keeping you occupied until Central's agents arrive. They suggested that an informal chat would be more pleasant and useful than leaving you in the holding corral. They didn't mention the guardianship."

Then he tilted the screen for Mean Cop to read.

"Shit," Mean Cop said.

Nice Cop gave Naomi a pained smile. "The custodial flag and contact list are right here in the court record, which means they should be in your intake file and hers, but they aren't. Someone has screwed up on a celestial scale. Here's what we're going do. We'll take you to Serena so you can calm her down. Then I will kick some asses up between shoulder blades about this screwup."

Naomi froze when they reached the elevator at the end of the hall. Even on a good day she wouldn't voluntarily step into a box outnumbered by unfriendly people who could overpower her. Tonight she kept seeing the crumpled doors in her building lobby: sheared metal and blocky rubble lit by emergency strobes. She stood in the hall with her knees shaking under her and balked. "Aren't there stairs? The detention area is still in the basement, right?"

Mean Cop rolled his eyes, but Nice Cop took the refusal in stride and pointed to a sign at the end of the hall. "It's your party."

The stairwell smelled like old grease and pepper. The commissary was still in the basement too. Naomi became acutely aware of her own odor: sweat, smoke and concrete dust. She stopped on the first landing. "I need to wash up."

Mean Cop said, "Not happening. I am not leaving you alone anywhere with an air vent or a window."

"If you don't, Serena will end up worse than incoherent. Look at this." Naomi tugged at her sooty shirt, wiped at her filthy hair.

"Smoke. Concrete dust. These are triggers for her. If she goes off, you won't be able to interrogate her for days."

"Give me a break," Mean Cop said. "Poor little rich girl reduced to sucking at the public teat is a good con, I'll give you that, but don't expect me to buy in. She'll be fine."

Naomi clutched at her temper. "It is not an act. She was sleeping in the rocks under the Old Bridge when the quake hit, and when it all came down, she was—"

She stopped and gritted her teeth when Nice Cop put up his hand and glared at his partner. "We know," he said. "We read the file. Three days before rescuers dug her out. Assigned full Subsistence support for mental disability. Not an act. Got it. If you want to help her tonight, get moving."

"Not like this! She hasn't had a major crash in over a year, but in the beginning she attacked everyone, even herself. I had to keep her hands in mitts when she slept."

Serena had also refused to eat because her food cried when she chewed it, and one month she'd sneaked onto the roof every night to let clouds lick her ears. Solo living had been a huge step up, even after five years of progress.

It might've been too big a step. Naomi shoved that doubt out of mind and plucked at her shirt again. "Please. I'm all she has. Her family disowned her. If I come to her like this, then your Central investigators will be trying to interview a berserker. Will that make them happy?"

Nice Cop exchanged a glance with his partner, who said, "We'll see what we can do."

ONCE THEY REACHED the ground floor, Nice Cop provided a comb and a rumpled shirt from a box behind the processing desk. Mean Cop donated a bottle of sanitizer and a towel. Naomi felt unreasonably grateful.

The general holding area was noisy, the corrals packed with the detritus of a busy night in the city. Drunks, fighters, prostitutes, political protesters, and a scattering of confused bystanders would all get sorted out later. Traffic was brisk between the pens and the guarded tunnel to the courthouse next door.

They passed a second security desk, and Mean Cop card-swiped them into another hall. This one was silent. Naomi hurried forward, checking into each cell she passed. Two cells held solitary men sleeping on the inset bed ledges. Further along Serena was leaning against her cell door: feet spread, hands and forehead against the transparent panel as if she might ooze her way out if she pushed hard enough.

Her short hair was a rat's nest of knots and tangles, and in the two days since Naomi had last visited, she had dyed the tips a coppery red. A well-worn CAF field uniform blouse sagged loose over narrow shoulders, and the beltless matching pants hung low on her hips. Her eyes were squeezed shut, her lower lip was caught in her teeth, and there were bloody scrapes on her palms, which were pressed against the clear barrier of the door.

The thick acrylic blocked sound. Naomi lifted her hands up high to match Serena's larger, calloused hands, desperate for even the illusion of contact. "Serena. I'm here."

Serena opened her eyes. They were clear and alert. Her lips moved. "Down, Bao. *Down!*"

Naomi hit the floor, and plastic exploded over her head. Sound arrived an instant later, a tremendously loud crack that hammered into her eardrums with deafening force. A weight fell across her back, blood splattered to the floor next to her nose, and she heard a distant, muffled pop. Time slowed, her heart raced, and she scrabbled and shoved at the heavy body above her, desperate for escape.

"Stay down!" Mean Cop's shouted voice was barely audible next to Naomi's ear, but it jolted her out of the panic. "Waist holster. Pistol. Keycard—*Jesus*—" His body jerked against Naomi.

He draped his left arm over her shoulder. "Key front right. God fucking damn. Pull me up. Cruz, cover us, dammit!"

Nice Cop responded in a murmur that was probably a shout. More pops followed. Naomi reached back for the weapon in the holster and the card in the pocket. Mean Cop moaned when the harness snagged against his ribs, but the pistol came loose, and Naomi tipped her head up.

Serena was crouched to the side of her door with her eyes steady on the weapon. Naomi pulled Mean Cop's arm against her shoulder with the hand that held the pistol, tucked up her legs, and heaved herself to her feet. Her back felt warm and wet, and Mean Cop came up cursing and heavy, dead weight against her spine but not dead, because when Naomi swiped the keycard through the lock, he planted his bloody right hand against the plate, and Serena's door slid open.

The pistol disappeared from Naomi's grip, and she hit the floor again. Bare feet flashed past her face. Dim pops of gunfire and muted shouts penetrated the buzzing in her ears, and she huddled beneath the protection of a man whose name she didn't even know.

Then Serena's feet were in front of her nose again. A pistol appeared, followed by a second larger gun and three ammunition clips. After Serena walked away again, Naomi pushed at Mean Cop until he rolled off.

He had a hole in his back, low on the spine, another in the back of one thigh. Both were big enough to hold a clenched fist. His eyes stared unblinking at the floor.

He was dead. Naomi couldn't make sense of it. Her mind kept rejecting what her eyes saw.

She knew what the aftermath of a firefight should look like. Mob violence and brutal domestic crimes were unavoidable facts of life in densely populated Subsistence housing blocks. Police actions were common. They were short but often intense and always resulted in piles of unconscious participants. These people were not unconscious. They were dead. They had been shooting bullets at each other like soldiers on a battlefield in some movie about the Pre-Restoration days, not like police and criminals.

The whole idea was absurd. It was incomprehensible. The Bureau's weapons of choice were compressed-air dart guns and ranged electrical stunners. Fast-acting paralytics could induce overdose or suffocation, and electrical shock could stop hearts or cause seizures, but those options were still less hazardous to bystanders than high-velocity solid projectiles. Only specialist units and officers on high-risk cases carried lethal weapons.

Blood spray and gore dripped down the white walls of the hallway, pooling on the gray floor. The lock plate on the entrance door still glowed red, but the other two occupied cells were open now. The prisoner who'd been in one of them lay dead inside his door. Serena dragged the other into the hall through a smear of blood. He was missing his right hand and most of his head, but that didn't deter Serena from checking his pockets and taking his shoes.

Naomi's brain caught up to reality. Someone must have classified her and Serena as deadly threats, authorizing her guards to carry lethal weapons. Someone else had wanted them dead, wanted it enough to risk staging an ambush here. She was only alive because others had died for her.

Nice Cop lay behind his partner. His head was mostly missing on top, and his belly was an exploded mess. Cruz: Naomi concentrated on remembering his name. Cruz had been kind and he had been competent, and now he was dead. He deserved to be remembered.

Serena brought another handful of salvaged items to Naomi, knelt beside Cruz and started looting his corpse. Naomi picked up Mean Cop's bloodstained keycard. She felt the first serious shudder of reaction as she looked for his name. It seemed immensely important that she know it.

She owed her life to Leonardo Sanchez. She was soaked in his blood, and a little voice in her mind was screaming, *whywhywhywhywhywhy*, and while she stood there shivering, Serena collected everything Sanchez had left in his pockets right in front of her.

Serena murmured, "Gray Dog wants to go, Naomi, and Red Dog wants off the leash. Are you ready to run?"

"What dogs? A red dog? Run where?" Naomi's ears popped, and she could almost hear her own voice properly again. "I don't understand you, sweetie. They said you—" Best not to mention incoherent raving, under the circumstances. "Never mind. There's nothing we can do, Serena. We're trapped in here."

"No, we're not." Serena's smile was a small tired thing. "There are two stun wands, four slug pistols, sixteen rounds of bang-ammo for them, a knife, and two active keys. I have a big red dog who wants to play. This'll be easy. I know I'm crazy, but I can do this. Will you trust me?"

They were in a secured cellblock with four bodies, two of whom were police investigators. Naomi was shaking so hard that her teeth were chattering, and so dizzy she could barely see. Her ears were ringing, her guts were turning inside out, and Serena was babbling about dogs.

Naomi looked up into her friend's dark bloodshot eyes, and she saw passion and purpose there for the first time in what felt like forever. Her throat went tight.

They'd shared first adventures and childish dreams, and later they'd shared three years building roads and laying foundations and repairing bridges together. They'd shared *everything* until Serena went away to learn how to break people and Naomi went home to learn how to fix them.

Serena had tested Naomi's patience to the limit many times, but when she had that look on her face there was only one possible answer to the question of trust. "Forever and always," Naomi whispered. "Lead and I'll follow."

CHAPTER FIVE

USTIN'S DRIVER TURNED THE limousine onto the
highway and picked up speed. Carl braced his feet against
the floor and pushed against the back of his seat until joints
popped and eased the stiffness in his back. He wished he had an
equally simple way to dispel the churning dread in the pit of his
stomach, but that wasn't under his control. He glared at his
brother. "Eddie, can't you turn down the weirdness volume?"

Parker gripped his hands together in front of him and offered
an apologetic shrug from his seat on the facing bench. He wasn't
doing it on purpose.

"What's going on?" Justin asked. He was sitting beside Parker
with his arms crossed and his weak left leg tucked behind the
protection of the right.

Carl said, "I don't know. I've never gotten more than a sense of
condition and location from him in thirty years. Tonight it's like
he's on loudspeaker, and it's incredibly distracting. He's never
reacted this strongly to malice directed at anyone other than him
or me."

Parker ducked his head. His ears turned red. It was as good as
a confession. He was more than gaga over Naomi. He was

emotionally *attached*, which meant more for him than most other people. He'd been keeping that little truth well hidden.

Carl kicked him in the ankle. Parker looked up, squinted at Carl, and kicked back. Carl considered throttling him.

"And what the hell was that?" Justin looked from one to the other.

"Sibling spat. Apparently he feels a more serious connection to Naomi than he's been letting on, and that's bumping up the weirdness. I do not appreciate being left out of the loop." Carl squelched a stab of concern. "She won't appreciate it either. What if she hates you when she finds out who we really are?"

Parker shrugged. He would worry about consequences later, when he knew Naomi was safe.

"Not my business," Justin said. He laid his head back and closed his eyes. The partition to the driver's compartment next to him sparkled with reflections of passing lights as they headed north from Seattle city center. "Most days I wish I was still allowed to drive."

Fielding the occasional non sequitur was a typical hazard of conversations with Justin. His mind went on tangents, and listeners either followed or got lost. Carl traced the associations back from the spoken words through an old joke—*stop bickering or I'll turn this car around*—to discomfort over intruding on a private quarrel. Aloud, he said, "As a car owner, I'm glad you're banned from the roads. One seizure at high speed would be one too many. But speaking of cars, how are you paying for this?"

Justin yawned without opening his eyes. "The limo? Dawnstar Foundation is picking up the bill. There's a whole auto division, and Manny wanted me and Allie to arrive in style. The Foundation started in-house transport back when I was in charge. The shipping and dock storage units run right through Restoration Week, since the rest of the world doesn't shut down too. Manny snapped up a ton of contracts. Hard to believe I started up Dawnstar trying to get rid of money." He frowned. "Wait a minute. What did you ask me about?"

"Don't play absentminded eccentric with me, Justin."

"I'm not playing," Justin said mildly. "I work very hard at it."

The only outward sign of the skull fracture that had nearly killed him was a sprinkling of white in the dark hair over one ear. The inner losses were incalculable. Appearing normal when he wasn't was an unending war, but he was a canny veteran who won more battles than he lost. He was adept at covering handicaps with humor.

He was also adept at dodging issues he didn't want to discuss, like his finances. Carl said, "I asked how you were planning to pay for helping us. A chartered plane isn't cheap. I thought you were on a fixed income since coming back from the dead. Did you have the will voided after all?"

"Hell, no. Can you imagine the legal hassles? No, a few licenses reverted without challenge, and I've been blowing up shit for Adam Berenson's construction firm too. Do you know him? It's fun and absurdly lucrative." Justin yawned again. "He'll get an exclusive on that power cell configuration when I get around to licensing."

That deflection was an interesting one. Carl said, "You're talking about those little super-batteries you won't share with the world? I thought you were dead set against weaponization."

"Dynamite isn't a weapon. Fission is." The last two words slurred together. "Suppression was always a stopgap. I can shape the change or let it break me, but I can't sit out the game forever. I'd rather be Nobel than Oppenheimer."

By the end, Justin's voice was barely a murmur. Feigning a nap was another weapon in the pretend-to-be-normal arsenal. Fatigue, stress, and environmental changes could all knock him out of contact with reality.

Carl sat back and conceded the fight. The problem would correct itself in time.

A few quiet minutes passed, and then Justin's cargo pants emitted a deafening trill. Parker nearly hit the ceiling, Carl flinched, and on the third ring Justin jerked upright and looked around in confusion. It took another jarring alarm before he pulled a phone from the lower pocket and silenced it. "Sorry. New toy. New settings." He gave the device to Parker. "Preliminary reports on the explosion."

Parker physically shook off tension when he found Naomi's name on the confirmed-safe list, but the internal turmoil barely ebbed. The look he shot Carl as he handed back Justin's phone was more frustrated than anything else.

"We'll go after Naomi as soon we clear the house," Carl said. "Pete's call made no sense. If it was a legit trip, then an advance team would've contacted us before he left Minneapolis. If it isn't legit, there should've been a Bureau response, even if Rydder kept it out of the headlines. We would've heard."

Justin checked his handset. "Naomi was the one in the explosion, right?" He started adding notes. "And who's on your doorstep again? A neopsych like you?"

"Technically speaking I'm not a neo these days, but Pete is one, yes."

"What's speaking?" That nonsense question was followed by more typing. "I thought Bureau escorts were a mandatory safety precaution."

"They are. Certified neos do not travel alone. Ever. It's one thing I don't miss." Carl waited a few beats. Justin didn't respond. He was gone again. Multitasking was tricky for someone who had to work hard for every second of mental focus. Carl settled back and considered all of the restrictions he had left behind when he'd abandoned his first career.

The Rydder Institute for Applied Neuropsychiatry had spent forty years building a solid track record for working miracles with an ever-expanding arsenal of medical interventions, but "arsenal" was more than a metaphor. Their most effective tools were drugs and coercive neurological procedures originally designed as tools of war and subterfuge. Abuse of power was a legitimate concern.

Those same tools had been put to work keeping nervous critics happy and ensuring that the Institute built a reputation for inviolable integrity. Protective patient protocols and codes of ethical conduct were as deeply ingrained in practitioners' brains as most survival instincts. The death-before-dishonor precautions were a little less than absolute, as it turned out, but the record stood at six deaths. Technically speaking, Carl counted as a seventh.

That was past. He needed to concentrate on the present. There were still questions to be answered. He'd given Justin plenty of time to regain focus. "Justin, how long have you been keeping a bug-out bag on hand?"

"Bag?"

Justin could've simply loaned them the car, but he'd come along. There'd been a duffel in the trunk of the limo when Carl tossed in his own bags at the train station. It might be a practical emergency protocol, or it could be a sign of a frustrated adrenaline junkie desperate for a fix. "Bag, Justin. Are you going somewhere this week?"

"Two years in November," Justin said, answering the earlier question. "Tyler's motto is 'Always be ready to run.' Took me forever to convince him that spare power cells and a charger were more important to me than freeze-dried food. I think he's infected Ryan too. The kid's Duty Day list was all survival gear. Which is why I've blocked Helen's comm account for the week. She'll go ballistic when she sees the hunting knife."

"Mothers are protective like that, even ones who aren't bitter ex-spouses."

"I've never understood the bitterness. Why is it my fault that she got bored with me? Even if Prickface hadn't gotten her pregnant, she would've left me soon enough." His attention never wavered from his screen. The question was rhetorical, pairing incisive observational skills with a glaring lack of self-awareness.

Carl let the conversation flow away from the initial question he had asked. "Do you spoil Ryan to put Rob Armstrong's nose out of joint? Because he got your wife, but he would never be rich enough to give his son what you can?"

"More or less. The lawyers thought I was bonkers to add the trust for the kid as a condition of the contract release after the paternity tests. They had fits about the visitation rider."

"You still loved Helen."

Justin looked up and smiled. "Of course you see it right away. Protecting her baby from her bad decision was all I could do for her." His eyes narrowed. "Wait. You're distracting me. Go back."

"To what?"

"You started with my go bag. Why? Did you think that I was skipping town? Tyler nearly stroked out over a joke I made earlier this evening. Why does everyone think I'm ready to run off and join a circus?"

Because he was, even if he didn't know it himself. Carl bit back that analysis before he said anything aloud.

Parker cleared his throat. "Join this one. Two's company, three is a fire team. The more the merrier. Safety in numbers."

Justin eyed him suspiciously. "I don't know how useful I'd be. I'm coming off a bad patch, mentally. Loud phones and blank stares will be the least of the annoyances."

Parker rubbed one hand over his hair. "You're made for recon, Justin. Please."

"That's a lot of words. You must really want it." Justin brightened. "Sure, why not? I'm yours all week if you want."

Parker turned a frown on Carl: a plea to take over the effort of communicating. Carl accepted with a shrug. "All right, Justin, here's the local situation: Pete mentioned that 'the volcano gods want a new sacrifice' when he called. It's a private code that means he's in trouble, but it doesn't mean he's here. This stinks of strange."

Justin grimaced. "The stinking thing is that I have no idea who Pete is. The way you say it—I should know him?"

"You should, yes." Carl paused. "That's twice in five minutes that you've admitted to weakness. What will I do for fun if I don't get to shake you by the ankles to make you cough up important details?"

The other two both stared at him, and then Justin said to Parker, "Was that a joke? I think it was. Amazing. I should call Alison so she can mark the date on one of the millions of calendars she keeps for me."

Carl put together shifts in eye contact, posture, voice, and facial cues, and shock value slipped a comment past his internal censors. "You two split up."

Justin's smile turned brittle. "None of your business, nosy bastard."

"Sorry. I thought it would last, that's all."

"It goes like this: I gave up pretending my condition would improve after a bad patch last year. Allie gave up pretending that I wasn't breaking her heart every time I went blank. She has legal access to my account profiles and holds my financials in trust, and I have my own apartment and a cold, lonely bed. How's that for open and honest?"

"Better than I deserve for accidentally prying," Carl said. "Speaking of privacy, do you have our current call codes, and can you turn off the tracker on your comm account?"

"Allie updated your info for me. I checked. And I've had a celebrity tracking exemption forever. Helen's people insisted." Justin shook his head. "Now, before I forget, tell me who Pete is and how you'll deal with his problem and take care of your refugee in San Francisco too."

Carl said, "How is easy. We drag him along, if he's there. If it's a trap, we spring it and go. As for who, Pete was Rydder's public sector liaison back when they tried satellite clinics. He specializes in clinical pediatrics now, but he also—"

"—is your last remaining link to the Institute and acts as a cutout between you and the Bureau." Justin tapped his temple with a finger. "Found it. So that's why you couldn't get intel on the explosion? He's missing. All right, say it's a trap. What comes after I sneak up and take a peek through the windows?"

One lifted eyebrow and a quirk of lips from Parker, and Justin said, "Oh, you're going to love the new toys. I've stayed busy, between demolition jobs."

THE CAR DROPPED them at the end of a long residential street north of Discovery Park. The street lights were haloed in fog, and the dark shape of a wooded hillside rose away to the left and led down steeply in front of them beyond a traffic barrier. From there the rocky ground dropped steeply to the shores of Puget Sound, on the point where the sea turned inward towards the locks into Lake Washington.

Justin regarded the hillside with irritation. Someday he might get used to Seattle's terrain, but he doubted it. At times like this he felt deeply nostalgic for the flat Nebraska fields where he'd grown up.

He stepped into the brush, out of view of any nosy neighbors, and dropped his pack next to Parker's. "You had to buy a secluded lot on a dead-end street at the top of a hill, Carl? I'm back in decent shape, but I still limp. Slowly. You do remember that, right?"

"This isn't a game, Justin. You do remember that, right?" Carl's voice started as a vicious parody of Justin's, then deepened. "Call your car back and go home if the bitchy attitude is all you have to offer."

Silence fell, disturbed only by wind in the shrubs and waves lapping the shore far below. Justin pulled damp salt-scented air into lungs emptied by the shock of Carl's brusque dismissal. His temper cracked, and cold anger stabbed through. "You know what? I don't need your attitude. I don't need to be here at all."

He was turning to leave when Parker stepped past him. "Hold on," he said, firm and angry. "Carl, stand down."

Carl froze as still as a statue, pale hair shining in the moonlight. The solid bulk of him loomed over Parker, who stood there silently staring back with his hands loose and his weight on the balls of his feet. Eventually Justin lost his patience. "Somebody talk, or I punch you both."

"Neopsych voodoo got out of control," Parker said. "Are you back on top of it now, Carl?"

"Yes, dammit." Carl blew out a sigh. "I pushed you, Justin. Snap hypnosis. I swear I didn't do it on purpose. Eddie's jitters are wreaking havoc on my concentration."

Justin replayed Carl's words in memory, and rage shredded what was left of his self-control. "You cheating bastard. You pushed me to leave, to keep me safe? It isn't your decision. If you *ever* pull that manipulative bullshit again, I will beat you senseless as soon as I figure it out."

Parker said quietly, "Cut him some slack, Justin."

Justin stared. "You know I hate it when you talk normally. It creeps me out."

"I know." Parker waved at Carl. "That's why I did it. Stop worrying, both of you. Move, Carl."

The contents of Justin's duffel bag rattled when Carl grabbed it up. He headed downhill into the underbrush, and Parker gave him a few steps before beckoning to Justin and following.

They cut south along the wooded hillside to a narrow concrete stairway illuminated by the rising moon. Carl stopped on a landing and looked up. A steep roof shingled in cedar was visible above them, framed in security lighting. Other homes dotted the curve of the hill, all with glorious views of Puget Sound.

"This is the only route to the house besides strolling up the driveway," Carl said. "Please be careful. You aren't trained in covert work, however uniquely proficient you may be at it, and there's definitely trouble. My security system is down and won't respond to remote access."

His voice was rough with stress. Justin bit back a facetious response and took back his bag. "I'll tell you what's up there in a second."

The scanner's range barely extended far enough. The one he'd designed for wide-area use wasn't easily portable. Carl turned the device over in his fingers while Justin explained its commands and icons. There were at least three people waiting in the house above: two moving, one stationary. Broad shading indicated sensor fields.

"Your system's not down, it's been co-opted," Justin said in conclusion. "Trap, no doubt about it."

"That is an impressive toy," Carl said. "Thank you. I truly didn't mean to force your response earlier. I am sorry."

"And yet I don't hear you promising to never do it again." Justin looked up when Carl didn't reply. "I will take your head off. I mean it."

"Good. If I can't control myself, I'm better off dead."

"Now you're being creepy too. Here." Justin offered Parker two smaller gadgets. "This one spoofs most IR and UV detectors. The other jams wide-spectrum. Takes out cameras, phones, and radios, and it screws with electrical grids. They're both power hogs. Ten minutes charge at best, even off my power cells. Helpful?"

Parker nodded, raising the second one. "You first for intel, me hot behind you. Carl to keep eyes on scene for both of us."

"Here's a gift for you." Carl handed Justin a lightweight communication headset with an inset camera and a night vision eyepiece. "The camera will let me know you're safe even if you don't feel like reporting in. I'd loan you my tactical vest too, but you'd drown in it."

"I'm probably bulletproof," Justin said. "The invisibility is a threshold effect, but the armor reaction is proportional to the force applied. The harder I get hit, the harder my skin gets, and the faster the strike, the faster the response."

"Probably does not reassure me. Are you ready?"

"Not yet," Justin said. "I need to zero out before I crank up the power."

He sat in the dirt and reached down to flip a small power switch from one setting to another, but Parker grabbed his wrist. "Zero out?"

"Turn this off." Justin lifted his pants leg to display the power cell in its ankle cuff. "I've been boosted all day. If I don't pay off the existing debt before adding on, then you'll be carrying me home in a bucket later." He stopped and regarded the blank faces watching him. "Do either of you know what I'm talking about?"

"Apparently not," Carl said. "You have been busy. Last time we saw the fancy suit, the battery was on the collar."

"Easier to reach down here. Asymmetric power distri-bution was a bitch to design," Justin said, "but worth it to have more options with the suit. If I have to be a freak, I might as well have fun with it."

Tyler wanted to buy him a tee-shirt that read: 'I plowed my plane into a mountainside in the Big Nowhere, and all I brought home was this freaky new skin.' That incident had left Justin with a mangled brain and a shattered leg too, but skin capable of emit-ting electromagnetic interference under certain conditions was by far the most interesting souvenir of the bunch. His epidermis was also practically invulnerable whether it was visible or not, and that had come in handy more than once.

The side effects of his condition were less entertaining. Over-heating triggered the invisibility effect as easily as electrical charge, so opportunities for social awkwardness abounded. Other tedious issues included muscle cramps and chronic pain, and his fancy skin tried to kill him if he didn't keep it warm and happy. Typical room temperatures could send him hypothermic when his skin demanded diversion of core heat, and that would be followed by fever that kept his outsides heated but cooked his internal organs. He wore custom-designed base layer every moment of every day because freezing to death in a delirious fever on a sunny summer afternoon would be pathetic.

The condition did have its upsides, however, and the base layer material was conductive, which made a handy foundation for adjusting the electrical effects. Fun was a precious commodity, well worth the effort of tinkering with his underwear.

"One of the things I've worked out," he said, "is that at the right micro-voltage the aches disappear but I don't. So I run powered up most of the time now. Sorry. I thought you knew." He must've come up with the idea after they'd left town. "There's still backlash, though, so I pace myself."

Disappearing was painless and as easy as applying current to flesh, but powering down hurt like hell in a mathematically predictable relationship. The longer he spent charged up and the more current he used, the harder he crashed once the power was off. If he wanted to dance, he had to pay the piper every so often.

"Zero," Parker said and nodded understanding.

"Yes. Move back and let me get it over with."

Powering down hurt as it always did. A cascade of hot pain poured from the marrow of his bones into his gut and chest and tried to burn free from there. When the worst of the backlash passed, Justin pushed the power output all the way up to maximum, and the remaining discomfort disappeared.

So did his body.

He got to his feet once he caught his breath and accustomed himself to the heady sense of physical well-being that came along with the invisibility. "Now I'm ready."

The other two were staring at him again.

CHAPTER SIX

T HE SILENCE GREW UNCOMFORTABLY thick, until finally, Justin said, "What's wrong?"

Carl shook his head. "You did that in front of Alison, didn't you? That's why she distanced herself."

"Yeah." She'd burst into tears when Justin refused to promise he wouldn't do it again. "The only painkillers that won't kill me leave me fogged. I'd rather take the pain in big short doses than feel like shit every waking minute."

That was enough to satisfy Parker. He finished prepping his own gear, which included a mag-powered slug rifle and pistol as well as a knife and a pair of pointy metal rods. Then he keyed through a sequence of visual enhancers on his helmet visor. "Gone. Nice."

Carl said, "But I still see him on my screen. Are you sure you can't be detected, Justin?"

"I'm certain. That isn't a normal scanner, remember? I played with the reception until I registered. It gave Tyler a whole new dataset to analyze. Best he can figure, current models for electricity and magnetism are totally wrong. He's started his models from scratch three times. When he's feeling pissy, he tells me I'm a figment of his imagination. Someday he'll figure it out. Somebody has to, and it won't be me."

He could still come up with results at a production bench with a goal in mind and components at hand, but only if he was careful to avoid thinking about *why* a given *how* would work. Not that he'd ever been good at explaining ideas.

Pondering his flaws took him all the way up the steps to a walkway facing a shrub-lined driveway and the side of a house. Fireworks were exploding in the air over Puget Sound, starting off Restoration Week with a bang. A long-absent voice whispered in Justin's memory: "Not with a bang but a whimper, boyo. That's how it all came down."

Justin blinked back a rush of tears. "Oh, William," he whispered. "I wish you'd made it this far. You owe me ten dollars. We're going to make it to a referendum after all."

He could almost hear the lawyer's throaty laugh at the thought, and that raised a fleeting memory of the man's smile, which had been as subtle as his sly intelligence. It was hard to picture the life-lined face and the tidy gray hair. Mostly, Justin remembered the suits, always impeccably stylish no matter the circumstances.

The man had taught Justin how to view the present in the frame of the past, had always reminded him to look beyond his own future. William had loved to pontificate about the social and economic upheaval that his generation had survived, and he'd loved the country he'd helped hammer and weld back together as much as he'd loved revving its chugging economic engine.

Once upon a time Justin had played an integral part of that engine's maintenance, and the company was still doing well two years after he'd turned his back on it. Because he had once been so involved in the nitty-gritty, because he'd *listened* to William's lectures, Justin also knew that the situation now was terribly fragile.

The Fed held all the old state governments and all the new

little city-states together through a balance struck between the strength of the Combined Armed Forces, the financial support of multinational corporations, and the watchful oversight of the investigative divisions—both local and national—of the Civilian Security Bureau. Or in William's more pithy words, the Republic's stability was protected by a triad of military muscle, monetary blackmail, and meddlesome spies.

That precariously balanced system would go up for grabs in less than six months, when the constitution forged after Restoration faced its first vote of confidence. A mandatory approval referendum was an ironclad component of the document, and five years were reserved for framing a new covenant if the current one failed its vote.

Renewal was far from guaranteed. The voting population was restive. Every op-ed these days contained new radical proposals. Those ideas were stoking a heated public debate, and if reforms were voted in, certain segments of the business community stood to lose a lot of political power.

Most corporations liked things just the way they were. Qualified companies could buy voting seats in the Senate right alongside recognized local government bodies, and money would always find a way to the top.

It was tempting to see the hand of influence in tonight's events. The political consequences of tragic events were volatile at best, but in general they made people leery of change. In two out of the last three years, tragedies had cast a pall over Restoration Week. It was enough to make a paranoid man believe in conspiracies.

William would've been that kind of man, except that he'd fallen victim to an earlier plot, one that Justin should've seen brewing. He had died, and Justin was still alive, and that was just one of many injustices in the world.

"*Justin!*"

When the deep, insistent sound of Carl's voice registered, Justin found himself looking at a sky empty except for the moon and stars. Boat lights and moonlight twinkled on the dark water. He looked around but found no clue to tell him how long ago the fireworks had ended.

Carl said, "Ah. You're back."

Justin nodded. His knees ached. He had been standing motionless long enough for his back to stiffen up too.

"Sorry. Next time I'll rattle your cage sooner," Carl said. "Contact One is five meters ahead, twenty degrees right. Two is behind the house. Get us visuals."

Justin got moving and did what was needed, went around the house and did the same there. On first glance the intruders were innocuous, men in casual clothes enjoying the fresh night air outside a large brick house.

On second look, the man in front had a rifle with a big scope and a bigger ammunition magazine leaning against the wall in deep shadow while something with a short wide barrel lay flat on the floor. The man in back of the house had similar weaponry under his feet where he rocked on a porch swing. Both had flex-screen on their shirt sleeves that flickered softly with video imagery. That was expensive tech, prone to rotting fast and not commonly seen in the private sector, but to Justin's mind the porch swing was the most incongruous element in the scene.

He could not imagine Carl relaxing on a porch.

"Hold at the back door," Carl said. "Then as soon as Eddie hits Two, you go inside and up right to get eyes on Three. He'll go through for One out front. Don't take any chances. Watch your back and let Eddie handle the mayhem, got it?"

Justin nodded his head sharply. Knuckles that turned to stone on impact could generate lethal results with only moderate momentum. He knew how to pull punches, but avoiding the potential for fatal mistakes was a better strategy.

His headset began transmitting static ten seconds after he reached his position. The security lights died next. The man on the swing grabbed his rifle and glanced at the blank screen on his arm. Then he moved behind a support column and watched for trouble.

Ten minutes and more passed. The static died, the outside lights flickered and pulsed back to life, and Carl's quiet cursing filled Justin's ear. He tuned it out.

A wide swath of hillside between the house and the tree line had been landscaped with terraced flowerbeds. Justin never saw Parker cross it. A hand came up, the guard's rifle muzzle dipped, and he went over the edge before he could make more than a strangled prelude to a shout.

Justin went in the door and up the stairs at full speed, which wasn't all that fast. His left foot lagged. Sprinting led to falling like night followed day, so he jogged slowly and checked each door as he reached it.

A man and a woman were lying prone on the floor of one small, bare room. A ceiling fixture illuminated wood moldings and pale blue walls, and a wide irregular black stain marred the deep blue carpet beneath the room's occupants. The single window was open, and thin white curtains lifted in the light breeze. The air stank of blood and feces and buzzed with flies.

Only one contact had registered on the scanner Carl was using, which meant that one of the two was dead.

The dark blotch in the carpet squished underfoot, and the scent of blood intensified. Energy still coursed through Justin's nerves. He exhaled slowly, riding out the reaction. Sometimes the barrier between exhilaration and panic got very thin. He held himself detached from the scene, anchoring himself on the right side of the line.

Justin rolled the woman over first. Her eyes were blank and starting to cloud, and her left arm had been slashed open to the bone twice, in long diagonal lines. She was dressed much like the two men outside. An empty knife sheath rode her leg above one hiking boot, and an empty pistol holster sat at her hip.

When Justin moved her, the man lying on her far side made a

startled noise and started to wriggle. His ankles and his hands were bound with plastic ties, but he still managed to roll over twice, stopping on his back.

His eyes and mouth had been taped shut. Justin's heart lurched, looking at that, and as he fought to keep his breathing under control, he realized that Carl had been talking in his ear for a while.

"—hear me, Justin? I can hear you breathing, but I've lost your video and Eddie's, and his scanner signal is gone."

"He was heading to the front, last I saw," Justin stepped through the blood to the prisoner's side. "The lights-out box probably trashed the cameras, sorry. The surge is hard on components. I have one dead female here, one live male prisoner. He's maybe six cems taller than me, black hair going gray, brown skin, built like a small tank."

Carl sounded a lot calmer when he said, "That could be Pete. And now Eddie's back on radar too. I hate you both, by the way."

"Two more," Parker said. "Driveway. Secure now."

Justin gave the prisoner a closer examination. He wore torn clothing that was filthy with dried blood and other fluids, and some of the fresh blood might have come from him too. His face was bruised and swollen, and his nose looked broken.

If the gag didn't come off he was going to suffocate.

Justin's hands were shaking so hard that it took three tries to pry up a corner of the tape. He paused before pulling it off. There was no point in taking chances with anyone who had Carl's abilities.

"I'm here to help," Justin said, "but you have no reason to trust me, and since I'm kneeling in blood I'm not feeling very trusting either. I need your name. If anything else—*anything*—comes out of your mouth, I will hurt you so badly that you will never speak again. Name only, or I rip out your tongue. Hear me?"

He received a vigorous nod and yanked off the gag. Skin came off too. The man gasped and whooped for breath, then said, "Pete. Peter Rafiki Hamil."

His voice was a tenor copy of Carl's expressive baritone, although right now a plugged nasal tone distorted the mellow inflections.

"Hear that, Carl?" Justin pushed Pete onto his side and tugged at the wrist restraints to see if he could snap them off. "He needs a doctor. I know somebody, but I can't remember her name. Call Allie or Tyler. They'll tell you."

Pete began squirming so frantically that Justin lost his grip on the slippery, sticky restraints. Wiping away some of the blood revealed the cause of the man's agitation. He didn't have a pinky finger on the left hand. He also didn't have nails on any of his remaining fingers.

Justin let go, and Pete fell back against the floor. He arched convulsively when his back and hands hit the carpet, but even then he didn't cry out. Tears leaked from behind his tight-shut eyelids, and his face was red from holding in sobs. Justin demanded, "Why the hell didn't you tell me—"

The question died in his throat, choked by cold understanding. He'd threatened to cut out Pete's tongue if the man spoke. Remorse blasted away Justin's eroding sense of detachment, and suddenly he couldn't breathe. He staggered upright and got as far as the doorway, where he rebounded off Parker and hit the wall both literally and figuratively.

"Why don't you call Alison yourself?" Carl asked, but it was a sound heard dimly through the blood beating in Justin's ears. Bands of pain tightened around his chest, and vertigo rolled over him in a black tide.

Parker caught him before he hit the floor.

———

CARL LEANED against the corner of a short hallway where it

entered Tyler's small living area while he decided where to go from there. He'd gotten Pete settled in a tiny office with a thin, intense woman introduced as Doctor Patience. Now he needed to tackle the migraine developing behind his eyes before it grew from painful to debilitating.

Couches, camping gear, and an entertainment unit clogged the tiny main room. The kitchen was a protected nook behind a partition, the office and bedroom behind him were on the exterior side of the hall, the bathroom on the interior, and the whole of it was sixteen floors up.

A screen in the office had showed views of the building stairwells and the elevator as well as feeds from the lobby and outdoors. An "always be ready to run" philosophy made for a secure little bachelor's pad.

The big couch looked inviting. Carl sank into the sagging cushions and fished his medicine case out of its flat compartment inside his belt. Some of the contents were meant for professional applications, but most were for personal use. Conditioned allergies had more than a few inconvenient side effects. Without biochemical tweaking a lot of simple medications would kill him outright.

Better to save the painkillers for a real emergency, he decided after sorting pensively through the selection. Pete had been his only source for the tailored pharmaceuticals. The remaining stash might have to last a lifetime.

He sealed up the kit and concentrated on evicting the headache through deliberate relaxation. He wouldn't be interrupted. Tyler and Parker were assisting the doctor, Justin had slunk off to hide in the apartment's only bathroom, and Alison was puttering in the kitchen.

The pain slowly ebbed to an ignorable ache, and the auras cleared from his vision. Three dusty pictures on the far wall caught his attention once he could focus again. One was a photo of a restaurant with checkered tablecloths and dark wood beams wrapped in grape vines. Justin and Tyler were both grinning at menus. The middle image showed Tyler following Justin and a distinguished older man up a gangway into an airplane, and in the one on the left, a gangly younger Tyler and a man with the same strong jaw and laughing eyes stood together on a snowy mountain.

The triptych wasn't as overtly artistic as a neighboring series of images that documented the demolition of an adobe home on a sandstone bluff, but it still invited closer study. Alison set a mug of coffee, two glasses, and a bottle of Irish whiskey on the coffee table. "Not my best work," she said. "But not my worst. How is your friend?"

"He'll live." Carl withheld the details. Pete's bloody condition had given Alison a bad case of green-around-the-gills when she'd first seen him, and the weakness embarrassed her. "Thank you again for everything. For being here, for getting Pete help. All of it."

"This? It was easy. Dr. Faisal is always on call for Justin, and Tyler and I were planning on an all-night movie festival here already."

She smiled at Carl's outstretched legs. "I always forget how big you are. Tyler, Justin, and I can all sit on that couch with Toby on my lap, and Toby is not a small animal. Make room for me, please."

Carl looked at the neighboring love seat. Alison looked at him. He made room.

Alison sat down so close that she bumped his elbow when she poured herself a splash of whiskey, and she put her fuzzy socks on Tyler's coffee table with the easy familiarity of a regular visitor. She was small and warm and kindhearted, and her steady presence was an encompassing comfort. Carl sighed as tight muscles slowly, finally began to loosen.

Alison wiggled her toes in a little "I-knew-it" motion. "You're mixed up in trouble again, aren't you? Tell me everything. You know I won't leave you alone until you do."

Carl considered the beverage selection. Headache suppression argued for caffeine. The rest of his brain argued for alcoholic oblivion. He decided to postpone the decision.

Alison said, "Your brother is a bad influence. Are you really stooping to the silent treatment?"

"Not intentionally." He needed to talk to someone, no matter how difficult it was. "I don't know where to start. This whole impossible situation is tied into what I am."

"Oh? Are you finally bursting out of the closet in a spray of pink glitter?" Alison bumped Carl's arm with her shoulder. "I have wondered from time to time."

"I hate glitter." The image was still amusing, and Carl smiled at the affection which had inspired it. "Teasing me to lighten my mood? Not bad for an amateur."

"You were looking tragic. Besides, I couldn't resist the straight line." Alison smirked at her whiskey. "So to speak. You Midwesterners and your inhibitions. Justin is bashful, but you're so repressed you're unreadable. It's all very puzzling to a West Coast girl like me."

"Repression minimizes awkwardness. I could shock even your liberal Coastie sensibilities."

Alison sat up straight. "And now you're teasing me with all the big words. What's that mean?"

"It means I'm careful. Neopsych training leaves its practitioners with a lot of compartmentalization issues. The social side effects can be problematic for me now, especially when it comes to sexual attraction and emotional intimacy."

"You retreat into major jargon when you're feeling stressed, did you know that? Spit it out, will you?"

"Fine." Carl gave Alison full eye contact and let a thousand tiny physical cues that he normally suppressed crash into the interpersonal feedback loop. He was suddenly, fiercely conscious of the pressure of Alison's thigh against his, swamped by the warm scent of her body.

He took a lock of Alison's hair and tucked it behind her ear. "I respect the boundaries others set because I have none whatsoever. I cherish my few friends deeply. This is the result. Do you think Justin would be comfortable with it? Or Tyler? You're not."

Her eyes were wide, pupils dilated. She said breathlessly, "Comfortable? Good God, Carl. You're like a giant-sized box of erotic dynamite. I would say, 'screw comfort, find me a ladder,' but I'm pretty sure it still wouldn't work."

The laughter burst out of him, taking tension with it. Alison sat back and patted him on the leg. "That's better. Score one for me. Now, box up the explosives and explain yourself before I get so horny I can't concentrate."

Her brisk, earthy practicality was indescribably precious. Carl mentally packed away all the unspoken possibilities like keepsakes too fragile for daily use. "What I am, as I just demonstrated, is a neopsych. Even if you take away the drugs, equipment, and controlled environments, we still affect people. That's why the Institute enforces compliance to set protocols with conditioning."

"I know. And you're the exception because you broke your conditioning leash and survived." Alison sighed again. "If there's a point, I'm still missing it."

"The first point is that people like Pete don't travel without protection teams and approved itineraries. They literally can't. Second, his kidnapping didn't raise a single police alarm. That's also impossible. Third, it looks like some of his conditioning has been compromised. That's the most dangerous point of the three."

"How can you tell?" Alison cast a worried glance down the hall. "And is he dangerous?"

"Not now, not normally, but even a good man can snap. At some point after his call to me, he was beaten to a pulp and left to choke to death beside a fresh corpse. Kidnappers don't destroy potential leverage without good reason. I think he goaded someone into suicide. What's dangerous is that he isn't catatonic now, and he should be."

Alison opened her mouth. Carl spoke before she could ask. "Yes, I'm speaking from experience. I didn't break my conditioning leash. It broke me, and—"

He brushed away the ghosts. "Never mind. The point is that someone must have unbuckled Pete's collar for him, to use your analogy, and no one should be able to do that."

"That does sound ominous, but not urgent." Alison finished off her drink in a swallow and shrugged away the problem for future consideration. "Are you going to report the kidnapping?"

"No. For one thing, there's a bloody mess in the house we can't afford to waste time explaining."

Alison looked down, and the implied censure in her silence scraped at Carl's conscience. He leaned back and closed his eyes as the headache made a triumphant return. "Dammit, Allie, do you think we wanted them dead? Eddie is ruthless, but he isn't stupid. We have no idea why they took Pete or wanted me, and now we may never know."

Alison's hand was warm on his knee. "I'm sorry, Carl. The down-and-dirty makes me cringe, that's all. You know I can't help it. Please don't look so grim."

"How should I look? Dumping dead bodies in a park is grim. I have a head full of grim images just as bad that I can't erase, and I'm sure these won't be the last."

He'd accepted a devil's bargain, back when Rydder had nothing left to offer him but a future bounded by walls and devoid of purpose. The CSB had offered him a new identity and freedom in exchange for future services, and sometimes the work left stains on his soul. Not that security consulting was much better. He'd done his share of watching Parker's back, the last few years, and he'd seen more of the violent side of human nature than he wanted to contemplate.

This was not a life he'd ever intended to lead. He rubbed his eyelids to push back the pain. "Sorry. The down-and-dirty gets to me too. I became what I am to heal people. I don't like much about my work lately."

After a pause Alison said, "I hear you'd rather spend your days with a lap full of bunnies and baby lambs."

Carl looked at her through the fading visual auras. The strained comment was a peace offering. "That's a daydream, nothing more. Eddie must be worried if he mentioned it to you. He would take a perpetual firefight over farming."

"I think it sounds sweet: rabbits, goats, chickens, and all. Think of the photo ops." Alison pursed her lips against a smile. The smile won out, but it had an edge of sadness. "I will try to contain my judgmental prickles. What went wrong, at the house?"

Carl took the horrific memory and tucked it away with the rest of a collection he'd never wanted to accumulate. "The kidnappers flatlined after waking up captive. It looked like poison or suicide programming or both, which is just another frustrating impossible mystery to add to a huge stack of things that have to wait."

"One mystery at a time." Alison gave his leg another reassuring pat. "Bloody mess and no official report means your house needs cleanup. Let's write up a caretaker agreement so I can hire a crew. One less detail for you."

She retrieved a datapad from an overnight bag sitting near the kitchen. "Do you think it would it be safe to take your friend back there tomorrow if Dr. Faisal okays it? Am I being insensitive? I'm selfishly thinking of multiple bathrooms and space for Toby, so I won't have to commute home to feed and walk her."

"It isn't insensitive unless you're planning on locking Pete in the room where he was held, which you wouldn't."

The arrangements were handled with brisk efficiency. Alison conspicuously didn't mention that Carl could've saved himself some work if he'd let her oversee the property from the start. It was true, so Carl kindly didn't point out that Alison might be dead now if he had.

She finally asked the question Carl had been expecting from the moment he'd arrived. "What's Justin's problem? Blood doesn't make him green and wobbly. Neither does risking his neck. I had to aim him at skis to keep him off snowmobiles. Can you imagine?"

"Vividly. As far as tonight goes, he had an impressive panic attack on scene. By the time he shook it off he was—and I quote —'in no fucking mood to talk to anyone.'"

"Ah." Alison called out, "You were warned, Justin. Stick to a routine, eat regularly, and avoid stress or pay the price in brain tantrums. Stop sulking and come out before I pee on the floor."

He opened the door and stood there looking pale and shaky. Alison went to embrace him. They stood glued together long enough to leave Carl lost in the thicket of body language cues before Alison went into the bathroom.

Justin limped to the wall near the front door, leaning against it to take his weight off his left leg. He smiled at Carl. "You are pathetic when you look confused. We're not a couple, no, but we're working things out. Maybe it isn't normal, but neither am I."

Alison returned to the kitchen and emerged with a tray holding cups and a carafe. She handed a handful of energy bars to Justin. "Here. I do what I can," she said. "Eat them all."

Justin's smile was a studied balance of melancholy and contentment. He began dutifully chewing. Cups rattled as Alison maneuvered the office door open, and Tyler's voice drifted out: "—would've helped you."

The door swung shut on her reply. Justin said, "I wish they would work things out. Boy genius is good for her, but he thinks he's Lancelot to my King Arthur, the moron, and Allie insists that he's too young."

And Justin had no objection to his ex-lover and best friend pairing off right in front of him. "You are a strange and complicated person," Carl told him.

"That's what Connie says. That's my therapist's name." Justin swallowed a mouthful. "Carl, why can't I shake the panics and nightmares? I'm grateful I don't get full-sensory replays the way you do, but looking at Pete sent me into a fit, and I'm sweating at the thought of boarding that plane."

"That is a topic for your Connie," Carl said. "I have no clinical perspective."

"Yeah, but you have a personal one. The stupidest shit still sets me off. Why? It's been two years, and compared to—" Justin stopped and polished off a third energy bar.

Carl reached for the coffee cup, slugged back half the tepid contents, replaced it with whiskey, and choked down the result. The alcohol made his eyes water and the caffeine hit his veins in a warm flood: simple pleasures to balance complex pain. "Don't measure yourself against me."

"Is that a height joke?"

"No, I'm serious. It's an invalid comparison. Healing doesn't follow timetables, and the effects of trauma are unpredictable. Neos also process memories differently. We don't lay in neural pathways like normal adults."

Alison came out of the office in front of Parker, forestalling further discussion. "You should see this," she said. "Tyler had a news feed running in the office for background noise. Look."

She turned on the wall screen and muted a babble of competing narrations for a clutter of images, lists, timelines, and bullet-point speculation. Views and diagrams of the still-burning complex of buildings predominated. The common thread was the word *bomb*.

"Firefighters ran into residue from obsolete military ordnance." Alison's voice wavered with emotion. "It wasn't an accident. It looks like a real political statement. Gas explosion, yes, but someone helped it along. Still no power for blocks around, and the death toll's over 250 now. All travel is under inspection watch until noon Tuesday too, by the way."

Parker came forward, eyes fixed on the changing data. Alison put a hand on his arm. "Don't get sucked in, now. Tyler and I will keep the home fires burning. Go take care of your friend, then come back and deal with—what is it?"

Parker traced a breaking-news crawler with one finger.

"Suspects in custody?" Alison read. "What about it?"

It was an unconfirmed rumor. The authorities hadn't released names, but a sudden cold rush of fear told Carl all he needed to know. This was the reason Parker had never settled. The explosion had not been the threat looming over Naomi after all, or not the only one.

Parker was halfway down the hall to the stairs a second later. Carl was on his way out the door before his brain kicked into gear and he turned back.

"You'd better run on ahead," Justin said as he limped up. "Otherwise we'll need another ride. The plane won't lift without my say-so, but he has the keys to your van."

DUTY

RESTORATION DAY 2

Freedom is not free, citizenship is earned, and while we stand united, no one of us will fall. When everyone offers time and talents to the greater good, then we all share in the benefits. We are all in this together, like family members who don't always agree but who do always pull together to help one another. Respect your family. Take pride in your service.

—*A Young Citizen's Guide to Restoration Week*

CHAPTER SEVEN

T HE TRANSIT STOP AT the shopping center was filled with
late-shift city commuters who crowded their way onboard
the bus. Serena and Naomi were the only ones who got off the
vehicle. All the holiday surfers and beachcombers had departed at
the previous two stops.

Naomi glanced around the retail strip as Serena started walking. The fog was thinner on this side of the hills, and the sun
peeked wanly through haze above the eastern ridge. The shops
were closed, the parking zone empty. Corporate operations
remained open through Restoration on short shifts, but these were
family-owned shops whose owners had obligations elsewhere. No
one would notice two women in fitness gear taking a morning
stroll here.

The road uphill looked just as long and steep as it had on
Naomi's last visit to the Nguyen home. Once again she was
escorting Serena home for a tense family visit. This reunion would
be even more awkward than last year's had been, but it wouldn't
be a surprise. Naomi had called ahead.

Hiding until the furor died down would be the smart course,
but Serena wanted to come home, and when she was stubborn,

she was unstoppable. Naomi trudged along behind her and hoped for the best.

Mams had loved Duty Day. Naomi pushed that painful thought aside and reflected on the many times she'd come up this hill at dawn. She'd been ten the first time she followed Serena home after spending the night committing one felony after another. So much for leaving her youthful indiscretions behind.

Serena stopped when they reached the parking circle at the end of the road. She looked west and down, across the bank of fog that obscured the ocean.

"Why are we here?" She dragged her hands through her hair and tugged the red-tipped strands. "Oh. The big, brown stupid watchdog took over. Bad dog."

"I don't know what that means," Naomi said. "We're here because you insisted on making your Duty visit even though your family is usually under surveillance." Even though Serena's family had abandoned her twice over when she needed them. Aloud, Naomi added, "*I* suggested holing up in an empty condo and hopping a freight train tomorrow."

"Brown Dog wanted me to have my army gear." Serena frowned. "Oh, no. It's Duty Day, and I don't have any presents for Meema and Ba. Neither do you. Oh, Bao. Your mother—"

Her eyes filled, and she started to tremble. Naomi swallowed her own tears. "Don't break down now, sweetie. Be strong for me. Please."

Serena laced her fingers with Naomi's and took a deep breath. "I'm here. Gray Dog was saying go-go-go, but I put a muzzle on her, and Brown Dog will behave too, I promise. I'll be strong."

"If you say so." Understanding this strange new presentation of Serena's instability was not as important as accepting it. If imaginary dogs kept Serena functional, then Naomi would buy them steaks and build them a kennel with her bare hands.

They continued up the long drive leading to a sprawling estate home. A stooped man with wispy gray hair and narrow scowling eyes opened the door. The scents of soy and steamed vegetables wafted past him into the chill air.

David Nguyen looked up at his tall daughter, and the first words out of his mouth were: "Are you a murderer? A terrorist?"

"No, Ba," Serena said without any sign of the resentment Naomi would've felt. "We're both innocent of those crimes."

He nodded sharply and opened the door wide. "Inside, then. We're having a family meeting about the crapfest that's going to hit once your name leaks. Hello, Cupcake. Thank you for keeping her safe for us, as always."

Naomi rolled her eyes. The English translation of her nickname to cupcake wasn't remotely accurate. For years she'd thought Serena's father was delivering a calculated insult. What a difference maturity made. The affection was sincere. David Nguyen merely had an odd sense of humor to go with his odd family.

"Hello, Mr. Nguyen, sir." She bowed and stepped indoors, and he sighed at her formality, as he always did.

"Was she a target?" he asked. "Is this a move by Flores? Or Chi? Maybe Guo?"

The questions were asked with the resigned tension of a man who considered the quality and number of his enemies to be a point of pride, and with the shamed concern of a father who was unable to give his daughter the care she needed.

"I can't see why it would be," Naomi said. "It's obvious she's no threat to anyone's operations. Is someone trying to reach you through her?"

"No one's claimed it, if so." He ushered her after Serena, who had gone to the kitchen to greet her mother. Mrs. Nguyen's graying coppery curls made a bright contrast against her daughter's short black mane, but the fading red was an exact match for Serena's highlights.

A crowd waited in the airy living room. Two brothers, their wives, an uncle, and three cousins: half the neighborhood was perched on seats, sitting on the woven-reed floor covering or standing near the patio door watching an assortment of young-sters run in circles on the backyard lawn.

Naomi's skin went cold and flashed hot, going damp with sweat as her heart started to race. Seen through a different filter, she was looking at four successful business owners, a lawyer, two teachers, and most importantly, a CSB sector captain. The captain was sitting in Mr. Nguyen's favorite recliner.

Serena laced her fingers into Naomi's. "Uncle Phil, why are you here? You always volunteer for Restoration duty."

Her uncle crossed his legs, adjusted his trousers. He was taller than his brother and thinner, and the hair wasn't as gray. The scowl was the same. "Administrative leave. You've put us all at risk, coming here."

"We'll be gone in ten minutes," Serena said. "Once we figure out what's going on, can we come to you?"

Phil's eyebrows rose. "She sounds normal. Is she?"

That was directed at Naomi, and the tone hit her exactly the wrong way. "She's standing right there. Ask her."

Mrs. Nguyen came into the room with stack of bamboo steam-ers. Mr. Nguyen followed, dragging along a large duffel behind him by its strap. "Answer Serena's question, Phil. Do your loyal-ties lie with the Bureau or with family?"

"I'm praying there's no conflict, David." Phil rose from the chair, and came to look Serena straight in the eye while he said, "Naomi, you legally speak for her. It's a formality I need. Is my niece in her right mind and innocent of the crimes of which she's accused?"

"Yes, she's innocent, and so am I," Naomi said, wincing as Serena bared her teeth at her uncle. "Judge the rest for yourself. Why do you care?"

"Because I can help in good conscience as long as I believe you're both innocent. Which I do. Into the basement with you. Dave and I will get you off the radar. After that, you're on your own."

"Of course we are." Naomi clenched her fists around frustration. Mr. Nguyen shrugged unhappy acceptance, and his wife hid behind him, lowering her face. Serena's erratic behavior had long ago worn out her family's welcome. Of course they would renounce her now.

"We'll do all we can," Phil said. "Investigators sniffing after you two will use the excuse to dig up any number of expensive transgressions. If you find evidence that clears you, I'll do my best to put it in the right hands. That much I will promise and gladly. Come on, everyone."

With sighs and groans and muttered protests the whole group gathered close. The intimacy was uncomfortable, but if anyone was watching the house, imagery would show only a single contact. After children came running inside, muddying things further, the coffee table and the mat were pulled aside. The trapdoor was invisible until Mr. Nguyen unlocked it.

Naomi went down six narrow steps and remembered to stay bent over. Serena came down tugging along the duffel and carrying a pair of steamers balanced in one hand. The trapdoor closed, the light disappeared, and Serena whimpered.

The scent of spicy hot vegetables made Naomi's stomach growl. She groped her way to the workbench and turned on the light. Bulk merchandise was stacked along one wall, with packaging materials, scales, and shipping containers stowed in neat rows nearby.

It was the tidiest smuggling operation Naomi had ever seen. Not that she had seen many. She pulled up a crate and took the food from Serena.

"Let's eat," she said. "Then tell me about these dogs."

Serena began pulling things out of the pack instead: stun baton, knives, body armor, communications equipment, socks, boots, clothing, tactical helmet. Serena's parents had kept the mementos even though they'd exiled their child. The equipment had never frightened them. The daughter had. Serena repacked everything and bowed her head. "I'm acting crazy again, aren't I?"

Naomi moved around her to put her hands on those tense shoulders. "Wanting defenses when people are trying to kill you is entirely sane. You've been amazing except for the fade on the walk. Stubborn and obsessive, yeah, but maintaining. Even last night—you were grounded, not on a crying jag or in a blind rage."

"I didn't kill any patrollers." Serena ran her hands into her hair and squeezed her head. "Somebody mugged me, and I might've killed him, and I tried to call you, but it didn't work and then they said I killed police, and they shoved me in the box and all the dogs got loose. They were trying to keep me safe, but I didn't have a weapon and I saw—I knew—they were stalking—nnggh."

She bared her teeth and yanked at her hair. Naomi caught her hands, brought their arms down until she was spooning the taller woman in a hug. "Serena, stop. We need to rest and trust your Ba and Uncle Phil now."

"I smell dirt," Serena whispered. "Dirt wants out. Out-out-out."

"Shh, relax. This is the earthquake shelter, remember?"

Naomi got her settled against the wall and brought over the food. After the silent meal, she leaned in, shoulder to shoulder. "I've been meaning to tell you that you saved me last night. I was trapped and panicking, but I reached out and you were there for me, like old times. Like always."

Just saying it took her back to the morning five years past when she'd awakened to shaking walls and a roar of noise, terrified to her toes and feeling an inexplicable relentless need to *move*. After settling Mams, she'd walked halfway across the city until she was staring at San Francisco Bay and the emergency crews and all the destruction. It took two days to convince them to look in the right place, because no one was supposed to be on the rocks at night, but Naomi had *known*.

She'd known Serena like she knew her own body from the

instant they first laid eyes on each other. The connection was real as the air she breathed and just as impossible to describe or explain. They'd never talked about it much, partly because it wasn't useful, and partly because they'd been afraid that talking might make it go away.

And then it had, from soon after the quake until last night. Naomi had forgotten how good the togetherness felt.

"You saved yourself," Serena murmured against her neck. "You save me."

They fell asleep like that, huddled together. Naomi came awake to the sound of the trapdoor opening. A familiar voice said, "Time to get busy, lady friends."

Serena stretched and yawned, and Naomi did the same, wondering how Jaylin Byrd could be here. She must be dreaming.

A shadow crossed the light. "Don't make me crawl into that hole to get you."

It had to be Jaylin. No one else in the world could issue an effective threat in a chirpy soprano voice like that.

"Is that Jaybird?" Serena asked. "Or am I all crazy now?"

"I can't answer that second one, but I am myself, and unlike the rest of our old dorm mates, I don't scare easily. Up and at 'em, girls, the papa and the policeman want you safe and think I'm the woman to help with the job. Lucky for you, I agree."

Daylight streamed in through the tall picture windows on the west side of the house now, painfully bright against dark-adjusted eyes. Naomi climbed out, squinting, and Jaylin wrapped her in a hug that smelled of lavender and pine.

Naomi pushed her to arm's length and looked her up and down. Mostly up.

Jaylin was a big, voluptuous beauty on her worst day. Today she was deliberately outrageous in a sleeveless print dress and stiletto heels. Her wiry hair was dyed orange and twisted into dreadlocks, and earrings dangled to her caramel-brown shoulders. She gave Naomi a broad smile. "First thing we do is get you some decent conditioner. Then you're going to let me braid that amazing hair."

It was what Jaylin had said when they first met more than ten years ago, fresh out of police detention and waiting for the government bus to take them to service training camp and a future none of them could've ever imagined.

"I think we need to get safe first," Naomi said, and Jaylin grinned.

"You always have your priorities straight. Here's the plan. Mr. Nguyen will be delivering us to the train station, where a rental coupe was reserved by my company despite my checking 'no,' which turns out to be a good thing. You will be driving it. No, I still haven't bothered getting a driving license, thank you very much, Miss Big-Rigs-Are-Fun-Toys, and I will never let Serena drive again, not *ever*."

Shortly after being discharged from the Armed Forces, Serena had crashed a very expensive stolen sedan straight into a wall at high speed, without leaving tire marks on the pavement. Everyone but Naomi had believed that it was a suicide attempt.

"That was early in the after," Serena said from the bottom of the stairs. "I didn't understand yet how traffic would be so distracting. I would do better now."

Jaylin hesitated before saying, "That's nice. Bao will take us to the lovely furnished place that the company comped me this year. No pesky hotel cameras or documentation trails. The current travel restrictions expire tomorrow midday, and then you can drive me home to St. Louis. Isn't that a clever plan?"

The nattering speech made it hard to believe that Jaylin was a brilliant financial analyst, but that was the point. She could turn the breezy earthy attitude on and off at will. Her skin color and her sex were still handicaps in the business world, and she wielded her disguise as a powerful defensive weapon. Enemies underestimated her.

Serena's pack launched upward through the trapdoor and

landed on the living room floor. She climbed after it and stood with both hands over her eyes until Jaylin said, "I always said my beauty was blinding, but that's taking it too far. No hug for me, Serena-Ballerina?"

Nearly a minute passed before Serena let her hands fall to her sides, but then she laughed, and Jaylin beamed as they embraced. "There's the smile I remember."

They headed out together into the afternoon sunlight.

TYLER GRABBED the phone handset before it went from vibration to audible and punched acceptance with his right hand while his left kept tracing the line on his workstation screen. The idea was there, in his brain. He'd seen something critical in the emissions spectrum data he'd pried loose from Justin a few weeks past, and he could feel it sitting there behind his eyes. He just couldn't math it yet.

"Hey, Tyler, it's Dan. What's up? I got your message."

Tyler looked at the handset in confusion.

CSB Agent Dan Patterson looked back: medium-brown face, darker brown eyes and a thin white line of teeth. The smile looked genuine, but Tyler hadn't trusted looks since Dan's partner, Neil McAllister, had demonstrated the tricks an expert could play on a comm network. The pair of them had destroyed Tyler's faith in a lot of fundamental beliefs about law and order and privacy.

Dan contacting him wasn't confusing. The confusing part was that Tyler hadn't sent a message. He'd been too busy, first helping Alison with Pete and then getting distracted by the pesky idea.

"Is that sarcasm?" Tyler glanced at Pete, sound asleep on the couch behind him, and shunted the call to his workstation screen. "I'm sorry, but things are crazy—"

Dan raised a finger and looked to the side before nodding. "Right. You're you, you're not being coerced, and the line's secure.

Good job. Remember how I said you should always have an insurance plan and two escape routes, back when you asked for paranoia lessons after your big adventure?"

"I remember." His big adventure had left him with a profound hatred for adventures that involved people trying to kill him. His pulse skyrocketed. "Why?"

A loud noise preceded Dan's answer. "You're my insurance, and Neil's too. Call it a favor, call it cashing in the favors we've done for you. Call it what you want, but we need you and yours."

Another bang and a series of quiet whines made Tyler's stomach tie itself in knots. He'd grown up in a house full of hunters, and his lack of proficiency with firearms didn't affect his ability to recognize them. The bangs might be firecrackers, but the whines were not. Dan and Neil were dodging gunfire.

Neil McAllister was the kind of federal agent who made people and problems disappear; one who called the plays when the letter and spirit of the law disagreed. The world was gone to hell in a handbasket if he needed *Tyler's* help.

They wanted Parker and Carl or maybe Justin. Not him. That must be what "you and yours" meant. He shook off the numb fear. "What do you need?"

"A safe house, to start with. Do not tell a soul we're coming, Tyler. If we're not there in twenty-four hours, we're not coming, and I would suggest emigration. Jamaica's nice. Or Argentina. I'm not joking."

Tyler jumped in his seat when Alison slammed a cabinet door in the kitchen. Within the hour they would be moving out to Carl's place, with its tighter security system and wider variety of escape routes. Tyler bit his tongue to get moisture into his mouth. "What if I'm not home?"

"Keep your account on at least one piece of hardware. We'll come to you, and we'll explain when we get there. If we do. Watch yourself, Tyler."

"I will. Wait. Is Neil going to bring that monster cat with him? Can he leave it at home this time?"

Someone laughed, off-screen. It had a hysterical edge. Dan disconnected.

Tyler erased all evidence of the call as fast as he could enter the commands. Fear twisted inside him the whole time, and nausea sent him running for the bathroom the instant he finished.

Luck smiled on him. Alison didn't notice.

THE FRONT DOOR lock released with a click just loud enough to break Justin's concentration. Panic shot through him when he looked up from his reading and recognized *nothing*. His feet tangled in chair legs when he tried to rise, and a flailing attempt to regain his balance sent him crashing to the floor.

Consciousness made contact with memory after a few horrible seconds, and the disorientation receded. He was in San Francisco, catching up on Carl and Parker's case at the apartment the pair had rented as part of their cover.

He adjusted his belt and reclaimed his chair. "I suppose that looked hilarious."

Carl stood just inside the doorway with an odd expression on his face. His hair was hanging in wet strings, and the shoulders of his coat were soaked. "Hilarious is not the first word that comes to mind when I watch you go blank," he said. "Do you spray on that shirt, by the way?"

Justin looked down. The stretchy black thermal fabric shaded to gray over every contour down to the seam where it met the leggings, below the waistline of his pants. "It is getting tight. I've been gaining back muscle ever since Allie twisted my arm about physical therapy."

The words came out in a mush of syllables. Carl pinned Justin with one of his more intent looks before kicking off his shoes and peeling off the coat. "You slur after blanks now too, not just before them?"

Justin's attempt at "Not every time" came out as "Narr-ever-rime." He waited to be written off as a liability. There were still good days when he didn't fade out once. Sometimes he had good days for weeks in a row.

He'd also spent one long terrible week floating in and out of blanks and being a combative shit the whole time. At the end of that week, he'd taken Tyler and Alison to see lawyers about setting up the trusts, because he had no idea how many good days he had left in him.

Carl said nothing, only stood watching. The silence dragged until Justin gave up and tried speech again. "How'd your morning go?"

He did better that time, and Carl nodded, looking relieved. "We haven't learned much," he said. "Naomi was in custody, but she isn't now. Rumor says she and an accomplice shot their way out of Central Detention. There's no official word but the wanted-for-questioning alert fits her description. The worse news is that the CSB may go to a street curfew tonight. Social Aid is catching protests from all sides, on everything from Subsistence crime statistics to police interference and harassment. Mob tension is building up."

"So you have no idea where to look for this woman, but we need to find her and get out before the city shuts down to stop riots and panic migration? Fantastic. Is Parker still out hunting?"

"Yes, practicing his intimidation skills to get hospital and morgue intake records. Trying to confirm or refute the escape rumors. Hoping against hope for another weirdness attack to give him a better line on Naomi's location."

"And you got stuck keeping an eye on me?"

Carl sighed. "No, Justin. It isn't always about you. I wanted a shower, a nap, and lunch. Oddly enough, I like to rest and eat when I'm cold, tired, and hungry."

Justin had meant it as a joke. He tried another one. "Well, at least you'll warm up fast enough."

"Yes, because you turned up the thermostat to 'surface of the sun' as usual." Carl stripped off the jacket and the wet shirt and walked toward one of the apartment's two bedrooms. "For once I'm grateful. This city's weather is insane. Who ever heard of cold fog in August?" He paused to shed the pants, and dropped all the wet clothes on a weight bench before turning back. "I'll start on lunch as soon as I get into dry—"

He stopped and scowled. "Do not say you forgot about the scars. You've known about them since we met."

Justin shook his head. The disfigurations were as unforgettable as they were unsettling: a broken-lattice pattern front and back, from scalp to feet. "I don't mean to stare, but it's a shock every time."

"Too bad. I will not hide in my own apartment." The bedroom door slammed.

Something about Carl's short temper ate at Justin's nerves. Everything was bothering him, really. The whole place was full of things that looked wrong.

His table sat next to a pass-through that separated a small kitchen area from a shared living space with the front door in the center and doors to two mirror-image bedroom suites on either side. It all looked indefinably odd, from the untidy piles of clothes to the metal bucket full of yarn.

Carl came out wearing only dry black work pants and started doing things with vegetables and knives and bowls in the kitchen. "I can see you didn't bother to shower or shave yet," he said. "Have you eaten, or did you forget that too?"

The question was loaded with indulgent patience. Indulgence was the child of sympathy, sympathy was cousin to pity, and Justin hated the whole family. "I wasn't dirty, and who shaves on vacation?"

"Meaning you did forget." Carl kept chopping. "Everyone has

issues, Justin. You will never catch me voluntarily stepping into closets or crawl spaces, and Eddie's never going to be anyone's choice for chatting up witnesses. Your faults are a little more problematic, true, but—"

He set down the knife and turned, leaning against the counter. "I just realized that I'm getting wound up because *you're* wound up tight. What's wrong?"

"I don't know." Justin couldn't meet that steady blue gaze for long. "I can't explain it. Nothing fits."

"You keep looking at all the—ah." Carl's frown cleared. He went back to dicing. "Schematic dissonance."

"Can I get that in English?"

"You have a hard time processing changes, and we're not living exactly the way you remember us. Here's some context: the toys are from a service animal center where Eddie volunteers, and the yarn is his too. Naomi recommended knitting for motor therapy."

Justin blinked. The idea of hypervigilant, hyperactive Parker knitting didn't fit in his mental universe. "Knitting."

Carl grinned at him. "Now that look, *that* is hilarious."

"I live to amuse you."

"Word of advice." Carl pointed the knife at him. "Keep that orphaned-animal charisma of yours to yourself once we do find Naomi. Eddie is thoroughly besotted, and he might cut your balls off if you make him jealous."

Justin let his head drop forward until it was resting on the tabletop. "You joke, you cook, and you use the word *besotted* to describe your slightly sociopathic brother. You are making my brain melt."

"Relax. You'll get over it." Carl put a dish into the oven and started cleaning. "Adrenaline does odd things to memory formation. Did I wipe out your work when I startled you?"

"Let's find out." Justin propped his head on his hands and tried to put ideas in order. "There's a legit pipeline from Rydder

Institute's drug synthesis unit to a center here that supplies clinic pharmacies. You think the psychiatric medications are being filtered through dispensaries and out again as street-saleable garbage like Ghost, and the Bureau okayed a covert investigation. The clinic where—shit." Names were impossible. "*Shit.*"

"Naomi."

"—where *Naomi* works is a leaky distribution point that you hoped to backtrack. You've ruled her out despite a clear money trail, and you were looking hard at the clinic director and the head of an associated psychiatric unit before the Restoration break." He sat up. "That's now."

"And here we are," Carl said. "Pete was poking into the Institute end of the pipeline. It was months ago, but if I add him to the picture, there's another scenario: someone's filtering the drugs through the clinics straight into the hands of people who are using them the way neopsychs do. Without their training or ethics code."

The right medications in the hands of rigorously trained experts could produce changes in behavior both dramatic and subtle. In the hands of the unscrupulous, the same drugs had the potential for wreaking societal havoc.

"Could anyone get away with that on a large scale?" Justin asked after Carl put away all the cookware. "The CSB's screenings are solidly designed. That's why Dominic Walton was so selective about his victims. Somebody would notice, right?"

"Someone would, yes, but the Bureau is more rotten than solid in some places these days, San Francisco being one of them." Carl sat down on the couch. "You've kept the bones of it. What about the briefs on Naomi and known associates?"

"Lives for the job, and her patients love her. Two legal dependents: sick adoptive mother, dead now, and a childhood partner in crime who went batshit crazy and washed out of a CAF training program. Is that her accomplice?"

"It might be. The description fits. Go on."

"Bio: safe-haven newborn, single-parent Subsistence adoption, thanks to our federally subsidized 'take home a baby, get a live-in servant' program. Looks like she rebelled: chose extra government service at sixteen instead of prison for petty theft and vandalism." Justin shut his eyes to concentrate. "Worked off the debt, got licensed in physical therapy, got off the Sub rolls. Went on probation for absenteeism and tardiness. Her leech of a mother picked up one of the nastier nanobugs a few years ago. Until recently the batshit crazy girl was sponging off her too."

When Justin opened his eyes, he was facing a disapproving frown. "What?"

"You can be breathtakingly judgmental, and they do have names."

Justin winced. "Things only stick when I strip them down. And no one who strips naked to sing lullabies to flowers in a public park has a right to complain about being called batshit."

A smile twitched at Carl's lips. "Point. Batshit-crazy is Serena Nguyen. Her enabler is Naomi Kwan. Please try to memorize both names if you can. What else?"

"Nothing." Justin rode out a spike of frustration. "But you wouldn't ask if there wasn't."

"You lost a few names and sketch bios. Associates that Naomi was supposed to meet over the break." Carl checked the oven. "I'm taking a nap until this is done. You should catch some sleep too."

Justin called Ryan instead. Duty had come to mean family in the shifting culture of Restoration, and the boy was family, even if not in the traditional sense. His conception had betrayed his mother's infidelity and ended her marriage to Justin, but he was also a smart, sweet child who had his mother's smile.

The boy was looking for sympathy today. First his father hadn't made a visit or even sent a message, much less a gift. Then Helen had packed away the presents from Justin and cried, saying that Ryan must think she was a horrible parent.

Ryan was feeling indignant and guilty at once. Justin found it easier to relate to the boy's discomfort than his mother's distress. Helen traveled nowhere without a security detail and a publicist. Nothing about her life or Ryan's would ever be normal or safe, even if their public profile was lower now that Helen had finally divorced the boy's egotistical celebrity father.

Once Justin wrapped up that call, he spent some time pondering the stupidity of twice locking himself into legal relationships he couldn't emotionally sustain.

He'd learned a few tricks in the process of protecting assets from the consequences of his bad judgment. Carl's datapad had a lot of tracking and data aggregation programs stored on it along with the case files. The current activities of Naomi's friends might contain hints of her plans.

Captured message threads provided travel plans for the out-of-town friends, and a little effort confirmed that five of six on the list had checked out early from hotels they'd mentioned booking. Justin skimmed their bare-bones public profiles and started some additional searches.

"Don't jump," Carl said behind him. A loaded plate landed on the table. "Eat. You could still stand to gain a few kilos."

"I'm working on it. Doc's best guess is that whatever lives in my skin skims off my metabolism, but she can't keep samples alive to study. Allie worries."

"Meaning that you'll starve if Eddie and I aren't careful. Noted. Now, dig in." Carl started on his own meal.

Justin's query results started trickling in before the food was gone, and after he confirmed them, he slid the pad across the table. Carl put down his fork, looked over the address and other information and reached for his phone.

"Hey, Eddie. Good news."

SERENA PULLED her knees to her chest, folded her arms over the top, and rested her forehead on her arms. The darkness was cozy, the walls were close, and she was warm and clean. She felt alive.

There'd been a time when she felt like this more often than not. There'd been a time when brief storms of bleakness had been separated by long stretches of laughter and love. There'd been family and friends and beauty in life. That had been *Before*.

All the dogs stirred and growled warning when she drifted close to the dark *After* where she'd lived for so long. It was their territory now, not hers, and she was content to leave it to them. She enjoyed *Now* for an unmeasured stretch of heartbeats, happily cataloguing the current occupants of her wonderful inner menagerie. The dogs were the most active of the bunch, easiest to identify, but it felt as if she might have a whole zoo in there creeping and bouncing and fluttering around.

Someone knocked on the door. Serena noted the size of the shadow against the dim light filtering between the door slats, caught a hint of scent. "Hi, Naomi."

"Sweetie, are you okay?"

"Yes." Serena waited. Amusement snuffled at her throat, tickling her with wiry fur and tugging at her with little monkey paws. The door opened to let in a stab of light and a harsh brush of cooler air. Naomi closed the door and sat beside her.

Clever Naomi always approached from the side. Never confronting, never challenging. Her hair was a damp black cloak over the shoulders of the tight exercise outfit, and she smelled of water and lemongrass and lavender soap.

After a lovely silent moment, Naomi said, "You're hiding in a closet with no clothes on, and now you're whuffling in my ear. In what way is this okay?"

Serena drew back so that she could make out Naomi's face in the gloom: grumpy frown with the lower lip pushed out, thin brows together, eyes narrowed to slits. The amusement escaped Serena's control and leaped free as a giggle.

She put one finger on the pouting lip. "I. Am. Okay," she said with slow emphasis. "Really-really. I'm naked when cloth hurts my skin. I'm in the dark when light hurts. The bathroom was cold. The closet is perfect. I like Jaybird's soap. Everything here smells like her. Safe."

"Is it like a migraine?" Naomi asked. "Are you queasy? I'm asking because lunch is here. Well, late lunch, early supper. Whatever. Food. Are you hungry?"

"Hungry, yes." She hadn't had an appetite in so long that she hadn't been able to identify the roly-poly kitten for what it was. She picked it up and hugged it until it squirmed. "I'm hungry, Naomi."

"That's good?" was the wary response.

Serena stood and pulled Naomi to her feet. "It's wonderful. Let's go eat."

CHAPTER EIGHT

SERENA DRESSED IN THREADBARE fatigues, soft from wear and washing, and Naomi switched off the hall light on the way to the main room of Jaylin's rental unit. "How often do you get migraines, Serena? I never knew; I'm sorry."

"It isn't a headache. Everything is too much."

Jaylin dimmed the rest of the lights and closed curtains, then pointed them to the table where bags and boxes, bowls and plates awaited. The food was delicious, and Serena savored every bite before swallowing.

"If I buy pancakes for breakfast, will you let me record you eating them?" Jaylin served herself more rice to soak up leftover oyster sauce. "The way you're seducing that fried tofu, I could make millions on food porn."

Serena stopped chewing with quite so much enthusiasm. "Sorry."

"Eat up." Jaylin's dreadlocks swung as she pushed a container of sweet dumplings closer. "I'll live vicariously."

She turned to Naomi. "I ordered clothes online while you two were cleaning up and sleeping, and I've set up a delivery drop. You can't wear stolen spandex and army surplus forever."

"Thank you," Naomi said for them both.

"I also did some groundwork." Jaylin tapped her chopsticks on her plate. "The police don't toss out the word *terrorism* for shits and giggles, and that made me curious. Your comms and financials are frozen, of course, but they haven't been purged. I'm sorry, Naomi, but I can see why they snapped you up. Hand to God, you look guilty as sin. There's a big red financial trail, the last few months."

Naomi pushed back from the table. "You got into my accounts? How?"

"The same way I got your body specs for the clothes order today, of course."

Jaylin went back to eating.

Naomi sat there waiting for the rest of the explanation. Serena smiled at her plate. Naomi could be aggressively patient when she wanted. Jaylin rolled her eyes and conceded the answer. "You had me do your taxes, way back when you took on Serena, and you gave me full profile access. You never erased the permissions. You're far too lax about security, you know. And you—"

The chopsticks pointed at Serena. Her muscles tensed as her bigger, more dangerous protectors stirred in the den. She let them prowl outside to show them that there was no threat, and for a few heartbeats she saw the world their eyes saw: weapons, ranges, strategies, angles. Felt the rush in her blood. Attack, control, dominate, win: those were the reflex reactions. It took a moment to override them with the concepts *Jaybird: friend: protect.*

Jaylin carefully put down her utensils and licked her lips. "Put away your mask-of-menace and back it the hell down, Serena. I am not the enemy."

"I know." Serena shifted uncomfortably as her stomach clenched around the food she had eaten. "Sorry, Jaybird. They know you now. It won't happen again."

"You'll have to buy me new underwear if it does." Jaylin chuckled. "It is an impressive mask, I'll give you that. I didn't mean to set you off. I was only going to make a point about not letting your bills fall behind."

"I know, I meant to send them yesterday, but it was all too much, and I screwed it up." Serena got up and paced, tried to soothe Gray Dog back to sleep. Worrying was silly now, she *knew* that.

Naomi came to her side and pulled her close. Her heartbeat was steady and certain, and it brought the world into balance again. Serena smoothed down the soft length of Naomi's hair, and it felt like a million strands of calm.

Naomi said, "Say good-bye to it, sweetie. I've convinced Jaybird to lop it off. It's in the BOLO. I know it soothes you, but if I can cut it now, of all times, then you can bear it too. Please don't be upset. Mams would be so disappointed—"

Grief was thick in Naomi's voice. Serena squeezed it away with a sharp rush of sympathy. Naomi's mother would've wanted her hundred days, her wake, all her traditions, and Naomi would've given her full honors, but there was no body to bury and she couldn't even leave her hair uncut in proper mourning.

Serena stroked her hair once more in farewell and dug deep inside in search of words to ease pain. "Your mama would've frowned and waved her hands and said 'Ungrateful daughter,' but she would've spent hours making short hair toys, after. She loved you, and I will be strong for you, I promise."

"Oh, a promise," Naomi said with a hint of bitterness. Then she smiled and stretched up to touch noses. "Thank you. Your colored hair has to go too, you know. Jaylin will trim it out. We'll face it together."

Jaylin said, "I'm warning you, I'm dangerous with scissors. Hair care isn't genetic, you know." She clapped her hands together. "Enough warm fuzzies. Let's get to work."

Work included questions about Serena's purchases and deposits, utilities and rent, Subsistence payments and waivers. It also involved letting Jaylin play with scissors. The questions were embarrassing because Jaylin kept asking about dates when Serena couldn't remember what she'd been doing. The haircut was worse. Serena ended up with itchy hair everywhere. She could feel it even after she showered under a pulsing-hard shower spray and scrubbed herself raw.

She curled up in her nest of blankets in the closet and whimpered. Her skin prickled from scalp to toes. Naomi kissed her on the cheek as if she were a fretful baby and apologized for having no meds to help. Her new pixie bangs tickled Serena's skin, and the touch was no comfort.

"I'm strong," Serena said. "I can do this alone."

Naomi left her the astonishing gift of solitude. It was a precious statement of trust to leave her hands free and her nails bare when she was feeling like this. She could scratch herself bloody. She'd done it in the past. In the After.

She'd promised, and Naomi believed in her.

Serena sat on her hands and tried to live up to that faith. She was crying before sleep finally came to release her from the maddening discomfort, but it did come, with a whisper of silky feathers that wrapped her in downy oblivion.

SHE AWAKENED BLIND AND BREATHLESS. The closet was pitch dark, her arms were pinned in the bedding, and someone's knee was on her chest. From the scents of knife oil, gunpowder, and sweat, "someone" was male and armed. A hand pressed steady against Serena's throat, and another covered her mouth. A simple message: either she remained silent or she would not remain conscious.

Red Dog woke in a howling fury, which wasn't helpful because Serena would already be dead if she were meant to die. Before she could push the growling aggression out of mind, she bucked and twisted. Her captor exerted pressure. The darkness faded into snowy dots of oxygen deprivation. Serena got one arm loose and tapped the man's wrist, signaled surrender, begged with a touch of nails as terror ripped free.

Suffocating. Trapped. Buried. *Dying.*

Then she was sitting up and sucking air into her tight, aching chest, and the monstrous fear dissolved into relief. A brief touch on her bare shoulder was followed by fingers at her lips: reminder of the terms. She nodded, and the man retreated with a muted jingle.

Soft weight hit Serena's lap: her clothes. She dressed fast, and the lights came up. It was the lowest setting, but it still felt like nails driving into her skull, and she struggled to keep her defenders muzzled, because now she could see that she wasn't truly outmatched. He was wearing a tactical helmet and ballistic vest, but he was barely taller than her. His knife was sheathed, his pistol holstered. She could take him. Maybe.

He dropped to a crouch, one knee on the floor. *No threat*, the rugged face declared when the helmet visor was retracted. *No threat*, insisted the splayed hands and lifted chin. Then his eyes met Serena's and held fast. Bright with intent, they were full of forest colors and the certainty that no, she wouldn't win.

A grin said he would enjoy the challenge all the same. Promised: another time, a different place. Just for the fun of it, and it would be fun. Curiosity pricked up pointy ears and flared its whiskers, but Brown Dog growled about the lines of *not-safe-not-safe* urgency in the man's shoulders. Away would be safer, that tension said.

When he nodded to the door, Serena walked out in front of him.

THE VAN TOOK a corner a little too fast and then halted, and both maneuvers caught Naomi off-balance. Being blindfolded complicated life, and her hands being tied together made matters worse. She slid across the slippery bench seat and banged her already bruised elbow on the cup holder again.

The motor shut off. A door opened.

Engines rumbled in the distance, and the air smelled like ocean. Jaylin's spicy hair gel was nearby, and behind her Serena occasionally sighed. Things could be worse. No one had hurt her, at least not on purpose, and if the situation changed from mysterious to actively dangerous, a blindfold and bound hands wouldn't stop Serena for long.

Whatever was happening, it wasn't official. Police broke into homes in the dead of night, yes, but they didn't sneak in and slink away in silence. They came in with breakage and bright lasers and shouting and left under an umbrella of press coverage and helicopter spotlights. Police didn't transport blindfolded prisoners in vans that had cup holders and smelled of commercial disinfectant. These people did.

The man Naomi thought of as Mr. Shivers helped her out of the van. His touch raised goosebumps. He'd held her by the wrist or arm at several points on the drive when the van was slowed or stopped, and each time the electric static had raised every hair on her body.

"Please don't fight," he'd whispered when Naomi hit him, and he'd apologized when he blindfolded her and walked her to the van. All the polite courtesy had been oddly reassuring, and Naomi would've said so, except that her mouth was taped shut by then. Her knuckles still ached from the one punch she'd landed. Hitting him had felt like hitting a brick wall.

She was walked up steps and indoors. Her new seat smelled like leather. Items rattled, voices murmured, and bodies moved. Engines roared to life, the air pressure changed, and the world tilted steeply to the whine of turbines. Then the noise and the floor leveled.

"Okay, we're in the air. I'll free your hands so you can take off the blindfold," Mr. Shivers said in a raspy soft voice. "Let me get this first."

Astringent liquid dabbed against Naomi's face, and the gag came off without pulling skin. He'd used medical tape and solvent, yet another gentle oddity.

Strangest kidnapper ever, Naomi thought, and she removed the blindfold. Everyone knew what airplanes looked like, but she'd never expected to be riding in one. She had to look all around.

This looked like a small but expensively appointed aircraft. She was facing another couch, and four seats on swivel bases flanked a small conference table to her left. Jaylin sat beside her, twisting a piece of cloth in her hands. She wore sweatpants and an oversized tee shirt similar to the one she'd loaned Naomi. Bits of adhesive showed white against her chin and cheeks, and her eyes were hot with fury behind an orange tangle of bangs.

She was looking at two men in matching black outfits on the opposite bench. Serena was sitting free and easy between them in her ratty camouflage, and the pain of betrayal shattered Naomi's heart into a million pieces. Serena's eyes widened, and then she flung herself across the space with a wail of distress.

Sixty kilos of pure unhappiness slammed into Naomi's lap. Serena squeezed tight, and babbled protests with her face pressed against Naomi's belly. "No, Naomi, no, please don't look like that, we weren't safe and he promised, and they got us away and we need to be here and we are safe and *I only wanted to help*."

She burst into tears, distraught beyond hope of consolation. Naomi rested a hand on her head and looked at Carl. There he sat, he and his brother, the one so damaged, the other devoted. She should have known it was too good to be true. They were not who they'd claimed to be, and the blame for mass murder was being laid on Naomi's shoulders. The line was easy to draw.

She wanted to shriek and scream, but she couldn't even draw a breath. Serena grabbed her shirt and whimpered.

"Well, this is going well." The sarcastic comment came from a disembodied voice right above Naomi's seat: Mr. Shivers, except that he wasn't there. "Carl, I need to zero out. Is it all right if I crash in back?"

"It's your plane, Justin," Carl said without taking his eyes off Naomi. "Take care of yourself. I've got this."

"You've got a shitload of nerve, that's what you've got," Jaylin said. "And you've kidnapped us. Why?"

Carl raised an eyebrow at her. "We had to move fast to get you out of the mess you were in."

The statement implied that they hadn't been the ones to put Naomi *in* a mess after all. Confusion made it hard to hold onto anger. Carl looked familiar and strange at the same time. His face was somber, his eyes held none of their usual warmth, and with no smile to buffer its power, his deep voice was a hard authoritative force.

Parker was still Parker: tan, trim, and twitchy. One leg jiggled, a hand tapped on the bench, and his gaze touched Naomi in passing as he watched everyone at once. Suddenly Naomi felt more exhausted than anything else.

Jaylin said, "Oh, for pity's sake, will you all stop mooning at each other?" She stomped her way to the table and took a seat. "Naomi, what's going on?"

"I don't know." Naomi coaxed Serena into lying on the seat but couldn't convince her to lift her head. "Shh, baby, I'm sure you tried to do the right thing. I'm sorry I doubted you." She went back to glaring at Carl. "Why did you lie to me? Why did you set me up to take the blame for the apartment explosion?"

He'd been about to speak, but he hesitated, looking startled. "We didn't. Set you up, that is. The lying part: because we had to."

Jaylin made a rude noise. "Don't be cryptic. Fork over a rational excuse for treating us to a luxury pajama flight."

"Pictures speak louder than words," Carl's voice took on a

sharp edge. "Look out the window on your left. Tell me what you see."

Jaylin responded with uncharacteristic meekness, and then turned back with a stricken expression. "The whole downtown is covered in emergency lights."

"A bomb went off in the county courthouse. Minor structural damage, lots of secondary fires. Broken glass and chunks of rubble ripped through the crowd at a Duty Day event in the square, too. There's also a big hole that used to be the Oakland Point railyard on the other side of the Bay. The city's going to a zero-tolerance street curfew with door-to-door occupant surveys, which would've been impossible to evade and could've resulted in you being shot dead."

"So you had to steal us from our beds?" Jaylin made another rude noise. "Try again."

Carl crossed his legs and clasped his hands loosely together over one knee. "If I'd shown up on your doorstep saying, 'Come with us, your lives are in danger, and we need to drive like maniacs to get wheels up before they shut down the airport,' what would you have done?"

Naomi thought about it. So did Jaylin, with a shared look that made them burst out laughing at once. Serena lifted her head. Naomi suppressed the chuckles before they turned hysterical. "I would've argued. And fought. And we'd still be there. But who *are* you? Why help us?"

"Those are good questions." Carl gifted Naomi with the familiar warmth of his smile. "I'll start with the most important point. We misrepresented exactly two things. Last names and employment particulars. Those were the only lies either of us told you."

Parker snapped his fingers: the ones on his right hand. When he'd first managed it in therapy, he'd laughed out loud, and the joy on his face then had made Naomi's heart leap. That warmth was still there. She blinked away tears. She wanted to believe that it was real, wanted it too much to trust her feelings.

Jaylin rapped knuckles on the table. "All right, big boy. Why don't you come over here and start at the top? I like my explanations all businesslike and tidy."

EVEN WHEN CARL wasn't vague, which was most of the time, he got to his points by the longest route imaginable. His initial employment description, "we look into things," translated to freelance work for the federal government, for example, and Mr. Shiver's identity was passed off as "Justin helps with logistics." Following his exchanges with Jaylin took most of Naomi's concentration. She missed the transition when Serena's clingy anxiety lapsed into sleep.

Parker brought over a blanket and inclined his head at the table. When Naomi lifted an eyebrow at him, he sent the gesture right back at her with interest.

I'll take care of her for you, that look said, and Parker dropped to the floor in front of the bench with a declarative, proprietary thump. *Go on.*

Some things in life were inevitable. The sun rose in the east, tides rose and fell, and men were drawn to Serena like bees to a thorny, bright flower. This felt different, though, so Naomi tried to listen to her heart and be hopeful.

Once she got to the table, she took Jaylin's hand and started a massage exercise. The activity helped them both relax while Carl explained things badly and Jaylin made him explain his explanations.

"That's all of it, then," Carl eventually said. "Everything I can share without violating confidences or launching into irresponsible speculation."

Naomi couldn't blame them for initially thinking she was

involved in an illegal drug network. Her record spoke for itself: she was an unreliable ex-felon who'd been trouble since the day she was born. Carl refused to say which of the clinic's drugs she'd been suspected of distributing, but it hardly mattered. She had looked guilty.

Within hours of every shipment that went through the clinic, someone had moved unrestricted funds through Serena's Subsistence account. Naomi had been responsible for that account. She should have reported unauthorized activity, but she never had. Keeping everyone clean, fed, healthy, and happy had been an exhausting challenge, complicated by the need to keep her head above water professionally as well. She'd never had the energy to poke through endless lines of numbers after paying the bills. It wasn't as if her mother's or Serena's stipends ever changed.

Her accounts and her every traceable activity had been monitored for months before Carl had traced the financial indiscretions to her manager, Lucy. The invasion of privacy should have left her outraged, but right now she could only feel grateful for it. All the collected records would prove that the unexplained cash deposits and purchases *Jaylin* had found were bogus.

There were still mysteries, and Carl had some odd ideas. One was a belief that the bombing might have been planned because Naomi had been cleared of involvement in the clinic scheme.

She knew she should've died. She'd thought it herself more than once. Serena could've died too, in the attack that had ended in her arrest. Carl's warped perspective did make the attack in the holding pens look like an improvised follow-up by someone determined to see both of them silenced. It just didn't make sense for anyone to kill hundreds to cover up the murder of a couple of pawns.

Carl was firm in his belief. It made Naomi wonder if tonight's events were more acts of conspiracy, if other crimes were being erased or obscured under cover of greater violence. She couldn't bear to think about it for long before it made her want to cry.

The murky depths of motivation made her equally uncomfortable. Appreciation for her therapeutic skills could not account for this rescue. Her usefulness as an informant couldn't justify it either. She wasn't worth all this trouble.

"What happens now?" she asked to fill the tired silence.

Carl said, "We lie low and wait for the storm to blow over. It's clear that we've been caught up in the edges of something huge: you by intent, us by association. We'll get safe, throw out feelers to some federal contacts regarding the legal situation, and go from there."

"What about all that?" Jaylin waved at the windows. "Don't tell me it's coincidence that Day One saw a major bombing and Day Two had two. The group supposedly funneling cash to Bao, Kali's Disciples, they're small players. No way they pulled off a coordinated attack."

"Revisionists took credit for tonight." Carl folded his arms across his chest. "And hundreds of them are currently being incarcerated for it. I don't believe in coincidence either. I did say 'huge' didn't I? We many never know the whole story. I say to hell with whoever's behind it."

"To hell with them? What's Day Three going to bring? There are millions of people in the Bay Area. If you're on the edge, then you can dig your way to the middle. At least alert the authorities to all this. You have to do something."

"I disagree. Picking which battles to fight is critical to surviving them."

Jaylin gently placed her hands, palms flat, on the table. "Well, I disagree with you disagreeing. In fact, I find cowardice disagreeable in the extreme."

The emotional atmosphere went from heated to frigid in an instant. Carl pushed back from the table and strode away, past the wall divider at the rear. Naomi took a breath and shook off the chill. Serena put out a hand and groped blindly until she found

Parker's shoulder within reach. He put his hand over hers, and she quieted again.

Jaylin slumped back in her seat. "Touchy son of a gun, isn't he? If he can't take a little insult, then maybe he shouldn't be so selfish."

Parker dismissed her with a glare and settled those bright eyes of his on Naomi. "Cautious, not cowardly," he said with quiet intensity, as if he deeply cared what Naomi thought. "Experience teaches caution."

Naomi's stomach went sour, thinking of the scars on Carl's wrists. A *work accident*, he'd called them. She got up immediately and went to see if he would accept an apology.

———

THE DIVIDER SHIELDED a small galley that opened over a bar into another seating area with two facing couches. Naomi almost fell over Carl before she caught herself on the counter. He was on his knees, bending over someone on the floor. The man named Justin had mentioned the rear of the plane and something about zeroing out, whatever that meant. If that was him, then 'zeroing out' evidently meant passing out cold.

"Can I help?" Naomi asked.

"No, I've got him." Carl carried Justin to one of the benches, then retreated to the opposite bench and hunched over to face the floor. His hands were so tightly clenched together that the knuckles were white.

Naomi considered opening lines and went with, "Is he okay?"

The question would pull Carl back from whatever emotional edge he was teetering on. Caregivers were predictable that way, and that was one thing that Naomi was *almost* sure she hadn't mistaken about Carl. It took one to know one.

Carl sighed. "Okay is a relative concept with Justin. So is

normal. What do you want? I'm busy licking my wounded ego here. If you can't be grateful, can you be elsewhere?"

He couldn't have picked a better way to hurt Naomi's feelings if he'd tried. *Selfish child*, whispered the memory of Mams voice. Naomi's throat went tight around her next words. "Jaybird didn't mean for her comment to hit so hard. She didn't mean to hurt you like that."

"Let her apologize for herself if she wants. It isn't your job." Carl put his head in his hands. "Please do me the favor of leaving me alone."

The odd phrasing left little room for discussion. Naomi turned to go, but when Justin moaned, concern made her pause. "Are you sure he's okay?"

Carl sighed again, more heavily this time. "And he calls me nosy. Go on, take a look, satisfy yourself."

Justin looked normal enough. He was broad-shouldered and wiry like a gymnast, on the short side of average height, with dark wavy hair and Caucasian features under sun-browned skin. Touching him didn't make Naomi's fingers tingle now, although the stubble on his throat was scratchy and thick. His skin was moist and hot, and his pulse was thudding along much too fast.

Naomi checked for signs of injury. The man's left leg was impaired severely enough that she would've suggested corrective surgery, not that anyone had asked her, but it wasn't recent. She sat back on her heels. "Unconscious with elevated pulse and fever doesn't worry you?"

"Not yet. If he starts shivering, or he doesn't wake on his own by the time we land, then I'll panic."

"Whatever." She was hardly in a position to argue. "What's on his ankle here? It isn't rigid enough to be a brace. And it isn't a bond cuff." She knew what those looked like. "Those don't have buttons and switches."

"Don't touch—"

Carl's warning came a little too late. Naomi fell back from the

107

bench as its occupant abruptly disappeared. Her rump hit the floor, and a slight breeze warned her just before something landed on her feet. Static tickled her legs.

"Shit." Plastic crunched. The panel under the bench developed an elbow-sized dent. "*Shit.*"

Invisible Justin cursed the whole way to the rear of the cabin. A pocket door slid open to reveal bathroom fixtures and slammed shut again. Naomi looked back to Carl. "Normal is a relative term with him?"

"I did warn you," Carl said.

CHAPTER NINE

T HE NOISES FROM BEHIND the bathroom door were
barely audible, but every suppressed whimper made Naomi
feel worse. "I am so sorry. I barely touched him. I didn't know it
would hurt him."

"Not your fault." Carl yanked on the handle. "Idiot. Didn't.
Cover. The. Controls. Come out, Justin."

The noises stopped. The door stayed closed.

Jaylin peeked around the corner into the galley and hefted a
suitcase into view. She was wearing a bra under the shirt now and
had replaced the sweats with black trousers. Her eyes widened.
When Naomi waved her away, she left the suitcase on the counter
and retreated.

The bathroom door latch gave way under the force of Carl's
shoulder, and he hauled Justin back into the lounge by the legs.
Justin rolled onto his knees the instant Carl let go, curling up tight
with his face to the floor and both arms locked over his head.

Naomi retreated to the galley, behind the comforting barrier of
the counter, and dug into the suitcase. The way Carl's hands were
flexing into fists and opening again made her feel a little too

vulnerable. Even Jaylin's too-big sweats would be better than no pants at all.

"Did it never occur to you that you might bump the thing?" Carl asked.

"No, and I never did, all right?" The answer was a hoarse whisper. "Not once. I'll fix it now, believe me."

"Good." Carl folded himself into a crouch and rested a hand on Justin's shoulder. "Do that."

Justin pushed himself upright, swaying dangerously off vertical before Carl helped him onto the bench. His eyes were glazed, and his breathing was as labored as if he'd been running a marathon inside the tiny bathroom. Being invisible was apparently hard work. Or else not being invisible was. Naomi wondered which state was natural. Then she wondered, a little less calmly, if she was insane for being curious rather than mired in hysteria.

Mostly she wanted to know why Justin's skin felt prickly when he was invisible. His skin was grayish and sweaty at the moment, and he abruptly bent forward and retched, although nothing came up.

"This sucks," he whispered. "So much for helping."

Carl said, "You got our fugitives through all the police road-blocks and onto a plane under the noses of paranoid airport security. What do you call that?"

"Easy?"

Carl dropped to the bench and rubbed at the bridge of his nose. Seated together they were a study in contrasts, big and pale next to little and dark, broad and solid beside sick and shaky. Naomi pictured lean, tawny Parker sitting between them to complete the spectrum and smiled inside. Whimsy made everything better.

Carl said, "You didn't mention that your new gadget would knock you flat for more than an hour. Or that it would leave you like this."

"I didn't know. I'd never tested the contact booster for that long or with multiple people. And I *did* explain this. Avoiding this is why I zero out regularly." When Justin stopped speaking, every measured breath was audible.

"I didn't mean to bump you," Naomi said.

Justin jerked upright and went white around the eyes looking at her. Then he made another of those whimpering noises that tore at her heart.

"Naomi," Carl said, with an inflection that made her name sound like a reminder. "Don't worry about it, Justin. We'll take care of you. Let it go."

Tyler came downstairs into Carl's living room while Alison was completing last-minute paperwork. When she asked after Pete, Tyler waggled a hand and headed into the kitchen. His hair was wet, and so were the sleeves on the dress shirt he wore unbuttoned over running shorts and bare feet.

Alison crawled off the huge couch and went after him. The dark floorboards squeaked when she hit the edge of the thick gray rug. Carl's house had all the character of a hotel lobby, and she was coming to appreciate that squeak. Tyler was digging randomly through cabinets while he finished chewing the handful of crackers he'd shoveled into his mouth.

"Pete's awake and cranky," he said indistinctly. "I thought I'd feed him."

When Alison didn't respond, Tyler stopped rummaging. "What?"

She took the leftover stew from dinner out of the refrigerator and started reheating it. "I'm endlessly amazed by your talent for understatement. Pete has a broken nose and broken ribs, he lost toenails and fingernails, and someone amputated a whole finger, *and* he's at the mercy of total strangers. I seriously doubt 'cranky' covers it."

Tyler broke into a grin. "Yeah, well, compared to Justin, he's an angel."

When he smiled like that, with sun-bleached hair falling into his eyes and the smile a little crooked, he looked about twelve years old. Alison said, "How is he, really? I nearly threw up on him last night. I've been afraid to even look ever since."

"You aren't afraid of anything. You're squeamish. I'm the scaredy-cat. Let's see ..." Tyler ticked off points on his fingers. "His fever broke, he's been showered and bandaged, he's on fresh morphine and antibiotics, and my clothes fit him, sort of. You want charts? I do great charts."

"I know you do." Alison had to smile. "I saw all the ones you did for Justin's persuasive presentation titled 'Let's Invest Millions in an Old Nebraska Homestead.' "

"You liked it?"

"It dazzled the trust lawyers. I especially liked the part where you glossed over the existence of a decommissioned missile silo on the site. Perfect for an underground lab."

"Can you blame him for wanting a hidey-hole?"

A squalling noise, a heavy thump, and a startled shout occurred within seconds of each other upstairs. Tyler's face drained of color. "You let Toby loose? I left Pete's door open. He got antsy when it was closed."

"And I forgot to warn you that I was letting her explore." Alison filled two bowls with stew and listened for trouble, but peaceful silence reigned. She put a spoon in Tyler's hand, handed him one bowl. "Sounds like they're getting along."

"Unless she killed him already."

"You are such a chicken. Toby is fifteen kilos of fur and purr. She isn't scary."

"Not to you, maybe." Tyler wilted when Alison glared at him. "She swats at me, Allie."

"If you didn't jump every time she did it, then she'd get tired of the game."

"She's big enough to reach my balls with those hooks. You'd jump too if you had any balls." He blinked. "Wait. That came out wrong."

Once Alison stopped laughing, she took the tray up to their guest.

TOBY WAS on her back in the middle of Pete's makeshift bed with her white belly fur on display. Pete was sitting bolt upright against the wall with his legs off the side of his air mattress.

His salt-and-pepper hair was still curled damp from the shower, and he looked fragile despite the width of the chest stretching out one of Tyler's tee shirts. The damage around his bandaged nose was a mask of colors from black to yellow and all shades in between, and an IV line trailed down to his left arm from a bag on a wall hook.

"Hi." Alison peeked at his left hand. The dressings were neither bloody nor gooey. "Toby's a sucker for belly rubs. Are you allergic?"

"No, just cautious." Pete's eyes were a gorgeous light brown around the pinpoint pupils. His voice was nasal and a little slow, lagging behind drug-fogged thoughts. "Where did Carl find a cat built on the same scale he is?"

"She's mine, and she's not all cat. Toby, come here." Toby slunk over to sit on Alison's feet. "She was a gift from the CSB agent who covered up Justin's adventures after the plane crash. His uncle is one of the few people in the country licensed for genetic animal research. He sells culls to finance the breeding programs."

"So you own a giant mutant—oh, Christ. I can't even look at you." Pete shut his eyes. "It's Alison, right? Where's Carl? I need to talk to him."

"He's on his way, but you're stuck with me for now." Alison set the tray beside the mattress. "He talks to me, if that's any help.

Tyler said you were hungry. Was he hearing his own stomach, or do you have an appetite?"

"I know I need to eat, but—Jesus, I get dizzy just looking at you. Move back. Get away." Pete's neck was rigid with tension, and he smoothed his right hand over his hair. "What the hell is wrong with me?"

"Carl mentioned that morphine would knock you for a loop, and there's some in that drip along with saline and antibiotics."

"Morphine? Oh, thank God. An explanation." Pete looked up and shuddered. "This is only morphine? No wonder Carl hates dosing up out here in the wide world. Cog stimulants or neural blockers must be awful with all these side-streams."

He was nearly as oblivious as Tyler was about inflicting jargon on the uninitiated. Alison let it roll past without questioning. "I can ask Tyler to use something else now."

"Not when I hurt this much. Just go away. Far away."

She retreated to the desk under the window. Toby took up her official job of lap warmer, and together they watched Pete eat. He was left-handed. His struggles made Alison's heart ache. "Are you sure I can't help?"

"No. Stay away." When Pete was done he pushed away the tray and sighed. "I apologize. The rude just keeps dribbling out."

"No worries. I prefer blunt to the smokescreen of fancy words that Carl throws off when he's moody."

"Well, I'm not Carl. God knows I've proved that." Pete took a series of shallow, gulping breaths, and between one gulp and the next he was crying. He hid his face in his right hand, the only physical retreat he could make.

Toby crept across the room and onto Pete's lap, and he sobbed out a laugh when she started purring. "Giant mutant therapy cat. Fabulous."

Toby slanted her ears sideways and chuffed happily.

"I can't do this." Pete rested his forehead against the cat's skull. "Not even for another hour. The way our memories work, God, I keep flashing—I need to bury it, but Carl needs to know what happened *now*, not in weeks or a month when the edges are dulled —oh, *God*—"

"I have an idea." Alison cued up the workstation camera. "You talk, I'll record it, then you do whatever."

"Of course. Yes. Obvious to anyone sober, right?" Pete held his breath a moment, then continued in a flat, detached tone. "Way back, I filed a report about a leak in our pharma storage. I did the bookwork to pinpoint shifts and suspects and forwarded the case to CSB Central Admin per protocol. Weeks turned into months, and I got impatient. I wish I'd thought it through, but I didn't. I sent a back-channel query expecting to hear about some bureaucratic snafu. Two minutes after I sent it, my unit shut itself down, security showed up, and I was escorted to an isolation room."

He pulled Toby closer. The purring intensified. "We have a traitor at the top. Or the Bureau does. Maybe both. I was scooped off Institute grounds in broad daylight without a single challenge, and they took me—and—"

Alison tensed, but Pete only sighed. His next words were fast and stumbling. "I gave them a ton of codes and protocols I should've died before spilling, and I let—I gave up Carl. I don't remember if I brought it up, or if they pried it out of me, but I know I told them where he lived, that he was away, working—"

He sighed again, a shuddering exhalation. "So stupid. They were going to kill me, but I said Carl wouldn't walk into a snare like I did, that bait would work better, and they bought it. They thought they'd have hours or a day to wait, thought they could pressure him by threatening me, and I hoped Carl would—he was always …"

The disjointed words trailed off, and his eyes filled with tears. Alison came down to Pete's level, moved the tray to sit on the floor beside him. The look on his face made her want to cry too. "It worked. You warned him about the trap, and he rescued you. Not stupid."

Pete picked at the IV lead until Alison put her hand over his. Then he lifted his chin to look at the ceiling with bloodshot eyes the color of gunpowder tea. "I hurt so much after they made me call, and she had that knife she always used when she was bored, and I told her she should just take herself out of the picture if she was so unhappy.

He shuddered. "I meant it, God, I meant it, and then she put the edge to her arm and she didn't even hesitate—oh, *God*. Why won't that stay buried? I shouldn't talk. I can't talk to you. What if you—I don't want to—no. No."

He closed his eyes and pressed his lips together. Tears were flowing freely down his cheeks. Toby nosed in and started licking them. Alison shut down the recorder and pressed a hand against Pete's hair, the only spot she was sure wouldn't hurt.

"I have to head to the airport now," she told him. "It could take hours. There are checkpoints on every bridge. Go ahead and do whatever you need to do. Would you like Toby to stay? You don't have to worry about talking her into doing anything. She is mostly cat."

Pete gave a small nod, then snuffled. "I like cats."

He scratched Toby under the chin, and she purred louder. Alison held back her tears until she got to the privacy of the garage.

THE PLANE SHOOK, bumping up underfoot and dropping out in twisting jerks and hops. Haze stole Justin's peripheral vision, and fear shuddered through him as if each nerve were doused in ice. The flight data on the screen beside the bench wasn't reassurance enough. There had been too many nightmares of fear and pain and obliteration.

He wanted to be in the cockpit. If they went down, he wanted to see the ground coming head-on this time.

Carl came forward with him, along with someone who Justin was probably supposed to know. She reminded him of Alison for no good reason. The woman was slimmer than Alison, not to mention taller and darker skinned. It had to be the way she moved: worried and watchful.

She undoubtedly had a name. Justin had no idea who she was. Frustration stole what little coordination he had left, and he stumbled, coming through the galley.

A small hand caught his arm, and a sweet soft voice said, "Careful."

He didn't quite yank his arm loose, but he couldn't be gentle when he felt like screaming. Carl said, "Justin," in that way of his that meant "Don't be an ass," and a new voice said loudly, "Oh, my God. When you said Justin, you didn't say you meant Justin Wyatt. *Oh. My. God.*"

The last two words rose into a squeal. Justin looked up from his feet and tripped again evaluating the obstacles blocking his route. Farthest was a big dark woman with orange hair, who was sitting with her mouth open and eyes wide with the stunned reverence he utterly loathed. Reality would inevitably disappoint.

Closer was a lean tanned man in black fatigues, coming to his feet on the alert. On the bench next to him sat a tall young woman with black hair and tilted dark eyes. She was dressed like a soldier too, frowning and tousled, and with that realization Justin *knew* her.

Relief was a giddy force. "You're Batshit-crazy," he said. Other pieces fell into place, and he turned to apologize to Naomi for forgetting her name.

Something slammed into his back, right over his left kidney, and the force sent him staggering. He turned and raised his arms to deflect Serena's next punch before she hurt herself. Parker took her to the floor with a leg sweep and pounced on her.

By then Naomi was pressed trembling against Justin with her

hand pressed over her mouth. Carl edged past them to stand huge and overpowering in the center of the small space.

"Enough," he said. "Back off, everyone."

Turbulence rattled the plane, and the floor dropped again. Justin fled to the cockpit.

TYLER WAVED good-bye as Alison pulled Carl's big utility van onto the drive. Then he doused the yard lights and stepped onto the back porch to take a huge leap of faith. A moment later two shadows appeared at the edge of the woods and came jogging up the porch steps.

Neil McAllister nodded in passing, as casual as a banker hurrying home after a long day staring at accounts. Nothing about him screamed out *warning: danger*, not the office-pale skin or the black curly hair in need of a trim, certainly not the lanky body draped in a travel-creased charcoal-gray suit.

Only the icy eyes gave him away, touching on every security point with unerring accuracy. Those gray eyes gave Tyler a chill even when the man smiled. As Neil hit the spill of brighter light from the door, he stripped off the jacket to reveal dried blood on the back of a white dress shirt.

Dan Patterson came next. The man's brown face had been pretty a few fights back, and his black hair was shaved close in a no-nonsense cut. Heavy-soled boots, black leather, and black jeans completed the tough camouflage. He enjoyed letting people think he was nothing but muscle right up until he cut their intellectual legs out from under them.

He also had a way of moving that made him easy to overlook, even when he was walking backward to keep an eye on the surrounding area. When he stopped to survey the yard one last time, he basically disappeared.

Alison's hurried synopsis of Pete's situation had contained the warning that the Bureau itself might be a threat. Tyler tried to concentrate on possibilities that didn't involve treachery, and then Neil's damned cat arrived.

Tom made Toby look like the oversized housecat she was. Both animals were the same mottled gray-black-white color, but Tom's head came to Tyler's thigh, and he massed closer to thirty kilos than fifteen.

Tyler left ample space before following, and his palms were sweating by the time he got to the couch. His guts churned with fear.

Tom's tail was disappearing up the stairs. The two men were standing in the center of the room staring at the muted news program on the San Francisco situation.

Tyler said, "Had you heard about tonight's bombing?"

"No." Dan holstered a pistol Tyler hadn't noticed in a rig under the leather jacket. "We avoided anything that could transmit biometrics, including public screens."

The tactic wouldn't work forever. If the CSB chose to issue itself the proper warrants, it could eventually track anyone down. That was one of the many things Tyler had learned from Dan. "So, why are you guys on the run?"

"Hang on." Dan waved long brown fingers in front of Neil's face. "You're blank. I don't like blank. Please don't tell me their flight transferred through there."

"Early today," Neil said without looking away from the screen. He snapped his fingers in Tyler's direction. "Phone."

Bargaining for information was tempting. Survival instincts argued for cooperation. Tyler tossed over his handset.

Neil turned his back and sent a quick message. The answer arrived on a ping of sound a minute later. He put out a hand, the phone dropped, and Dan caught him around the waist as his knees buckled.

Dan carried him to the other couch and pushed his head down.

"Do not faint on me. You're not weeping, so Deecie and the little buns must be safe, yes?"

Neil bent forward with a wince. "They're nearly to Perth. And Dee will erase your bank balance if you don't stop referring to our children as baked goods. They've been out of the oven for three —*ouch*."

Dan finished peeling the blood-soaked shirt collar off Neil's neck. "Tyler, you're doing that salty pillar of panic thing you do. Can you shake it off, please? We could use first-aid supplies and something stronger than aspirin."

"Not until I get my explanation." Fear erupted into defiance. "Why are you here? Was this all some bullshit story to make me let you in here? Are you here for Pete?"

Not that Tyler had a chance in hell of stopping them, but he didn't have any choice about trying. He had taken on the responsibility.

Dan looked up, and Neil did too. Light eyes and dark blinked at Tyler with identical looks of surprise, and Dan said with an air of dread, "Pete who?"

FOR SOME REASON Naomi had expected Seattle to be cold and rainy. The view from the top of the flight steps revealed a clear sky hazy with city lights, and a warm breeze caressed her face.

The air smelled like fish and fuel. Cars, vans, and trucks sat in neat rows on dry asphalt, in the shadow of a hangar not far from the airplane. She closed her eyes and came down the steps at a snail's pace. Her wrist hurt, her head ached, and grief felt like a raw bleeding wound.

She wanted a kiss that felt as dry as paper and smelled like gardenias. She wanted to listen to news she'd heard ten times already, and to waste her evening picking up the forgotten debris of a day's unfinished chores and projects and meals.

She wanted her mother, but her mother was *gone*.

When she got to the ground, she opened her eyes and was treated to the unusual experience of looking down at someone. Her surprise emerged in a squeak.

The tiny woman offered a steady hand and a stunning smile, and Naomi immediately dubbed her Queenie for a manner that was both kind and aloof at once.

"Hi, I'm Alison," the woman said.

Her brown eyes were a lot like Justin's, dark and expressive, and her long hair was dark brown and wavy like his too. She wore it in a lumpy braid, which she tossed over her shoulder after their handshake.

Naomi stopped before she made the same habitual gesture. Her braid was gone. Another pang of loss hit, and her heart stuttered over it. "I'm Naomi Kwan."

"Justin told me. I made him lie down, or he would've come back to brag about remembering." Alison offered a supportive arm. "Such a bunch of boys, leaving you to stumble along on your own. Never fear, I'm here to help."

The car's headlights flicked on, and tires squeaked on damp concrete as it pulled away. Serena peered out the rear window, and Naomi raised a smile for her.

Alison opened the front passenger door on the van and settled on the first bench. "You take the front," she said. "The chair is more comfortable."

The silence lasted until they hit a traffic jam in a few blocks.

"It's going to be slow through the checkpoints." Alison put her feet up on the bench and crossed her legs. "You'll have plenty of time to explain why you wanted the extra car, and why I feel like I should be hiding all the sharp objects."

"I think separating the combatants will be enough." Carl glanced back. "Thank you for the extra work. Renting a car at midnight during Restoration break—well."

"Wondering how much it cost?" Alison's grin turned into a

yawn that made Naomi's jaw ache in sympathy. Alison said, "Relax. Prometheus Auto is a Hermes subsidiary, just like Raven Airlifts. Argue money with Justin later. Now tell me why you split up."

"Things got a little fraught near the end of the flight."

The man did have a way with words. Naomi's mood lightened at the diplomatic understatement, and when Carl sent a smile her way his cheery sympathy made holding onto selfish heartache impossible.

"Fraught," Alison echoed. *"Fraught,* Carl?"

"Wait."

He maneuvered past a waving patrol officer and onto a highway. A few minutes later the tale was told. Alison looked over the back of her seat. "Batshit, Justin? Pots and kettles much? Speaking of crazy, Helen has started leaving threats about lawyers. What did you tell Ryan?"

Justin muttered something that made Alison laugh. She unbuckled her seatbelt and moved to the rear seat to continue the conversation in private.

"Brother and sister?" Naomi asked softly.

Carl smiled again. "No, but they're getting there."

A chorus of message alerts filled the van before Naomi could question that bit of nonsense. Justin sat up with a grimace. He was squinting at a handset. "Dr. Burke's Halfway House for Wayward Superheroes? Mutt and Jeff? What does any of that gibberish mean? I owe Tyler a pummeling, I swear."

Alison plucked Justin's handset out of his hand. "No nasty calls, please. You love his obscure jokes. Mutt and Jeff are those two fancy Central agents he bonded with. Whatsis and Whosits, you call them, when you're not calling Neil an asshole. I'll send our ETA."

"Bureau agents?" Naomi's heart raced. "Here?"

"Not for you," Carl said. "They're here looking for help. I seem to be collecting fugitives."

COURAGE

RESTORATION DAY 3

Rebuilding our nation was not a safe, easy undertaking. Do you hold fast in the face of physical danger? That is one form of bravery. Do you speak out when you see others are belittled or abused? Do you embrace those who scorn your personal beliefs? Those things require courage too. Be brave today.

—*A Young Citizen's Guide to Restoration Week*

CHAPTER TEN

J USTIN MADE A COVER for the power cell controls as soon as he woke up. The thought of slotting a charged unit into the cuff was a serious temptation, but he resisted it. The worse he let the overload get, the harder and faster it built up the next time. Grounding out for ten or twelve hours wouldn't kill him. Another backlash episode as bad as the last one might.

The new cover clicked into place over the empty slot, and he stuck his leg out straight. Ripples of unease chased along his nerves when he looked around.

He knew he'd slept in the recliner behind him, he recognized his tool kit and spare parts collection, but the knowledge floated in an abyss of ignorance. He had no idea why he and his supplies were here, much less where *here* was. Most troublesome of all, he didn't recognize the two men engaged in a snoring contest across the room.

One was pale and rumpled, lying on the bed across from Justin with an air pistol gripped in his left hand. The other was dark and slick in leather, sprawled on a cot under the window.

When Justin blinked, the light outside was brighter. Now he'd lost some unspecified amount of time, and he still had no idea what to call the man currently sitting awake on the edge of the bed. Some days sucked. Other days completely sucked.

"What was that?" Thoughtful gray eyes gave Justin a once-over. "Seizure? Meditation? A flash of genius?"

"Keep guessing." Justin prodded at his memory in hopes of shaking loose a name. Facts fell into place. He was in Seattle. This was Carl's house.

The man said, "You're not going to call me an asshole? I'm disappointed, Dr. Wyatt. And I was only teasing. I don't need to guess. My wife gets that lost look now and again too. In her case it's permanent neural damage caused by an adverse drug reaction."

Living with that would require a lot of patience. "Lucky her."

Silence. Finally the man said, "You really are off-line, aren't you? From the top: I'm Neil McAllister. Big, black, and noisy in the corner there is my partner, Dan Patterson. Sound familiar?"

Justin wasted a glare on him. The man sighed. "No? Try this: we're here because my boss Stephen Webster got shot yesterday, and Dan and I escaped the same fate by the skin of our teeth. Five others in my unit didn't make it, which is saying a lot. Any bells ringing yet?"

Dan's snoring was a steady drone in the background. Justin leaned back, tucked his bad leg under him and waited for another hint. He was probably supposed to know who Stephen Webster was, but he didn't feel like looking it up.

The door rattled, then opened to admit a huge gray and black spotted cat. The beast swung its head around to check on Neil with pale blue eyes, then stretched out full-length beside Dan.

"Traitor," Neil said. The cat yawned to reveal a mouth full of sharp teeth.

The cat's name was Tom, and he was from the same breeding program that had produced Alison's Toby. That one association was all it took to jar other chunks of knowledge loose. Their release was accompanied by a blinding headache, and Justin pressed both hands against his skull. It suddenly felt much too small.

He had referred to Neil as 'you fucking asshole' more than once shortly after they'd met. In his defense, he'd been under a lot of stress at the time.

Neil had proceeded to reconstruct an otherwise hard-to-explain year of Justin's life. If he'd decided to feel insulted instead of amused, he could have murdered Justin without penalty. The man was one of twenty people—fifteen now, from his earlier words—empowered by the Civilian Security Bureau to break any law of the land.

The existence of Delta-clearance operatives was an open secret exploited shamelessly by fiction producers in every format. Most Delta-level work involved building new backgrounds, erasing incriminating data, and destroying or creating evidence. Some of it involved eliminating people in ways that could never be proven as homicides.

All of it made for great drama because Delta operatives submitted to some of the most extensive mental and physical modifications ever designed by science. They were analytical combat machines given carte blanche legal coverage.

Those few agents were each monitored full time by at least one handler, and they answered directly to the head of the Bureau's Central Investigations unit. That was Dan and Neil's boss, Stephen Webster, the man who had called a meeting for all twenty top-clearance Delta operatives and their handlers the previous day.

Such meetings were rare, and Neil still had no idea what its purpose would have been. Someone had started shooting. He and Dan had fled before the smoke cleared. At least five agents were dead, as were seven handlers, and possibly Webster himself.

Speculation was all Neil had to go on. News of the bloodbath had not been released to the public and never would be. That was how things worked in those circles. His name and Dan's were currently on apprehend-with-prejudice watch lists issued to every local CSB unit in the country. That meant things were moving behind the scenes, and that was why he was here.

In his opinion the attack on the Delta cadre had happened too soon after the West Coast incidents to be coincidence. Whether the shooting had been an inside job or an outside hit, the central division of the Bureau would be deeply preoccupied with its aftermath.

Like Carl and Parker, when Neil looked at civil disruption he saw shadowy hints of a larger plot. He wanted to be in position to counter whatever the underlying power play turned out to be, even though he had to stay under the radar while doing so.

"Don't Delta agents face summary execution for working without clearance?" Justin scrubbed at his face to encourage the memories to settle. "You're crazier than I am. And I hate being called Dr. Wyatt. Everybody knows that."

"That's what made it a good test." Neil smiled. "Online. Good. This isn't about sanity, Justin. It's about the law. Sure, the Fed is hugely flawed. Fine. Let the public vote it out in six months and take five years to come up with a better idea. That's the system. No one has the right to usurp its process through force of arms or clandestine manipulation. My job is to keep that from happening."

"Nice speech. Very idealistic." Idealists got other people hurt.

"If I'm right, then I won't get shot. If I'm wrong, or if I get caught before I can prove my case, then I won't care because I'll be dead. It's worth a try."

"Do you really think the system is worth defending?"

"I think it's too early to argue politics." Neil raked a hand through snarled black hair. "Have you decided yet?"

The question made no sense. "Decided what?"

"If you're sticking around to help. Dan and I need all the backup we can get. I promised Carl to renegotiate his deal with the Bureau, and his brother is in for the low price of clearing two framed innocents. What will it take to persuade you to lend a hand? We need you."

"No one needs me." *Gimpy, mentally questionable, sick with pain half the time*—Justin cut off the inner litany. "You want my money, my contacts list, or access to my toys. You're welcome to the first two, but I only opened up the toybox to get Naomi out of the mess she got caught in. She's safe, I'm done, and the toys stay with me."

"It's all the same mess." Neil waved a hand in a frustrated gesture. "I'm sure it is. I can see pieces coming together."

Pain ran up Justin's spine and buried itself behind his eyes. He hauled himself to his feet and headed for the door. "Well, I can't see straight at all, and I don't feel like talking any more."

A LONG HOT bath eased some of the aches and cleared the worst blurriness from Justin's brain, enough to improve matters from intolerable to unpleasant. As if to balance that positive development, when he emerged from the bathroom he realized that his sense of direction had gone off-line.

There were stairwells at either end of the hall leading down, but that was no help at all. He went through the mental gymnastics that sometimes worked and sometimes didn't, and got nothing. He had four doors to choose from, two on either side, all slightly ajar.

A warm draft of air eliminated one door on the left from the list. Hints of citrus and lavender added their bright notes to Alison's lily-of-the-valley scent. That would be the room where the women were bunking. Justin vaguely recalled a laughing conversation about slumber parties and shared bathrooms.

Serena had a lovely laugh. Justin remembered that. He'd called the woman batshit to her face. Not his finest moment. He resolved to apologize later, once everyone was up and moving. With luck he would've found his clean clothes by then.

Luck happened in the form of Tom. The cat came slinking into the hall from one room and shouldered open the door across the hall. Common sense urged Justin to take the offered hint, but a faint mewing sound came from the other room.

Curiosity sent Justin after the cat.

Pete Hamil was sleeping on an air mattress inside a room that looked like a walk-in closet. His blankets looked dry, which meant that the cat pacing back and forth over his legs probably wasn't to blame for the stench hanging in the air. Carl was sitting with his back against the wall beside the pallet. He too was sound asleep.

Tom seized Toby by the scruff, backed the smaller cat off the mattress and carried her, still burbling protests, into the hall. Neither Carl nor Pete stirred at the commotion.

Justin laid a hand on Pete's shoulder, squeezed gently, then harder until the man's eyes popped open. Pete's expression went from dazed to mortified in a blink, and he rolled onto his side with his weight on his right elbow. "Well, hell. Color me all kinds of embarrassed."

"Don't be stupid." No one should ever have to apologize for the indignities of being injured and immobile. "You want humiliation? Try being stuck in a tent in the Arctic with a cracked skull and a broken leg."

Pete looked away. "Christ. You win. This is nothing."

"That's not—never mind." Helping was easier than explaining. Justin collected fresh sheets from a laundry basket on Carl's far side, and clothes from a backpack that looked exactly like Tyler's go bag.

When he turned back, Pete was staring hard at him. Maybe he didn't want help from someone who couldn't keep his foot out of his mouth. Maybe he would rather be alone. "I don't have to do this," Justin offered.

"Jesus Christ." Pete looked away again. "Help, please."

Justin's helpfulness ended at making the bed and assisting Pete into clean clothes. Changing empty IV bags and dirty dressings were tasks better left to steadier hands. Justin was still feeling pretty pleased with himself right up to the moment he tripped and went crashing to the floor with an armload of dirty cloth.

He got slowly to his feet and dumped the sheets in the hall while Carl took in the situation with a bleary scowl.

"I was letting you sleep," Justin said in apology.

"By kicking me? Interesting tactic." Carl yawned and reached for the medical kit next to the backpack. "Pete, I told you to wake me if you needed anything."

"Hard to wake you when I didn't wake me. No more poppy juice, please. I suppose pissing myself is better than the pipes shutting down, but the other side effects—saints on roller skates, Carl, I never knew it got this bad."

Pete had pulled up the covers and was back to staring at Justin while hugging a pillow to his chest. Carl looked up from prepping an injector. "I have complained about the side effects from free dosing for years now."

"You never told me about the shiny." Pete finally blinked. "My God. I'm going to go blind. I need to dim this. What's left in your field kit? We match profiles on painkillers and dampers, don't we?"

"Can't you last a few more hours?" Carl hesitated less than a second before digging into one of the cargo pockets on his fatigues. He pulled out a zippered case. "Once this is gone, there's no more for either of us."

"I know. I don't care." Pete watched with a look of desperation as Carl peeled open a dermal patch, and he sighed a few seconds after its application. Then his eyes slid up to Justin, and he blinked again. "He's still really bright."

Every muscle in Justin's body went tight. "What is that supposed to mean?"

It came out sounding even more hostile than he felt, and Pete's face paled under the bruises. Carl said, "Give it time to kick in, Pete. Justin, please ignore him."

That was an impossible request, so Justin left the room. When he was feeling charitable he could laugh at the self-consciousness, but he wasn't feeling charitable today.

"Justin, please." The plea was barely audible.

He looked back to Carl in the doorway. The anger drained away. "I know, it isn't always about me. It's only that I'm—" *Feeling clumsy and stupid.* "I hurt."

"I see that. For once it is about you. You're a little intense, and he's a lot sensitized. Do you still do t'ai chi? The park out here sponsors sessions every hour from five to nine. The view's gorgeous. Turn right at the end of the drive, less than a block, you'll see them from the entrance. Eddie's up there now."

Meaning that Justin would have protection and supervision, if either was needed. "I won't offend anyone by barging in?"

"The sessions are public, drop in, drop out. And you could never offend Eddie. Offhand, I can't think of anyone he respects more."

A flash of memory: dizzy exhaustion and air scorching down a throat scraped raw by screams. Guttural sounds in darkness and Parker in shadow nearby. The sour taste of despair and the feel of his voice shredding to ruin, falling away unheard.

Justin shivered. "I can't imagine why."

"I know you can't." Carl made a shooing motion. "Go. Get your aching body out for a stretch and some fresh air and drag Eddie back for breakfast."

THE CATS WOKE SERENA.

The big one stopped inside the door. His absurdly long tail twitched, and the smaller cat he held in his mouth squirmed and growled a protest. Serena rolled onto her side and felt Naomi's warmth against her back as she returned the big cat's impassive stare.

His name was Tom, and he wasn't the wild animal he resembled. He wasn't even as feline as he looked, being a descendant of a lab-constructed hybrid. He was smart, he was trained for tracking work, and he belonged to one of the two human predators who'd been lying in wait here at the house.

Chimera was the word Neil had dropped during introductions. All Serena remembered about him was that he moved like a gray-eyed cat himself. She remembered the other man better. Dan could stand still better than anyone Serena had ever met. At first, she had mistaken him for a statue carved in smooth stone.

Her shock at finding out he was alive was the reason she couldn't remember anything else. Snarling, flat-eared Brown Dog had taken over, placing her big, overprotective self between Serena and harsh reality until someone brought her to this room to sleep.

Safe, the close walls and closed blinds murmured now. *Safe*, declared the smooth fabrics on the big bed that Alison had insisted Serena and Naomi share. *Safe*, whispered the mingled breath of sleeping friends. Serena wondered what crime Toby had committed, that Tom felt he needed to bring her back to the security of the den.

She patted the bedspread, but Tom rejected the offer with a flicked-back ear and deposited his burden on Alison's cot instead.

Toby hissed at him, and Tom's tail and ears drooped as he backed away.

"Hey, beautiful," Serena whispered. "Don't be sad. If I say 'Here, kitty-kitty-kitty,' will you come to me?"

Tom deigned to have his chin scratched. His fur was even thicker than it looked: slick on top, soft underneath. After a few minutes of slit-eyed bliss, he began to cough, a low rolling noise loud enough to wake everyone else.

Toby hissed again and lashed her tail when Alison sat up. Naomi sat up, scooting to Serena's side with a noisy yawn. Tom slanted his ears and snuck out the door. Jaylin groaned and put her pillow over her head. "Dogs in your head. Cats on the bed. What next, ballerina babe? Frogs in our pockets?"

"I'm sorry. I didn't know he'd get all loud and upset."

"No harm done." Alison gave Toby a stroke to settle the cat's temper. "That's his idea of a purr. I am *so* glad she didn't inherit that trait."

"No harm." Naomi flopped back. "Except that I'm wide awake now."

So was Serena. "Me too. Want to take a walk?"

"No, I don't. I want to lie here. I want to be asleep. I'm scared and sad, and I want to crawl under the covers and never open my eyes again because what I really want is a hug from my mother, only she's *dead*."

The room went still and silent, no breathing, no motion. Naomi brushed at her new wispy bangs and then covered her eyes with both hands. "And wasn't that a useless fit of self-pity? Sorry, sweetie. Of course we'll go for a walk if it will help."

An ache coiled under Serena's ribs as something new stirred and flexed, waking up inside. She needed to be stronger for Naomi's sake, and if any day of the year was meant for stretching wings, it was this one. The trick would be finding a way to leave the nest without kicking Naomi in the face, a path to freedom that didn't look like rejection.

"Toby could use a good long walk," Alison said. "You can take her for me. She has a tracer on her harness."

Serena looked across at the rounded little woman sitting straight and poised while the cat flexed agitated claws against her thighs. She was serene and unruffled, a black-feathered swan on a still, quiet pond. Not a predator, no, but fierce in defense of her own.

Fly, her smile said, and when her eyes went to Naomi they were shining.

"Thank you," Serena mouthed, and she placed a kiss on Naomi's scalp. "It's perfect, don't you think?" She inhaled a breath of home and love, exhaled the pain of failure. "You rest, Naomi. You've been brave for both of us long enough."

THE LIGHT WAS different in Seattle, and within a block Serena wished she'd thought to ask for sunglasses. The air was soft, warm against her skin, and scented with sap and wet grass. The whole menagerie was delighted by all the gentle newness, and she had a hard time keeping on top of them. Toby was an unexpected help. Whenever the leash went slack or yanked tight as Serena drifted, the cat dropped flat and dug in claws until the proper tension between harness and hand returned.

The cat led the way uphill to a park where a slow dance of motion and colors soothed away the ache behind Serena's eyes. Gray hair, black and blond, loose clothes and tight all moved in unison. Near the back, one tan, familiar form was impressive stripped to shorts and hiking sandals. *Steady*, his solid body said. *Safe*.

A gesture invited Serena to join in, but her control wasn't up to going through the motions without craving the melee, and her worn-out fatigues were soft but none too durable. She perched atop a wood rail fence and resisted the urge to let air and itchy skin meet.

Eventually the soothing unison shattered into individual people who came too close on their way to the path and bikes and a waiting bus. Defenses came charging up, and Serena closed her eyes to wrestle herself into order.

She opened them and found herself face-to-face with hazel eyes dancing and narrow lips lifting into a smile. Parker had slipped in close under the cover of her distraction.

Serena took a firm grip on growling temper. "Sure, laugh at me. It would be a huge joke if I beat up some poor old granny in a berserk fit."

A shoulder lifted: Parker had faith in her self-control. He knelt to scratch Toby's ears, and the cat responded with enthusiastic chirps as if making a report. Parker looked a question at Serena.

"Yes, she helps," she answered. "Are you the one who trained her to sense when someone's acting wonky? Why? How? And why don't you talk? You're not brain-broken like me."

He pondered the questions carefully before saying, "Words are hard work."

And Serena didn't need him to make the effort, which was an unexpected wonder. Parker said that with a tight jaw, looking up at the sun, and then he tilted his head in an order to follow him.

He took her to a bench placed to overlook the ocean from the top of a hill. Serena pulled hard on temper's leash again when she recognized the man sitting there. "I don't want to talk to him. He called me names."

Parker frowned his disappointment. He sat on the ground facing Justin and leaned back on his arms. All that bare muscle looked even more exposed compared to the shorter man's long pants and gray sweatshirt. Serena would have melted into a puddle of sweat in that many layers, but Justin looked cool and relaxed.

Toby tugged at the leash to pull Serena to the bench, then leaned into her. Serena sat down to humor the animal, careful to leave space between herself and Justin. The cat jumped into the gap, shoved her nose into Justin's hand, and gnawed gently at his thumb.

He sat up straight and frowned, looking around.

Comprehension took Serena by the throat. She'd missed it last night, distracted by her own howling mob, but Justin was no more whole inside than she was. No unruly zoo for him, though. He was made of fractured crystal, some pieces clear, others clouded, all flawed by cracks that were sharp enough to cut.

The shock of understanding shouldered aside temper and gave curiosity her voice. "He trained the cat for you. You have a before and after like me. You weren't being rude last night. It was only a label like the ones Bao uses for remembering, a way to see me through the cracks."

"Cracks?" Justin's bafflement was as clear as sunlight on his face. Confusion clouded the dark eyes for a moment, and then concentration sliced through it. "It's a memory tag, yes. I didn't mean to be insulting. I'm sorry."

"I'm not." Serena bared teeth at him and let playfulness out to bounce in the sunshine. "Say it again. What kind of crazy am I?"

"Batshit crazy." Justin's answering smile was slow and tentative. His eyebrows drew together. "What about Toby?"

"I trained her for Allie." Parker held out a finger for Toby to lick. "To track you when you wander. Bad day?"

"I couldn't even hold a stance. I hate it." He watched a glider catch an updraft over the water, and his throat worked. *Want*, his eyes said, but his hands flexed *can't*. The broken pieces rubbed together and drew blood inside. "I hate all of it some days."

Serena muzzled curiosity and reached into the dark to grope at memory, careful to only stroke the smooth surfaces, not the dangerous depths. She knew this story. Jaybird had told it like a fairy tale last year.

Rags to riches, that was Justin's *Before*. Mechanic turned corporate bigwig on the strength of genius products, childhood sweetheart turned media star at his side for the rise until infidelity divided them. *After* would have started when he went missing and was declared dead, with the next wife taking the company and fortune before she died too. He had spent months in protective custody during an investigation. Serena remembered that from the tidy story, but no one had mentioned the disappearing trick that his friends seemed to take for granted.

She drew a finger down Justin's jaw, along muscles that muttered about secrets unspoken. Looked at Parker's wary muscles protecting secrets shared. She cupped the hand to Justin's face, skin to scratchy skin with a ghost of spice in the air. "There's lots more to your After, isn't there? It didn't happen the way the stories say."

Justin drew back, and *threat* exploded in the space between them on a blaze of alarm from Parker. Serena flung herself away with Red Dog scrabbling for control of her muscles. She refused the challenge and kept her head down, vitals covered and spine bent.

No-threat, no-threat. She quivered with the urgency of convincing herself, caught her breath in relief when warm pressure settled across her shoulders, and the message was reinforced with a whiff of moss and darkness. Another heart beat against her skin. Steady-safe. Steady-safe. *Steady.*

"Wow." Justin's feet scuffed. Weight thumped. Serena raised her head and found him sitting splay-legged on the ground in front of her with a lopsided frown on his face. Shiny dark eyes under wavy dark hair. Sharp eyes. *Dangerous.* Serena slammed Red Dog to the ground again.

Not angry at her. Angry. Not at her. *No threat.*

"You look adorable with Parker draped all over you like an erotic sculpture, but what the hell is going on?"

"My fault." A huff of breath beside Serena's ear. "I tensed, she overreacted."

Warmth receded as Parker moved to her side. Still touching, fingers to forearm. Radiating control for Serena to emulate. She sat up, spine straight, head back. Sun too bright against the inside of her eyelids, cloth against her skin, itching.

Beautiful, Justin's breathing whispered, which made Serena wonder how many shirt buttons she'd lost. She didn't dare look yet, there was too much going on inside.

She gulped air for words. "Sorry, curiosity got off the leash when I saw all the holes in what people aren't saying, and then the whole pack wanted out, but I didn't want it, I knew threat wasn't real, only Red Dog wouldn't behave until I grounded him."

"Literally." Justin scratched at his chin, a quiet rasp of sound. "Next time just haul off and hit me. It won't be as dramatic, but you know I can take a punch."

Serena opened her eyes. Justin's gaze was on her chest, and his body was saying happy-happy-more-please. Serena secured the remaining buttons and tied the shirt tails so her breasts were covered. The man's attention shifted to her belly button, of all silly things, and the shattered focus of it was dazzling.

She squinted. "You are very, very bright."

"I used to be." He went still, and his eyes flashed up to hers. Thinking hard, so fast, so sharp. "Parker, what does Carl say about her?"

Parker approached the fluffy and indignant cat now hiding in the nearby bushes. "Idiosyncratic reaction to abuse or trauma. Stabilizing. Why?"

"Pete thinks I'm bright too. Guess who also has threat-response conditioning, reads body language, and hears what people aren't saying? Botched psychiatric work would be traumatic. I'll bet you anything someone stirred her brain with a poker."

"Not the CAF." Ferocious. "Never."

"Never authorized," Justin corrected. "You know that they turned a blind eye to Walton's illegal tampering when it was only contract personnel—" *Secrets*, that pause screamed, before his focus shifted to Serena again. "I'd bet you don't remember any of that 'classified training' listed in your service jacket."

After yawned black and terrifying in the back of Serena's mind. She swallowed a whimper and let fur and fangs push her away from it.

Justin returned to the bench, sat down to rub his left leg. "Looks like Whatsis gets me after all. He's right, this is all one big messy interesting puzzle. This, Naomi, Pete, the Bureau thing. All of it."

Parker whistled sharply. Toby came creeping out of the bushes so low to the ground that she seemed to flow over the grass. Her leash dragged along in her wake, and Parker snagged it. "Won't find answers here. Home. Food. Plans."

"Food." Justin brightened. "Hey. Alison's cooking."

Serena caught Parker's hand as he passed, squeezing it with

her appreciation and gratitude. *Teacher*. Parker scowled, rolling the idea around, rejecting some parts, adding others. Fingers entwined: *teammates*. The walk downhill was companionably quiet until they reached the driveway and Parker stopped to let Justin catch up.

"I'm trying to translate batshit-crazy talk into English," he said as he reached them. Breathing hard from an easy stroll, every joint tight and stiff. *Hurting*. "Help me out, will you? I think 'red dog' involves combat conditioning. You mentioned a brown dog last night. And the way you talk about curiosity—do you see all your emotions as real and separate creatures?"

"They aren't all separate." Astonishment had a tall crest and downy feathers that settled when Serena shook herself. She'd thought Justin was watching her ass, but he'd been pondering her menagerie. Amusement jumped after surprise, yipping that no, he'd been multitasking. "The dogs are. Everything else comes and goes in and out of me. Sometimes solid, sometimes not."

"Must get crowded up there in that belfry." The dry comment was a tease, yanking on the floppy ears of self-consciousness and offering it the treat of a shy grin.

He'd given Serena's craziness its own name. He was broken and whole all at once, and that meant it could be done. She could be whole too, in her own way.

"It's comfortable as long as it isn't noisy," she told him, feeling quiet and warm inside.

CHAPTER ELEVEN

A MUG OF TEA appeared on the counter in front of Naomi. Steam rose in threads from the pale gold surface and teased her nose with a familiar scent.

"I have Keemun if you'd rather. Or coffee." Alison pulled up a bar stool and gazed worriedly at Naomi from the kitchen side of the counter. She made coffee sound as appealing as dirt. "You smiled, watching me make mine."

"Jasmine is my favorite, and my—" Naomi blinked away the tears. "And my mother's. Sorry. I'm like a faucet today. Yesterday I was fine."

She'd sniveled in the shower. She'd cried getting dressed in Jaylin's borrowed shirt and a pair of sweatpants donated by Alison. Now she was weepy over tea.

Her life was over. Her mother was dead. Pain was only one ingredient of the toxic stew of emotions bubbling away in her heart. She had no idea what to do with the searing anger, and the fear only made her want to cringe. The mixture kept boiling over.

"Yesterday you were busy." Pots hit the stovetop, cabinets and drawers banged open and shut, and Alison set a knife and cutting board in front of Naomi with a clunk. Onions, peppers, and tomatoes followed. "Be busy now."

Gone. Naomi heard the word in every slice of the knife. The brutal reality was that her mother had been a shell of herself for years, and Naomi had been grieving over her for almost as long. Relief was a huge, shameful feeling that she kept shoving into the enormous empty space in her heart where she shoved all the other painful emotions.

Jaylin made her entrance in business dress, with her hair in a turban and her eyes on her datapad. She was given coffee and settled at a tiny dining table. Everyone else arrived in last night's rumpled clothes. They were provided with coffee and chased into the living room. Carl brought in a new addition, an injured man who asked for tea and fell asleep on the couch before it got to him.

No one introduced him to Naomi. Carl turned on a news feed from San Francisco while Alison efficiently saw the crowd supplied with food and returned to the counter to eat her own meal.

"You made that look easy," Naomi said.

"Four years on the kitchen line in a busy restaurant, remember?" Alison smiled. "Food is a comfort. Good meals make bad days better, my landlord used to say."

Naomi lifted her mug. "Here's to your landlord."

"Mario is the only thing I miss from that life."

Creative rule-bending was a common way to break through the Sub wall without selling one's soul or body. Alison had bartered rent from a restaurant owner. Jaylin had turned sketchy high-risk investments into a career, and Naomi stretched her pay by living on her mother's couch and paying a small cash cut to the building supervisor to turn a blind eye.

The principle was the same for all of them, but Naomi felt humbled when she compared herself to the other two. Jaylin moved in ever higher circles with each promotion, and Alison had gone from filing clerk to legal secretary to business manager and picked up a sideline as an artist. Naomi could never find time for more than work and sleep, and she barely scraped along month to month on her own salary plus the stipend for her mother.

What she would do now without that extra money and the free housing was anyone's guess. Assuming she ever got her life back at all. Her food went dry and tasteless in her mouth. She pushed it aside in favor of people-watching.

The count stood at eight, missing Serena, Parker, and Justin. The CSB agents were paired off in a corner, Tyler sat at the table across from Jaylin, and Carl had established himself in a big chair with the best view of the wall screen. Naomi finished her tea on the thought that he wasn't very Wow today. He looked sad.

Jaylin came over with her datapad in hand. "Bad news, Bao. One, CSB SanFran bumped out national warrants for you and Serena. Names, biometrics, the works. Two, Gonzalez-Yao has a crisis. My Restoration leave's been cancelled. Air travel over the Rockies is down through Sunday, but roads and rail east are only on inspection delays. I have to go home."

"What? Jaybird, no." Naomi's heart sank. "I need you."

Jaylin's eyes shimmered with tears. "Oh, no, Bao, not the baby-bunny face."

She pulled Naomi off the stool and right off her feet into a hug, then set her down and smoothed back her hair. "Look around, honey. Rogue CSB agents, your two thug boys, and Justin Wyatt, for pity's sake? What can I add? Get me an autograph if you end up meeting the first wife, that's all I can say."

Jaylin turned to face the room. "I'm on a company ticket for a zip-train that leaves in three hours, and I'll be buried in Asian market manipulations for at least six weeks. I promise to keep my head down and my mouth shut, if you'll let me leave."

Carl lifted his chin and his pale eyebrows rose high. "You're not a prisoner, Ms. Byrd. I thought that was clear from the start. Safe is good. We'll get you to the station."

He sent Alison a glance. She nodded. "With emergency cash,

an account code for contact, and a briefing on danger signs and how to disappear, just in case there *is* a conspiracy. I'll take care of it."

Commotion in the small front foyer announced the arrival of the missing trio. Parker breezed into the kitchen hand in hand with Serena. He smiled at Naomi over his shoulder, and she let herself smile back. He was trying to impress her by being helpful. It was working.

Justin came in next, but he stopped dead when he saw the crowd in the room. Naomi's neck ached just from watching the tension building up in his body. Finally he announced, "I am not up to this today," and limped straight through the middle of things to the stairs.

The CSB agents exchanged a look. Dan said, "Every time I meet this crowd, it's like a trip to the circus, I swear. A never-ending parade of wackiness."

Carl said to Alison, "How's your list coming along?"

She consulted her handset. "Jaylin to the station with comm, cash, and conversation. Personal kit for Serena and Naomi. Med kit resupply. Cat food. People food." She paused. "Justin's big toy box is here already. Tyler insisted I bring it for safekeeping. The equipment caches in the attic looked pretty comprehensive. Are you set for action? Do you want to keep the rental car?"

Carl considered it. "A medium-sized work truck would be better if you can do it without a money trail."

"Did you hear the part last night about Hermes Transport? There's a fleet of trucks sitting idle down at the port. I'll have them pull off logos the way they do for Justin's projects. Truck is on the list. Anything else?"

"Yes. I want you to take Toby, finish up these last favors, and lie low, preferably at Tyler's place. You both need to step back from this."

"Seriously?" Alison snagged her cat's leash from Parker and

moved into Carl's personal space, so close she had to lean back to look him in the face. "You are serious."

Tyler edged past them both, into the hall that led to the garage. "Is this the part of the movie where we're supposed to say that they need our help too much to let us go? Not me. Not again. When the scary people say go, I go."

Serena leaned over the counter to watch his departure. "Glittery like Justin," she said in Naomi's general direction. "Only scales, not crystal. Not broken. He's a pretty lizard."

Naomi shushed her.

Carl tucked Alison's hair behind one ear and dropped his big hand onto her shoulder. "You've worked wonders, but peace of mind is more important to us at this point than material support. Get safe and stay safe."

"What about your friend?"

Carl shook his head. "I'd better keep Pete close."

"Okay, then." Alison reached up and poked him in the chest with one finger. "But when I get back from shopping I will be setting up a call schedule, blind comm accounts and all. You *will* keep us in the loop."

She waited for a nod before turning to Jaylin. "Whenever you're ready."

"I'm ready." Jaylin hugged Naomi once more, a warm comfort that ended too soon. "Don't forget me."

"Don't forget me." Naomi made herself smile as she gave the ritual response that stood in for all the other admonitions: call when you can, if you can, be careful, take care of yourself. Live large. *Live.*

The room seemed much emptier after they were gone. After a moment, Dan said, "If the show is over, can we can get down to some serious work now?"

NAOMI'S STOMACH GROWLED. She concentrated on the biographical profile she was reading on Jaylin's datapad and sighed. Breakfast had been a long time ago.

"Are we boring you, Naomi?" Carl's voice was blandly indulgent, and when Naomi looked up from the datapad, he was sporting a tolerant smile. The combination pushed Naomi's temper to the bloody edge.

"I'm not bored," she said. "I'm steaming mad. You've talked over me every time I tried to ask a question for the last three hours, and I'm sick of being snubbed."

She was done being good and swallowing insults. She'd done that for more than a decade and earned nothing but grief. "Someone tried to kill me. I have a right to help catch whoever it was. Serena and I both do."

She glanced warily up the front stairwell. Serena had fled under the pretext of needing a shower some time ago, and Parker had gone after her, with a look at Naomi that said: *Do what you need to do, I'll watch over her.*

Naomi wanted to be glad, because Carl's unsubtle belittlement would've long since worn down Serena's temper. Instead she couldn't help wishing that *one* of them had stayed to support her. Alone or not, if she wasted this opportunity Carl might never slip and give her another. She would lose her nerve and let him sideline her if she didn't act now.

She stood up and then nearly wilted when the CSB agents turned her way. All the attention felt impossibly heavy. She stiffened her spine against it and used her datapad to highlight items on the main screen where the men had been organizing their ideas.

"I'm also confused," she admitted. "You've tossed around a lot of names, but you keep coming back to these five."

Gordon Hughes, senator. Camille Chen, CSB chief for NorCal. Carlos Sanchez, president of Santa Fe Shipping. Martin Singh, CSB city captain for the San Francisco district. Haley Reese-Patel from

PacRim Financial. Jaylin would've known a lot about all of them, but Naomi had recognized only two. From her brief recent studies, she never would've expected to hear any of them being accused of murder and conspiracy.

She said, "You must have reasons, but 'She has the connections' and 'He could swing it' are so vague it's maddening. And this is the worst." She tapped one name, and it highlighted onscreen. "Dominic Walton. Deceased, listed clear as day. Why include a *dead* arms dealer on the source list for Sunday's explosives? Also, why are you ignoring Serena? Why did they use her account and not my mother's? I never checked either one. I have an idea, if anyone cares. And speaking of ideas, if you want to connect those people to your terrorism conspiracy, then data raiding everyone on that shortlist would be a good place to start. That'd be my advice, and speaking of me—"

She took a deep breath. "I am not a piece of furniture, and I won't sit in storage while you clean up my mess, so you need to stop ignoring me."

"I'm paying attention, I swear."

That came from the man she thought of as "Mr. Maestro." She still hadn't been introduced, and from her exile at the table she couldn't see him. His left hand appeared, gauze-wrapped and waving. "Hi, I'm Pete, whoever you are. Are you really three meters tall and breathing fire?"

"Stop it, Pete," Carl said, but he frowned at Naomi. The intensity of the disapproval made her knees go rubbery, and she sat down fast to hide the weakness.

Neil traded glances with Dan, then said, "I would apologize, but we didn't realize we were ignoring you. Why the smoke-and-mirrors routine, Carl?"

Carl redirected the frown at the floor. "To see if she wanted inclusion enough to fight for it. There was no way to ask without pressuring her. She has some useful skills, but better to do without than to *use* her."

"Skills, is it?" Dan asked. He smile was all dimples and humor, and his brown eyes were sympathetic. "Do tell."

"Let her catch her breath, Agent Patterson." Carl beckoned. "Naomi, if you're joining us, join. Bring a chair."

The carpet next to Pete's couch was soft. The legs of Naomi's chair sank deep. She clamped her hands on the seat beside her thighs to steady herself. "Smoke and mirrors?"

Neil turned to Carl. "She doesn't know?"

"Twelve hours ago she thought I was an electrician, Agent McAllister, and it isn't exactly a casual confession."

"What don't I know?" Naomi asked.

"That's an impossible question," Carl said. "Answer this one first: what do you know about the Rydder Psychiatric Institute?"

"What everybody knows about neopsychs, that they're miracle workers, plus it's obscenely expensive. They rejected Serena because she's on Sub, and a promissory note from her father wasn't legal payment. Why is that—oh."

Details came together so abruptly that the force of under-standing was a painful, visceral jolt. Carl's charisma and charm, the indefinable aura of authority and credibility. Other stray comments. Pete's injuries. Drugs. *"Oh."*

Spots in front of her eyes warned her that she'd stopped breathing. "Why are two neopsychs playing house in Seattle? I had to drag Serena all the way to Minneapolis for testing. And if someone's selling psychogenic medications, isn't that a huge prob-lem? *International* huge? Anyone who could do that would be powerful enough to arrange bombings as a cover-up too, wouldn't they? But why would they target me? What is going on?"

Dan said, "How in hell did you put all that together from one obscure question?"

Naomi nodded at Pete. "Hands, feet, and face says beating for information, not revenge or spite. And his voice and how he moves—it's like Carl only different, and he brought up Rydder, plus drugs, and me and Serena, and—well, everything."

Neil narrowed those eerie gray eyes of his at her. "It's still an impressive chain of guesses."

"Accurate intuitive leaps from minimal data," Carl said. "A handy talent for people whose survival depends on flash-reading environments. Naomi, for example, was a successful pickpocket and sneak thief before she hit puberty, according to several frustrated detectives."

Naomi's eyes shot to him. "I was never charged. Ever."

Carl stared back: blue eyes shadowed, big body relaxed in the chair. "No, vandalism was all they could ever prove. Interesting that Serena had a multiple-page misdemeanor sheet that put her into petty-crimes service too."

"We wanted to serve together. Her uncle brokered a deal for us, which you probably know already. How did you get all that information?"

Carl put on a smile that didn't reach the sad eyes. "I got nosy and did some prying. People talk to me."

Naomi shook her head, trying to clear it. "Prying. So much for those famous neopsych ethics."

"Sorry to disappoint you, but all I have is a standard-issue conscience."

It was an odd statement, and an odd silence fell. Naomi resorted to pulling out the "you don't impress me" face in a ploy to get someone to explain it.

Carl finally said, "A few years ago some ambitious criminals forcibly hired seven neopsychs away from Rydder. The arrangement didn't last long, but it did cancel the Institute's prior claim and the associated restrictions."

Forcible hiring was a fascinating way to describe a kidnapping that had been a top news story for weeks. Video clips of the unsuccessful rescue attempt at the end had been impossible to avoid.

Naomi said, "I thought those neos all died."

"Two died outright. Five of us were locked away 'for the good of the Institute.' The other four were too damaged to care. I sold my soul to escape."

Neil said, "Meaning that the Bureau covered his disappearance and lets him run loose as long as he does ethically gray work for us now and then."

They were serious. Naomi stared at Carl. "Definitely not a casual confession."

Carl lifted his chin at Neil. "How much more dirty laundry do we air?"

Dan stirred in his seat. He looked like a big grumpy crow: dark skin, sharp eyes, black leather. "She's already spotted Walton. Brief her on Justin's mess before she guesses half of it and hyperventilates into a faint."

"What mess? The scandal over his second wife trying to murder him? Jaylin went on and on about divesting from Wyatt Industries over the break that year—" Naomi paused to wrestle with a rising sense of disbelief. "Walton? The dead arms dealer? Is every tragedy that makes it into the headlines connected?"

"There's a frightening thought," Neil said. "No. Dominic Walton wanted the rights to an arsenal that Justin refused to develop. The second wife was willing to deal, only they didn't quite eliminate Justin, and he stumbled onto some motivated allies."

A glance tossed the conversation back at Carl, who dropped it by refusing to look up from his shoes. Neil went on, "Walton started on the dirty side of paramilitary ops, before mergers and buyouts made him legit. The criminals Carl mentioned? They were a fringe outfit, operating on Walton's orders. Neopsych protocols have a lot of potential military applications."

Dan jumped in with, "Justin and Carl plotted an elaborate revenge scheme, got outmaneuvered, and had to be rescued by the Bureau at great expense and effort. Walton didn't survive the experience."

Carl leaned forward, somehow taking up even more space than usual. "You didn't *rescue* us."

"No, we didn't, but we are completely sidetracked," Neil said. "Back to Walton. He's on our lists now because the ordnance used Sunday should've been destroyed by one of his companies five years ago. Decisions to hide that much materiel would've been made at the top. Whoever knew about the bombing was probably a close associate."

Dan said, "We do need more data, Neil, and we need it fast. We need to confirm and arrest. Day Three's half over. I'm dreading the sight of a new red-box alert any minute now. Who knows when they'll hit next?"

Naomi gratefully accepted the change in topic. "Not until Hope, I would think. If there's a political thread, I mean. Today's Courage, tomorrow's Sacrifice. Anyone who dies is a martyr. The Fed will have to lift the tightest restrictions soon or get blamed for hardship complications, and by Saturday people will talk themselves into acting brave to keep—what?"

Neil's stare was nearly as intimidating as Carl's. The pale eyes and the stiffness of his posture gave him a belligerent air. Dan was staring too, and he was equally daunting in a more muscular way. Pete had a hand over his face, which did nothing to hide the fact that he was snickering. Naomi directed her next words to Pete, because he was fatherly and injured and the least threatening of the bunch. "Sorry, I was only thinking out loud."

"We," Carl said. "We are all thinking aloud."

Neil said, "Yes, we are, so let's take a closer look at those names I honestly hadn't realized we'd emphasized." His hands danced over his datapad, and the huge array of names on the wall screen melted away, leaving only the ones Naomi had highlighted.

"Next problem: how to raid all five in the minimum possible time," Neil said. "It's a long drive down the coast. Naomi, I'd also like to talk about those other ideas of yours. If you were implying that Serena's relatives factor into this in some way, I agree. There also might be a tie-in to another situation I'm watching—"

Dan cut in. "Don't we have enough to worry about already? Let it rest." He rolled his eyes at Naomi. "He's been building a criminal conspiracy chart for years now and tries to work every case we get into the Big Picture. I think one crisis at a time is plenty, don't you?"

Dan had a warm smile. He was asking her opinion. Naomi smiled back. "One is more than enough for me."

SACRIFICE

RESTORATION DAY 4

Count your blessings, and honor those who fight and die to ensure that you might keep them. What have you sacrificed? What have you given up, to help others and to add to the community? Today, take time to reflect on the balance of your life.

— *A Young Citizen's Guide to Restoration Week*

CHAPTER TWELVE

THE LIGHTS ALONG THE roadway flared, then returned to normal. Serena watched them carefully. Such flickers were typical of surges in rural electrical supply, with generators and collection systems going on and off for maintenance in the dark hours of the early morning. That was the price the rich paid for privacy and security.

Nothing unusual in a quiet area far from the more robust and better-integrated city power grids, except that it happened again and again at three-second intervals, a sequence Serena knew well. She went up on her toes and fingertips, anticipating her signal. The distant building sat exposed and vulnerable now, its protective web of sensors and cameras now telling lies to the four guards working the property.

She moved the instant Carl's voice whispered in her headphones: "Go." A sweet fiery rush of energy danced through her body. Data rippled pale across her visor: targets, positions, movements. The darkness hid nothing.

Her body armor was hot, but it fit well and rode lightly on her shoulders, and the black bodysuit beneath it was soft and tight and comfortable, like skin on skin. She wasn't allowed the armament that Parker carried—no slug pistol or grenades for her—but she had the weighty comforts of knife, darts, and stun gun, plus her feet in hard boots and fists encased in gloves. No chance of silence dressed for combat, but quiet enough for stalk, sprint, and blitz.

She slipped past Naomi, a shadow lying in shadow inside the perimeter next to an access station. Naomi raised a hand, and Serena paused close enough to let those questing fingers rest on her arm. She trusted instinct that said Justin was there too, and trust paid off with a hint of spice and a husky laugh as she brushed against him too.

He shimmered into visibility, lying flat on his back with his left leg propped up. The way he held his body whispered of weariness, but his grin laughed it off. Pain lurked under the exhilaration, though, waiting for a chance to strike.

Careful, Serena warned him with a touch that lingered longer than she'd planned, because his warm brightness felt so inviting. His grin went quiet and thoughtful.

"Move," Naomi whispered, and tapped Serena on the back of her helmet. "Go play soldier."

Naomi had a low opinion of combat gear. She had refused to even consider using light protection or a radio headset. In her experience electronics made unexpected noises outside windows or went rotten at the worst moment, while bulky layers left forensic material to snag in tight spaces, or fell off while upside down in elevator shafts.

Serena had persuaded her to carry a powered-down phone. Just in case. Just like old times. Justin had donated one with assurances that he hated it anyway, and he wore the comm headgear that kept them in contact with the support team.

No arms or armor for him either. No skill with the first, and no need for the other, he'd said, and threatened to shoot himself in the foot to prove both points when Parker tried to insist. He wore a black bodysuit and soft shoes like Naomi's, and they carried only tool kits and flexible sensor screens that could be folded into belt pockets.

Alive, the dawn-soft air murmured. Serena opened her mouth to taste it and savored pine and oak in the dusty dryness. *Hunt, chase, win,* whispered the breeze. Small things peeped and chirped in the towering bushes that the home's owner had unwisely planted right up against the building.

They were hunting information, not playing pranks, but it still felt like old times. The thrill was the same. Two down, three to go on their mission, soon to be three and two. They had moved fast overnight, too fast for word to spread if any of the targets were working together. The first, in Portland, went down in broad daylight before dinner. They hit the second outside Sacramento in the late night after a rest break. Now they were nearly home again, although still inland and warmer than Serena liked, with daylight eating away at the night.

She crept to the house, not silent but quiet. *Ready.*

On the opposite side Parker reached his position. Mirror to her, kneeling in place. Serena saw the blinking dot and his camera feed on her visor, and more than that, she felt the crunch of leaves against his knee, the thump of his pulse in her throat from twenty meters distance.

Steady.

Carl's voice: momentary disruption, necessary focus. "Go or no-go on you, Thing One. Thing Two, step to the left for us, please."

Blood rushed to Serena's face. She'd lost herself the last time. Not the first—she'd been careful—but on the second run, she'd lost control. Red Dog had left an embarrassing wake of damage. She stepped to her left now, proving she was in charge, and Parker stepped right, and then he breathed out the signal to go after their prey together: *Go.*

It was glorious fun.

A DEAFENING squeal hit Justin's left earphone. He rolled onto his stomach and snatched off the headset, muffling it under his body. His eardrum felt shredded.

"Nothing but trouble, those things." Naomi pressed close. "What happened?"

"No idea." As Justin replaced the headset, Carl was saying, "—rena says, quote: 'One of the local trips didn't listen to Bao, but we caught it in time.'"

Justin passed along the news and wondered if the "we" Serena used was referring to Parker, her collection of personas, or some combination of both. One thing was certain: she had a complicated inner life. She also had remarkably soft hands. Her passing caress had distracted him from the muscle cramps for several pleasant moments.

Naomi sat up, which was also distracting, since the maneuver put Justin's face in her lap. He stayed put. Moving would hurt, and the view was nice right where he was.

"Is that necessary, Justin?" Carl was speaking from two kilometers away, inside the cargo truck packed with assorted useful equipment from Carl's house. He and the rest of the backup team were enjoying the same scenery Justin was.

He winced and lifted his eyes to Naomi's face.

She smoothed out the map against her upper thigh so Justin wouldn't need to move see it properly. She smelled like lemons and clean sweat up close, and when Justin glanced up again, her lips were curved in a smile.

"Flattery and honesty will get you all the eye candy you can handle," she said. "But I'll warn you: touch me, and I'll sic Serena on you."

That threat should've been as effective as a bucket of ice water, but it had the opposite effect. Justin censored every comment that came to mind and kept his eyes on the map, where Serena and Parker's indicators pivoted in unison away from two separate dots that indicated the house's security guards. They kept perfect pace in opposite directions, making beelines for the second pair of guards.

Back in the truck Carl's mike picked up Dan saying, "I was already miffed because you kept this ungodly surveillance system to yourselves. The synchronized destruction routine is enough to make me weep."

Parker and Serena had shown the same swift precision on the last two operations, as if they'd trained together long enough to know where the other one would be at all times. Watching them work raised the hair on Justin's arms.

"Exterior secure," Carl said. "I'm adding data to your channel, Justin."

Neil's signal blinked to life on the schematic while Parker's and Serena's dots moved together into the outline of the building. Carl said, "I need to ask Naomi some questions about those two when you all get back."

Naomi shook her head when Justin relayed that message. "I don't have answers. She's never played mirrors with anyone but"—her sigh was wistful—"me."

Justin said, "That doesn't expla—ow!"

His left leg chose to cramp into a solid bar of pain. He muted his microphone and rolled away, reaching for his power switch. Naomi grabbed him. "Wait. Let me see."

She pulled Justin's foot out straight, and fire shot through the knotted muscles. When she pressed lightly, the cramp tightened further, but she slapped Justin's hand away from the power cell controls. "No, don't disappear. I can fix this. Don't you monitor your electrolytes? Cramping like that isn't healthy. And why haven't you gotten this repaired properly? Are you opposed to replacement parts?"

Justin couldn't draw enough breath to speak. Naomi took his

headset and keyed the mike. "Hi, we're having technical difficulties here. No, I've got it."

She returned the headset and worked on him. "Better?"

Justin nodded. He was dizzy from holding his breath, but the leg did feel better. Naomi kept kneading gently, and his throat relaxed enough to attempt speech. "My teeth grew back," he said.

The soothing hands went still. Justin tried again. "The leg happened before the skin. I lost teeth, later. They came in with the wear patterns intact. Cuts and burns heal without a trace, but old blemishes reappear. Splinters work their way loose no matter how deep they get. Imagine synthetic bones popping out."

"Ick." Naomi went back to rubbing.

"And do you really think no one ever thought of low potassium or dehydration? There's some kind of neurological disruption."

Neil arrived with barely a rustle of sound. Black fatigues and backpack, matte-black weapons, night-vision lenses covering his face: he made the outfit look natural. "Intermission's over," he said. "Ready for round two?"

Tom came slinking up, nearly invisible himself. The spotted gray was surprisingly effective camouflage. He slid into the brush on a gesture from Neil, back to prowling the perimeter and sending site data to the support team.

Neil's skills were the ones that pried open systems and left no signs of the electronic violation. He could've done the infiltrations all by himself too, although not as fast and not without effort. Justin suspected that the rest of them fell into the same category as Tom in the agent's mind: useful labor-saving assistance, not fundamentally necessary.

Serena and Parker met them in a foyer decorated with glass art pieces on spindly tables, and thick woven rugs on the walls. Serena was stroking the wall with one hand while she monitored the stairs and hallway.

Her strong features, muscle, and height made the idea of

calling her pretty an absurdity, but when she was fully alive inside her skin, like she was now, she transcended pretty and achieved stunning. Justin spent several enjoyable moments watching her pet things while Parker added building data to the maps and consulted with Neil.

The house held five neutralized occupants. Parker and Serena took up watch posts, Neil and Naomi split up to explore, and Justin tagged along with Naomi.

On-site storage from an office, entertainment center, and the family's personal devices were all dead ends, as expected. Neil copied files on principle and cleared a panic room in the master bedroom. Naomi found a safe and a stash box in the kitchen, but neither held anything useful. Any offline unit holding juicy illicit information was either carefully hidden or didn't exist at all.

Justin was doing one last check before declaring defeat when he spotted an anomaly between map and reality. Two interior walls didn't quite match. Naomi returned to a first-floor pantry room off the kitchen. Soon a panel opened to reveal a steep stairwell descending into darkness. Naomi grinned. "Yay, me. Take that, secret agent man."

"I heard that," Neil said from wherever he was. "What did you find?"

"Hidden stairs," Justin said. He shifted his eyepiece to IR, and steel-braced concrete walls appeared. "Goes down at least thirty steps."

"Wait."

Justin grabbed Naomi by the wrist when she started down the steps. She turned her arm to slip free and danced back a step. "What's wrong?"

"Neil says to wait."

"Why? Doesn't he trust us to check it out?"

"I don't trust anybody," Neil said on arrival. He gave the doorway a quick look. "This building has twice as many generators as it needs. When push comes to shove, this is my job, not yours. I'm not risking your skins to find out why there's extra power."

He had decent morals for an idealist. Justin said, "My skin's tough, and two sets of eyes are better than one."

"Fair enough," Neil said. "But I'm still taking point."

He'd been right to worry. Before they got to the bottom of the steps, the roof blew in.

THE FLOOR BUCKED UNDERFOOT, the house shuddered, and the lower half of the stairwell disappeared behind a veil of falling concrete. The noise was minimal, all things considered, the shaking barely noticeable to anyone accustomed to life on a major fault line. The stairs were just gone, the air suddenly hot and stifling. The results looked fuzzy in the monochrome tones from her IR system.

Naomi wiped dust off her lenses. Her hands shook. She'd wanted to go first. She'd been *disappointed*.

Serena came barreling past at full speed, down into the dark pit full of unstable rubble. Naomi shook off the numbness and ran after her. "Serena, no!"

A helmet bounced on the steps and gave off the sound of whispering voices. Harness, armor, and belt came off next, and then Serena waded into the debris. Naomi grabbed her with both hands and heaved back.

"Stop it, Serena. Stop digging. It's too dangerous."

Her efforts were as effective as yanking on a tree. The quiet noises Serena was making were too controlled for crying, and she scrabbled with both hands, raising thick plumes of dust. "Out. Out. Outoutoutoutout. *Out.*"

It was the same low chant she had been making when the searchers finally reached her. She'd left sanity far behind by then, but she had never stopped fighting to live.

Naomi tugged until her left wrist gave out, and then she pulled with the right one alone and sniffled back tears until someone shoved her aside. Her shoulders hit the wall with bruising force, and Parker brushed past. He clamped an arm around Serena's waist and swung her onto his hip as easily as if she were a misbehaving toddler, and then he pivoted, looking up. His eyes were obscured by the helmet visor, but the bared teeth sent a clear message: *move.*

Naomi backed up as fast as she could and squeezed herself against the pantry wall. Parker stomped upstairs with Serena kicking and fighting the whole way. He pitched her sprawling to the floor, crashed to his knees next to her, and slapped one hand over her mouth. His other hand clutched the back of her neck.

Serena crumpled into a fetal ball, head down with arms and legs tucked beneath her. Parker left her like that, stomping down the stairs again without even a glance at Naomi. She stood frozen until he passed. Then she ran to Serena, cradled her friend's head to her chest, felt the heat of panting breath against her skin.

She pressed her cheek against Serena's hair. Justin's face flashed into mind: convincing Neil of his usefulness with earnest insistence; sticking his tongue out at Naomi afterwards; smiling as he followed Neil away. And then *gone.*

Justin, who apologized for staring, then grinned like a naughty little boy and kept doing it, who called Serena crazy as if it were a compliment and made her smile. *Gone.*

Serena twitched against her. "No, no, no, not dead. Not, Naomi. Out. We have to get them out. Out. Out. *Out.*"

Parker emerged from the stairwell with Serena's discarded equipment and dropped to a crouch beside them. Naomi turned her face away, cringing inside, but the expected violence never materialized. Her IR headset was removed and replaced with Serena's helmet. Rough fingers retracted the visor and flicked controls. The babble in the earphones disappeared, and a headlamp sprang to life.

Warm hands cupped her face and tipped it up.

Skin smeared half-clean of black paint. Eyebrows wrinkled together, narrow lower lip caught between gnawing teeth. Green irises flecked with brown, warm and bright. Parker's face held none of the contempt Naomi had expected. She saw only desperation and sorrow in the tight cheek muscles and clenched jaw.

She looked down when Serena started to whisper. "Her fault, me and the dogs, he's all tangled up in me, through you, and she's too scared to let go, they need help please, they need out-out-outoutou—"

Naomi *felt* the growl that stopped Serena midword and sent her cringing to the floor in a ball again. The vibration shivered through Parker's fingertips, and frustrated intent lodged itself somewhere between Naomi's ears.

He couldn't find words with Serena howling inside his head, but if he shut her out, she would be back in the stairwell in a heartbeat, digging until her hands were broken and her sanity shredded. He needed help.

"Wow." Naomi put her hands over Parker's and raised her head. "Hello."

The flash of relief in his eyes amused her. He'd actually been afraid Naomi wouldn't understand. Which was stupid, really, but that could wait until later.

Had to wait, came the inner echo. She tapped the helmet. "You want me to make your report for you? Then make this work for me."

He hit two buttons, and the air filled with angry voices. Then he leaned in to kiss Naomi on the lips.

It wasn't a friendly little thank-you-for-helping kiss. That, she could've handled. This was more like being swallowed up and rolled by a breaking line of surf. By the time Parker drew back, Naomi was dizzy and breathless, flattened and boneless in the best possible sense.

Some small stupid part of her soul wanted to get up and dance.

The rest of it, raw and bruised by betrayal, still quivered with doubt. Parker closed his eyes and rose to his feet. His jaw knotted, and Serena whispered, "*Mine.*"

"All things considered, that's still ambiguous." Naomi closed her eyes too, pushing aside the confusion until later.

Boots thudded on the main stairs: Parker was off to make sure none of the house's inhabitants had gotten loose or started any mischief. Naomi spoke over the questions hammering at her ears. "Please shut up and listen."

That brought silence. She gave as concise a summary as she could, leaving out the personal parts, and then out of nowhere, heartbreak welled up. "Serena thinks they're still alive. I don't know how—I don't know what to tell her."

Carl said, "Tell her she's right. We're coming in."

JUSTIN SAT UP. Debris cascaded off his body. His back felt stiff, and his head throbbed. Even skin that could absorb a hit from a sledge-hammer had its limits. A lot of things had hit him very fast and very hard, and at least one thing must have landed on his skull.

He was somewhere dark, quiet, and cold. The headset had come off in the tumbling fall, which accounted for dark and quiet, and he'd been literally stripped of his insulation. The bodysuit and the thermal layer beneath it now consisted of more holes than fabric, and the power cell had blown off with the material under it. Even his shoes were gone.

There'd been an instant of warning, a bare tick of sound familiar from months of working with explosives experts. He'd shoved Neil down and forward, below the main collapse, but he had no idea whether the tactic had made any difference.

There was nothing within arm's reach, which was a good sign. The darkness had a red tint and a chemical smell.

Justin licked dry lips, coughed up dust. "Neil?"

"Here."

The soft reply came from the right. Justin crawled straight until he hit a wall and pulled himself upright against its support. One hand landed on a switch, and light fixtures flashed to life overhead, illuminating a cloud of dust that obscured the room almost as much as the darkness had.

"Do you have a death wish?" Neil sounded amused.

"Clumsy. Are you all right?"

"I doubt it."

A heavy-duty ventilation system kicked into high gear. The dust cloud thinned. Indistinct objects and glowing indicator lights appeared first. As cold swirls of clear air pushed through the haze, more shapes emerged: countertops and tables, retorts and distillation tubing, vats and bottles and centrifuges, analytical equipment and manufacturing units. Telltales blinked red everywhere, and liquid dribbled and dripped and pooled on the floor. Justin shivered in the draft and limped carefully through the mess.

The room was roughly ten meters by ten. Neil became visible in a few steps, at first a tall form leaning against a counter, then a person at a workstation. Neil had the cover off, and one of his diagnostic devices was attached to it.

Blood seeped down the agent's face from a forehead cut to mix with smears beneath his nose. More blood straggled down the sides of his neck from both ears, and the pale irises of his eyes were swimming against a background of burst blood vessels. Dust had turned his black hair gray.

"Comms are shot, and there's no other exit. I got bored, so I started—holy shit." He stopped waving the device around. "You look horrible."

"Says the man whose face is leaking."

Neil opened his mouth to reply, but then dropped to his knees to vomit up blood onto the floor instead. When he was done, he said, "Definitely not all right."

"Doesn't look that way."

In spite of the cold, Justin's hands started to sweat as he helped Neil move away from the mess. Panic swelled in his chest. He took care of Neil's damages as best he could between bouts of quaking terror while the agent made electronics jump through hoops.

The backpack provided splints for Neil's broken fingers, gel bonder for the scalp wound, and tape for the reopened bullet graze on his shoulder. Justin handed over a water bottle and took one for himself. "How do you feel?"

"I *feel* fine." Neil's eyes had never wavered from his work. "My body lies like a rug, courtesy of the nifty Delta tinkering. We go until the blood's gone, the brain's gone, or the mission's done. Or until pain-stimulus failure results in a moronic death by accident: 'Oops, too busy trimming hedges to notice the missing foot.' "

That had the ring of a true story. "Gruesome."

Neil smiled, which looked ghastly. "I volunteered. No point in crying now. Can you take down the other workstation? I'm getting stand-up-equals-pass-out signals. The brainsucker is plug-and-play. If you can run that, I can try to rig a radio beacon from parts here."

His chances of success were too minimal to calculate, but Justin understood the sentiment. Better to do anything than nothing. Better to concentrate on activity than on the way his vision kept fading because fear wouldn't let him get enough air into his lungs. Better to work than sit and think about how fast the cold would kill him.

Uncontrollable shivering began while he was hooking up the unit, and by the time the download was done, his fingers and brain were numb. He spent some immeasurable amount of time struggling to remember what he was doing, then staggered across the room with the equipment. Someone needed it.

He stopped next to a man lying on the floor. "Hey."

After a long hesitation the man opened his eyes. "God, you seriously look like shit now."

"'M f-f-f-fine." Justin gritted his chattering teeth together. The name came back to him. "Your name is Neil."

"Yes, it is. New chore." Neil held up a roll of tape. "Sit down. I'll secure that brainsucker. Then you take it up that ventilation shaft. You'll have to stop the fan. Short the main breaker here. That'll help your shakes too, if I recall correctly. Short the power, climb out, find the big angry black man. Repeat that for me in sequence."

Justin got it right on the second try.

There was a flaw in the plan. He was sure of it. He already would've tapped into the electrical supply if getting relief was that simple. He wouldn't be putting himself through this for no reason.

"Do it," Neil slapped him on the shoulder. "Go."

CARL JUMPED BACK when Naomi came sliding out of the airshaft headfirst onto the flagstone patio. He'd known she was coming, but the soundless arrival was still startling. Her hands slapped against stone, and she somersaulted to a halt.

"What's wrong?" Carl asked. "You never checked in."

"No signal. Probably shielded to jam up aerial recon."

Naomi dodged his offered hand and hopped onto the low wall that hid the access to the underground room. "I found Justin. He's nearly to the last vertical here."

The patio sat twenty meters from the house and a deeply buckled patch of lawn that corresponded to the collapsed stairwell. Carl consulted the little sensor unit Justin had designed. Naomi's report made Justin's icon the flickering one and Neil's the steady dot near the house. "How is he?"

"I'm not sure." Naomi shimmied halfway into the shaft from above. The provocative move showcased both her shapely rear end and her flexibility, and she yelled, "Can you climb? It's designed for emergency exit, there are grips."

Muttered echoes rose from inside. Naomi unfolded herself. "He says he's fine, but he's shaking awfully hard."

"I told you shivering was a bad sign. Why didn't you stay with him?" Carl quelled the stab of aggravation when Naomi flinched at his tone. Then he turned and called out to Pete. "Dig up the climbing rig, and prep some heat packs, will you? Kick up the heater in there too."

Their truck was parked with its lights shining on the work zone. Pete waved and crawled into the back for the supplies, and Naomi whispered, "I'll get the rope."

It would only save a few seconds, but Carl let her go after one look at her face. She wasn't nearly as tiny as Alison, but her delicate build and the brittle emotions in those watchful eyes made her seem infinitely more fragile. She wore her air of resigned deference like a ragged cloak over old fears, and his inability to regain her trust was getting on his nerves.

The reflected headlights cast an oblique glare along the side panels of the truck, highlighting the slight change in color where the company logo had been removed. Carl stared at the dim imprint of a runner with wings on his feet, trying to channel his thoughts away from worry and anger.

When Justin decided on a theme he stuck with it. All the subsidiaries of his nonprofit's transport company followed the example set by the foundation itself. Dawnstar owned Hermes, Hermes operated Raven Air, Mercury Shipping, and Prometheus Rentals. They were all rebel gods and tricksters, every one. Carl wondered how many people ever spotted the joke. He hadn't, until now.

When Naomi returned, she stood back until given ample room to pass, and she kept her eyes on Carl's hands while she gave him one end of the rope. Then she bolted past him into the air duct with the harness.

Pete settled cautiously on the patio wall with the other supplies. "I see why you didn't take her at face value now," he said. "She sets my teeth on edge. Emotionally reserved, major shifts in affect and proximity tolerance depending on whether she's near males or females, exaggerated submissive response to force—that's a classic reaction matrix. You dug into her background because you didn't want Eddie hooking up with a sex worker, even one clever enough to avoid arrest. Tell me I'm wrong."

"Selling sex is legal in California for adults with a license, but the timeline didn't work for anything but child prostitution." Carl coiled up slack in the line. "Am I a twisted sonofabitch for even suspecting it?"

"Christ, no." Pete thumped a heel against the wall and winced. "Nothing about her quite fits. Rape, incest, or other relational abuse would set up those patterns, but the trauma residue isn't there, and that high-tactile profile doesn't match—"

"Hold that thought." A firm yank told Carl that Naomi had gotten the harness attached. He walked the rope back until Justin landed on the patio. His body was shimmering, and the night air was cool enough to feel the heat rolling off his skin without touching him. Pete got the blanket over him, and he accepted the heat packs with a groan of relief.

Fever-bright eyes slid up to Carl's, daring him to say something about being more careful. Carl bit his tongue. After a few moments Justin groped between his shoulder blades and ripped loose an object wrapped in tape. "'S for Whosit. There's a lab down there. Whatsit dumped the workstation."

"You mean Neil?"

"Whatsit, yes. *Shit*. The vent closed. Breaker pops, fan stops, vent shuts." Justin staggered to his feet and glared at the airshaft. "Fucking asshole."

Pete said dryly, "Can I get a translation, please?"

Justin's teeth chattered. "No."

A flurry of subdued activity followed. Carl helped Justin to the truck and sat with him among the crates and bags in the smothering heat. It was easy to see why his appearance had unnerved Naomi. The manic gleam in his eyes was disturbing, and the shivers made him look spastic. He was also mostly naked, and he had huge red blotches across his back and thighs.

"Bruises, Justin?"

"Do they look impressive?" Justin dug up base layer and a power cell from his go bag. Next he rummaged up black pants, a shirt and boots from a box, and he fiddled with his ankle cuff.

"There," he said triumphantly when he was done. "Now I don't feel them. All set."

"Is that a good idea?" Carl asked. "Not the clothes. Clothes are good, although Eddie's don't fit you very well. I mean boosting above your baseline. What are you up to?"

"Improvising." Justin threw items into a sack: pliers, tape, wire, and a half dozen fist-sized power cells from the big crate he called his toy box. "Where is everybody? Are the bastards who set that deathtrap still in the house?"

"No. Eddie and Dan moved our hosts out front, wrapped up nice and tidy for the local Bureau station. We could lose our cover here any minute now. Dan's retrieving Neil's furry perimeter scout, Pete took him whatever you brought back, Eddie's sitting on the house security until we're ready to retreat, and Serena—"

Carl watched a fire blanket and an IR headset go into the bag. Serena had explained earnestly that air on her skin and green in her nose would push the dirt out of her head. He edited that to, "She's hugging shrubs by the front door. Naomi took the scrapes-and-scratches kit and joined her. What are you doing?"

Justin shot him a puzzled glance. "What does it look like I'm doing? I'm getting Neil out of that hole in the ground before the air runs out."

CHAPTER THIRTEEN

C ARL STOOD UP AND moved to block the rear door. "Are you delirious? We might have enough rope, but I doubt it. Besides, if he has internal injuries, then being dragged out would kill him anyway. Is he going to suffocate or bleed to death in an hour or two? We can send in an anonymous tip and let emergency responders extract him."

"No, but—" Justin rubbed both hands over his face. "They might shoot him as soon as they ID him. Carl, I'm concussed and cranky, and it's hard to explain. Move."

"No. Alison will murder me if I can't keep you alive for twenty-four hours."

"She will not. Move, or I will move you."

"Try it," Carl said.

The truck door squeaked open, and Dan spoke from the front. "Whoa, now, kids. Wait for me."

The truck swayed as he squeezed himself into the rear compartment through the access hatch. He pointed a finger at Justin and used the other hand to pull a pistol from beneath his leather jacket. "I'm not writing off Neil until I see the body rotting," he said. "What do you need?"

"Space. Back off." Justin picked up the sack and ducked under Carl's arm, heading outside on a gust of cooler air.

Dan raised the gun when Carl moved to follow. "I don't think so, Goliath. I'm on David's side. Sit back and relax."

When Carl didn't move, Dan said, "This thing fires pellets that can penetrate cloth and act on skin contact. It's a Delta perk. Illegal as hell. It will drop you in five seconds, and then you'll enjoy five minutes of excruciating, paralytic cramps. If your squirrelly little genius wants room to work on a plan, then he gets it."

Carl sat down, suddenly feeling old and tired. "Justin doesn't plan. He jumps off cliffs secure in the belief that he'll learn to fly on the way down."

Dan's laugh had a bitter undertone. "I know the type."

"No, you don't." Carl hunted for words to soften the blunt contradiction. "Justin leaps past decision points to sidestep crippling uncertainty. It isn't bravery. It's a coping mechanism."

"Can't it be both?" Dan holstered the gun and pulled out the little device Justin had brought back for him. "Look, it's clear we're both praying our birds sprout wings one more time. Do you want to sulk in private, or will you help me harvest the fruits of this fiasco while we wait? I could use a hand."

All the equipment boxes were still open from Justin's raiding. Carl gestured an invitation. "Take whatever you need."

NAOMI COMBED stray foliage off the top of her head and sniffed it. The needles did smell green, if green meant spicy and fresh. A thick bed of mulch covered the roots of the tall shrubs where Serena had taken refuge. It made reasonably comfortable seating. The house security lights were dim here, filtered through the protective branches. It felt safe.

Her left wrist ached under the tape. Serena pressed both hands over the old injury, stroked it with fingers that had been scraped raw even through the protection of gloves. "You never let go. I was so scared when they found me, but you didn't let go even when I broke you."

Once the search team had made contact, after the quake, once they'd made the first hole, Serena had started throwing herself against the rubble. They'd needed time to engineer a safe extraction. Naomi had stayed the whole time, holding Serena's hand through that tiny, tiny opening.

"I'll never let go," she said now. "How are the itches?"

"Better." Serena lifted her head as irregular footsteps rapped along the stone pathway outside their hiding spot. She was out of the bushes before Naomi could gather her legs under her.

"Hey, Batshit." Justin's voice sounded much better than it had only a short time earlier. He also sounded more blasé than Naomi would've expected under the circumstances. "How's the belfry?"

"Quiet," Serena said. "You give off quiet."

Naomi emerged from the bushes at the end of the exchange. Justin was wearing rumpled too-big black fatigues now, and his appearance was much improved from the feral apparition Naomi had glimpsed in the tunnel. Serena bent slightly to kiss him on the forehead.

"You stink like dirt and sweat," she informed him.

"And you are magnificently naked. Hey. You." He squinted at Naomi. "I need you. I'm going back. You fit."

"What?"

Serena began shimmying into her clothes. "He's going back into the dirt, out-out-out-out, but he's all crackly and cloudy inside. He needs help."

"Not useful, Serena." The repeated 'out' plucked at Naomi's nerves, but Serena wasn't acting frantic, and she was getting dressed without fussing about it. "I'm sorry, I don't understand either of you."

The truly strange part was that they seemed to understand

each other. Naomi wrapped her right hand over her left wrist and pushed down twinges of worry and envy.

"My brain locks up." Justin tore his eyes away from Serena again. "I can get Neil out, but if I lock up at the wrong time we'll both be fucked. I need help that can move fast in small spaces. You."

Naomi's pulse sped up, prudence and reckless curiosity vying for control. When Serena said, "Please, Naomi," that decided things.

Soon she was climbing down the air duct after Justin, who slid down without gloves or harness while Carl anchored the line for him. As Naomi finished a more conventional descent, she said, "What is locking up? How do I help if it happens?"

"If I start babbling, or I stop moving and go quiet, then yell or hit or do whatever it takes to get a rational response." Justin ducked out of sight where the shaft bent from vertical to a gentle slant. "Carl's been doing it for me, but I heard you say this area's shielded."

"I thought he was just naturally—um." *Rude.*

"He does get cranky, but it helps. Too bad nothing helps when I get panic attacks or my coordination cuts out …" He trailed off. "I bet you're wishing you'd said no."

"Actually, I was thinking that you're putting a lot of trust in me." Naomi peered into the slanted section ahead. Justin's boots receded into the darkness.

She caught up to him and slithered to a halt beyond a ventilation fan in a hinged and dented frame. Justin turned and twisted, looking all around.

"What's wrong?" Naomi asked, but Justin said nothing.

He'd stopped talking. He wasn't moving. Naomi's heart withered at the thought of hitting him, and her head hurt at the thought of shouted echoes. She said, "Move, Justin. Move. Go, go, go."

She poked at his legs until he squirmed forward, banging

knees and elbows hard. He kept moving until he abruptly crashed through a closed vent to a floor below. Naomi moved more carefully and dropped down.

The room was full of shadowy lumps, and the air was unpleasantly pungent. Justin was turning in place, head swinging. Naomi grabbed his face in both hands. The contact tickled, but she forced herself to hold on. "Look at me, Justin. The stairs blew up, and you were trapped. We're back to rescue Neil. Anybody home in there?"

His head twitched and so did his arms. Naomi hastily moved back into a defensive stance. Justin tracked the motion, his IR glasses gleaming opaque. Then he took a step away and lifted his hands, palms out, fingers spread.

She lowered her fists. "Are you okay?"

Justin shook his head, then wrapped his arms around himself. Air whistled in and out between his gritted teeth.

He had mentioned panic attacks. Naomi approached slowly, put a hand on his shoulder, pressed into the prickling static with long, slow strokes. "You're okay. In and out. Slower, now. Let it go. Let it wash out and away."

"Sorry," he said when he had the reaction under control. "And thanks."

"How often—?" Naomi stopped. "Sorry. None of my business. That was impolite."

"I can go days without one episode. In a bad patch, I'm off more often than on. It's so *much* fun to be me." Justin scooped up the bag and headed for the wall of rubble in one corner. One hand flapped at the opposite wall. "Check on Whatsis."

She nearly jumped out of her skin when a voice nearby said, "Still breathing."

"Good." Justin emptied his sack of goodies onto the floor and sat down next to it. "This won't take long. It specs like a job I did in January."

Neil was reclining against a counter with his knees raised and both arms pressed tight over his belly. The floor next to him was speckled and splattered black. Naomi stopped, and Neil grinned. "I hear scared little feet. Naomi, isn't it?"

"Yes." She gulped at the thick air. "There's blood in your teeth."

"I haven't eaten anyone's brains, I swear. I can't even shamble." Neil raised his voice. "I kicked you out, Justin."

"You tricked me, asshole. Idealistic martyr-complex bullshit."

"Guilty as charged. No point in both of us dying. Why are you back?"

"Stairwell's intact and the lab too, for the most part. Means it's reinforced, designed to be cleared and reset. No time to dig, and blasting from above would pulp you with overpressure. I'll do it from here, and you get carried out. Simple."

Simple. Naomi felt a horrible giggle rising up inside. "Simple," Neil echoed. "All those years of pacifist posturing, and now you're an expert on bombs?"

"They aren't *bombs*, and—" Justin sighed. "And there go my hands. My day is now complete. Naomi, I need you."

"What if I do something wrong?" What if Justin did something wrong? "Do you know what you're doing?"

"Yes. It's safe as houses, I swear. Hurry. *Please*."

She hurried, because the alternative was unthinkable. They couldn't just leave Neil here now. Justin's hands shook as he pointed out what to do, and after the access panels were off the little boxes, he elbowed Naomi aside and poked at the innards. The work style didn't inspire confidence, and Naomi backed away.

"All right, that's done." Justin looked around. "Why are you over there?"

"I'm waiting for the boom."

He laughed at the admittedly ridiculous safety precaution, and the sound was so infectious that Naomi couldn't help laughing too.

Next, Justin started digging holes in the rubble with his bare hands. Naomi packed up the tools for him. The air burned her nostrils, and when she stood up, it left her dizzy. She crawled to Neil and waited until Justin joined them.

"We're set," he said. "Make sure they cleared the house and backed the truck off. Fumes, you know? Shout down, and I'll give you thirty seconds more."

"You're not coming?"

He shrugged. "I can't use a timer on this config, and I don't have a wired trigger. Shielding means transmitter has to be close. I'll keep Neil company." He knelt as if to tie his shoe and faded from sight. "We'll be fine. Move it."

Naomi went up the duct as fast as she could crawl.

Carl looked profoundly unhappy when she informed him of Justin's orders about the truck. Later, lying flat in a dip in the terrain at the end of the driveway, Naomi understood his concern a lot better.

The ground shook, and the noise of the explosion was immensely louder than the original collapse. A plume of dirt and pulverized concrete rose above the roof, and windows shattered even on the front of the building.

Then the brightening sky behind the house lit up with a towering column of flame.

JUSTIN'S EARS POPPED, and heat washed past the corner where he was crouched over Neil. The blast ripped the fire blanket from his fingers and smashed them both into the cabinets with bone-jarring force.

Justin rolled away and kept rolling until the licking flames died, until the black, stinking smoke cleared. Then he lay there in humming, eerie silence and savored the taste of cool, sweet air in his throat.

Dim light shone down the empty stairwell, revealing a raw

gash of lawn above. Burned sod had peeled back in thick black ripples to expose the battered edge of the foundation and a hole in the pantry wall past the top few stairs. Justin threw off the smoking blanket and stood up.

Neil pulled himself up the cabinets and leaned against the counter. He looked like a lanky, walking corpse, but he was alive, and there was access for rescue. Mission accomplished.

Justin limped closer. Satisfaction lifted his spirits to giddy heights. Most of the secondary explosion had safely followed in the wake of the first, exactly as he'd planned. Not even the bleak prospect of the bruises he would have to face when he powered down could dampen his mood.

Neil punched him in the chest. Justin staggered. The rebound sent Neil to the floor again, clutching his fist. "Damned reflexes," he said loudly. "You are there, aren't you? That is you? I can smell … something."

Justin put a hand on the agent's shoulder and spoke into his ear. "Can you walk? I can't carry you, and we'll have emergency crews on us fast after that show."

"Go, if you can. I'll wait. My legs are made of butter."

That image stuck in Justin's brain all the way up the ruined steps. His own legs were starting to feel a little buttery by the time he reached the top. He rested in the kitchen while Dan, Parker and Serena ran past him. They collaborated on Neil's transport and were gone again before he remembered that they couldn't see him.

Trying to walk out alone would be a bad idea. Better to wait for someone to come back than to trip over his own feet and knock himself out.

The little patio area was a crumpled mess of scorched stone. He was admiring the blast pattern when Parker crunched to a halt beside him. The man wrinkled his nose and looked into shadows. "Where, Justin?"

"I'm right here."

Parker caught his arm and dragged him stumbling outside.

The van was gone. Carl had the rear of the truck open, and the vehicle started moving as soon as they were inside. Naomi glanced back from the driver's seat. "Ick. What is that—"

Parker closed the cab access, cutting off her question. Justin settled to the floor between two boxes and powered down a few notches. Zeroing out properly could wait until he was on the far side of a long hot shower and within falling distance of a bed. With luck he might pass out from exhaustion before the backlash hit.

His legs shimmered into view. The pants were singed, but the thermal suit and power unit looked intact. His boots were black with soot and a little melted, and his left hand was blistered on the back. Not bad, all in all.

"I thought we had an agreement." Carl stood against the rear doors with his hands wrapped around cargo straps hanging from bolts in the ceiling. "About secrets. You might've warned us that the place would go up like a torch."

"I told Naomi." He tried to remember. "Didn't I?"

"No." That was Parker's furious word on the subject.

Being criticized for success was an emotional sucker-punch. Justin's satisfaction evaporated, leaving a residue of disgust. "The room was full of volatile chemicals in damaged containers. Of course it was going to blow. I deflected the worst of it, didn't I? Nobody died, right?"

His bruises began to ache, and his mood took a downward turn into resentment. He rolled a shoulder to stretch the strained and damaged muscles, easing the outer hurt to distract himself from the inner one. Whining about life's unfairness was pointless.

A massive itch sprang to life behind one shoulder, but when he reached up to scratch it, Parker caught his hand and scowled fiercely. "No."

The itch began eating into Justin's back, a painful, prickling, *burning* feeling. He'd only felt the briefest sear from the blast. Now dismay rose in a dizzy tide. "Did I get burned? Is that why you're both so crabby? How bad is it?"

"Bad doesn't begin to cover it." Carl lifted a hand to rub at his forehead. "The shock and that adrenaline high won't last. There's nothing safe to give you for pain, not even from my kit. Not between your damned allergies and two concussive shocks in under five hours. What are we going to do with you?"

"Nothing." If he zeroed out he would undoubtedly pass out, but at the risk of making things worse if he thrashed around. "Burns only take a day or two from scab to whole once I debride any charred stuff. It's disgusting, but I can grit my teeth until I get to a hot shower, and I'll crash fast after that. I'll be fine."

A small motion sent fire blazing out along every nerve and threatened to turn his body inside out. Tears spilled over when he blinked. "I will be fine," he repeated, because that future was his only defense against the present.

"Fine." Carl brushed a hand over the top of Justin's head, held it there as if in benediction, and Justin knew what was coming from the tone of that one syllable.

The next soft-spoken words were gentle and inescapable. "Go to sleep, Justin. I know you told me to never do this, but I can't— you are not fine. Sleep and heal. Close your eyes and rest until I wake you. Go. To. Sleep."

DAN SYNCED the van into the highway traffic control system. "Okay, Carl's route is in. Neil, how are you holding up? How much patching up do you need?"

Serena closed her eyes against the urge to challenge when Dan's gaze slid past her seat. Angry, his face shouted. *No threat,* she reminded herself. *Ally.*

"Neil?" Dan glanced over his shoulder.

"He's out." Pete was reclined next to the agent on the folded-down benches, and Tom was pressed against his legs. Pete stroked the cat's ears. "I've only had basic medical training, but I know a fast shallow pulse and a swollen, rock-hard belly are bad news. He needs a hospital."

"And all he has are me, you, and the head case, because we cannot risk the CSB catching him from the bio-ident a hospital would run. Great. Just *great*."

Serena studied Dan closely. No, this time she wasn't wrong. He meant "head case" as an insult. Dark skin and darker eyes were molten hot with disdain. Fury seethed under the smooth stony surface.

Dan's laugh was a nasty sound. "Look at this, all the weak links in one place. Where did Parker go? He was supposed to drive this thing. You think anyone will be at the end of the route they sent? I'm starting to wonder."

His voice was like stone, and Serena twitched at the effort of keeping Red Dog from rising up to crash against it. She let temper loose to growl and snap at him instead.

"No one could've planned this. Parker ran back for Justin; Neil could only lie flat in the van, which is what Pete was doing when we got in; Naomi would never ditch me; and don't call me a head case where I can hear you. I'm crazy, not deaf."

Temper wanted more, but Serena hauled back on its scruff and stepped on anxiety's tail for good measure. Once they were settled, she firmed up a glare to throw at Dan's rocky shell. He shut his mouth and glanced at Pete.

Pete waved a bandaged hand. "Oh, no. Don't look for sympathy from the other weak link. You kicked her, you deal with the kickback."

Then he looked at Serena with more than just those peaceful eyes. It was a whole-body smile, strong and gnarly and as broad as his shoulders, like a hug from a meter away. The core of him was a twining strength like a vine grown in high wind: bent and knotted, but powerful.

"That is quite a stare," he said. "What do you see, I wonder?"

"Vines. But it's not on the outside. It's an inside view."

Dan groaned loudly without taking his eyes off the road. Serena's temper pulled loose again and shouldered aside gentler feelings to ask, "Why are you being such an insufferable shit?"

Dan blinked, and tears filled those midnight-dark eyes. Pain had been hiding under the hot rage. Serena's temper dropped flat, whining apology, and Dan said, "Because he's dying, and there's nothing—I can't even—when I said weak links, I was including me. This isn't our range, I have no resources and no contacts, I am out of ideas, and I can't trust anyone, and I don't know what to do."

Despair bubbled through the whispered confession. Serena waited until Dan wiped his eyes dry, until she was sure her words could get through those cracked defenses without breaking them completely. "I know what to do," she said. "Maybe I'm a head case, but I'm a head case who has a bunch of cousins who run an unlicensed health clinic. Now what do you say about me?"

Pete laughed, a rustle of leaves on strong branches.

The van rocked when Dan leaned across the console and kissed Serena hard on the cheek. *Fast*, Gray Dog noted, always worried, and Dan said, "I say give me a damned address so I can plug it in, and I'll pass along the news."

TYLER JAMMED a stylus into the port that silenced the elevator alarm and then hit the stop button. Alison's loft apartment was the only residence on the level, but the elevator wasn't private. He didn't want it being called away.

Alison edged past him, but Tyler barred her way with his arm. "Wait. Justin has cameras, but you don't. I want to run a sweep with his gadget first."

"Why? Rabini's kids from Three did this. We saw them snickering downstairs." Alison wasn't silent or gracious about waiting, but she did stop. "Stupid kids. Sacking is a *stupid* fad."

"Humor me." The kids were fifteen and fourteen and twice Alison's size.

"I'm waiting. I already waited through checking Justin's cameras on the way up, didn't I? This is spite, pure and simple. Why does Day Four bring out the jerks? God, is that *flour* in those footprints?"

She kept talking, but Tyler tuned her out. It was only venting. Carl's early-morning call regarding Justin's second- and third-degree burns had brought Alison to the edge between worry and anger. The security alert here had pushed her right over it.

The remote viewer was giving off some odd flickers, but it showed no occupants. "Okay, Allie, go ahead. You know, if you'd let us put in cameras like mine in your place, then we might've caught them red-handed. Here, give Toby to me. I want her to stay on guard."

He tied the cat's leash to the stairwell door handle. The loft door slammed open. Alison snarled, "Thanks, Tyler. Thanks for making this my fault for wanting privacy. Oh, no. Look at this mess!"

Paints, brushes, draped fabrics, beads, wire, and other art supplies had been dumped in a pile and doused with the contents of every container in the kitchen. The furniture was slashed open, and the knives were jammed into the gutted remains.

Tyler took a walk along a line of tall windows past bamboo dividers. The two bedrooms were disgusting. The last room was a den whose walls had been covered in a collage of photos and memorabilia. The chunky leather recliner had been a great place to watch the night skyline.

Not a single item was salvageable. Tyler picked up a sparkly chunk of rock and hefted it. If he knew for certain whose skull to use it on, for once he wouldn't feel the slightest qualm. "What if it wasn't Sackers? What if someone was searching your place?"

"Oh, for God's sake." Thump. "What if one of the kitchen gadgets developed sentience? What if it was gremlins? Don't start with 'what-ifs' today. Please don't. Oh—"

Her voice broke into a gasp. Tyler returned to the main room at a dead run.

Alison was on her knees in the middle of the jumble, crying her heart out. "I'm sorry," she whispered. "I'm all in pieces, and I'm scared for Justin, and I'm scared for us, and I'm taking it out on you, aren't I? I'm so sorry."

"We're safe," Tyler said. "I've activated my taps here. If anyone comes calling then I'll get a heads-up, so we can dodge onto one of the routes I mapped—" He couldn't tell if Alison was about to cry or laugh. "What?"

"You mapped out escape plans for *my* building?"

"It's your home, and Justin's too, even if he moved downstairs. Of course I watch over it. Do what you need to do, and then we'll go off grid, just in case. Public transit, cash cards. I have a stash."

"Of course you do." Alison sniffled. "Once again you are my cheerful knight in shining armor."

"Justin's the armored one, and you take care of everything for us all the time. Someone has to take care of you." Tyler slotted chips for a generic account into his handset and earbug. "We'll need a place to flop. I'll try Mario first. The restaurant makes a public buffer, and there's no paper relationship, only the personal one. Good food, a quiet retreat and someone to watch Toby if we do have to bolt. If he agrees."

Alison went back to work. "He will. That's perfect, Tyler. I don't know what I'd do without you."

"You'll never have to," Tyler said.

Alison looked up, but instead of rewarding him with a sarcastic reply, her eyes went wide. "Dear God in heaven," she said. "No wonder Helen's been frantic."

Tyler spun to see what was behind him.

The front door was open. A small boy was standing there with one hand on Toby's leash and the other holding a backpack by the straps. He had spiky dark hair and wide brown eyes, he was dressed in rumpled dirty clothes, and he looked miserable.

After a moment Tyler's manners caught up with his confusion. "Hi, Ryan. What are you doing here, kiddo?"

NAOMI UNLOCKED an apartment door with a keycard and stepped back. Carl carried Justin inside, turning to keep Justin's boots clear of the door jamb. Parker handed Naomi the big red box he'd been carrying and walked off.

Someone had to move the truck off the loading zone and get the operation back on track. Someone had to stay focused on the mission and not the casualties.

Naomi hefted the box. She needed to persuade her feet to move her body into the apartment, and Parker's intrusive determination was more distraction than help.

Carl disappeared into a room on the left of a cluttered living area, and Naomi's feet lobbied for a full retreat. Her mother's judgment echoed in her mind: little girls who let themselves get trapped by big angry men deserve whatever happens next.

"*Safe*," Parker said.

Naomi nearly jumped out of her skin. He was standing right behind her. His shoulders were hunched, his face emotionless. His eyes were sympathetic and cold at once.

Reassurance and a hot tendril of vindictive fury circled his declaration. Carl would never hurt her, and Parker would never let her be hurt again. Not even if he had to hunt down people and kill them to keep her from harm.

He didn't kiss her this time. This time he only lifted a finger and touched her lips. He was gone before Naomi caught her breath.

"Thanks," she whispered to the stairwell door. Her lips were tingling, but she wasn't afraid. Confused, yes, but not afraid. It was a strange feeling.

Dirty footprints led her through a messy bedroom into the attached bathroom. The aromas of smoke and cooked meat were thick in the air.

The bathtub was huge, big enough that Justin fit in it without folding. The rough handling hadn't roused him yet, and Naomi hoped he stayed unconscious a little longer. He was still dressed in the scorched uniform, wrapped in blankets to keep him warm, and removing it all would hurt.

Naomi handed over scissors and a scalpel so Carl could cut away the ruined clothing. "Why didn't you take him to the clinic? It's a fly-by-night operation, and I'd honestly forgotten about it, but they're good and discreet."

"Discreet isn't enough." Carl started the shower and pulled down a wand attachment. The steam softened the burnt odor to a disgusting amalgam of cinders and charred flesh that turned Naomi's stomach, and her first clear view of Justin's back brought bile into her throat.

"Not in here, please," Carl said tightly.

She got as far as the kitchen sink before she lost the fight against nausea. By the time she cleaned up and returned, Carl had finished a preliminary rinse and was pulling off Justin's boots with brusque efficiency.

Naomi tried to match his detachment. "I'm back," she said. "How can I help?"

Carl looked up. His face was greenish, and flecks of char spotted his skin. He lurched to his feet. "Take over?"

Naomi hurriedly stepped aside to let him pass.

CHAPTER FOURTEEN

NAOMI GOT JUSTIN UNDRESSED and cleaned up, and her stomach slowly settled. As she finished scrubbing off dead skin she noticed the edges of the burns turning pink. New flesh developed under the hot water, while surrounding areas shimmered in and out of visibility.

A shadow fell over her. Carl said, "You are curious like a cat, aren't you? I'll tag in now."

He'd washed up and was wearing fresh clothes, olive green now instead of black. His hair was damp and tied back behind his ears. Round, dark scars showed along the nape of his neck. More scars dotted his bare feet, and pale lines on his shins and arms were revealed when he rolled up sleeves and pants cuffs. Naomi wondered idly how much trouble he had with splitting and numbness.

"Like a cat," Carl repeated. "Better than disgust, I suppose."

"Why would I be disgusted by healed skin?"

An alarm beeped loudly before Carl could answer. Naomi handed over the sprayer and pulled the loaner phone from her belt: she'd never turned it off after calling from the tunnel a few hours past. It felt like days ago already.

"That's Justin's, isn't it?" Carl knelt down, stiff and careful. "Who's calling?"

"The screen says X1—DO NOT ENGAGE—DO NOT RESPOND."

"X1 would be Helen Armstrong. Turn it off."

Naomi glanced at the packed message queue before putting it away. "I see why you didn't want him in a hospital now. They would go bonkers over this. The hot water seems to speed things up a lot."

"A nice surprise, for once." Carl rinsed down the tub and started filling it. Steam rose, and Justin literally disappeared into it. Carl arranged him to keep his head above the water even as it faded from view. "You did a good job with the cleanup," he said. "Nursing experience wasn't in your files."

Exasperation bubbled up to fill the void where fear had been. "Maybe I'm not defined by a file. My mother's first intern from Home Health Support was abusive. Serena terrorized two replacements. I persuaded the fourth to teach me enough to get by. Mams needed continuity. She was so frail—"

Her throat closed around the emptiness that kept slipping up on her unexpected.

Carl looked sidelong at her, one eyebrow raised. "And once again I demonstrate my talent for upsetting you," he said. "I'm sorry. For the insult and for your loss."

The bathroom wasn't silent, not with hot water pounding into the tub, but for a while it was peaceful, and the humidity masked the tears on Naomi's face until she recovered. Finally Carl said, "At least I didn't terrify you this time. Eddie will break every bone in my body if I don't stop doing that."

As if Parker would ever harm him. Naomi reached out to touch his arm. "Don't be silly."

"I'm dead serious." Carl's eyes went to the bandage around her wrist. "I thought you wanted the first aid kit for Serena. What did you do to this?"

Letting him capture her hand seemed perfectly natural, until his fingers closed around it and applied pressure. Then Naomi jerked back on reflex. Carl promptly let go. "And there I go again. I am sorry."

"Don't be. You can't stop being big, and I can't stop being someone who grew up small and female in a neighborhood full of bullies." Naomi flexed her hand. "It's prone to tendonitis, and I strained it. I'll survive."

"Yes, you will." The words carried more weight than the comment warranted. The conversation drifted into another silence until Carl frowned in Justin's general direction. "Burn coverage like that means dehydration, plus the tissue growth has to be pulling fuel from somewhere. Can you set an IV, or would you rather hold his head above water while I do it?"

"I can do a peripheral IV." Naomi accepted the D5LR bag that Carl pulled from the medical kit. "How do we get his arm to show up?"

Carl's smile was lopsided. "Ice, maybe?"

Ice worked, but Naomi broke the first two needles. The third kept trying to unseat itself until she secured it with surgical glue and tape *and* skin sealer. When she finished, she hung the bag from the showerhead. "Now what?"

"We wait. Why don't you go ice that wrist? You can crash in Eddie's room if you want. He won't be back until he finishes scouting the next site for data raiding."

"He's getting breakfast first. And groceries." The words came out before Naomi could stop them, and she was so tired she couldn't think of an excuse for knowing.

Her heart raced. Honesty was dangerous. Serena's family had doubted her sanity for years before she'd actually needed help, because she'd refused to pretend their closeness was an imaginative childhood game.

Carl lifted both eyebrows. "Groceries, then breakfast," he said. "If I'm reading it right."

Amazement flooded through Naomi. He'd already known before she told him. He *knew*. Carl looked down at Justin again. "Coffee would be nice if you get a chance. Make yourself at home."

The invitation resonated with acceptance. Naomi nodded, still light-headed, and went to explore.

Light cut across the darkened ceiling when the bedroom door opened. "Anybody home?" Pete asked.

Other impressions chased along Carl's senses: the odors of rotting flesh and fresh blood, the sound of moans and whispers. He sat up, bracing against the wall on one side and Parker's bed on the other. The blinds over the window above him were swinging back and forth, letting in flashes of daylight.

Pete closed the door and flipped on the overhead light to inspect the room, a tidier mirror image of Carl's quarters. "Where are you? Hiding under the bed?"

"No." Carl smiled. No matter how bad things got, Pete could make him feel ridiculous rather than pathetic. It was an important distinction. "I didn't fit."

"Can you breathe, all squashed in the corner like that?" Pete sat on the end of the bed and fell back, bouncing. "When we got here, Naomi told us you were asleep. That crash I heard says otherwise. You're running replays, aren't you? You hit a wall you weren't seeing. How bad?"

"Bad enough." Phantom pain chased along his nerves, and his vision wavered, overlaid by shadows of a dank concrete bunker full of monsters. "Reality's pretty slippery."

"I'm real." Pete's brown eyes were full of regret. "How long, now? Seven years? Seven years since we pushed that interview and saddled you with permanent stress triggers."

"You had other hostages to find. I've been doing better." Carl

191

consulted the log inside his meds case. "Four hundred fifty-three days since the last replay."

"Until now, he says. Cue dramatic music." Pete waved one hand. "What set you off?"

"Is there an 'all of the above' option?"

"Don't sass me, Doctor Grumpy. It was the smell, wasn't it? How many times did they brand you? You smelled like a pork roast when we dumped you out of that packing crate."

The words hammered at Carl's grip on the present. The stench of seared flesh rose to clog his nostrils, and horror sucked him down. Then and now fused into a bright, agonizing blank. Scent drew him back, led him by the nose past memories of sleepy mornings and busy nights.

He stared at the mug in front of him until it came into focus. His throat felt raw when he spoke. "Hard slap shot to clear the neurological deck?"

Pete set the coffee on the floor and backed away. "Fast and dirty reboot. Did it work? We're lucky no one called the police, as loud as you yelled."

Carl wiped his face against his sleeve and touched the mug. It was hot, and his fingers quivered. The first sip burned going down. "Did I wake Justin?"

"You woke deaf grannies a block away. He's awake and furious." Pete sank onto the bed again and scooted back against the headboard. "Christ, I hope you're done for a while. Tears unnerve me. Crawl out of there and use a chair, will you? My back hurts looking at you."

The teasing complaints were a steadying emotional lifeline. Carl got himself to the desk and put both shaking hands around the coffee mug. "So, where is he?"

"Justin? Dan has a lid on him. Did you really put him down cold, facing active resistance?" Pete leaned forward, eyes clouded with doubt. "Can I do that?"

"It's a snap hypnotic induction. Child's play against a shocky patient."

"But to do it like that, no prep, no pharma, no contract? Sure, you could do it, but tapping skill sets doesn't work that way for me. It can't. Someone would have to rework my full conditioning profile to shift those restrictions. What happened to me?"

The desperation under his questions meant it was too soon to answer them. "Don't pick at that memory scab, Pete. Give it time. I'll say this. You'll need—"

The doorknob rattled. Someone pounded on the panel. "Unlock this door, or I will fucking break it down."

Carl unlocked and opened it. Justin stood dripping in the doorway as naked as the day he was born. His arm was bleeding where he'd ripped the IV loose, and Dan stumbled to a halt behind him, sopping wet from head to toe and smoldering with embarrassment. He watched Carl over Justin's head with an apology in his eyes but no expression at all on his face.

Naomi appeared in the opposite doorway. She was hiding worry behind a veil of wet black bangs, and she clutched a knotted towel in both hands.

Justin shoved Carl back, glaring up at him. "I warned you." Another shove. "Said I'd beat you senseless."

"Technically, that's a threat." Carl sat on the edge of the desk, putting them nearly eye-to-eye for once. "But yes, I knew the price. Can I ask you to be careful with those fists? Or would you like me to talk you out of the whole idea?"

The boiling rage in Justin's eyes chilled, and an open-handed slap rocked Carl's head to the side. The backhand made his vision swim. By the time he could see straight, Justin was limping away.

Patches of pale skin on his back alternated with areas that looked like raw meat. He got halfway across the room before he pitched forward. Dan stepped in and grabbed him. "Gotcha, wild man. Are you done rampaging?"

Justin's mumbled reply was unintelligible. Dan got a shoulder under the man's arm and frowned at Carl. "I could barely see the squirmy little shit, and he was knocking holes in things. I should've used Neil's pistol, but I—couldn't."

He already felt guilty about the injuries Justin had sustained on Neil's behalf.

"You did the right thing," Carl told him.

"The apology's mine." Pete handed Carl the coffee mug. "I didn't realize what I was asking. He is an *impressive* squirmy little shit, isn't he?"

"You're all horrible." Naomi came up with the towel and wrapped it around Justin's waist. "He's bleeding and naked, and you're making fun of him?"

"It's either that or shake in my boots." Dan hefted Justin a little higher. "Please take an arm, will you? The sticky bits are disgusting. Back in the tub with him?"

"No, Serena's still mopping up the mess. The cat thinks it's all a big joke too, which is not helping. I thought cats hated water." Naomi cast a harried look toward the bedroom. "I guess we'll find out if the heating blanket works as well as the hot bath."

They retreated with their burden, and Carl gave Pete a weak smile. "As I was saying, you'll need to find yourself a good moral compass and forgiving friends."

"Where does a broken jaw fit in?" Pete went into the kitchen. "I don't know if that's a healthy—"

He stopped as Dan came out of Carl's bedroom. Dan pulled his wet shirt away from his body and flapped it. "Is there something I should know?"

"No."

Carl's denial came out in chorus with Pete's. Dan rolled his eyes. "Less than convincing. Never mind. Time's slipping away on us, and we still don't know if something else is coming up on the disaster agenda. Where is Parker? And why do I feel like I'm always asking that?"

"Because Eddie is the only one of us you trust, other than

Neil." Carl paused to concentrate. "He's across town, finishing recon on Singh's office."

"You couldn't pretend he sent you a message or called?" Dan gave up on his shirt and pulled it off. "My fragile belief in a rational world is rapidly dissolving."

"Rydder's Esoteric Research division called it 'resonance' and gave up on quantifying it." Pete opened kitchen cabinets. "Gnashing of teeth was involved. Nothing here but booze and coffee, Carl? How do you keep that huge carcass of yours fueled? I'm starving."

"It's a crash pad, not a restaurant. Drink your lunch or wait for Eddie." Carl pushed yarn and dirty clothes off the couch and sat down. "Here's a thing to distract you from your stomach: Dan could've asked Naomi where Eddie was. There might be a tactile element, given her career choice and how careful she is about social distance."

Pete stopped rummaging in the refrigerator to peer at Carl across the breakfast bar. "That's the missing piece of the puzzle? Interesting."

"What's interesting?" Naomi asked as she dragged a wet and smug-looking Tom into the room by his harness. She had a whole armload of towels now, and she sat down at the dining table with the cat at her feet.

"You, evidently." Dan grabbed two of the towels. "Carl, please tell me I can take a turn hiding now. The conversation is getting way too woo-woo for me. I need to leave before anyone mentions secret breeding programs or forbidden genetics research or aliens. I can only handle one conspiracy nut in my life, and Neil has that slot filled."

Pete lifted his beer bottle in a toast. "Go get some sleep, Agent Patterson. We have booze and we have weapons. What could go wrong?"

Dan shut the bedroom door gently, which was somehow more emphatic than a slam.

CHAPTER FIFTEEN

SERENA POPPED OPEN THE passenger door of the car that Dan had stolen for their most recent excursion, and cool wet air stroked her face. Sunlit fog made the redwood forest around her a fairyland of mist and leafy shadows. Light dappled the low stone wall around the graveled parking turnout.

She fought to see the beauty in it, to see more than *threat* and *no-threat*, but her wild rowdies were tired of obeying orders. She and Dan had done well together, finishing one job while others prepped this last mission, but control was eluding her now when she needed it most.

Dan shut the door on his side of the car. "Are you listening, dancing girl? Neil confirmed Singh's involvement from the correspondence we scooped from his office. We want him and the senator too, and they're at the same party. Naomi and Parker are in place—what's wrong?"

Growling inside Serena's head wiped away the words she wanted to say. Brown Dog and Red pulled free and clenched her fists before she could stop them.

"Serena? Are you ready to graduate to kidnapping or not? Yes, or no?"

"My head is loud and crowded." She wrenched back enough control to toss away her harness and the weapons she might use to hurt allies. "Crazy-dangerous-unsafe. Can't dance now."

"That's a no, isn't it?" Dan sighed. "Please, don't make me shoot you. Stay right there."

Crazy, the breeze murmured as Dan headed for the truck parked nearby. Serena crunched over gravel that muttered *crazy-crazy* to a spot where a hiking trail led into the woods. There she dropped to her knees and closed her eyes, lifted her face to the scents of resin, rot, and life.

Red Dog quieted, intimidated by the memory of the awful little pistol that froze people in two heartbeats and made them cry when they could move again. Illegal, Dan had said, and no, Serena couldn't have one. She'd asked, in Singh's office after the guards went down. Now she breathed deep and tried to hold herself together.

Hints of smoke and a distant touch of lavender and lemon drifted in the green. *Too far to help*, she thought, until steps approached on just the right angle to avoid alarming her. She smiled. "Hi, Bao. I thought you were far away."

"She is." The voice behind her was deep and soft like feathers. "You are in bad shape if you can't tell us apart."

Serena shot upright, but Carl grabbed her before she could turn on him. Warmth enveloped her, and lips brushed her ear. "Crazy-dangerous, are you? Eddie can pin you. I can pin him. Go ahead and cut loose."

His tone was heavy with authority, and his grip was secure. Serena shuddered with relief and let all the wildness loose. The next thing she knew, she was lying on her back, arms immobilized, legs entwined and trapped. Red Dog gave a last pleased bounce before sprawling down with the rest of the tired pack. Serena squirmed too. All the itching was gone, and she could think again.

The springy surface beneath her vibrated with Carl's chuckle, and he released her with an push. Serena sprang away. "Better. Better-better-better. Thank you."

"Any time." Carl got to his feet slowly, brushing off gravel and settling the torn shoulders of his shirt.

Dan and Pete were both waiting at the trailhead. Pete was seated on the stone wall with a blank look on his face and one hand on a pile of assorted equipment. He offered the gear to Serena and said to Carl, "That is not the holding therapy I remember learning."

Carl rolled up a sleeve to inspect a rising bruise. "I've been perfecting that technique since I was five. Eddie threw hellacious tantrums. Serena, when this is over we seriously have to talk about safe ways to channel that energy."

"Yes, please." She touched scarred skin over thick muscle, looked into blue eyes so dark that they were black in the shade. So much strength over such a delicate frame.

"Hollow," she said, and Carl blinked at her.

A snort jarred her out of the contemplation. "Hollow?" Dan asked. "Are we looking at the same bleached-out walking brick wall? No, don't answer that. Just tell me if you're back on the dance floor or not. Sounds like not."

Irritation stole Serena's tongue and snarled, "Are you ever *not* a smartass?"

Dan stood still as stone and matched her stare for stare. "You blow off steam by pummeling people. Sarcasm gets the job done for me. Answer the question."

The shiny brown eyes and the polished onyx skin insisted on respect. It was only determination, but it was unyielding. It got the job done. Serena nodded approval. "I kept my clothes on," she pointed out.

Dan's eyes crinkled around the edges. "Now who's a smartass? Be sure. My rusty field skills are fine for milking electronics, but if you're not up to backing Parker on the action, then we'll have to scratch this plan."

Serena shrugged into her vest. "I'm ready to dance."

Dan's grin came out for real, and it was a hunter's smile like her own: bright and sharp. "Glad to hear it."

PETE PICKED rocks out of the scrapes on Carl's back and dabbed them with antiseptic sealant while Serena layered on gear over skintight camouflage. She tested her electronics and tucked silky black hair under a hood, and the whole time she kept darting little glances at them, her eyes intent beneath thin arched eyebrows.

"She calls that her inside look," Pete said softly. "I call it eerie. She has some interesting quirks—hang on." He paused as noises came from the earpiece Carl had handed to him earlier, then hung the device on Carl's ear. "The peanut gallery wants an update. All yours."

Carl provided Neil and Justin—who were supposed to be resting and recuperating back at the apartment—with a briefing that stuck to action and skimped on details. Meanwhile, Dan went over the estate layout with Serena. He kept offering suggestions until she raised a hand to his lips.

"Don't fuss. I know this dance." A sharp jerk of her chin. "Well, someone in here does. Bao and Parker have a hidey-hole, I slip in, we scoop fast and scram once we get an exit window, after dark. Easy."

She turned away and jogged down the path.

Dan put his hands on top of his head as if surrendering to the inevitable. "She is going to be the death of *somebody*, that's certain. God willing, it'll be the bad guys."

Serena turned in a patch of late-afternoon sun. Leggy, muscular, and fey, she went still and all but disappeared against the ferns and underbrush. Then she was gone, without a leaf moving to mark her passage.

Dan sat beside Pete. "I need a cold shower. Where the hell did you find her? I thought she was a CAF washout."

"We found her with Naomi," Carl said, "and I'm only speculating, but I think that's what you get when the CAF tries to reverse-engineer a CSB Delta agent without proper vetting. I'm no fan of the Bureau's devotion to security conditioning and drug-assisted interrogation, but at least you screen your candidates properly."

Dan's eyes narrowed. "Your precious Institute gets half its funding from contract work for the Bureau, so you can get off your high horse any time now."

"It isn't *my* Institute."

Pete gave Carl's shoulder a poke. "Stop. This isn't the time for a debate on the ethics of forced confessions."

The rebuke stung. Carl pulled down his shirt. "Any idea why Serena called me hollow?"

"My guess is that she sees you as a bird. Hollow bones." Pete packed up the supplies. "If it makes you feel better, I'm a vine. Remind me to ask her if I have berries."

"Are you sure you want to know?" Dan headed for the truck and the surveillance monitors inside. "I thought you people were all about head games, not hand-to-hand. What's with the fancy wrestling moves, Carl?"

Pete hopped off the wall and went white-faced with pain as his feet hit the ground. Getting him to the truck without hurting him further or bruising his pride drove Dan's question out of Carl's mind.

When they arrived, Dan blocked the way by holding the rear doors shut with one spread hand. "It trips my alarms when people don't answer idle questions," he said. "Makes me think they aren't idle. Why does a headshrinker who won't carry a gun do martial arts?"

Dan was a tall man and a smart one. After a few seconds, recognition dawned that he was feeling the strain of looking up. "That's why," Carl said gently. "Submission holds won't hurt anyone if I can't avoid a brawl. Some people just can't resist picking fights with me."

His tone sent Dan back a step. Pete yanked open the door and climbed carefully inside. "Will you two please stop the posturing and posing? Whip 'em out and measure, or agree that you're both big boys and start acting like it. She likes me better than either of you, anyway."

The tense silence broke on Dan's laughter.

FIRE GLINTED through the heavy tree cover, and smoke blended with mist to obscure the view of a crowded deck party. That was Serena's destination, the private compound nestled under spreading tree limbs, where the event being thrown by Senator Hughes was shifting from afternoon moderation to evening extravagance without missing a beat.

The site was isolated by regulation as well as terrain. The diligent sentinels who guarded the property had only one road to patrol. Laws designed to protect a fragile ecology made life easier for intruders who could evade electronics and move in cover.

Naomi and Parker had cleared the way and marked the route. Serena moved faster but just as silently. She crept into their ready position while glasses clinked overhead. Voices muttered, and greasy smoke rolled on the moist air.

Too close to the action for speech, they huddled together and passed along intelligence by signal and map. Six guards on grounds patrol, one at the gate, four covering the house, two in the monitor station. Thirteen total, keeping watch over thirty guests on or near the party deck.

She stretched, knees straightening over bent toes as she eased forward and ran her tongue over wet skin, tasting warmth and salt. Naomi swatted her. A nuzzle of her cheek against cloth next, and then a darker, musky taste from the exposed neck she took gently in her teeth. Parker's growl buzzed against her lips, and he turned to breathe *steady* over the top of her head. Knuckles brushed her jaw. *Ready.* His other hand moved, firm against her back. *Go.*

Pulse stuttered fast, skin tingled, nerves simmered with energy. No room for mistakes. *Alive.* Serena eased herself back while Brown Dog and the others did the hard work. When Parker confirmed success, Serena's helpers obediently nosed their way back under her hands with happy little bumps and lolling tongues. Together they all burrowed deep to wait until they could properly retreat with their prey.

Chaos erupted overhead as she went to ground.

MARIO USHERED Alison to the chef's table in the kitchen with a flourish, and then he hugged her until her ribs creaked. The man cultivated his stereotypes with a showman's flair, from the interior decor of his bustling trattoria to his own bristling gray mustachios, and if his accent occasionally slipped into a drawl from the south of this country rather than that of his restaurant's ethnic origin, no one cared once they tasted the food. He had accepted Alison's hard work when that was all she had to offer, and he'd never mocked the dreams he neither shared nor understood. Alison thanked him profusely as usual, and he huffed at her though his mustache, as usual. He did good deeds for their own sake, and gratitude embarrassed him.

Ryan crawled to the center of the bench seat with the backpack he refused to let out of his sight, and he sat tense and trembling until Alison and Tyler were seated on either side and holding his hands. He'd barely said a word since appearing on her doorstep. There'd been a sleeping bag, empty snack boxes, and candy wrappers behind her overturned mattress, and Tyler had found the precision tools and the master key Ryan had used to gain access.

The boy was eight.

He scowled, whispering, "I don't want to talk. I won't call Mom."

The thought *paternity tests be damned* drifted into Alison's mind as it always did when she saw him wearing that particular mulish expression. She would've tried to persuade him to cooperate, but Tyler spoke first.

"All right, little man. You're in charge. I hope it was okay that we called for you, so she knows you're safe here?"

Ryan sighed and nodded.

"Great. She'll meet us here later, you know. She's on a plane now."

"I know. I knew she would come, only I didn't know Mr. Justin was gone."

Alison squeezed his hand. "It's okay, Ryan. We know. You were brave."

The call to Helen had revealed that she was already en route to Seattle, not just in a bid to regain custody of her child, but in preparation for her Saturday appearance at a charity ball. Once the situation had been explained, she'd showered Alison with gratitude for "saving Ryan."

A server brought beer, wine, and a cheese pizza sliced into strips. Tyler tackled the beer, Alison took a sip of wine, and Ryan started inhaling pizza. He was halfway finished when Mario dropped by with a message that Helen would be arriving shortly.

Ryan gazed up at Alison with fear in his eyes and tomato sauce on his chin. She wiped his face clean. "You don't ever have to talk unless you want. Not even when your mother gets here. Eat your dinner."

He dug into the food again with an enthusiasm that lasted until dessert arrived. The dish of gelato sat in front of him untouched, and his lip quivered.

"Ryan? What's wrong?"

"I hate ice cream. It melted after my birthday party. It all *melted.*" He crawled onto Alison's lap and pulled the bowl closer. "They had the biggest fight ever, and Dad left, and it's all my fault."

"No, sweetheart." Alison placed a kiss against the back of his neck. "It is not your fault. There's different kinds of marriages so people can try to pick what works, but sometimes they still make mistakes."

Ryan picked up a spoon and poked at his dish. "I wouldn't leave if I promised. He signed papers to stay until I was grown up, I saw them in Mom's scrapbook, and he knew all along I wasn't his, only he stayed because who wouldn't want to put one over on a genius, but I'm weird and I made Mom ugly, and so he left. I *hate* him."

The grouchy recitation was as informative as it was disjointed. Alison's heart started beating faster, and she was torn between a desire to shout "I knew it!" and an urge to hug away the pain in Ryan's voice.

She opted for the hug. Tragic, that Ryan had learned the truth in such a painful way. Alison set him on the seat beside her again and glanced at Tyler over his head. He said, "I thought I spoke little-boy pretty well, but does he mean what I think he does?"

"Let's find out." Alison brushed back Ryan's hair. "Ryan, are you saying that your mom and dad were fighting about Justin? Because Justin is your father?"

"Genetic donor," Tyler murmured. Alison hushed him.

Ryan picked up a spoon and poked at the gelato with it. "Dad said stupid, they could've been lots richer with proper child support, except Mom was selfish like always, and he never should've agreed to help her lie, only he loved her then, but he doesn't now, so he's the liar, and now I hate him."

The gelato fell victim to a ferocious spoon attack. Alison stifled a sigh. Now was not the time to try and explain the infinite ways love could make people behave badly. "Your birthday was months ago, Ryan. Why didn't you call right away?"

"Dad is mean when he's mad, and he lies, and so I thought it was only more lies like always, but then he *left*, so I did the test, and it came out not a lie, but Mr. Justin hates phones, and I wanted to see him, only he didn't say he wasn't home when we talked on Duty so it was all empty, and those boys came, and I had to run, and then you were there. I wish Mr. Justin was here."

"Me too." Ryan had found a way to obtain a genetic test without adult supervision, he'd made his way alone to Seattle during a travel lockdown, and even when his plan had gone wrong, he'd kept his head and improvised. His motives were a child's emotional tangle, but that only made his competency all the more terrifying. "I'm sure he'll come as soon as he can."

"Unless he doesn't want me either. Unless that's why he left us. Because of me." Ryan mashed down icy slush and began smearing it everywhere.

Alison watched the demolition in silence. In time, Ryan turned in her lap and wrapped his sticky arms around her neck. His face was blotchy, his eyes puffy, and his breath slowed to the steady rhythm of sleep while Alison gently rocked him.

"Wow." Tyler stretched his legs under the table, and his thigh nudged Alison's leg. "Poor monster. He definitely got his father's temper."

"No, Ryan got that from both of us." Helen Armstrong swept into the kitchen from the dining room with her usual exquisite timing. She stopped in front of the booth: a pale, unpretentious beauty in a sensible green dress, perfect in the role of distraught, loving mother.

Two of her staff came stalking after her, and another moved through the prep line from the rear of the kitchen: unobtrusive protection, ever-present audience. Helen's blue eyes filled with tears at the sight of Ryan. "I should've ended the charade years ago. Every time Rob saw them together—do you think he'll ever forgive me?"

"Which one of them?" Alison asked. She wanted to be angry,

but Helen couldn't help being dramatic. It was her nature as well as her profession, and she did love her son. She even loved Justin, in her own wounded, self-centered way. "If you're playing up the penitence and sorrow for Justin's benefit, you can stop now. He isn't here."

"I apologize." Helen sat down on the edge of the seat, and the tears spilled over. Alison relinquished Ryan. The boy murmured into his mother's collar and settled against her, not quite waking. Helen's relief was obvious. "I knew he was unhappy, that he'd heard, but—oh, Ryan." She pressed her cheek against the boy's hair. "I never expected him to be so sneaky."

"You should've known," Tyler said with typical bluntness. "You know how devious his father can be."

Helen snorted, an inelegant, honest expression of aggravation. "What is he doing this time? Climbing up a mountain? Hang gliding off one? Or is he buried in a huge pile of new widgets? How soon can he get here?"

Alison swallowed guilt at the ignorant optimism behind those guesses. "Helen, we don't know. He said he'd call when he could, but he might not be back until the end of the break or even later."

Helen's martyred sigh accompanied a masterful eye roll. Then she shook away that mood and put on another. "Well, then. Can I ask a huge favor? Restoration Week appearances have been cancelled left and right, but I still have this fundraiser in Bellevue. I don't want to take any chances with Ryan. He trusts you, clearly. Could you stay with me—with him—until we get a chance to straighten everything out with Justin?"

Tyler said, "Sure, why not?"

He nodded at the bodyguards when Alison silently questioned his prompt agreement. As long as they stayed out of the limelight themselves, they could hardly ask for better defenses than a professional security cordon.

Alison looked at the exhausted child clinging like a limpet to his mother and dredged up a smile. "Count us in."

TIME TICKED SLOWLY BY, and Naomi grew to despise the odors of mulch and mold. She'd hated this whole plan from the start because of the waiting. If Parker had been up to the fiddly task of tinkering with the security electronics, she would've sat out the whole operation. His hands still shook badly when he was tired, so Naomi had come along, and now she was stuck here in the cold muck with him spooned close behind her and Serena pressed in face-to-face.

Shouted voices came and went, engines revved, and quiet settled over the compound again. The main search had long since expanded in all directions, but it still swirled too close, and they were still waiting. The joy of uncovering secrets was what drew her to sneak into places, not this sitting helpless while others hunted. This was unbearable.

Serena took Naomi's hands and squeezed them.

Carl's deep voice buzzed in the irritating earpiece he'd talked her into wearing this time. For Parker's sake, he'd said. "Still no-go. No pickup. Lie low."

Naomi swallowed a nervous giggle. They couldn't get much lower physically, half-buried in deep leaf litter with concrete decking overhead, behind a baffle where they could lie hidden from sight and masked to sensors. They couldn't stoop much lower morally than kidnapping, and they'd already accomplished that.

A senator lay trussed and gagged beyond Parker, and Serena was leaning against the police chief for all of San Francisco.

And if they didn't move soon, then Naomi's bladder was going to burst, and her heart would give out from the fear that wouldn't go away.

Parker jogged her elbow, questioning. He didn't like the direction of her thoughts, which was understandable. She didn't like them either. Heat nuzzled against Naomi's jaw, and she twitched back. Parker leaned in again, put his cheek against hers, and breathed softly past her face. *Safe. Wait.*

His hand also pressed against Naomi's spine with unyielding force: if she panicked, he would subdue her without hesitation. That implacable discipline was a consolation of sorts, but she still wanted to run so much that she felt like she was drowning in the need.

Serena stirred. Her hand slid under Parker's, adding *please* to the ferocity of Parker's silent *stay*. Naomi squirmed forward to bury her face against Serena's neck, and Parker burrowed closer too, slipped his arms around them both.

And from the earbug, Dan's mock-petulant voice: "What the hell are they doing, and why wasn't I invited?"

Serena snorted, barely audible, and fingers brushed Naomi's cheek. It was as natural as blinking to reach out and slip into Serena's skin, just as it had been when she arrived. They'd played all their pranks together like that once—so many adventures, so many good memories, so long ago now.

Watch with me was the name of this game. Naomi smiled, seeing all over again the shock and lust in Senator Hughes's eyes when Serena walked up to him bold as brass, right through the crowd of guests, right under the eyes of his staff.

Not one guest and precious few of the security team stopped staring long enough to wonder where Serena had come from. Naked athletic women without a shred of self-consciousness tended to have that effect on a crowd.

She stood with her hands out and raised her chin at the bodyguards, silently made a joke of their presence with her harmless submission.

Hughes pushed past them. Serena leaned in to cup his balls in one hand, set her nails against his chest beneath his shirt, and spoke truth loud enough to be overheard and remembered.

"I was sent. Pick a sacrifice. Pick me and lose dignity. Pick dignity, lose me."

Her hand moved. Hughes inhaled. "Who sent you?"

"Choose." Serena breathed it against his lips and squeezed hard. Hughes waved off his people and led the way into the house without a moment's hesitation.

Powerful people used to sycophants could be stupid, especially when taken by surprise. A patter of applause and laughter followed them indoors.

The strategy wouldn't have worked with other men. It wouldn't have worked at all without good timing and bored staff watching house cameras that had been eased onto a time delay. Serena had asked for thirty seconds. Naomi gave her a full minute. Hughes might have expected a gag and snap-restraints to come into play, but not that his fun would end in a drop out a window and a roll in the mud.

Serena had pushed past Singh on her approach too, enough to put him at the edge of the deck where Parker could yank him out of sight in a swift and nearly soundless exit. For that precious short window of time, the man's neighbors were too busy ogling Serena to notice his disappearance, and her show distracted them afterward.

A sharp pain at Naomi's ear shook her back to her own flesh and the present, which meant wet, cold, and afraid. Parker had nipped her earlobe. Naomi swung an elbow back. He effortlessly deflected it, and Serena gave her face a reassuring pat.

Naomi settled between them and accepted the hand Parker slid into hers. It was quivering, and he ached. Naomi let her fingers work along the sore muscles, eased the pain, and took solace from his relief.

They were really going to have to talk about proper boundaries at some point, but for now, this was better than waiting alone.

FAITH

RESTORATION DAY 5

Believe in a world larger than yourself. Skepticism is healthy, but cynicism is an ugly strangling disease. Look in your heart and ask yourself: what do I believe in?

—*A Young Citizen's Guide to Restoration Week*

CHAPTER SIXTEEN

C ARL SHOVED A LAST box into the space under the van's rear seats while Pete eased the rear doors to the truck closed. The cargo compartment was all but empty now, ready for its new role as prisoner transport. Pete gingerly handed over a last bag. "A lot of work for nothing if we end up with no prisoners."

"We'll have them." The darkness under the tree cover was impenetrable, but he could tell Parker was irritable and getting closer. He would've been furious if he'd had to ditch the hostages to escape. "I can tell."

Parker had used Justin's "lights-out box" to cover the initial departure from the senator's compound, and the gadget had completely fried their comm gear. The loss could've been disastrous, but they hadn't needed electronics to negotiate a rendezvous well off the beaten track and beyond the current search perimeter.

Carl rapped the side of the truck. Dan opened the cab window. Carl handed him the bag. "They're almost here."

The truck headlights sprang to life, illuminating a gap in the trees. Pete said, "You used to be more discreet about the homing pigeon trick."

"I used to be a lot of things. Have you noticed the company we're keeping?"

"True. What's a little magic navigation with legally exempt and occasionally invisible on the scene?" Pete squinted through the van window. Neil was snoring quietly on the folded-down bench with one arm around Tom, and Justin was slumped in the front passenger seat. "They're both down for the count."

"Not surprising. It's past midnight, and it was a rough ride up from San Fran for both of them."

Jostling over dirt roads was hard on a healthy passenger's body. Justin had powered up after one too many painful encounters between healing skin and hard surfaces. He'd crashed hard on arrival. Neil was in worse shape. His surgical repairs were draining, and given his internal injuries, it would've been wiser to not move him at all. Unfortunately they had little choice.

"Speaking of rough—" Pete said.

"Stop volunteering to do it for me. We went over this. Interrogation was never your specialty, and attempting it would rip that memory scab right off. It was one flashback. I can do it. I've had plenty of practice. "

Neil sat up with a groan when the side door on the van slid open. Tom put a paw on his chest and growled at him. Carl returned the man's gray-red zombie stare until Neil

blinked, proving he was awake and not on autopilot. "Ready?"

"I'm functional," Neil said. He shoved the cat's head out of his way and held him down by the scruff. "But I think Justin's hibernating."

Carl looked in. "That isn't sleep. He's in reset mode."

"Really? I haven't seen that up close." Pete crawled past Neil to sit on the edge of the bench. "Looks unconscious."

"Not quite. There are markers. Muscle tension, eye motion, breath rate. He also does 'thoughtful stare' and 'absentminded reverie.' "

"Processing dysfunction, not true seizure, right?" Pete asked.

"And he comes out fast if you give him enough sensory input. Otherwise known as yelling in his face or shaking him till his teeth rattle?"

"Those aren't optimal solutions, but yes, that works up to a point. And before you ask, the underlying etiology is a mystery to me too. Rydder kicked him loose as soon as he black-flagged the pharma tests, and he hasn't pursued treatment since."

"That streak of physical denial runs pretty deep," Pete said. "I wonder where it comes from."

"He is sitting right there," Neil said in a dry voice. "Wake him up and ask."

"How? A bucket of cold water?"

"Don't push it. He's already threatened you with tongue amputation." Carl pounded on the van door. The noise echoed. Justin grabbed at the door handle. Plastic crunched.

"Shit," he said in a voice acid with self-loathing. He wiped his mouth against the back of his arm before huddling up in a ball. "What's going on?"

"We're back on the road," Carol told him. "At least an hour, possibly as much as two. Can you boost again safely? It would be a big help. With Neil in the truck up front and you as witness in back, I can make a start on questioning."

"Why me? I can understand wanting Neil around, for the legalities, but what good is an invisible audience? Are you trying to make me feel useful?"

"No." Carl picked the easiest explanation. "It's late, and I'm cranky and it's hard to explain. If you can boost, I want you there."

Justin barely hesitated. "Not about me, right. I'm in."

He helped Neil change vehicles with minimal hassle. Persuading the cat to stay in the van with Pete was a more difficult task, and that fell to Carl. They'd just settled matters to everyone's satisfaction when leaves crunched and branches snapped in the woods.

Naomi's lithe form appeared at the edge of the trees first. She skidded to a halt in the headlight glare, and then Serena and Parker jogged into view, pushing along the two men they'd gone to such lengths to secure. All five of them were covered in mud from head to toe, and the captives were shackled and gagged. Naomi walked over to Carl and tried to scrape muck out of her hair while the prisoners were loaded.

"Never again," she said in a squeaky voice. "Never-ever-ever. I was a specialist. Elevator buildings with fire escapes and alleyways and plenty of—"

The semi-hysterical rant stopped on a gasp, and Serena came scrambling out of the truck with a squeal of laughter. She was equally muddy and bedraggled, and she slid an arm around Naomi's shoulder in a sideways hug.

Naomi shuddered and looked up at Carl. "Your brother tickled *her* to distract *me*."

"Not even remotely the weirdest thing he's ever done," Carl assured her.

She looked like a baby bird with her shiny eyes and her hair sticking up in all directions, and Carl desperately smothered the urge to smile. They had reached a fragile détente, he and this fierce, complicated woman, but even a hint of ridicule might cause irreparable damage. Serena's protective posturing indicated that she would fight Parker for the privilege of gutting him over any perceived slight.

"You two are the advance team for the next phase," Carl told them. "Dan pulled data on some places for us to go to ground. You secure one of them, call us, and we'll join you. He'll explain the details on the road."

"Places, everyone." Pete made a sweeping gesture to the van. "Seat yourselves and await our fearless leader's arrival. I'll get started on the boring details."

Naomi still hesitated, looking doubtfully at Carl until Pete added in a stage whisper, "I'll tell you where the cleaning wipes are packed."

That did the trick.

THE WORK LIGHT on the floor of the truck compartment threw harsh illumination against one wall. Deep shadows pooled against the ceiling. Parker had already stripped Singh and Hughes of their outer clothes, blindfolded them, and stuffed earplugs into their ears. Their wrist cuffs were secured to cargo bolts so that they could neither stand up straight nor sit down. Their leg muscles were visibly cramping already.

The warm air was stuffy and smelled like dirty, sweaty, fearful humanity. Carl exhaled sharply, inhaled again, and let the emotional associations fall away. "All right. I'm ready."

Parker gave him a long hard look, then nodded. "You're cleared for action."

The coded permission lifted artificial barriers on certain skills, and that brought to the surface personality traits that were not fit for normal company. Remorse and empathy dove under less-civilized emotions, burying themselves deep. Without their buffer, training designed to make him a phenomenal observer and a charismatic counselor became weapons as sharp as any blade wielded by a mugger.

Power did corrupt. Carl had long ago put Parker in charge of making these judgment calls. Some people might not approve of his taste in moral custodians, but they hadn't lived his life. They didn't have the right to judge his choices.

Later he would have to live with ineradicable memories of exactly how brutal he could be, and how much he could enjoy it. Now scruples slept, and power stretched free.

His heartbeat slowed, and every sense began delivering points of data that could be combined and refined to create the perfect approach for *this* moment, honing the right tools to breach the minds of *these* people.

Martin Singh was a tall man built on a delicate frame, with thin shoulders, narrow wrists and long toes. His face was lined and settling with age, but his body testified to diligent exercise and careful diet. Dark smooth skin, manicured nails, and an expensive haircut had all taken damage over the course of the evening.

Gordon Hughes was more physically substantial: broad and thick-necked, soft around the middle, with a jowly bulldog face. Those puffy features were twisted into a grimace of discomfort now. Sweat dripped off his chin onto a mat of graying chest hair.

Tactics rose into mind, coalescing into a plan of attack. "I'm up," Carl said.

Parker handed over a knife and a wide roll of tape before ducking through the low access door to the cab. The panel slid shut without a sound. Carl cut strips of tape and placed them where he would need them later, and the truck lurched into motion.

"I didn't actually punch you senseless," Justin said. "Still looks painful."

His voice came from empty air near the cab access. Carl shelved the strategic priorities and considered the non sequitur in context.

Justin was referring to the bruise on Carl's jaw, which led to the reason it existed: an inflexible belief that acts should have consequences no matter what the intentions. He'd correctly connected that ruthless attitude to his presence here, and he didn't want the job after all, not if it meant hurting Carl again.

That was what he'd meant, anyway.

"You're especially cryptic tonight," Carl said. "Even with all my unfair advantages on max I could barely follow that from A to B."

"Fuck your advantages." The curse was halfhearted. "You are seriously creepy right now, Carl, and I don't like it. I don't want to be your conscience."

"You aren't. You're more like a beacon reminding me where

I've left mine." That external brake would be enough to keep him on the upper slopes of the abyss. "It has to be someone I trust implicitly. That's a short list of two. I know it's a lot to ask."

"Yeah, it is." Justin's boots scraped the floor as he fidgeted. "I feel like I'm reliving the worst year of my life on time compression."

That train of thought had started with "a lot to ask," gathered a thread of stress, picked up other resonances, and then jumped the tracks completely. Carl gave up on it. "Decode that for me, please."

"First there are murders and bombings, then I demolish myself physically, and now we've kidnapped people. Only the time frame's in days instead of months, and this time you're asking me for help instead me begging you. I do not want to repeat the last act of that play, Carl."

"Neither do I. In fact, let's call that a goal." He contemplated their prisoners. As long as Justin was invisible, the illusion of over-sight would be preserved even if the man sat there with his eyes shut and his hands over his ears. "How long can you stay boosted without passing out? I'll work them as long as you can hold up."

"I can do the hour and more. Do what you have to do."

Carl removed blindfolds and ear protection gently, a contrast to the brutal force Parker would've used. He made eye contact, delivered kind smiles, and unhooked the cuffs to allow both men to sit relaxed on the truck floor.

Singh had served over two decades in law enforcement. He'd studied the texts and participated in his share of hostile inter-views. Hughes was a career politician. He'd been through abduc-tion drills. They knew Carl's every move was calculated for effect.

He watched with great satisfaction as they realized that knowl-edge was no defense. Instinct trumped intellect. Even hardened experts trained in resistance doctrines felt the desire to roll belly-up when rendered powerless and offered compassion. These two were already cowering.

"You're here because you have secrets," Carl told them. "Secrets I want to hear. Things you won't want to tell me."

He took off his shirt, sat down cross-legged, and spun the knife in a circle on the floor in front of him. Air drafted over his skin, barely discernible where the scars were thickest. The hum of the motor traveled through the floor into his bones as the truck rocked over the unpaved road. Reflected light flashed off the blade.

"You will talk to me." He pitched his voice low and intimate, and it still carried. "You will tell me what I want. You will give me everything I ask and more."

The knife spun. Light flickered. Singh made a sound in the back of his throat, and Hughes squirmed against his restraints, only to stop short when Carl spoke again.

"Oh, no. There will be no bloodletting, no rending of flesh, no exotic tortures. The sadists who practiced on me were adepts in the old science, but it is time-consuming, and it doesn't work well on people who enjoy pain."

The twitch of Hughes's foot was a minuscule betrayal. Carl filed away the reaction and caught Singh's eyes. The pupils were dilated and muscles jumped in the thin skin beneath the sockets, but resignation predominated.

A tap kept the knife in motion, rotating bright-dark-bright, hilt and blade.

"I won't be using any of the so-called humane modern drugs either." Carl gave the news a thick coating of smugness. "Not when artificial defenses are standard for law officers and seated representatives. There will be no early exits for you, no clean escape from defeat and surrender."

Despair drained the blood from Singh's face and paralyzed the muscle twitches. Carl said, "I don't need to mortify your bodies or pickle your brains to get what I want. Tonight you've fallen into the black chasm between the bad old days and the bright new order. That's where nightmares were bred. That's where I came from."

He slapped his hand down on the knife to stop the spin. The cracking sound of his palm hitting the floor jolted through both his subjects like an electric shock.

"When the time comes," he said, "you'll do anything to make me stop."

———

THE TRUCK RATTLED OVER A BUMP, and Justin grabbed at the frame of the access panel to keep from sliding over the floor. If he moved, Carl might hear the noise and look in his direction, and Justin didn't want to see those cold eyes again any time soon. Listening to the man's voice roll through the confined space was bad enough.

He'd seen analytic intensity in Carl's face before, but never that callous, unblinking indifference. *Creepy* didn't begin to describe the way it made him feel as if every flaw were being laid bare. *Bloodcurdling* came closer.

Carl sat beside Martin Singh, slipped a bare scarred arm around the man's naked shoulders when he tried to wriggle away. His other hand came up, cupped Singh's jaw and trapped him in place. He bent to whisper in Singh's ear.

The scent of urine joined the stink of sweat and vomit hanging in the air. Singh brought up his bony knees and tried to cover his ears with his shoulders. Carl kissed him softly on the cheek and sliced the plastic cuffs off the man's wrists. Singh curled into a fetal ball near the rear doors. Hughes was already in an identical pose on the opposite side, lying with both flabby arms covering his head.

The truck ran onto a paved surface, and the tire noise diminished. Carl stood up, looming and pale, with one hand pressed to the low ceiling, and started peeling the precut pieces of tape from the wall. They came loose with ugly little sounds. Carl used them to cover the eyes, ears, and mouths of his unresisting victims, then made his way to the cab.

Justin kept his eyes down and his breathing shallow until a boot nudged his leg. Carl slid open the access panel and crouched, and his face went from frigid calm to molten disgust on a blink.

"ETA?" he asked in a voice so saturated with misery that it hurt to hear.

"Five to ten from your tap out." Parker looked over his shoulder. "Carl?"

"Now," Carl exhaled low and slow. "I can't hold it."

Parker slammed on the brakes, and Carl was out the back doors before the vehicle was stopped. He crashed into the brush at the side of the road, and the cab door slammed open against the cab when Parker followed in his wake.

After a pause Neil said, "Anybody still here?"

"Me." Justin powered down and hissed as backlash rippled through his body and lit a fire in his bones. The hot pain was followed by a familiar dizziness. "Shit. Talk, please. I need input."

"Sure. Are they feeling any more cooperative yet? The regular Bureau liaisons usually need—hot damn." Neil peered into the compartment, squinting against the glare of the work light. He wrinkled his nose. "Suddenly I'm very glad that I could supply the thin veneer of legal sanction from out here."

Justin concentrated on the words, and the worst of the mental fog receded. He said, "All he did was talk."

Neil stretched his body across the gap between the front seats and rubbed one hand over his stomach. "Rydder's curriculum was built on the scavenged bones of a failed military intelligence program. Operatives specialized in intimidation and emotional manipulation." He hesitated. "You sound drunk."

"I know. How was it a failure if it produced *that*?"

"It's all a matter of perspective, I suppose. More than eighty percent of the trainees went insane before completing the program. Carl's the closest thing to the original working model that the world has seen in decades. God, it reeks back there. How can you even breathe?"

He'd smelled worse and for longer. "Perspective."

Neil didn't have a witty comeback for that.

The sole remaining box in the truck contained rags. Wiping down the floor didn't improve the air quality much, but the activity kept Justin's brain working. Then Carl climbed aboard again, and Parker started the motor. Justin retreated to the cab access, where the air was fresher. The dashboard display shimmered in his vision, defying all attempts to bring it into focus.

Carl stayed by the rear doors with shoulders stooped and head bent so that sweat-tangled hair hid his face. Eventually he picked up his shirt, regarded the stains on it, and let it fall on the pile of soiled rags.

When he came forward to join Justin, Hughes and Singh both responded to the vibration of his passage with muffled cries and twitches. Carl sat down and glanced their way with a haunted expression.

"What do you need?" Justin enunciated carefully. "You aren't doing your weird flashbacks, are you?"

"No." Carl tipped back his head and sighed. "Just be there. It helps."

He looked ready to shatter into pieces at any moment like a large, quietly ticking emotional time bomb. Justin scooted closer. If being there helped then it seemed logical that greater proximity would help more.

Experimental results confirmed the hypothesis. He found himself scooped up and back against Carl's chest as if he was no more substantial than a pillow.

All the best intentions in the world couldn't make the role of human teddy bear a comfortable one. Carl pressed his face against Justin's shoulder blade, and when he shuddered the tremors shook them both.

"Good thing I'm not fragile," Justin said once that horrendous shaking had eased. "And please tell me that's not what I think is pressing against my backside, because no, thank you."

Carl's laugh was strained, but he released the death grip and shoved Justin off his lap. Next he rubbed at the bridge of his nose and raised his knees so he could rest his forehead on his crossed arms.

Neil craned his head around the edge of the access panel to look at them. His face was thoughtful, the bloodshot eyes sharp. "Here's another bit of perspective, Justin," he said. "Of the five people who were still sane when they mustered out of that spy program, four committed suicide before age thirty."

Justin watched another shudder run through Carl. "And the fifth?"

"Well, there's some debate concerning—" Neil began.

Carl interrupted. "He collected himself the brain trust and corporate backing he needed to bury his stolen military data and start Rydder, and then he got himself shot in the head before the doors opened. Technically, none of them saw thirty."

He rubbed at his left temple. "Why are we discussing this? All the records from that period were heavily redacted, Agent McAllister. The original files were burn-before-reading material. I won't ask how you came across the story, but you know it's highly classified, and Justin isn't."

"He is if I say he is. Sharing secrets is the fun part of my job. Sometimes it almost makes up for the parts that try to kill me."

"I'm thirty-seven. So much for your hypothesis."

"My *theory*. Don't make me quote Rydder Institute's own statistics on early retirement due to psychiatric—ah, forget it. Is this where we're going?"

Lights came into view as they rounded a curve. Ahead down a straight, steep drive was a tall house with a gabled roof, elaborate scrollwork trim, a round tower on one corner and a wide porch. It stood proud on a wide swath of lawn cut out from the forest, and every window glowed. A familiar van was parked on the grass outside.

"Perfect," Neil said. "A gingerbread house. We ask for a dungeon and end up with a classic piece of Victorian architecture."

"Who cares what it looks like?" Justin said. The words came out as mush. Carl reached out and turned his face to the light, and he wanted to sink through the floor. "Hate when you do that." Another unintelligible mumble.

Carl let go of his chin. "Justin, if this is how often you lock up when you're coming off a bad patch, how the hell does Alison handle you when you're in the middle of one?"

"Gas pizzed off and y'lls allah juslike you're d'ing. *Shit.*"

At least the curse came out clearly.

"Settle down. I'm not pushing you this time, I promise I'm not, but you can't drive yourself into the ground like this forever. You've been stalling off crashes with sensory overload and adrenaline for days now. You're healing and exhausted. Stop fighting so hard."

As if his brain would give him a choice. Justin's vision hazed over in earnest, and the warmth of Carl's hand on his arm was the last thing he felt before reality fell away completely for a time.

THE EMPTY GUEST house boasted ten tiny private rooms on two upper floors. Each room had its own cutesy decorating theme. On the main floor, a pleasant open seating and dining area on the main floor faced a spotless showcase kitchen, while a corner tower held a library full of antique books. An addition at the rear hid a separate private apartment.

Naomi had chosen the place off the list Dan provided in part for the number of rooms. She hated the way resentment bubbled up sour in her mind when she was tired and achy and dirty like this, but it seethed there all the same. She needed doors and distance tonight.

Once the minimal security measures were disabled and the van was unpacked, she took refuge upstairs in the first available bedroom. Tom crept along beside her with his ears flat and his big fluffy tail dragging. The poor animal looked as distressed and overwhelmed as Naomi felt.

When Tom tried to slink under the bed, his head thumped into a solid frame hidden under the dust ruffle. He hissed and gave Naomi a reproachful glare.

"I'm fresh out of sympathy," she told him. "Go bother Dan or Pete."

Tom draped himself across the lacy bedspread. Naomi moved his tail and set her little suitcase next to him.

Alison had filled the bag with clothes that were comfortable and comforting, and she had an excellent eye for color. Naomi gratefully set out a fleece top, twill pants and fuzzy socks in soft pastels and pretended that the gifts were *not* the only things in the world that she could currently call her own.

Thumps and bumps rose from the first floor. Serena said she needed to introduce herself to the house, and the project might take all night. She was opening every door, drawer, and container, sometimes more than once. Gray Dog didn't like new places, she said.

Voices echoed up the narrow stairwell too. Pete said, "You couldn't fit three sardines in that room. Carl would pitch a fit. Why not in here?"

Dan replied, "And put on a show in the bay window? Are you nuts?"

The search for an interrogation venue had started as soon as Naomi put the security system to sleep and unlocked the front door. She was ready to christen the two men Bitch and Moan if they didn't stop sniping at each other.

"Sweet Jesus, you are the pickiest man I've ever met."

"No, you have no grasp of basic security—damn. Dancing girl is making a silverware sculpture. Is that safe?"

"Do you want to fight with her over steak knives? I don't. Let her play."

Naomi fled to the itty-bitty bathroom and stepped into the shower stall fully dressed. Turning on the water drowned out all of the noise and most of the guilt. Pete had promised to keep an eye on Serena, and Naomi could hardly ask for better than that. She had earned this respite. She *needed* it.

Scrubbing off the filth with herbal-scented soaps made her feel almost human again. Perfection would've involved a large tub of steaming water, bath oils, and an intoxicating beverage, but Naomi settled for the petty pleasure of leaving her wet clothes and boots to clog the drain. It wasn't as if she had to worry about the mess upsetting anyone.

That thought sent grief coursing through her, but the sting was softened by the quiet realization that for once putting herself first would harm no one. There was a measure of peace in that. She felt a little giddy at the idea of guilt-free selfishness.

Her fragile tranquility shattered when Tom began to yowl in the bedroom. Naomi yanked open the bathroom door. "Shut up, you awful creature. I am not taking care of you no matter how much you cry. I am done—"

The words dried up when she saw what was upsetting the cat. Parker and Dan stood in the open hall doorway with Justin sagging limp between them. Parker was still covered in dried mud from scalp to boots, and the slant of his shoulders inside the tight stealth uniform said both arms were hurting. Dan was scary and somber wearing black leather and a hard, dark scowl, and Justin hung between the pair looking like a child in someone else's too-large fatigues.

He also looked staggering drunk.

Tom darted past them into the hall. Parker's eyes got as far as Naomi's chin before sliding down again in a slow, pleased appraisal. Heat flooded over Naomi when she remembered that she wore nothing but a towel, and other emotions churned up in embarrassment's wake.

Suddenly the only thought in her mind was *stupid*. Stupid to let two big men catch her in a room with no exit. She was trapped. She slammed the door, put her back against it, and got a grip on old terrors before they could become new panic. "Go away. Please go away."

She was being an idiot. No one here would hurt her.

Lust added a sharp edge to the intrusive force of Parker's weary resentment. It cut like a razor through Naomi's self-control. His anger sliced along nerves already sizzling with fear, and bitterness spilled out.

"Get out of my head," she said as loudly as she could past the lump in her throat. The order came out shrill. "Get out and go away. You never ask if I want it. None of you ever ask what I want. I never wanted any of this. Why won't everyone just go away and leave me alone?"

A murmur of voices was followed by the thud of receding footsteps. Naomi bit her lip, but the tears came out anyway. Of course they'd gone, she'd told them to go, and it was a relief, but she felt forsaken all the same.

Her whole body began to shake. She slid to the floor to wait for the reaction to pass. She was safe and warm and clean, and in a while she would get dressed, and she would be fine even if solitude felt impossibly lonely instead of liberating.

Tears ran down her throat. She was so sick of being scared and alone. So tired of being brave and strong for other people.

"Not alone," Parker said from the other side of the door. He was sitting with his back to hers, separated only by the thin sheet of wood. His head rested against the panel, and his eyes were closed. Emotions sifted through: remorse and worry and anguish. *Let me stay.*

Naomi closed her eyes too. "I asked you to stop."

"Can't." It wasn't about permission. He would leave if Naomi insisted, but he could not stop the rest of it. She might as well ask him to cut off a foot or stop breathing. He could not bear to leave her like this, not while her heart was pounding so hard he couldn't count the beats. Not even if Carl got six kinds of furious about the desertion.

The whole world could go to hell before he left her alone by choice when she was so desperately unhappy.

A different kind of heat crept along Naomi's skin. She couldn't possibly deserve that kind of devotion. "*Why*? Why do you care? Why me?"

Parker stood up. Equipment rattled, and his boots squeaked over the bare floor. He didn't have an answer, didn't need one. He was satisfied with *because* or even *why not?* The sun rose and set. This existed. It was like that for him. Some answers were simple.

"Let me in," he said with his forehead resting against the door and his heart in his voice. *Want* echoed beneath the raw words: a reverberation of feelings and needs and fears that spiraled around an empty, lonely core. *Please.*

Naomi opened the door.

CHAPTER SEVENTEEN

SERENA SPUN THE LID of a pickle jar on the kitchen tiles. The moving circle flashed blue, reflecting lit stove burners. Gray Dog was grumpy and wriggling inside the quiet bubble of *safe* she had created. Cloth rustled behind her: Pete was watching her from his seat at the counter between kitchen and main room. He made the room smell green and safe.

A door opened. Serena heard her name before it shut again, and her pulse spiked as the world pressed in. She held tight to Gray's bristling ruff and let Brown Dog out to confirm that the sights, sounds, smells, and tiny changes in air pressure were harmless.

She was strong. She could handle *new*.

The oily odor of feathers and fur nearby mixed with acid fear and dusty stone. Carl and the CSB agents had dragged their prey into the owner's first-floor private suite a long while ago. For some reason Carl wanted her there now, and Dan was objecting.

Spice, moss, and citrus-floral were farther away: Justin, Parker, and Naomi, all upstairs. Serena smiled at the contented murmur of *sleepy-cozy-safe* at the back of her throat, where itchy tears had lurked earlier. Naomi was happy. That was good. Better yet, there was no danger here. Best was Pete, warm and twining nearby like a thicket in summer sun.

"You look better," he said. "Let's try this."

Lights sprang to life overhead, and Serena saw herself reflected in dark glass cabinet doors. Her solitary form looked wrong. Gray Dog was in her lap, Red Dog was asleep at her side, and Brown Dog stood guard with ears pricked. Surprise had taken flight in a whir of feathers at Pete's words, and scaly caution coiled around her arms and legs, counseling stillness.

She was in the center of a crowd, but her reflection sat alone on the floor: eyes watering, skin itching, skintight clothes soiled in patches, hair slicked back and coated in mud. The menagerie was invisible, intangible—unreal.

Crazy, the running dishwasher hummed, and the stove burners jeered their agreement. The compressor in the open refrigerator beat out a rhythm faster than her heart. *Badbadbadbadbadbad*. Then fur and scales and feathers all pushed her away from the harsh accusations of *After* and settled her into *Now*.

She was crazy, yes, but she was coping.

Pete said, "Most of the clutter is harmless, but open flame is a hazard, and there's food spoiling. May I turn off the stove and close the fridge now?"

His gnarly voice had dry sharp thorns on it tonight.

"Yes," Serena said. "I'm sorry. I couldn't stop."

"I know." Pete came closer, every muscle declaring *no threat* the same way Naomi could. He stood right beside Serena with dirty bandaged feet and vulnerable bowed shoulders. "I have to wonder why you didn't react like this to Carl's house or the apartment, though."

"They weren't covered in new. They were dark-sky and steady-safe." Serena bit the inside of her cheek and sucked on words. "I knew their scents already."

"Very sensible," Pete said. "You do continue to amaze. Let's find out why Doctor Grumpy wants you, shall we?"

He offered an elbow as if he were dressed in a suit instead of a dirty tee shirt and dirtier too-long jeans. When Serena stood and laid her hand on his arm, he smiled broadly. "Stick with me, kid. We'll go places together."

THE INSIDE OF THE OWNERS' suite was a visual assault. The walls were papered in green and black with blotches of red, pink, and yellow that might be flowers. Lumpy furniture and chunky tables sat on a knotted rug that spread ugliness across the center of the room. Only the edges of the floor were calm: a dark wood that gleamed under too-bright ceiling spotlights. Serena took one look and closed her eyes in self-defense.

She found an empty spot and made herself small there, breathing through her mouth. The air stank like roses and chemicals and filthy bodies. Small noises of pain and fear were a low drone over a silence that murmured *waiting*.

The cool floor pressed against her palms and face and soothed her overloaded senses. Pete's stable presence settled at her side in a chair that crinkled. Brown Dog nipped and nosed at the sounds and smells, herding them into order, and Serena sorted through impressions until inner truth and outer reality fused together.

The shadowed statue by the door was Dan, being as hard as he had to be to get the job done, moving data over a sparkling screen. Singh and Hughes were trapped mice on chairs in the center of the room: bound, blind, deaf, and dumb. Two sets of pale predator eyes watched them from the couch—Neil, lying with his long legs bent up, using his cat as a shield to hide weakness. Carl was standing behind the couch with one hip resting on the edge of the table that had sacrificed its chairs to the mice.

He was holding a small rectangular case in his hands, turning it end over end. Feathers rustled in shadow, talons scratched frost.

"You be careful how you move," Serena told him. "It's too

messy to fly properly in here, and that is not a safe perch. The ice won't hold you if you fall."

"This is a sick idea," Dan said, and his steel-on-stone voice rang with disapproval. "The eyes-shut stroll was hot, yes, but she's speaking gibberish."

Pete said, "No, there's always a thread of logic. Unless I've gone blind, Carl has dosed himself up for observation work as if those two were hard-to-read patients in a nice, neutral clinic room. On thin ice surrounded by chaos. Accurate." The thorny voice stretched to Carl. "Why call plays from the sidelines when you're the best player on the team? Weren't you running a hostile interview configuration?"

"I was. Does everyone love bad analogies tonight?" Carl's words scraped and scratched. "My turn, then. I can't take the field without Eddie's permission, and he benched me. I can still call plays, though, and I get a much better view of the game up high like this."

"That'll be cold comfort when you're retching through the hangover." Pete's sigh was a leafy tendril of worry. "How does Serena fit into this ugly picture?"

Neil said, "Carl and I both think a little hormonal whiplash will put Hughes right where we need him. Dan has threatened to punch us both in the balls if we ask her to help."

"You want to use her to sweeten him up?" Pete paused. "That is vile."

"Yes, it is." Frost crackled under Carl's voice. "Want to hear the next three alternatives?"

Serena shivered. "Careful, he's a hawk, not a duck, he'll drown if he goes under. That ice is thin. Don't push him."

Pete sighed again. "Right to the heart of it once again. Sorry, Carl. I'm shutting up now."

Neil said, "Better yet, let's clear the room. Dan, put Singh down for a nap, then upload everything we have now into dummy accounts and run rot checks on your rig. I'm getting some weird glitches from my unit."

"They're brand-new."

"We've hard-plugged into a dozen systems between Seattle and here. No telling what we picked up, and no point in taking chances. After you're done sanitizing, dig through what Singh gave us. Ping me if you have questions for Hughes. Dr. Hamil, you'll go with them."

His tone growled with hidden pain, but it left no room for argument. Scrapes and a snuffle and other soft noises marked the removal of a chair to the back of the suite. Electronics clattered on a second trip, and a door shut.

Serena sat up and looked around the room. Carl stared back with a hunter's gaze full of twilight colors. Something slinky and mean rose inside Serena in response to the cold challenge. She bared her teeth. "Do I get to hurt him?"

"No." Humor twinkled in the icy dark blue of Carl's eyes. "You're the carrot. Neil is the stick. If you work up Hughes like you did this afternoon, Neil can take it from there. Can you do it? Can you seduce that?"

That question was a sheltering curve of wings, encouraging a last look before leaping. Serena wrapped herself in the soft concern and considered Hughes.

He was slumped in a chair with bare knees spread and pale belly jiggling when he breathed. The blindfold and gag were soggy, and damp gray hair stuck to the plugs jammed painfully tight into his ears. His hands worked at their soft restraints, and fat toes wriggled in the carpet.

Vile, yes. He had plotted mass murder and pointed the blame at her and Naomi because he had never imagined they might live to fight back. Wrong. He considered his private goals more worthy than those of any one of hundreds dead, thousands bloodied, or millions thrown into confusion. Wrong again. He believed he was stronger than anyone else. Superior. Untouchable.

Wrong. Spite wound through Serena, gnashing sharp little teeth. There was more than one way to torment a man.

"Oh, I can do it," she said, and she unsealed her bodysuit just enough to tease.

THE FLOOR CAME UP and hit Carl in the face when he stood, and he barely got his hands up in time to avoid landing directly on his nose. Even lying flat, he felt as if he were rolling sideways. "Better, but still woozy," he said.

"Strangely enough, I figured that out myself," Dan said. His voice was mocking, but the hands that returned Carl to the cushioned armchair were gentle, and he draped a blanket over Carl's shoulders. "Do you need the bucket?"

The jumble of words and the conflicting sensory data set off another round of vertigo. Carl pressed both palms against the top of his head. The drugs he'd taken had hellish side effects, and time was the only cure.

Dan slumped into a matching chair, arms folded, face brooding. The bay window behind him was open to a foggy dawn, and the scent of wet pine was sharp in the air. He said, "Putting yourself through hell doesn't make up for using a mental patient as a cocktease. That was despicable."

Memory flashed—eyes glistening with tears, the sound of a defeated, *grateful* sob—and cold sweat broke out across Carl's skin. He wrapped the blanket tighter around himself. "You still want to punch me in the balls? Go ahead."

"And do what for an encore? Kick a newborn puppy?"

"Truce," Neil said tiredly. He was sitting on the bed with a datapad in his lap and a second unit propped on a pillow. "Bottom line, it worked. That intel normally would've taken days to pry out, and he came up with the non-lethal cleanup plan too. Speaking of that—how did it go, Pete?"

Pete entered from the sitting room of the owner's suite with Serena lilting along in his wake like a grubby Amazon bodyguard. He sat on the end of the bed, while Serena took a seat on the floor next to Dan's chair. She smiled and put her hand on Dan's shoe. He yanked his foot away. "Well?"

"The last day is blurred, and they won't want to share what they do recall," Pete said. "Serena trussed them up and tossed them into the truck."

He yawned. "Sorry. Memory disruption is tedious. It's also on a long list of tricks that have serious consequences. Ones that aren't bothering me the way they should. Carl, would you care to explain me to me yet? It was your idea to sic me on them."

"Only because I couldn't see straight," Carl said. "I wish there'd been an alternative." The shadows in Pete's eyes were getting deeper, but contradiction still saturated every word he spoke. *Breakable*, was the message. "You are not ready for explanations."

"No one is—Jesus." Dan grabbed Serena's hand when she reached for him again. "Stop that. I don't know which ring of the circus you're dancing in, nympho, but leave me out of it. Have you no shame?"

Serena patted his leg with her other hand. "Touch helps me focus, and you are rock solid. Not sexy. Rock. And no, there's no shame in the den, not that I've found. Some of my monsters are ugly and twisted, but they're all righteous."

Dan stood up and shoved his hands into his jeans pockets. "God help me, I must be going crazy too, because that almost made sense."

"You're not crazy." Serena stroked the floor with her fingers. "Stone will crack if you don't vent all that heat."

Dan looked down his nose at her for a moment. His total stillness hid his thoughts. Finally, he stirred. "Neil, I'll take out that trash and score us some clean equipment now, if you don't mind."

"Go. I'll keep adding filthy points to my data web until this unit rots out too." Neil looked up, a pale flash of eyes in a paler face. "I have plenty to work on. Deecie sent back the decryptions from Hughes's office. She sends her love."

Dan's nod was a choppy, unhappy motion, and then he was gone. Pete inhaled deeply, then let it out with a theatrical sigh. "Oh, good. There *is* air in here."

"Who's Deecie?" Serena walked her fingers along the floor toward Carl's boots, making little patterns along the way.

Neil said, "My wife, who happens to be one of the best encryption specialists in the country. She's also safely out of the country at the moment. Luckily, computers never sleep, and the time difference is working in our favor."

"I'm glad something is." Pete turned to Carl. "What am I missing with Agent Patterson? Channeling guilt as hostility, sure, but where's that volatility coming from? He's like a pool of gasoline waiting for a match."

Neil set aside the datapad and gave Pete his full and amused attention. "Do you run casual psyche dissections on everyone you meet?"

"It isn't casual; it's a defense mechanism," Carl said. Shrugging made his vision swim. "I don't know what its source is, Pete."

Neil said, "He would tell you, if you asked. His experience with Bureau psych personnel hasn't been positive. Staff debriefing protocols were abused—it was a mess in the local unit where he started. It led to a total systems overhaul from Central Admin, in fact, but—"

He stopped talking. Blinked. "The *local* psych contracts with Rydder Institute and *Central's* security program."

Watching him think was mesmerizing. Ideas struck one after another, tightening muscles around lips and eyes as they bounced away and were replaced. The effect was intense. Carl looked away before he made himself sick.

"Well, hell." Neil picked up the datapad again. After a moment he said, "There it is. There was action the last couple of days, just not bombings."

"Action?" Carl asked when the agent fell silent again.

"There have been major fish kills all down the coast, always and only near dock frontages. Ports are being closed for bilge inspections. First bombs for the air lockdown, now biohazard. They're isolating the region." Neil returned to scanning data. "Some kind of spoiler op, has to be."

Carl exchanged a puzzled look with Pete, who prompted, "They?"

Neil ignored him and tapped his fingers on one of his screens. "I need to call Dan. We have to risk coming in from the cold. He's going to hate this, but—"

He started to swing his legs off the side of the bed. Pete grabbed him by the ankles. "Whoa there, Agent Invalid. Please, don't move. You'll hurt us both. Sit still and avoid bleeding on things. We'll bring whatever you need. Serena, go get Naomi, will you? Then find a bed and get some sleep. That part isn't a request; it's doctor's orders."

Carl nodded agreement, pleased to find he could do it without getting sick. They needed to get Serena away from Neil's agitation before she took it on some unpredictable tangent. He moved his foot away from Serena's stalking fingers. "You heard him."

Serena tensed. "Yes, because I'm crazy, not deaf or stupid. You're trying to get rid of me."

"Can you blame us?" Pete asked.

"No." Serena sighed. "I'll go if you promise to rest too. Soon. And only if I can ask Carl a question before I leave."

Neil said with admirable gravity, "I think we can all accept that deal."

Serena reached Carl's boot and put a hand on it. Then she looked up and frowned, serious and soulful. "I want to whisper it in your ear," she said.

NAOMI SAW Serena's feet first. A bare toe rubbed over the top step of the porch stairs, and then she sat down while balancing bagels stacked on steaming mugs in each hand. She still wore nothing but the filthy camouflage sneak suit, and she smelled like garbage. Sleepy eyes gleamed at Naomi over a secretive smile.

"I promised to go to bed," she said. "But you're on the way. Good morning."

Naomi took a mug and let tears spill down her cheeks. "I love you so much."

"It's only tea, Naomi. It isn't even good tea."

"It's more." She wiped her face and sipped the perfectly acceptable black pekoe blend. "You don't realize how much better you've been, the last few days."

"Don't get excited. I'm still a moody bitch." Serena wrapped her arm around Naomi's waist. "I love you too, Bao-bao. You held me up until I could run again."

Naomi put her head in the curve of Serena's shoulder. "Whatever."

Birds were peeping in the drooping evergreens somewhere, and the gray sky was lightening in advance of the sunrise. The breeze was light and cool. Naomi shifted the tea to one hand and took a bite of half-thawed bagel. While she ate, she went back to doing what she'd been doing before Serena arrived: wondering why Parker wasn't freezing to death out on the lawn in nothing but a pair of cut-off sweatpants.

He squared his shoulders and flowed smoothly from one t'ai chi form to another. His balance never wavered as he pivoted to face them, but surprise came through: he hadn't noticed Serena's arrival. His attention went back to the exercise, and then he smiled.

Naomi couldn't keep her lips from curving up, but she firmly put him out of her mind even as heat coiled through her. Boundaries were important.

"Why is 'threesome' the first thing every guy thinks when he sees us together?" Serena asked. She added loudly, "She doesn't share, sorry."

Parker came down flat-footed. Chest muscles and abs rippled when he took a deep breath, and his face flushed red. Serena hummed appreciatively.

Apprehension sputtered to life within Naomi's heart as Parker turned away and got back on task. "Serena, I know you, and—please, let me have this? I can't compete, you know I can't."

"No, no, no." Serena kissed her on the ear. "Silly Naomi. Very much no."

The cheerful emphasis was as confusing as it was a relief. Naomi went back to watching Parker. "Why not? You've been sniffing after him since you met."

"Only because I could feel him, steady-safe like you at my center. Secure, not sexy. You and I don't have sex." A moment passed. "Together, I mean." Another pause. "Except those couple of times way back when, but we were both stoned and drunk at once, so I don't think they count."

"Stop." Giggles bubbled up. Naomi stifled them. "You are not helping."

For a moment they were fifteen again, winding down from a night of harmless pranks and minor property crimes. They had been so *young*. So full of hopes and passion. Life hadn't been perfect, but the future had been infinite. Their limitless reality had imploded, desperation had crushed them both into tiny futures with no room for dreams, and then even those unenviable lives had been torn to pieces.

This morning felt like rebirth.

Serena set down her cup to nestle closer, but her breath stank and so did the rest of her. Naomi pushed her away. "Dirty girl."

"I am." Serena was still watching Parker. "He is hotter than a chili pepper, and you haven't even nibbled on him yet. What is wrong with you?"

"*Boundaries*, Serena."

"I can't help noticing. He's in the same place you are." She rubbed a fist between her breasts. "Steady-safe, the pair of you. Like my heartbeat."

"Notice away, but I will not talk about anything we do or don't do. Ever."

The previous night Parker had walked right past her to the shower, keeping to himself even though his body had made his thoughts obvious the whole time. Naomi was never going to look at a bath sponge the same way again in her life.

But after that—after he toweled off and kissed her until she was dizzy and melting inside—after that, there were only yawns and laughter. They retreated to bed, where Parker wrapped himself around her like a hot, muscular blanket.

The hair on the back of Naomi's neck rose, remembering the feel of his breath against the skin there as he'd sighed into sleep. She had never felt so *treasured* as in that moment, desired and trusted and protected all at once. She'd followed him into slumber within a minute.

"You never let yourself have any fun. No." Serena abruptly stood up. "No, no, no. Ugly, slinky mink is still worked up, and I'm dirty, and I should find my bed."

A throat cleared behind them, and Pete Hamil said, "Excellent idea. I need to steal your girlfriend anyway. Go to bed. No more detours."

"Bed," Serena said with a firm nod. "Yes."

After she left, Pete shuffled to the top step and eyeballed Parker. The bruising made his face hard to read. It might have been a smirk. "Ah-hah!" Pete said, looking down at Naomi. "So you're why he went AWOL."

Then he shook himself and grimaced. "My apologies. That was

nosy. I came to beg for help. You're the closest we have to a medic after Carl. Since he's busy vomiting—"

He paused as Parker arrived at the bottom of the steps. "Hey, Eddie. It's only neurostim hangover. He'll be fine, but I need dressings changed, and so does Neil. Neil also needs a sounding board who isn't sick or blind with exhaustion. That means you two. If you're up to it. So to speak."

Parker stalked up the steps, grabbed the tee shirt and the rifle that were sitting where he'd left them. "Clothes. Coffee. Food. Fuck off."

Pete watched the retreat with a frown on his face. "I think that was a yes."

"It was," Naomi said. "And of course I'll help. I didn't mean to be so selfish last night."

"Never apologize for knowing your limits. Taking the down time you needed was the sensible thing to do. I'm about to hit a wall myself now. Notice me asking for help?"

She helped him limp back to the owner's suite and pulled supplies from the med kit. He helped Neil to the couch and made him lie down. "Him first," Pete said, and then he disappeared into another room.

"There's a lot of blood," Naomi said when she finished changing dressings. "I don't know what's normal, and I can't tell if there's infection, but I do know you're exhausted, dehydrated, feverish—are you even listening?"

Neil looked up from the datapad he'd refused to relinquish. "Yes. Drainage is always disgusting. Give me a stimshot and antibiotics and hope for the best."

Naomi bit her tongue and followed orders. She was tidying up when Neil said, "Finally. Took you long enough."

Parker set a carafe and a box on the small dining table and looked for the side chairs, which were missing. He'd collected his sidearm and wore it with a casual air, and he looked as good in khakis and boots as he had out of them: tawny, powerful, and relaxed.

When the tops of his ears turned pink Naomi made herself stop watching.

"Do I smell coffee?" Neil pushed himself upright, then drooped when Naomi glared at him. "No coffee on top of stimulants, right. Sit and listen, then. Both of you."

Naomi said, "First I need to fix Pete—"

"I can listen while you work." Pete hobbled into the room barefoot, wearing fresh clothes that fit better than the ones he'd had on earlier. Stolen from the absent owners, Naomi decided, looking at the horrendous floral print shirt. The jeans and his hair were damp, and he had a towel over one arm. He sat on the floor and leaned back on his elbows to prop his bare feet on the couch. "Is that coffee, Eddie? God loves you for your kindness. Give me some."

Parker brought two cups but held them back. "Carl?"

"In the bedroom there, bird-watching with a bucket in his lap. Go easy on him. You know how he gets after session work."

The snort of Parker's answer as he left with the second mug was ambiguous. The flash of aggravation wasn't.

"I don't think brothers do easy," Naomi said, and she got to work on Pete's toes.

CHAPTER EIGHTEEN

P ETE WAS NOT A stoic patient. He jerked at every touch of antiseptic, and whenever Naomi tested the healing nail beds, he made little squeaks that tested her professional ability to keep a straight face.

Neil said, "Can we please get started? I've been collecting bits and pieces of this mess for over a decade, and I need to see if a new theory holds together when I explain it to someone else. If I *can* explain it."

The wall across from the couch lit to display a red-gold CSB shield being presented by a cartoon animal. The logo dissolved into a constellation of photos with text sidebars. Some of the names looked vaguely familiar to Naomi from the weeding-out process they'd used to pick targets for data raiding. Most were new. Lines connected the profiles, each one labeled with dates, place names, and other notes.

Neil said, "It's taken forever to get a grip on this because it isn't organized crime. It's *disorganized*. There's a loose collaboration of operators whose agendas sometimes coincide geographically or chronologically, sometimes politically or financially. Sometimes they conflict. It's a tangle. A snarl."

"A rat's nest," Naomi said when he paused.

"Yes, exactly, and every time the Bureau got near one rat, the others scattered. Cases fell apart. Accomplices slipped through legal loopholes, finances audited clean, evidence disappeared. But this time the rats have lost their escape tunnel."

"I love a good metaphor as much as—hey, ouch." Pete pulled his left hand away from Naomi, inspected the fresh layer of sealant where there'd once been a finger, and then thrust it back at her. "Christ. Hide that before I throw up. Neil, can you work back from our facts to your theories? It might be easier to follow."

Neil pulled up profiles for Hughes and Singh. "Facts. These two guided the Duty Day bombings from setup to knock-down. Singh wanted a chance to show off because the Remembrance blowup caught the local Bureau stations flat-footed. Hughes owed him favors, so he put Singh in touch with a player he knew engineered the first blowup."

Three new profiles panned to center screen, pulled there by their ties to Hughes. "Meet the cabal behind the Remembrance explosion. On the left, Gregor Pietrykowski of United Transport. He tipped Hughes in time to prepare a political response in return for later support on interstate tariffs. In the center is Diane Gomez from Gamma Personnel Specialists, who shared a common political cause with Pietrykowski and coordinated on supplies and strategy."

"Will you tell us the motive if I beg?" Pete said.

"Both Gomez and Pietrykowski are pushing hard for huge cuts in Social Aid obligations and benefits. Terrorist activity in SF's largest Subsistence housing zone backs their claim that Subbies are lazy, stupid, and unreliable. Classic 'blame the victim' strategy. Money was motive enough for the last fellow there on the right, Arjuna Gupta."

"Money from what?" Pete asked. "The note on his link to the others says, 'ordnance,' but I see 'financier' under his name. How did banking get us to bombs?"

"Indirectly. He got a kickback for introducing buyer and seller. He was socially close to someone who used to own the confirmed source of the explosives."

He paused there, clearly for effect, and seemed disappointed by Pete's blank reaction. Naomi stared at the lines leading off-screen from Gupta's picture to other as-yet-unseen conspirators. "Used to," she said. "Past. You mean Gupta knew the dead arms dealer. This is the investigative cusp you were hoping to find when you were talking Tuesday."

"Yes, it is. Good memory."

Naomi briefly considered kicking him. "It's only been two days since I had a crash course on this. Maybe I'm only a crappy therapy tech with a criminal record, maybe I'm a lazy, unreliable Subbie failure who couldn't manage a bank account, but I am not *stupid*."

Humiliation rose up, choking thick. She hadn't recognized just how out of place she felt in the company of all these educated, professional people until the moment Neil had tossed off those casual insults.

No one here had ever gone hungry because bartering food for clothes was better than being mocked for wearing a Subsistence-issue jumpsuit. None of them had ever faced police patrollers who treated the housing blocks like zoos. There were things even Serena had never understood, but she'd never made Naomi feel so fundamentally inferior with an offhand comment.

"Being a keen observer of the human condition," Pete said, "I believe I detect a sore spot. Scabs hurt when people knock into them by accident."

He moved his hand, a material example, and Naomi suddenly wanted to laugh rather than cry. She finished the bandaging job. "I am *not* stupid."

"I said that was their position, not mine," Neil said. "It was only one conversation, and it's been a busy—"

Carl's voice rolled over his. "Condescension is inherently

insulting, Agent McAllister. I'll remind you that you're the one who brought her up to speed on a decade's worth of security tech changes during a three-hour drive. You're not the only bright bulb in this light fixture."

Parker brought him into the room, moving slow and supporting most of his weight. Even as Naomi opened her mouth to protest the stress Parker was putting on his wrists, he shifted his hold, relieving the strain.

Neil turned back to Naomi. "Dan knocked me on my ass the day we met. He said 'arrogant,' not 'condescending,' but it's the same thing."

It was almost an apology. Naomi chose to accept it as one.

After depositing Carl on the arm of the couch, Parker tossed a look at Naomi that asked her along for a second trip into the bedroom. They retrieved armchairs and got Carl and Pete both seated, and Parker sat at her feet with a cup of coffee, which put him in perfect position to let Naomi rub knots out of his shoulder muscles. She took advantage.

"If you're quite ready," Neil said.

After a nod from Parker, the agent pulled a new profile on-screen. "Let's take a closer look at our cusp person. Dominic Walton, who was at one time director of CircleD Security, board chair of Suwon Logistics, head of—"

He stopped when Parker shot to his feet: fists clenched, poised on the balls of his feet. If he'd had hackles, they would've been up. His eyes were locked on Carl. His coffee cup rolled off the rug onto the floor with a sad little thunk.

Carl had barely been able to sit up straight when Parker helped him into the chair. Now he was a solid, menacing force standing directly in front of the screen. Chill dribbled down Naomi's spine, and she had to force air into her lungs. When Carl exhaled hard, the frost melted as quickly as it had formed.

"Ease off, Eddie," he said. "I've got it under control." He

turned to Neil with a wavering frown. "Sorry. It seems that I will never be fully rational about that man."

Neil said, "No, I'm sorry. I should've realized—ah, why don't you sit down?"

Pete added, "Before you fall over and squash me, thank you very much." He eyed Naomi. "For once you do not have a look of burning curiosity in your eyes. Afraid that Neil will melt down if we digress again?"

Naomi shook her head. "No. I got the basics Tuesday. That's enough for now."

It might be enough for forever. She'd seen Carl's scars, and the glacial force of his hatred was still vivid in mind.

Parker grabbed his mug and refilled it, ignoring the wet spill except to avoid it when he settled. Neil moved Walton's icon off to the side of the screen and pulled other connected icons up to prominence.

"This gets messy fast from here," he said. "After the Fed broke CircleD over those unauthorized maneuvers in New Mexico, these two divided the spoils, and they've been sparring over the rest of Walton's holdings ever since. They both lead to Gupta, and from there to the rest."

Next Neil brought up a whole spray of icons, each with its own set of spokes, and highlighted a tracery of connections to the three he'd named as the Remembrance masterminds. Naomi saw her own name and Serena's in the new cluster. One of the other names made her sit up straight. "Hey, that's—"

Neil spoke over her, firmly. "Naomi, this is how you and Serena factor in. Hongbo Chi is a confirmed associate of Pietrykowski and Gomez according to surveillance and financial records. He's a known organized crimes broker. My judgment is that he wanted a shot at some Nguyen operations and figured that miring a vulnerable family member in a major terrorist case might be profitably distracting. He suggests a scapegoat, Naomi is already on their radar for other reasons, and that ties it all up with a bow."

"I was about to say that Serena's father uses Chi's face as a dartboard target," Naomi said as soon as he was done, which made Pete snort coffee up his nose. She waited until he recovered before asking, "If this was all corporate backstabbing on an enormous, ugly, bloody scale, where does Pete fit in?"

"You would ask that. Pete." Neil stopped drumming his fingers on the datapad and pulled a profile headed by Pete's face onto the screen. Lines tugged forward Naomi's profile too, along with ones for Carl and Parker—and Walton—again. Several blank icons without sidebar data were also pulled forward from the field. "Dr. Hamil's investigation pointed to your clinic. Your employment reports and background made you a perfect goat to throw to the local CSB. The drug money groundwork was perfect. I've reviewed it. Why did you look outside the frame?"

That was directed at Carl, who glanced at Parker and sighed. "Because I thought she was a puzzle, and Eddie had a feeling. Once we got approval to expand the inquiry, the real picture came into focus fast."

"Which alarmed someone in this group." Neil brought forward the five black-box icons, which were connected to nearly every other name in the thickly-populated diagram. "They were nervous about that Institute pipeline. I'm positing that one of them brought Naomi to the attention of Gomez when you didn't take her at face value. Gomez liked the Sub facet, and the Nguyen connection clinched the deal." He started tapping the pad again. "And this is where I get nervous."

"Wait." Carl's eyes darted from spot to spot on the chart, tracing connections to the black boxes. "You've got to be kidding."

"I wish I wasn't," Neil said. "It'd be a lot easier on me. You see it?"

"I spent five years building a map like that around Walton. There were always loose ends and blank spots I couldn't fill. Meetings with partners who disappeared. People who I couldn't prove ever existed despite eyewitness accounts. Official records containing data that clerks didn't remember entering. Oh, yes. I see it now."

Pete said, "Am I blind? I see black boxes."

Neil highlighted the icons with glowing red outlines. "I just added those a few minutes ago, and I can't put pictures or data on them. There used to be a lot of lines that led nowhere. You were talking about Dan, I was looking at you, and suddenly I saw how adding these players here would tie everything together. I needed other eyes to confirm that I hadn't twisted facts to force a fit, but I can't—"

He stopped and made a pained noise. Pete stared at him. "Holy Christ. When you say can't, you mean *can't*? You're running into an aversion loop? What in the world is a Delta-9 agent not cleared to talk about?"

Neil said, "Exactly," as if that made sense.

Carl held out a hand. "May I?"

Neil surrendered the datapad. Carl moved the five blank icons up again. The pattern on the screen swung dizzyingly through three dimensions while he studied it. "Five of your rank died on Tuesday."

When Neil slumped back, Naomi realized he'd been braced against hearing a question. He waved at the chart. "I saw the two on the left go down for certain, and three from the side of the angels. That leaves two on the right unaccounted for." Another wave. "I'm in the middle. I was brought in to consult on cases. Handed data to analyze. I didn't know I was so close, but someone made sure the hammer would also fall on me if my boss brought it down."

"Two of five," Carl said. "Not an effective hammer."

"Six of eight—two of the four rats plus all the handlers, who were either betrayed or slower. I don't think the good guys wanted a bloody hammering. I was too busy guarding Dan's back to be sure, but it isn't Webster's style."

Parker growled. It was a mild sound, considering the frustration Naomi could feel rolling off him, and Pete raised a hand. "I feel left out, too."

Carl said, "It goes like this. For at least the last ten years of its forty-three-year existence, the CSB has been sheltering a group of extralegal agents who work for hire, and two of them are still on the loose despite a major effort to eliminate them. People died on Monday to keep that information from ever seeing the light of day, and technically all of us can be shot just for knowing about it now."

"As dirty secrets go, it's a doozie," Neil said, "but you're being melodramatic with the threats. Why shoot anyone when nothing can ever be proved? Our real problem is that it looks like the two who got away are the same ones who've been stirring up trouble out here. They're up to no good, and they have nothing to lose by going out with a bang."

MORNING WAS Justin's least favorite time of day. Sleep rarely gave up without a fight, and victory seldom came quickly. Rousing to the tickle of a cat's paw on his cheek was a familiar aggravation. It meant he'd slept through his wake-up alarm.

Justin pulled the pillow over his head and held it in place with one arm to keep the cat from pushing it off. A wet nose burrowed into his palm. "Toby, I swear I am going to turn you into a coat. Quit it. I'm awake."

The cat chirruped and pinned down Justin's wrist for a thorough tongue-cleaning. The scraping didn't hurt, but the rest of his body ached with an intensity that meant his power cell had slowly drained while he was asleep. That was a little confusing. Mornings

251

were bad enough without starting them off in pain. The last thing on his go-to-bed list was "fresh cell."

Toby had never been in that bed. Toby slept with Alison, and Justin hadn't slept with them since Alison had kicked him out. That raised the question of whose rough tongue was working on his wrist. It also raised the question of whose arm was resting across his chest.

Justin sat up, which prompted grumbling protests from both his bedmates. The cat was much bigger than Toby: dangerously so. His other companion was human, female, naked, and brunette, but she was definitely not Alison. The bed was a confection of lacy covers and ruffles that dominated a room packed with wicker furniture and decorative mirrors. Cool daylight filtered through a dormer window. Nothing looked familiar. Not a single thing.

Some days *sucked.*

The usual routine for kick-starting his brain began with name, age, date, and time. He'd grounded out on time and place, and the last event he remembered—

"Tom," he said as reality fell into place. The cat squinted at him. Justin scratched behind his ear. "Can you tell me how Sleeping Batshit got here?"

Tom swished his tail over the quilt. Serena slid her other arm around Justin's back and pressed her face against his hip. He tensed up. Skin-tight underwear wasn't much good at preserving modesty. If Serena moved a few centimeters in the wrong direction —or the right one, depending on how selfish he was feeling— things would get interesting fast. All other complications aside, there was the significant factor of legal competence to keep in mind.

He patted Serena's head. "Wake up, crazy woman. Time to explain things."

"You're very warm. He likes warm. He's supposed to be patrolling. Bad cat."

The words were a hot whisper across Justin's skin. Arousal was immediate, the rush exquisite to the edge of pain. He counted to ten five times. "Not Tom. You. Why are you here, Serena?"

"Carl needed air. I need clean, spice, and bright."

She rolled onto her back, stretching, and Justin hurriedly looked elsewhere. He might be a selfish bastard, he might entertain some high-quality fantasies on his own time, but he was *not* going to take advantage.

"No, look." Serena nudged her head under Justin's hand. He had to look down to grab her other arm before it slid into dangerous territory. He couldn't help getting an eyeful of details: breasts exactly large enough to make nice handfuls; fresh STI vaccination tattoos vivid on one lean thigh; bare rise of belly framed between delicate hip bones.

Justin clenched his teeth and forced his gaze up to meet dark, wide eyes filled with earnest appeal. It felt like drowning. Serena said, "I like the happy-more-please. It makes me feel clean."

"You're filthy," Justin told her.

Her hair was lank and greasy, and even the short glimpses had shown Justin the grimy imprint all that lovely golden skin had left on the lacy bedspread. He noted the dirty clothing in a line from the open doorway to the bed, and then he realized that the door was open.

His head began to throb, and his stomach knotted up. "How long have you been lying there?"

"Since we finished with the mice-men. Dan took them away. I do need a shower. You do too. We should both take a shower."

She meant they should shower together. Her suggestive grin left no doubt of that. The mental image left Justin as hard as a rock and aching worse than ever. He shut his eyes again. "Hell. No."

Tom thumped to the floor and away, and Serena's breathing became audible: in and out, steady but harsh.

Clearly that had been the wrong thing to say. Justin rubbed his aching forehead with both hands. "This cannot be a good idea. You are a box full of bedbugs, and I'm—"

Fingers brushed his lips, stroked down to his chest to press over his heart. He opened his eyes and got lost in Serena's liquid-dark gaze all over again. She huffed out a deep breath. "Maybe I'm crazy, but I know I want clean happy body-bumping to push out all the ugly. Your body is saying happy-please-now-thanks. So is mine. Stop arguing."

Justin opened his mouth. Shut it. Tried again. Nothing. Serena's smile came up slow and wicked. She went to the door and glanced both ways before shutting it. Then she came back to kiss him, light as a feather, on the lips.

THE SHOWER TURNED out to be less about sensuality and more about avoiding elbows, but Justin enjoyed it all the same. The scenery was glorious, the water was hot enough to dispel all his aches, and Serena was agreeable about playing in the filled tub, afterwards. A lot of water ended up on the floor, and eventually they ended up in bed again to cuddle and doze.

All too soon the pain returned in force, and then he started to shiver. Body heat didn't generate enough energy to satisfy his damned skin for long, not when he was lying still. Serena frowned when Justin slid out of bed and retrieved the clean, dampish base layer from the towel rack in the bathroom. He braced himself for after-action awkwardness, but Serena only sat up with the covers wrapped around herself and watched him dress.

"Pieces are rubbing inside," she said. "What's wrong?"

He should've known Serena wouldn't be normal about anything, including post-coital conversation. "I'm freezing. I don't wear long underwear in the summer as a fashion statement. Have you seen my go-bag? I wasn't awake when I got here. I need to power up."

Serena pointed at the foot of the bed. His duffle was hidden under the dust ruffle beside a neon pink suitcase. Serena watched with a rapt expression on her face while Justin shuddered through the relief of slotting in a new power cell. He set up a charger for the drained one, and he stayed on the floor when he was done.

"So bright," Serena said, and her thin brows lifted. Soft lips quirked into a smile. "Flickery. What are you thinking?"

"Wondering when you're going to ask what I'm doing. And when you're going to ..." Apparently he got to start the awkwardness. "Why me? Was it process of elimination? Everyone better was busy or uninterested?"

Serena fell back on the bed and pulled pillows over her face. The cloth didn't muffle her laughter much. Justin's temper started to fray, but someone knocked at the door before he lost it. He pulled open the door with every intention of snarling a dismissal.

When he saw Carl, the words that came out were, "Damn, you look like shit."

"Good morning to you, too." Carl's eyes were glassy blue around pinpoint pupils, and the bruises on his jaw were vivid black under pale stubble. The blanket he wore draped over his shoulders gave him the look of a disaster victim seeking shelter. He braced a hand on the doorframe and looked down at Justin with a crooked half smile. "You, in contrast, look positively chipper, not to mention clean and coherent. All good things."

Serena said, "Bad bird. You promised to roost. You're all splintered claws and loose feathers."

She sounded distressed. Carl looked at her over Justin's head. "I will stick my head under my wing as soon as I'm done annoying Justin by reminding him to eat today."

Justin resisted the urge to slam the door shut. It would break Carl's hand, for one thing. For another, the damage was already done. He loosened his grip on the knob when he heard crackling. "I'll eat. Soon. Satisfied?"

"Almost. I'd also suggest that you avoid hard-linking into the house systems—most of it is rotting fast—and get a briefing from Neil or Pete. We're waiting on word from Dan, but—"

"But nothing," Serena said. "Go roost, bad bird. We will take care of us."

"Hang on, crazy woman." Justin glanced at her and back to Carl. "Bad news doesn't get better with age."

"It's complicated, not bad. I doubt I *could* explain properly right now. There's no rush. Relax. Eat. Enjoy life while you have the chance."

His tone carried a million dirty ideas that the words barely implied. Justin managed to not say "Fuck you" out loud. Carl's crooked smile straightened to a grin. He rapped his knuckles on the doorframe before walking away to a room at the end of a hall.

Justin closed the door and rested his forehead on its solid, predictable surface. The world wavered. He flinched when Serena's arms slipped around him from behind. "Please," he said. "Please tell me he didn't engineer this. Please give me that small grace. Lie to me if necessary."

She rested her chin on his shoulder. "No lies. I asked him if this was crazy to want. He said no, not crazy, but you're dumber than a dill pickle about some things, and I would have to be very clear."

Teeth closed on his shoulder and released. "Truth. You're sharp and bright and pure inside even when you're asleep, and when you're awake, you are beautiful to me. My noisy head goes quiet when you look at me, and my body sings."

She turned them both to face a wicker-framed mirror across the room. He was listing to the left, and his face was sallow and bristly under a bad case of bed head. Serena grounded her chin on his shoulder again. Dark eyes glinted from behind a black fringe of hair, and her breasts pressed warm against his back.

Her hands slid under his waistband. "Nice pickle."

WHEN TYLER'S phone chirped he was flat on his back with both legs in the air. He wiggled his toes, which provoked giggles from the little boy balancing belly-down on his feet. "Down, kiddo."

Ryan said, "But I'm not done flying you yet."

"What if it's Mr. Justin calling?"

That possibility made Ryan squirm off before Tyler could bend his knees, and the boy landed hard. The impact bounced a vase off a nearby table. It shattered when it hit the hotel room floor. The neglected call went to account memory before Tyler got to the phone.

One of the entourage glanced into the suite to check on the noise, but withdrew when Ryan said cheerily, "Only an oops, not an ow."

Ryan was an odd duck. He had banished the bodyguard to the hall with an air of authority when Alison and Tyler first arrived today, and he seemed accustomed to solitude under observation. Press events and fan sessions for the upcoming charity gala kept his mother busy from morning to long past a normal child's bedtime. During one of her brief visitations, she had admitted that the boy usually set his own schedule on trips like this.

Tyler felt sorry for the poor kid. He glanced over his shoulder as he hit call-back from the workstation. "Sorry, squirt, it isn't Justin. It's a public access. I told you Alison would disapprove of pancakes for lunch, even if your mom doesn't care what you eat."

There wasn't much about Helen's laissez-faire parenting style that Alison did support. When she wasn't doting on Ryan, she called her involvement *contributing to child neglect*. Tyler privately thought of it as doing a public service. Someone had to teach Ryan that there was more to life than drama and upheaval. Bitter cynicism and genius were not a safe combination.

Ryan was almost to the desk when Dan's voice spoke from the desk behind Tyler. "First you miss my call, and now I get the back of your head? Am I interrupting? I can call later with my news of disaster."

The boy stopped in his tracks at the word *disaster*. His eyes went wide, and his lip trembled. Tyler scooped him up and settled into the chair with him. "Shut up, jackass," he said to the face grinning on the screen. "I was busy."

"And I was joking." The graffiti-marked beige background behind Dan's face blurred as he leaned in. His smile dimmed. "Holy cow, Tyler. You're babysitting?"

"He isn't a baby. He's eight. Dan Patterson, meet Ryan Armstrong, Justin's—" Tyler winced at the thought of Alison's reaction, should he spill that secret prematurely. "His ex-wife's kid. Ryan, this is—" He stopped again.

Dan said, "Subterfuge is truly not a strength, is it? Hi, Ryan. I'm Daniel Patterson, Civilian Security Bureau, Central Investigations. You look familiar."

"You don't," Ryan said. "Mom says 'jackass' is a bad word. I know nine more."

Dan's lips and eyebrows twitched. "Do you?" he said, and laughed when Ryan rattled them off.

Alison arrived with lunch, and after negotiations, Ryan departed to Alison's room to eat his pancakes. Alison bolted the door and joined Tyler at the desk. She looked good in jeans and a tank top, especially when she sighed.

"I don't know why that child isn't a spoiled rotten brat," she said as she pulled up a chair. "Hello, Agent Patterson. Please say everyone's safe."

"Everyone's safe," Dan said promptly. "And you know what? It's even true."

Tyler wondered if the agent was trying to provoke another sigh. Alison frowned instead, and Dan got serious fast. "I need to ask another favor."

"What kind of favor?" Tyler asked.

"Tyler!" Alison grabbed his hand, clasping it tight. "He means 'of course we'll help.' What do you need?"

Twenty minutes later, Tyler finished assembling equipment,

and Alison said to Dan, "We're ready. You don't expect us to leave you alone for this, do you?"

"No, I want you to stay." Dan was slumped back in his chair with his eyes shut. "I want witnesses. If this all goes south, I want someone to know I tried to do the right thing. All right, Tyler. Key in the first code."

CHAPTER NINETEEN

T HE MAN ON THE screen had a pale complexion and graying brown hair cut without care, and his face was a nondescript frame for muddy eyes and thin lips. If Alison printed a portrait of him, she would have to label it *Forgettable*.

Dan stared out of his own screen on the other side of the hotel desk. The scrolling text on Tyler's datapad was too dense for Alison to interpret, but she knew it involved telecommunications programming. He'd said so, and now he tapped a command. "Links are secure."

Dan said, "Yo, Finley. How's it hanging?"

"You took your sweet time checking in," Finley said. "We sent the all-clear with the reinstatement verification this morning. I know you got it."

Dan hesitated. "Who is 'we,' exactly? Are you still chief flunky, or are you Director Webster's replacement?"

"God forbid. No, Stephen's still top dog." Finley made a face. "When he's awake, which isn't often. To balance it out, the chief flunky isn't sleeping at all."

"My heart bleeds for you both." Dan's voice lacked sincerity.

"How's Neil? Recordings show he took a hit covering you from the bad guys."

Silence. Dan's jaw clenched. Alison admired the way he implied that Neil was dead without saying a word.

Finley's bland features sagged, and he raised a hand to his hair, brushing it back in a finicky gesture. "Damn. We lost too many good people in that fiasco. How much have you worked out already?"

"Enough," Dan said. "Stipulate that I know the conference was a gigantic tiger trap. What I don't understand is why Webster would leave Neil out on the shitty end of the stick and cripple him with lack of intel."

Finley said hotly, "Spare me. You were both suspects until we saw which way Neil jumped that day. His never-ending conspiracy quest could've been cover. If we've lost him too, then we desperately need every trustworthy agent we can lay hands on to clean up behind the scenes. Get your insubordinate ass back here on the double."

"After scraping Doug's brains off my face and being hounded across NDC by local patrols? No, thank you. We'll hop a freighter to Fiji before we come home without a lot more proof of safety than your word."

Finley's eyes narrowed, and a cold smile lifted his thin lips. "*We.* Oh, Dan, quit yanking my chain. Check the reinstatements any way you like. If it makes you happy, have Deecie lock down your personnel files so that your privileges can never be revoked. I don't care, not as long as you come back. Why are you being so spiteful if Neil's safe and sound?"

He looked off-screen with his head tilted, and the smile drooped. "Nice trick, doing screen-to-screen through Bellevue, but are you really in SanFran? What is wrong with you? That's hopping out of a frying pan into a fire."

Dan took a deep breath. "Sir, I think we may be talking across each other. I'm not angry about getting caught in the meeting cross-fire. I'm angry because I think you knew we would end up here afterwards. Stephen Webster is a cold-blooded shit who wouldn't hesitate to drop Neil blind and naked into a total clusterfuck if it helped the Bureau. I think he *planned* for us to be in San Francisco."

"Well, you're wrong." Finley took a deep breath too. "What are you hunting? My pinpoint trace is stalled, as I'm sure you know. You have time to throw me a bone even if you won't come home from safari."

"I have a full briefing packet for you. Show me the boss first."

"So you can tell me I'm faking the imagery?" Finley snorted. "I am not disturbing his rest for your paranoia. He's seventy-eight, he's missing a meter of small intestine, and he hit his head when I took him to the floor. I wish to God you two were here to take over the mop-up, and Stephen would sign off on it in a split second. Is that *clear*, Patterson? If it isn't, then board a boat and be damned, the pair of you."

Alison hoped Tyler was capturing the call imagery, because *Furious* would make a great pairing with *Forgettable*. Tyler elbowed her and murmured, "That is exactly what you sound like when I'm being thickheaded."

Dan made no answer for several seconds. Then he squeezed his eyes tight, and his left shoulder moved. A status bar blinked to life on his screen. "Update on its way, sir. Check Neil's regular drop. Who thought that siccing a lethally armed tactical platoon on a room full of lethally armed Deltas was a grand idea, by the way? You?"

"Good Lord, Dan." Finley ran both hands over his hair. "No one, of course. The Tac unit's munitions were compromised. Current theory is that our bad apples thought we were clois-tering the unit in preparation for an investigation, not to announce its findings. They came in wearing heavy ballistic coverage."

Dan winded. "So if the Tacs had fired normal stun suppression after Gonzales drew, the bad guys would've been the only ones left standing."

Finley nodded. "Exactly so. Too bad for them, we already had a good idea who to watch, so the shots were targeted. And do not ask me why we allowed weapons in the room at all when we can't even get D-9s to stop bringing pets to meetings. There's your answer. Now tell me what the hell you're doing out west."

"I did tell you," Dan said in a much lighter tone. "Grabbing the shit stick by the pointy end. Neil can't help himself. I'll be in touch if your story checks out, but in case you're lying—now, please."

Tyler moved his hand, Finley's screen went dead, and so did Dan's. The first workstation chirped to life again a few seconds later.

"You're probably curious," Dan said.

"Understatement of the year," Alison told him. "Start talking."

"Let's make a deal. You tell me how you ended up babysitting Justin Wyatt's junior twin, and I'll tell you my crazy tale."

OLD BOOKS LINED ALL the inner walls of the round corner room, and the afternoon sun made a muted rainbow of their colored spines. Naomi sat curled up on one of the cushioned window seats with Tom and Parker, and she felt more contented than she ever had in her life.

Parker glanced at the hall stairs just as Serena came running down in bare feet and underwear. Justin limped past in sweats and hiking boots, and they headed into the main part of the house without a glance at the library.

"I sense imminent disaster," Naomi said after a moment's reflection. Parker's snort was an agreement, but he collected the cat with a whistle and passed through the dining area to the owner's suite rather than sticking around to assist.

Serena was by the stove, standing balanced on one foot like a crane while she sampled the remaining stir-fry from lunch. Justin sat bleary-eyed at the bar counter with his elbows resting on top to steady his hands while he worked on a handset. Either he'd gained weight overnight or he was wearing even more layers than usual.

Naomi took the frying pan away from Serena, started it reheating, and checked the contents of the rice cooker. "Cooks wear clothes, sweetie. Justin, make sure you're backed up in case that's infected already."

"I am wearing clothes," Serena said, and Justin continued staring at his screen.

Naomi sighed. "No one listens to me."

"He's filling in cracks." Serena opened the refrigerator and pulled out a container of sliced meat. "Hey, pickle-pickle. Carl said eat. You promised. You're crackly inside."

Justin jumped when the food landed in front of him. After chewing down a few plain slices of meat, he paused and looked up. "You were talking," he said to Naomi. "Sorry. I do listen. Carl mentioned the rot. My phone will be fine."

He took off his sweatshirt and removed a tee shirt. "And about the clothes—she was ready to prance down here buck naked. The fabric smells wrong, she says. We're compromising." He jiggled the shirt at Serena. "Your turn. You promised too."

"Stubborn man." Serena boosted herself over the top of the bar with both hands and inhaled deeply, then swung her legs up and over to come down on Justin's side. "Stinky, itchy compromise. Kiss first."

Justin blushed. Naomi pretended to stir vegetables. Feigned disinterest didn't prevent her from noticing that the bizarre buddy system worked. By the time the food was hot again Serena was also wearing sweats, and Justin looked energized and alert.

Naomi lured them both to the big dining table and sat at the bar to enjoy her diminished caretaking responsibilities. Parker came out of the owner's suite with a boxy machine under one arm.

He placed it on the countertop and hauled himself up beside it, then proceeded to split his attention between watching its screen and playing with Naomi's hair. He liked it short. Naomi liked the way he played with it.

Serena ate her meal leaning against Justin's arm and tapping his plate to keep his focus on the food. As they were finishing up, Pete came yawning out of the owner's suite and stood peering at the room.

"Good Lord," he said. "A party. Am I invited?"

Naomi filled another plate and set it on the table.

"See how I'm not analyzing?" he said around his first mouthful. "See how discreet I can be, even when the whole room reeks of sex and bonding hormones? I am a saint, I tell you. A saint."

Justin said, "Will the halo fall off if you bring me up to speed on the situation? Carl said it was complicated."

The story still stretched the bounds of believability on a second airing, but Pete summarized it well enough. Naomi considered her part in the strange intersection of events and then started worrying about the warrants still hanging over her and Serena, about her job, and about her financial mess.

She was working herself up to a stomachache when Neil started cursing in the next room. The long string of expletives was so hostile in tone that it brought Serena to her feet.

When the outburst ended with a crash, Naomi headed that direction at a run. Justin followed, and Parker grabbed Serena to make sure she didn't.

Neil was intimidating when he was angry, even reclining on a couch with a bloody throw blanket covering one shoulder. He was glaring at Tom, who crouched low to the floor, facing the door with his fur puffed out, his claws flexed, and his ears flat back.

"Down," Neil snapped at him. "Stop it, Tom. Settle."

Pete stumbled into Naomi's side, and she caught him by the arm to keep him on his feet. He swayed there, shivering and looking dazed. "I don't—and—I can't—*Christ*."

His face was an appalling shade of grayish green, and his eyes were riveted on the throw blanket. Naomi turned him around and pushed. "Out. We'll handle it."

Pete stopped shivering as soon as he couldn't see the blood, and Parker pointed him at the library with a sympathetic frown. Naomi turned back. Tom had risen to his haunches and was flicking his ears up. Justin handed the medical kit to Naomi and edged past her.

He stopped at Neil's side. "Which broke first, the tech or your temper?"

"Which do you think?" Neil scowled at his datapad. "Power up, you worthless piece of shit."

The screen was blank except for blood spots and greasy smears. Neil pitched the device at the wall. It crashed down to join one on the floor. "An hour's work shot. Why did the worst damned rot outbreak in a decade have to happen here and now?"

He made a visible effort to calm himself when he noticed Naomi staring. "I'm sorry. I won't bite. Can you patch me up one more time? I ripped through the glue and tape on my shoulder. Again. Please don't make me ask Justin to do it. He doesn't like me."

Naomi stopped herself before she ruined his joke by admitting that she didn't like him either. Concentrating on the shoulder repairs steadied her nerves until she saw that the other dressings she'd changed only hours ago were soaked in blood too.

Neil pulled the throw over his lap. "Nothing you can do for that," he said with a determined look that made Naomi glad she'd spared his feelings. She moved back when Justin arrived with the electronic discards in a wicker container.

Neil waved him away. "No point in keeping those. I tried every trick in the book. It isn't critical. I just wanted to get a few things in order in case—well, in case. This is maddening. You made a fortune on rot workarounds: any brilliant ideas?"

Justin's laugh had a nasty edge. "Not in years, and I was never a tech wizard. Mechanical engineering, chemistry—my first license was for a sewage-flow control unit that bypassed the need for electronic sensors. Here."

He tossed his handset to Neil. "You want brilliant, talk to the people who designed that. It's rot-proof, and you can cable-sync to dead units for data recovery."

Neil's eyes went wide, and he tipped the contents of the box onto his lap to sort through things. Justin accepted the empty container and lowered himself to the floor with a pained smile. The box crunched when he leaned on the lid.

He raised and lowered it a few times, assessing the damage with a vague determined focus that made him look for all the world like an infant examining its toes. He was so caught up in the inspection that he didn't glance up even when Serena came into the room.

She ended up on the floor next to him and visibly relaxed once they were touching. She petted the lid every time Justin lifted it, running her nails over the wicker. The irregular scratching sound set Naomi's teeth on edge.

"Let's let Neil work in peace," she suggested.

"Okay." Serena tugged the basket. "Move, crazy man."

Justin planted a hand on her face, pushing her away. Naomi tensed, expecting violent consequences, but Serena only laughed and ducked back to give him space.

"I need—a thing." Justin wiggled one hand. "Makes marks. Shit. A thing."

Serena went to a cabinet on the far side of the room and brought back crayons and a pad of drawing paper. Naomi wondered how she'd known where they were, then remembered the obsessive explorations. Justin made several broad strokes and scribbled down numbers. Serena sat down again and rested a hand on his knee.

"I'll keep an eye on him, I promise," she said. "He's gone flickery bright."

Neil leaned over to look at the art project. "Huh. I wonder what'll come out of that."

Naomi started to suspect that she was the only normal person in the entire house. "What comes out of *what*?"

"That." Neil gestured at the sketchpad. "You heard him complain that he hadn't had an idea in years? I think one hit him over the head."

CARL CRASHED from nightmare into wakefulness with pain hammering inside his skull and the residue of the dream dragging at his mind. He untangled himself from the twisted sheets on the bed and waited for the shakes to settle.

He was *not* trapped. The tower bedroom had three windows and French doors onto a widow's walk. Thin curtains were drawn against empty dusk outside, and the dim light from a table lamp revealed an empty room. The half-open door displayed an unoccupied hall.

Logic insisted that the fear was groundless, but logic wasn't running the show. The sense of impending doom refused to lift, and the tension headache clamped down harder when he tried to pull his hair back. His spine ached too, and his left arm tingled from being bound up in the clothes he hadn't removed before falling asleep.

He scratched at beard stubble he hadn't gotten around to removing since Sunday and admitted the truth to himself: he was a mess.

The sound of footsteps sent his pulse shooting up again before he recognized the source. Parker stopped where his shadow fell through the gap between door and frame and made clucking noises under his breath. *Chicken*.

Carl's paranoia evaporated in the heat of annoyance. "Yes, screwed-up brain chemistry is highly amusing. Next time you babble through a shooting debrief on neoscope or catnip, I am recording every second and broadcasting it."

Parker shouldered his way into the room. The absence of visible weaponry meant that he considered himself off-duty. He was holding Carl's medicine case in one hand with a bottle of beer in the other. He lifted both: *which?*

Carl met worried hazel eyes he knew as well as his own and fought to control his wayward temper. "Neither. If I get my hands on those meds in this mood, I will flush them all, stupid as that would be. Beer would lead to other kinds of stupidity. I don't want to cheer up. Go away."

One corner of Parker's mouth drew up, and the concern faded. He'd been ready to face some of the more extreme mood swings that the drugs could inflict. Grouchy threats were healthy threats.

He sank onto the mattress and leaned in, shoulder to shoulder. Warm, solid, alive. Together. It helped.

It had always been enough. Now it was more: there was a burr of steady contentment in Parker's breathing, a measured focus to his presence that was Naomi's influence without a doubt. Carl sighed.

Once Parker's arms were back to full strength, he would be hunting down new employment. He wasn't in a safe line of work. Carl said, "What are you going to do if she wants a picket-fence life, Eddie? You're not built for it."

Parker snorted. "Neither is she. You're the one who bought a house."

"I'm well aware that it will never be more than a crash pad and a storage unit. The Bureau will never stop finding ways for me to be useful, and it isn't as if I can submit a formal resignation. It was a financial decision."

There was no point in pretending it was a home. Undercover jobs would require lies to explain absences, and going from hostile interviews to neighborly chats would leave him with a lethal case of emotional whiplash. Easier to avoid ties than to face the pain of severing them.

He'd known what kind of deal he was making at the time. At the time he'd had other priorities. He stared into the hall and tried not to feel depressed about how much had changed since then.

Parker elbowed him: sulking would not be tolerated. Most of the changes had been good ones.

Shadows flickered in the stairwell, by the front door. Dan called out, "Can Mohammed visit the mountain now?"

"Safe," Parker replied, adding to Carl, "Rolled in with a doctor and uniform squad a few minutes ago. He and McAllister are back on grid, full restoration."

That was the most optimal of all the possible outcomes they'd considered that morning. Carl said, "You are making it very hard to keep moping."

That netted him a chuckle and another elbow in the ribs, and Dan arrived at the door wearing clean black leathers and a tired grin. "Such a cute couple."

Parker flipped him off. Dan's smile faded into a yawn as he settled on the window seat. "Don't hate me because I'm beautiful," he said. "Hate me because I'm talented."

"I can do both at once," Carl assured him. "Talk to us."

"Where do I start? Neil hasn't quite managed to kill himself, and I brought fresh tech for everyone. Except Serena. Naomi has her set. Also, Alison and Tyler have a non-life-threatening problem. I'd make that a priority, Goliath."

Carl took the earpiece, handset, and datapad that were offered and waited for details.

Dan only yawned again. "God, I am dead on my feet. Glare all you want. I refuse to ruin the surprise. Just call. Alison made me promise that you would."

"Naomi?" Parker asked. "Serena?"

Dan made an expansive gesture. "What about them? Mystery solved, right? Their troubles are over, although the rest of the op could still end up being the biggest clusterfuck since Chicago almost seceded. That was the last time Neil went home on a stretcher, now that I think about it. CAF's moving up and down the coast in unit breakouts for emergency action. Officially it's a gesture to reassure nervous civilians, but in reality it's watchdog duty."

"Specifics, Agent Patterson." As hard as he tried, Carl couldn't keep his voice steady. "Who closes out the warrants, how long will it take, and should Naomi and Serena expect assistance or resistance when it comes to reparation? And not to be selfish, but do we get paid? When can we call this done?"

Dan leaned forward, folded his hands in front of him in a serious pose and schooled his face into sober lines. "Serena's and Naomi's administrative profiles have been squeaky-cleaned, along with all associated accounts."

"And payment?"

"Your case contract was cashed out, and your file's closed. Neil took care of the prep earlier today because he wasn't sure if he'd be alive tomorrow, and I pushed through the filings after I dropped the doctor on him." He broke into another bright grin. "In a word: now. Call it done now."

"My file?" Carl echoed that addition.

"Closed," Dan said impatiently. "Consider yourself released from all prior obligations. Retired. Expelled, even. Put out to pasture. Footloose and fancy-free. Grasping the concept yet? I'm running out of descriptions. If you'll be kind enough to keep an eye on Dr. Hamil for us for a few weeks, we'll put together an ID workup for him and get him properly disappeared too. That's gratis, by the way."

Parker made a strangled noise, and Carl struggled to absorb the news. The prospect was too good to be true. "Forcing me back to Rydder for sequestration was always an implicit threat, never a legal one. When a Bureau order shows up in my comm queue next week or next month, then what?"

"Tell them to suck rocks if you're not interested. Your life from today back to your birth is now under a Delta seal. Appended with 'service obligation fulfilled.' No more limbo for you. Neil muttered about carrots and sticks and not burning up nonrenewable resources. He's odd that way."

Dan folded his arms over his chest. "Two important caveats. One, Dr. Hamil is getting a free pass because of your good record. If he misbehaves, do not get between him and our unholy wrath. Two, we will be asking for your help when we get around to digging into his departure from the Institute. That is going to be an ugly snake pit to clear, and you are our only reliable expert."

Parker pushed to his feet and paced around the room, checking each window in passing. When he glanced Dan's way, his eyes were alight with the same guarded hope that Carl felt. "Ask," they both said on the same breath.

"Yes, ask, you nasty, suspicious, *strange* people." The agent's sigh was leavened with amusement. "When the time comes to negotiate, keep in mind that Neil has a massive budget. Now will you please call the tiny tyrant? If you don't you'll make a liar out of me, and if you don't do it soon, I'll fall asleep and miss the fun."

Carl looked down at himself. He wasn't up to dealing with any problem that would stump Alison looking the way he did now, not even with the camera turned off. "Shower first. And clean clothes."

Dan opened his mouth to protest and then thought better of it. "Yeah," he said. "Not a bad idea."

COMMITMENT

RESTORATION DAY 6

The Restored United States is committed to the proposition that all of us are created equal. What are you committed to achieving? Do you make dreams come true? On this day, commit to at least one goal for the coming year, for yourself and others.

—*A Young Citizen's Guide to Restoration Week*

CHAPTER TWENTY

SERENA LEANED CLOSE TO the stove and inhaled the scents of onion and chili peppers and honey. *Tasty*, the fragrance promised, and she jiggled the frying pan. Liquid sloshed under the steamer basket. Mist burbled through the lid, lifting in thin tentacles like an anemone waving underwater.

"I'm listening," she said, and she hummed along with the water's happy song.

The floor vibrated: someone was approaching light-foot quiet. Gray Dog tugged at her senses, worried about weapons and escape routes—boiling water and knife at hand, windows across the room over the breakfast bar, sight lines to the front door. Then she caught a dusty whiff of feathers in the air. She firmly muzzled the nervousness. "Hi, Carl."

He arrived in a murmur of clean stiff clothes: all in black with pale hair, face and hands invisible against the bright sun behind him. He brushed the countertop clean and laid down a stack of papers, then made a beeline for the coffeemaker.

"Who were you listening to?" he asked as he poured. "I haven't heard a peep from anyone since Neil and Dan and their friends left last night."

The question was serious, so Serena answered seriously. "The food sings *almost done*, the coffeemaker burps that it's full, the house breathes in and out, *lazy-sleepy-happy*, and pipes complain that Justin and Pete are both using water. Also the refrigerator says, *crazy-crazy-crazy-crazy*, but I try to ignore that."

"That's wise." Carl's voice smiled, and his body was laughing under the serious face as he sat down at the bar with his mug. "Refrigerators aren't known for their diagnostic skills. I need to talk to Justin. He's up, you said?"

"Not now." Serena grinned. "I took care of that. Now he's showering. I was still bouncy with celebrating, and he said, 'Go make breakfast, only be careful with knives and fire.' These are breakfast food, and I am being careful."

All the laughter in Carl's shoulders went silent, and he slurped at his coffee. Serena pulled the pan off the burner. "What did I say wrong?"

"Nothing. I knew you two would be good for each other, but I never—never mind." He shook his head. "You asked for my advice. Here's a little more: do not make me regret encouraging you. His life is already complicated, and it's about to get worse."

Serena focused on the defensive plumage she hadn't meant to ruffle, measured the emotions in flexing talons and night-bright eyes. *Threat*, growled Red Dog, but it was more of a territorial declaration, and she could respect that. "I am very clear with him," she said finally.

It was the best she could do with words, but Carl's smile told her she'd found good ones. "What are you making?" he asked. "It smells good."

"Naomi calls them cheater bao. There was frozen biscuit dough." She tipped the contents of the steamer onto a plate. "Honey, scrambled eggs and hot sauce, pickled vegetables."

"All at once?" Carl didn't wait for an answer to the silly question before he bit into a dumpling. "So. Justin. Last night he was an impossible mix of creative mania and aphasic temper. Is he

verbal again, or are you translating for him the way you're translating for the refrigerator?"

There were only two tiers in the steamer. Carl looked hungry.
Serena filled another batch of dough rounds. "I don't know what
aphasic means. He tried to stay up all night scribbling, but I tired
him out with sex instead."

She timed it perfectly. Carl had started to swallow, and he
nearly choked. Serena beamed at him. "He's all sharp and sparks,
but he promised not to disappear into his head again until after
breakfast, and breakfast comes after he talks to someone about his
idea. What do you need to talk about?"

Carl picked up another dumpling and fanned out the stack of
printouts with his other hand. The charts and text looked boring,
but there were also snapshots of two boys at ages from crawling
infancy to diaper-free toddling.

Serena frowned at them. "Baby pictures of Justin and who else?
They're family, yes?"

One of Carl's eyebrows swept up. "You do see things, don't
you? Those are comparison shots of Justin and his son at the same
ages."

"Son." Serena rolled the surprising word over her tongue.
Carl's voice said not-a-joke. "I didn't know he had living blood,
not since the Omaha plague."

"Justin doesn't know either. In fact, he's currently certain the
boy is *not* his child. Worse, he doesn't handle change well. That's
the reason for the other documentation. For him, the shortest route
to acceptance runs through analysis, and he can't resist a big juicy
pile of data."

The pages felt slick under Serena's fingers. "Why kill leaves?
You both have new datapads."

Carl tidied up the printouts with a sigh. "We do. Nice, heavy
units in metal cases. For new ideas to stick, Justin also needs to
anchor them deep in emotion. Since anger is his most likely initial
reaction, letting him work through it without interference could

get dangerous. His fists are lethal enough. I'd rather not give him weapons when he isn't thinking."

"He always hears me," Serena said. "If you want a hand."

SHE WAS PULLING the third batch of dumplings off the stove when Pete showed up, looking wilted like late autumn vines gone brittle with cold. He nodded at Carl in passing and started a pot of tea.

"I've been ordered to tell Serena that Justin will be down quote 'in another minute, I swear,' end quote," he said. "He's yakking on the phone in the hall. Bumped right into me, told me off, and walked away. Self-centered little shit, isn't he?"

"When did 'self-centered shit' enter the lexicon of personality classifications?" Carl said.

"He elbowed me in the ribs, and he has very hard elbows. Don't get huffy." Pete took up all the space gathering supplies to make toast, so Serena took a cup of tea away to the dining table. Pete tracked her hurried departure with a look of wounded surprise. "You too? What's got you riled?"

"You," Serena told him. "I know you aren't trying to hurt, only you're nothing but thorns right now. It's okay. I'll stay out of reach."

"And thus am I chastised with sweet courtesy." Pete's amusement unfurled, green and sweet and rustling. He plopped down on a stool at the bar. "My apologies, Carl. I take back every disparaging comment I ever made about your inability to manage insomnia without hypnotics."

"Memory bleed-through?" Carl asked. "How bad?"

"Bloody is an almighty appropriate description for the nightmares, and I triggered yesterday with eyes wide open. Ready or not, it's coming up. I'd rather not have a meltdown—*another* one, to be strictly accurate—somewhere public. Will you please work with me on this?"

"Can it wait a few more hours?" Carl laid out the papers again where Pete could view them. "No more than that, I promise. We'll have plenty of privacy and time on the road back to Seattle."

"Didn't we just drive *from* there?" Pete looked over the charts. "What's the rush? I thought we were done with pseudo-heroics."

Carl tapped the pictures. "Once Justin wraps his brain around this, there'll be no holding him back. Escorting him home is the least we can do to repay him for all his help."

"Gratitude, right." Under the leafy humor Pete was still prickly tempered, and his voice coiled tight. "Do me a favor, Carl. I'll be patient, but don't insult my intelligence. You and I both know how you feel about him."

He was frowning over numbers and didn't see Carl's reaction to the pointed comment, but Serena did. It was a look full of slashing temper and spread wings, mantling over nervousness, of all things. When he saw that Serena was watching, he swatted her with the same worried glare.

Red Dog bristled, but amusement nipped at her too, bumped Red Dog out of the way and stood dancing in its place. "Silly bird," Serena said. "I won't say anything, but I think he knows and doesn't mind."

She kept the rest of her thoughts hidden behind fur and dark-ness. Carl was more uptight than Naomi and Justin combined, and an offer to share might embarrass him to death on the spot. It would be fun to tease, though.

She was still wrestling with temptation when Justin came limping into the room. He kept one shoulder against the wall as a navigational guide, and every bright facet of him was focused on the earbug he wore. Affirmatives and negatives were his main contributions to a conversation, although he tossed in an occa-sional "Allie handles that, or the lawyers."

Serena got him to the table and fed him a steamer's worth of egg dumplings, a piece of toast, and orange juice before he finished the call. His eyes darted around the room, touching on

Carl, measuring Pete's studied disinterest, and halting on Serena's face. Sparks fell behind a cloudy frown where broken edges rubbed together.

"So much for that promise," he said. "I didn't even get downstairs before going into 'oblivious idiot' mode, never mind breakfast."

Pete said, "You did eat. You're welcome."

Justin tucked the earpiece in a pocket. "For what?"

"He took away the horseradish and the hot sauce," Serena said. "I wanted to see if you'd notice, but he said it would be mean. Maybe next time."

Her rough humor sanded down those jagged painful points, and Justin pulled out a handset to make some notes. The frown returned. "Hey, this isn't my—did Neil take my new phone with him?"

Carl said, "He tried to swap back before he left last night. You kept pushing it away and growling at him, so he said he'd keep it until you complained."

Pete leaned close and whispered into Carl's ear, then left the room. Once he was gone, Carl left the counter to take a seat across the table from Justin. "And before you get distracted again, there's some news you need to see."

He slid over the papers without explanation. Justin glanced at the pictures, and aggravation sparked high. "Again? I am so tired of this tabloid bullshit. Paternity was settled before the poor kid was even born. It isn't Ryan's fault his mother dyes her hair. Why won't the damned scandal sheets let it drop?"

"I pulled those from archives, to be sure you saw the resemblance," Carl said in a low voice: hard claws grasping gently. "There's a legal document signed by Helen underneath, plus four lab reports and personal notes from her and Alison both. Note the dates and the petitioning client names on the labwork, please. Compare the results."

Thoughts started roiling under Justin's crackled surface, dark and flashing by turns. Serena slid her hand onto his leg, smoothed her cheek against his shoulder. Worry was a bitter note in the spice of his scent. He put a hand over hers.

For a few minutes everything was quiet but for the kitchen equipment rumbling about being ignored. Justin took a deep breath, pressure built under Serena's hands, and suddenly holding him wasn't enough to help hold everything together.

The papers shrieked, falling to the floor in torn strips. Justin's handset squealed when his fingers slipped over codes. Carl's silence was so full of words *not* said that Serena had to put her hands over her ears.

Justin's voice was worst of all, a low screech of edges grinding. "Helen," he said. "No, you listen, you lying bitch. You made me a laughingstock and stole my own fucking son from me. Don't expect me to kiss and make nice 'for Ryan's sake.' Fuck, no. I'll see you in hell first. I will ruin you for this. I will *destroy* you. You just wait and see."

He rapped the handset against the table. "I'm going to kill her," he said. "Her and Prickface both."

"No, you won't," Carl said, steady and certain. Serena's skin prickled at the force of it. The irresistible sound drew Justin's sparking anger from distant targets to the immediate, accessible one.

"Who's going to stop me?" he demanded. "You? Are you going to *persuade* me to calm down? Don't even think about it. Do not do it. I will kill you if you even open your mouth, I swear I will."

The splintering flare of temper blinded Serena to everything but the need to choose between attack or withdrawal. *No-threat. Never-threat*, she told herself, but her heart still raced, and she couldn't see anything but that dazzling rage. She retreated, fumbling and stumbling into the close haven of sheltering wings.

Justin's eyes went dark, looking at her in Carl's arms, and it hurt just to watch him try to grasp all the serrated pieces of pain and betrayal inside.

The phone in his hand shattered, and shards of plastic spilled between his fingers. His left foot caught in carpet when he stood up, and he stumbled before catching himself.

Serena squinted past *threat/no-threat*, and fear stabbed at her with sharp hedgehog spines. She couldn't stop reacting, not with all that turbulent anguish so close. Defenses muscled up, red and gray and tight in shoulders and legs.

Justin kept staring at Carl with his face stiff and eyes cold like black diamonds. So angry. So *hard*. "Too hard," Serena whispered. "Too sharp, it gets everyone worked up. I don't want to hit you. See us as *no-threat*, Justin, please."

His gaze shifted to her, and his surprise was a blaze of turning facets. Then he looked down fast, trembling with the effort of holding still when he wanted to lash out. He set down the squashed handset with excruciating precision, dug out the earpiece, and slid them both across the table. This time when he looked up there was only pain shining in his eyes, pure and clean.

"I—" he shook his head. "I didn't mean—I need—"

His voice rasped and broke, became a sob. Upstairs, feet made floorboards creak and heavier weights thumped and scraped: people were moving and packing. Carl's arms tightened around Serena, and he said whisper-soft, "We know what you need. Ryan's in Seattle. Dan left us priority travel waivers. You'll see him before midnight."

THE TRAFFIC MONITORING system sounded an alarm just south of Portland. Justin heard the buzzer from his position lying flat on the van's rearmost seat, felt the vehicle shimmy as Naomi checked the situation. Next, a phone pinged. Justin rejected the idea of sitting up to see what was going on. There was no time like the present to learn when to keep his head down and his mouth shut.

After a short whispered conversation, Serena crept back to sit beside him. Justin hated the guarded look on her face. She was hesitant now, where before she'd been bold. He'd done that to her with his temper and his total lack of impulse control.

"I can't even blame it on the brain damage," he said. "I used to get into so much trouble with angry calls that my lawyer carried a jammer."

Serena frowned, thoughtful. "Do you want to compare tantrums? I killed two people Sunday night."

"Shit." Justin let his head drop back against the seat. "No. It's just that I'm predictable. Allie takes away my phone if I even look irritable. How could Carl not see that coming?"

"Ah." Serena touched his chin with one finger. "He saw. He said a storm would be better than no spark at all. Brave bird, flying through lightning to reach you, even when he knew you might strike him."

The inside of Serena's head was a strange place, but Justin liked it. He liked it a lot. "Brave you, stepping in and grounding me. Did I thank Carl? Did I thank *you*?"

"Not yet. Touch." She danced her fingers up his leg.

Naomi said loudly, "Don't you dare, Serena. I will stop this car and slap you silly if you hump him in the backseat."

"Not happening," Justin assured her. "Not."

"No, it isn't. Serena, give him the phone. Justin, it's your ex. She's gone to a lot of trouble to reach you, forwarding through Alison to Parker to Carl to me."

Serena waved a handset and flashed a mischievous smile. "I'll hold it."

Justin let her lie with her head on his chest. It made her happy, and he needed a dose of calm and happy. The idea of confronting Helen made his blood turn to ice.

He had to get past the raw hurt to the important things, like protecting Ryan from as much fallout as possible. They would have to negotiate new arrangements like civilized people. Helen liked hurting him, and he would have to let her do it, because otherwise she could put armed guards and an army of lawyers between him and Ryan. He'd provided more than enough evidence to be declared a threat.

"Ready?" Serena's smile was gone.

"No."

"Too bad." She pointed the phone at him.

CHAPTER TWENTY-ONE

HELEN WAS GLARING, FROZEN on the hold screen. Justin's whole body thrummed with the ache of lost chances and poisoned love. Helen's golden hair was immaculately arranged, and her creamy smooth skin was flushed with color. Clear blue eyes snapped with the expressive intensity that had made her an iconic entertainer.

She was as beautiful as she'd ever been. Justin wanted to cry. He tapped 'resume call' instead. "Hi, Helen. You look eager for round two."

Her frown took on an edge of martyred patience. "Don't start with me, Justin. I know all your petulant little snits and sulks. Just tell me you didn't mean any of it. Tell me you didn't mean any of those horrible things you said."

"Now or then?" At the time he had absolutely meant every word.

He winced as Serena poked him in the ribs, and Helen caught her lower lip between her lovely white teeth. "Please don't be like this. I am trying very hard to be reasonable. Don't start with the nit-picking and the nastiness."

Her voice wavered, and tears welled up in her eyes. "Please,

Justin. If you ever loved me, help me make this work. For Ryan's sake. I'm begging you."

Justin knew Helen was milking the situation for every last drop of pathos, but it didn't matter. It never had. She could always cut straight to his heart. "Helen, I loved you until you left and for a long time afterwards. Yes, I was only ranting, and of course I will sit down with you and your legal team and agree to whatever new contracts you think will be best for Ryan."

She looked away for a moment, regaining her composure on a single inhalation and a blink. "Good. That's good. I only want what's best for him, even if I'm afraid it's more of you and less of me in his life. We'll work it all out, I promise. But I want one other thing too. First."

Justin braced himself. He'd set himself up. He would deal with the consequences. "What?"

"You. I want you at my party tomorrow. Clean, groomed, and in a proper suit. Nothing less than a full evening of glam and glad-handing. If you do that, then I will erase that vile call record and be the most reasonable woman in the world when it comes to visitation and so on. If you don't—"

Narrowed eyes delivered a grim promise of retribution.

"Deal," Justin said with all possible haste. The satisfaction of embarrassing him was a minor punishment, all things considered. "On record and witnessed, so don't try to wriggle out of it later. I have two conditions of my own: I get to talk to Ryan as soon as possible, in private, and I choose my own escort tomorrow. Take it or leave it. I will not hang on your arm as if we're still a couple."

Helen's laughter rang with honest humor. "I have a very nice piece of arm candy already. Bring your whole harem if you want. Your girl Friday has all the details. She is quite good at the part of her job where she gets to wear clothes."

There was no good answer to that bit of nastiness. Serena stirred. Justin tightened his grip in her hair. After a moment Helen said, "Well, then. I'll stay in touch with your other minions. The big one offered his house for a private rendezvous, and my people like it, so we'll see you there. "

She puckered her lips in a kiss and disconnected. After a moment Justin remembered to breathe. "That went well."

Naomi said, "Jaylin is dying for that woman's autograph, but I don't know if I could ask for it without slapping her first. I can't decide if 'minion' or 'harem' was more offensive."

"For the record I do use the word 'keeper.' I never was exactly proficient with everyday details, as you may have noticed. Helen certainly did."

Serena dropped the phone on the seat and squeezed Justin tight. "Hurt and hurting, around and around. You're both dizzy-making."

"I'm trying to stop the spin." Justin put his arms around her in return. "I don't know if Tyler and Alison are enough backup. They get busy at parties, and Helen will throw high-society snobs at me all evening. Can I convince you to come along? It should be quite a show."

The phone buzzed again. The screen displayed a red and gold CSB seal but no name. The call was being forwarded from Justin's account again, but when he accepted it, nothing happened. He raised his voice. "What is this? *Who* is this?"

"Woop. Forgotta cam'ra." the caller said in a slow, thick voice. Soon Neil was peering out of the screen from a lens too close to his face. The gray eye, a slice of pasty cheek and black bristles receded to a civilized distance, revealing a white wall and medical equipment. "There y'ar, Jussin."

"Are you drunk, Agent McAllister?"

"I woke uppith idea—" Neil blinked owlishly. "Yurrahdam liar. Stupid rot-poof phone's stone dead. Gettin' autopsy now."

Shock made Justin's skin go cold and then hot. "What do you mean *autopsy*? That thing is a prototype. If it isn't performing to spec then the developers will want it back."

Neil's face was replaced by Dan's dark scowling profile and

then a random shot of wall. "You are a pain in my ass, hayseed. I turn my back on you for five minutes, and you pickpocket your nurse? Just wait until you wake up for real."

After a mumbled response Dan moved away and spoke directly to Justin. "Sorry. The handset died when he was in pre-op for repairs, and now he's got a bug in his brain. He's hard to keep down for recovery short of hard restraints, which are contraindicated, what with the suicide programming and all. Disregard the babbling. He won't remember it."

Justin said, "Consider it disregarded, but please don't let him dismantle that phone."

"Too late. He gave the carcass to some nice sober Bureau techs before surgery. I'll see if I can recover the remains for you. Gotta go."

He disconnected. Justin stared at the blank screen. "Is it me, or was that call strange?"

"Strange." Serena touched Justin's chin. "You're the expert on that."

"Funny." He looked up Alison's number. "I'd better pass along the bad news."

THEY REACHED Carl's house just before midnight, and the welcoming committee arrived an instant after the door opened.

Ryan's forward charge ended in a leaping bear hug. Justin got his hands up in time, but his balance was off. His left leg twisted under the extra weight and the predictable consequences followed. He landed on his ass with an armload of startled little boy.

The rippling shock of impact passed in an instant, barely noticeable, but Ryan squirmed and pushed back with a yelp. Parker took the boy by one arm, Serena took the other, and they lifted him away. Justin accepted a hand up from Naomi, bumped against Carl, and looked down at—

His son.

The reality of it hit him all over again, like a hammer straight to the chest. His ribs ached as his lungs and his heart just stopped. Everything stopped. He couldn't breathe, couldn't speak. Couldn't *think*.

Helen had barely let him touch her baby, so protective and resentful that she'd made every encounter hellish. Justin had still insisted on visitation, as much to annoy her as to reassure himself that a man he hated was treating them well.

The first time he'd picked up Ryan had been at the boy's third birthday party. Ryan was an irrepressible ball of energy at that age. He would run straight at any adult in the vicinity, confident that he would be picked up and cuddled on arrival. He said, "Hug!" to Justin as if it were an inalienable right, and then he said, "Down!" with equal imperiousness and continued his rounds of the room.

"What's wrong?" Ryan asked. He was gazing up at Justin with fear written across his face. He'd gotten his mother's nose, lucky child, but those eyes, the jaw—Justin felt ground to dust between elation and sorrow. He'd loved his ex-wife's child from the moment of that first embrace, but the emotion had been steeped in bitterness and poisoned by envy.

His son. All this time. What was he supposed to say? When the silence dragged on, Ryan's worry melted into disgust. "I *knew* it," he said. "You don't want me either."

Pete said heartily, "From comedy to tragedy in five seconds flat. That is impressive, Justin. It's also blocking the hall. Will you please skip ahead to the happy-happy part, so Carl and I can get past you?"

His tone held just enough sarcasm to tickle but not enough to cut. Ryan looked around with a tense frown, then turned in place as if only now realizing that he was in the middle of a crowd. "Who are all you people?"

The boisterous, loving toddler was gone, grown into a wary child who shrank from strangers and believed he wasn't wanted. Justin wondered when that had started. He also wished that he could get away with pounding Robert Armstrong's handsome face into a bloody pulp.

The past was beyond any power to change. Justin went down on his right knee, braced and secure, and spread his arms wide.

"Hug," he said, as if it was his right to ask.

HOPE

RESTORATION DAY 7

We are who we are today because the power of hope drove a select few to accomplish miracles. They kept the faith, committed their hearts to the service of others, and sacrificed their lives to our Restoration. Rejoice in their victory.

—*A Young Citizen's Guide to Restoration Week*

CHAPTER TWENTY-TWO

THE DRESS WAS NAOMI'S undoing. She shook it out of its wrappings and slipped it on, and the elegant reflection in the vanity mirror overwhelmed her.

The silver cheongsam and matching leggings were silky-soft, piped and embroidered in black, and they came with accessories that probably cost more than she'd spent on food in July. Call it an apology, Helen Armstrong had said with a breezy wave, as if clothes and cosmetics would make up for rudeness.

Maybe in her world they did. Naomi didn't know the rules, and Serena had never been good about following them even when she'd been surrounded by affluence. She had been born to privilege, but she'd seldom exercised it.

Helen had apologized in words too, a speech delivered with a sincerity that made the woman impossible to hate. On meeting them at the hotel, she'd worked her way through the group with fluttery hugs for everyone except Parker and then escorted them to these rooms.

She'd also pulled Naomi aside and whispered, "Someone tells me you know a fan who might like this."

Naomi picked up the datapad loaded with imagery, engraved

with an autograph, and carrying a provenance seal. Everything had changed forever. The proof was all around her, in an expensive hotel suite rented solely for the convenience of *dressing*, and she didn't know how to handle it.

She did know someone who would, and that someone was only a phone call away.

After a full minute of joyful shrieking, Jaylin delivered an earful of advice that swept Naomi's fears into a tiny pile and blew them away with laughter. Then Naomi spent a half hour being briefed on the incomprehensible misdeeds of Malaysian investment firms. She offered her ignorant condolences and made Jaylin laugh in turn, and they both said their good-byes with lighter hearts.

A knock came at the connecting door. Naomi's nervousness bubbled up again when Alison slipped inside. The woman looked more like a little queen than ever. Her deep blue dress hugged every curve, her skin was porcelain perfection, and her hair swept up into an elaborate crown of dark curls.

Naomi asked, "Am I late? I'll be ready in a flash."

Alison's smile lit up her whole face. "Oh, no. Relax. There's plenty of time. Carl and Pete just threw Justin into the shower and trundled Ryan off for supper. God bless them for volunteering to help tonight. Helen took all her staff away with her, and it's been crazy busy. You should see all the snapshots I've gotten."

Naomi wasn't given a choice. Alison activated the wall screen with a controller worked into her bracelet. That drowning sense of strangeness threatened to swallow Naomi whole again, but her lips still curved into a smile as the images flashed up.

The first ones were of Carl and Pete with Ryan a laughing blur between them. The angle of the shots made Carl into a big pale afterimage of Pete's solid darker form in the foreground, and both of them radiated exasperated amusement.

More pictures flicked past: Helen, a figure of poignant regret and hope in stark focus with Justin looking away; Naomi and

Serena framed by an elevator door looking shell-shocked with Parker watching them over one shoulder; Tyler giving the lens a cross-eyed grin.

The best image was one of Justin. He'd spent the night with Ryan curled up in his lap on Carl's big recliner chair. Alison had caught them backlit by morning sun, Justin's chin resting on Ryan's scalp, both of them sleepy and scowling. The affectionate pose beautifully underscored their extraordinary resemblance.

"Adorable," Naomi said, with a heady sense of joy because Alison hadn't cropped out Serena, dozing on the floor with her head at Justin's knee and her hand on Ryan's leg.

People mattered. Things didn't. She couldn't have asked for a better reminder. "Thank you. I needed that."

Alison nodded, which set her earrings swinging. "I'm delighted that you're joining us, but these things can be nerve-wracking. Let's finish getting you into your social armor, and I'll tell you all about the ridiculous excesses I've seen over the past two years."

In short order Alison had lifted Naomi's spirits with tales of various party mishaps, helped her primp her hair into a sleek black cap, and applied cosmetics. Then she grinned, saying, "Parker's eyes are going to fall out. Shall we tackle Serena now?"

"No." Serena had towel-dried her hair, tossed on her slinky black outfit with her nostrils pinched shut, and retreated to the balcony for fresh air. "She's dressed and excited. Let's not push our luck."

Alison's grin settled into a more guarded smile. "Are we pushing you? Oh, I hope not. It should be fun, or as much fun as life in a fishbowl can be. Is that what's bothering you? All the checking and double-checking?"

"Not at all." Naomi thought of the uniformed private security they'd passed in the halls, the posted signs alerting guests to enhanced surveillance and CSB officers setting up stations in the lobby. She recalled the CAF units she'd spotted on the roof. This gathering of so many public figures in one location was a risk that was being calculated very carefully after recent events. "No, it isn't the security, it's the guests. I don't want to embarrass anyone."

Alison brightened again. "Is that all? Put your mind at ease. Justin loathes snobs more than you can imagine. Whatever you do or say will be fine. You do know he invited Parker specifically to keep everyone else at arm's length and make them uncomfortable, right?"

"Yes, and honestly, I can't think of anything more fun than watching that." Naomi smiled as anticipation tingled to life, driving out the fear. "Except maybe watching Helen watch Serena all night."

ONCE THE EATING and the speeches were done, most of the round dining tables emptied, and the aisles grew crowded with socializing guests. Serena watched every eddy and whorl, listened to all of its random shifting murmurs: *happy-bored-busy-waiting-anxious-happy-bored*.

The motion around the perimeter of the room made patterns as intricate as anything the guests were attempting on the dance floor in one corner. The roving servers were avoiding zones occupied by bottom-pinchers and cleavage-bumpers, and Serena made certain she stepped on the right toes as she homed in on her own quarry.

A russet-skinned woman with sleek ebony hair was lecturing a captive audience. Helen was one of the five hiding yawns behind smiles. Justin had bet Serena that she couldn't drive away the bore. Naomi declared clothing, food, drink, furniture, and weapons off-limits. Alison was the referee. She sailed along at Serena's side, as graceful as a little swan with Tyler on her arm like a sparkly decoration that radiated *gentle-happy-giddy* with every step.

Wild and wooly feelings bounced around inside Serena's head, grateful to be allowed out even on leashes, eager to play. She got a good grip on everyone as she arrived. "Hi, Helen! I'm rescuing you."

The speaker stopped midrant. Helen frowned, kitten-soft, pale and beautiful. Serena wouldn't underestimate her claws, but she couldn't hate a pretty cat for hissing, not when its tail had been stepped on so often that it was crooked. She leaned in and said loudly, "Introduce me to the talking lady."

After the awkward silence, Helen said, "Aggie, this is Serena Nguyen, a dear friend of Justin's. You know how Justin is. Serena, meet Agnes Dudek. She produces a serial for my disreputable friends here. Are you familiar with her work?"

"Nope. Is it porn? I like porn."

"Serena!" Helen spluttered, and the men in the group all laughed.

Agnes spluttered too, flushing darker from her high forehead all the way to the generous décolletage of her gown. She gave Serena's tunic a look of disdain, saying "Helen, I believe your charity case needs sobering up. We'll talk later."

She stalked off in a swirl of heavy perfume and injured dignity, and Helen tittered. There was no other word for it. She put one hand over her mouth and waved vaguely at Serena with the other. The fingers said *thank-you* with a flash of irritation. Alison tugged Serena's sleeve. "That's enough. We need to get back now."

Helen might've assigned Justin a back table as an insult, but its location suited their little group. Justin sat slouched in formal penguin clothes rumpled and loose, and Parker stood sentinel behind him in the corner, all in black with folded arms and hard eyes holding the world at bay. Naomi was silver to his shadow, sitting with her chair angled between him and Justin. Serena sat where she could touch Naomi and Justin both, and contentment curled its warm and fuzzy tail around her shoulders.

Alison and Tyler joined a group standing just out of Parker's effective glare range. Alison pulled one woman aside and spoke with her in low tones while Tyler dazzled everyone else with his shiny smiles and chatter.

Justin said, "Tell me how you did it," and laughed when Serena did.

"You are incorrigible," Naomi said with a smile, but her eyes said *worried*. Serena returned the smile with a brush of fingers: touch to reassure, gaze steady to let Naomi judge for herself. She was strong. She could handle *social*. She didn't want to be the one to end the fun early, even if the fun gnawed at her self-control.

Naomi said to Justin, "Ask her about the incident involving a city councilor and a bowl of fruit."

Serena said, "Blunt words frighten bad people." She'd learned early that acting out was the fastest, easiest way to push others off-balance and regain her own. "But peeled grapes under the collar are more fun."

Justin laughed again. "I wish I could've seen that."

A whisper of *watch-beware-fear* passed through the swirl of voices and motion. Red Dog and Gray Dog came leaping up to the forefront of Serena's mind. Parker lifted his chin and looked at her almost as if he could see her alarmed companions. *Steady*, his frown warned her, and then the moment passed. The crowd settled into a harmless mumbling dazzle again.

She still felt itchy and unsettled, and she moved closer to Justin. He jogged her elbow. "Bet you can't get that guy in blue to give you a kiss in front of his boyfriend."

Her skin prickled. Fur and scales shifted insistently on the inside. The dogs weren't alone in their wariness. Every part of her whispered *move-move-move*. "Bet I can," she said.

PETE LIFTED his head from his losing poker hand. "Did you hear that?"

Carl kept his eyes on the cards while he listened, just in case

Pete was setting up another sleight-of-hand cheat. The voices in the hall were low and calm. Someone was being questioned by the on-duty guard stationed near the elevators.

The party downstairs had been going on for hours and would likely continue well past the approaching midnight hour. The CAF units and Bureau personnel coordinating with private security were all on high alert. Only screened guests reached the upper floors. The stairs were guarded, and elevators were running operator-on-call.

The door chimed, announcing that the visitor had passed muster. Carl checked the hall camera to be on the safe side. The screen displayed the infinitely unlikely sight of Daniel Patterson in snappy formal wear.

The tux was all in soft warm grays that brought out the cinnamon undertones to his skin, but it wasn't tailored. The line of the pistol holster showed. Neil McAllister was there too, wheelchair-bound and looking tired in gray sweats with a CSB logo on the sleeve.

Dan grinned when the door opened. "Speechless. I love it." Then he stepped up close, lifted his chin to whisper in Carl's ear. "Stay speechless and let us inside nice and slow. One sound, one wrong move, and this turns ugly."

Carl squelched the instinctive surge of fear and followed orders. Despite the threat, every observable cue insisted Neil and Dan still considered themselves allies.

As soon as the door closed behind Neil, Dan pulled out the pistol. "Hello, Dr. Hamil. Don't open your mouth. I will shoot you. Come stand with your buddy here."

Pete came to his feet in a rush, eyes darting from Dan to Carl and back. Carl held his gaze and nodded encouragement. He still sensed no aggression from Dan. The man was running defense for Neil, a message underscored by the way he backed up once Pete came past the couch to Carl's side.

That shift in position dropped the ambient tension below critical mass, but Pete was still about two breaths away from panic. Carl kept one hand in view, palm out, and raised the other to Pete's arm, gripping hard with a message: there was a time to fight or flee. This was neither.

Neil rolled to the seating area and levered himself onto a couch. "Relax. We're tying off loose ends, that's all."

Dan said sharply, "Get it over with, will you?"

Neil consulted his handset. "I'm working on it. Astrograph, bailout, oxy—"

The words stopped making sense. Carl felt a singular sense of dislocation. Neil's lips were moving, sound emerged, but no meaning registered.

Reflexes took over.

When he could see and hear clearly again, his heart was racing. He was looking over Dan's head at Neil, who was gray-faced and saying, "We're on the same side, Carl. Friends. See? Look at my hands. Empty. Look at me. *See* me. You can put him down now. Please, Carl. Please put him down."

It sounded like he'd been repeating himself for a while.

Dan shuddered, sweaty skin slick under Carl's fingers, sliding against his arm. Carl kept his muscles locked and motionless. If either of them moved even a centimeter in the wrong direction, this particular hold would crush either the man's spinal cord or his trachea.

Pete was sitting a few meters away: alive, dazed, but otherwise unharmed. Carl took three deep breaths. "I'm letting go. Do. Not. Move. Got it?"

He took Dan's gurgle for assent and carefully released him. Dan crashed to his knees, hunched over and panting for breath. "Goddamn, Neil," he said hoarsely. "You said they'd either drop or go after you. You couldn't mention, 'Oh, and by the way this might make Goliath go berserk.' "

"I didn't know," Neil said. "Carl's profile is verified. He

should've gone down like a felled tree. They're called *drop* triggers, and they can't be erased."

Neil had used hypnotic keys meant as a last resort control on a rogue neopsych, and he hadn't trusted the records he had on Pete. Carl put those points in context and made the connection.

"I thought you weren't looking into Pete's kidnapping until later," he said.

"We ran across the trail unexpectedly," Neil said. "Why didn't you drop, Carl?"

There was suspicion in those ice-gray eyes now. Carl struggled to respond to the question and not the antagonism. He wasn't a threat. Neil didn't want him to be one.

"Eddie and I had our own copy of the workup he brought out of Rydder with me. We aren't stupid. We knew why the Bureau made that a contingency on their assistance. Primary triggers can't be erased, but they can be altered. Four to six words in a drop sequence. For me, the first two induce temporary deafness. Keep going, and autonomic defense routines come online. Delta agents know all about those."

"Yours are strictly reactive, though. I caught that, thank God. Dan froze, you froze. I talked, you listened."

"I don't like hurting people, even if I am unfortunately well equipped for it."

Dan retrieved his pistol, which had ended up in a corner. He looked worriedly at Pete in passing. "Is he going to snap out of that any time soon?"

"After the week he's had? You must be kidding." Carl helped Pete to the couch. Physical contact provided emotional anchoring they both desperately needed. Pete's hands were cold and wet, his body trembling from physiological and neurological overload. Carl brushed back salt-and-pepper hair and ran his other hand down Pete's arm, just *so*. The silent directive was accepted with a blink and a sigh, and Pete slid into a doze.

Dan stopped next to Neil's chair. The pistol went into its

holster with a sharp click, and he pulled out a phone to send a message. "We couldn't ask," he said in a voice full of remorse. "We couldn't trust you. Not in this."

"I do understand that." Carl relaxed as much as possible, given that adrenaline rebound was doing his temper no favors. "What kind of loose ends put Pete's confidential records in your hands and put you here?"

"The kind of loose ends we're catching rats with," Dan said. "Neil, the locals need a come-to-Jesus speech about the tech confiscation order. Then I'll go hunting and pray for luck. You do the explaining and the apologizing. Do a lot of apologizing, will you? And stay *sitting*."

Once Dan was gone, Neil leaned forward and winced. "Update and groveling. Where do you want to start?"

"I'll start with getting Pete into bed. You shook his brain like a baby's rattle, and I care more about his comfort than easing your conscience. Then I'll check on the eight-year-old in the next room, since it's unlikely he slept through that. He's also more important to me than anything you have to offer."

Neil winced again. "Take your time. I'll wait."

Carl stopped himself before he said anything unforgivable. "Thank you."

AFTER THE FIFTH time Justin sent Serena off to cause trouble, Naomi knew she had to put a stop to it. Helen's attempts to avert the confrontations were amusing, but enough was enough.

"She isn't a toy," she whispered.

"She what?" Justin lounged back in his seat so he could watch Serena's eel-like progress through the crowd. His forehead was shiny with sweat, and he mopped at it with his napkin. Then he tugged on his creased suit jacket and sent Naomi the same silly smile he had been using on other people all evening. "Who?"

Until he'd started the poke-the-poseurs game, Naomi had actually enjoyed watching his harmless goofball act. Unlike those who dropped by to curry favor, she was in a position to see the notes Justin consulted. His opinion of his supposed peers was not flattering. That knowledge made his casual use of Serena as a social weapon all the more annoying.

"Stop sending her out to do tricks like she's a dog," she said. "You don't understand how brittle she is."

"Don't I?" Justin leaned forward, forearms braced on the table. He smiled vaguely at the room. "Guess again. Quietly."

Naomi followed the direction of his gaze. Her tone had carried, and people were watching. Self-consciousness boiled up, and with it came the realization that Justin was pressing *hard* on the table. He was also breathing deeply and very slowly, and the pupils of his eyes were huge against the dark irises.

He wasn't sweating because it was stuffy in the room. He was fighting an anxiety attack, hiding it so well that he'd still looked like he was enjoying himself.

Naomi snuck a look at Parker, met eyes bright with a concern that washed over her and cleared her perspective. Serena was having fun, proud of her coping skills. Justin was keeping her at a distance to avoid pushing her into a crisis.

"Never mind," Naomi said, and then Helen was bringing Serena back to the table personally this time, walking fast with shiny fingernails digging into Serena's arm. Her icy smile was a work of art.

Serena's grin was far more dangerous. She disengaged and retreated behind Naomi, saying, "You shouldn't climb up people with those teeny claws. I'm being good tonight, or I would bite them off."

Justin aimed his silly expression at his ex-wife. "Problem?"

Helen's smile stayed frozen in place. "You win. Leave early. I said you had to be on your best behavior for the whole evening, but of course you found a loophole. Get out and take your lawsuit-waiting-to-happen with you before she gives someone a heart attack. You beat me. Again. Happy now?"

Justin was heading for the doors into the hotel hallway before the last word left Helen's lips. Serena hurried after him. Parker watched until they reached the security guards, then went stiff as they turned away and headed for the outside entrance. A frisson of cold emotion brushed across Naomi's skin, lifting the hairs on her arms.

Parker pointed at her and angled his head in Alison's direction. Then he went after Justin and Serena at a pace just short of a jog. *You take care of that set*, was the meaning of the gesture. *I'll take care of the other.*

The trust would've been heartwarming except that Naomi had no idea what she was supposed to do.

CHAPTER TWENTY-THREE

NAOMI FOUND ALISON AND Tyler deeply involved in conversation with a gray-haired, black-skinned woman whose blocky tailored suit was a good match for her round body and emphatic voice. Tyler stepped back to include Naomi in what was apparently a technical discussion. At the first likely pause, Naomi delivered the news that Justin had bailed on them.

Alison excused herself to "pour oil on Helen's waters," and Tyler's casual introduction to Gina Hayabusa included only her name and the information that her company had made Justin's new phone.

"I liked it while I had it," Naomi said, wanting to be polite.

Gina pounced on the compliment with demands for a precise recounting of the functions Naomi had used and a report on the device's performance. Tyler made them both sit down and flagged a server, but even with drinks and Tyler's occasional interjections, the relentless questions felt like an interrogation.

Alison came back with a suggestion. "Why don't we head to the suite? Justin's on his way up already. We can relax in private, you can pick *his* brain, and I'll see if I can pry Manny loose for a strategy session. Dawnstar's exposed in this too, as an investor.

They won't leave you in the lurch, but he needs to know the situation."

Gina checked her wrist, which held a screen on a delicate band. "I won't relax until I have that prototype in a testing rig that proves it's rot-clean. If the software's glitching, that's disaster enough. Lydia, Abdul, and I have all been running syncing demos with our units all evening. Who knows how many people we've infected?"

Naomi told herself that it wasn't her business, and then hastily covered a yawn with her hand. Alison saw it and winked. "Let's have some tea while they plot," she said in a low voice. "We can compare catty party notes."

"Deal," Naomi said.

SETTLING PETE WAS EASY. Ryan proved more challenging. The boy's diffident dismissal of the commotion as "only thumps, not breaking" provided a chilling glimpse of what he considered normal, but his reluctance to leave his hiding spot in the closet was more revealing yet. Carl had just coaxed him onto the bed when the door swung open. Ryan elbowed him in the chin, diving to hide behind him.

The wheelchair had a squeaky joint. The noise stopped when Neil did, at the bedside. Introductions led to questions. Neil's relatively truthful answers reduced the fight to the kind of slapstick scuffle a child would see as amusing. When relief led to curiosity, Neil included a display of surgical dressings. That started a discussion of why losing a spleen was suboptimal but survivable.

Ryan found the grisly details fascinating, and once he was yawning instead of trembling, Carl whispered him to sleep without a single twinge of guilt.

On the way out, he said, "Interesting definition of wait."

"I frightened an innocent child. Taking responsibility for that and helping him get over it were both more important to me than humoring your bad mood."

His tone stopped Carl in his tracks. Neil looked over his shoulder, then swiveled the chair to face him. "Carl, I don't enjoy being the 'fucking asshole' that Justin calls me. Sometimes I have to be one in the line of duty, but I have two kids of my own. Give me a break, will you?"

Not many people could hold Carl's gaze for more than a second or two. Neil *stared*, deliberately laying bare exhaustion, bitter self-recrimination, and simmering hurt. Carl stepped behind the wheelchair to push him along to the seating area. "Justin considers the nickname a term of endearment, if that makes you feel any better."

Neil snorted.

Before long Carl was bundled up on the couch with hot cocoa and a blanket, ready for his own bedtime story. "Loose ends," he said. "Hold the groveling."

The agent sipped from the mug of cocoa Carl had brought him as a sign of goodwill. "Justin unveiled an operation called Biovitel on Sunday. The man has a phenomenal knack for angel investing, one of many things I learned because I got angry at a dead phone. It's amazing how much research a hundred techs idling away Restoration duty can get done overnight."

Carl gave him a look. Neil said meekly, "Bear with me. If I don't start at the beginning and work my way along, then *I* get lost. Biovitel is rolling out electronics protected by bio-engineered elements. Certain tech stocks started behaving oddly right after the announcement. Our markets are closed for the break, but ones in Hong Kong showed a bubble in similar ventures within hours. Bizarre, since those companies will be at a disadvantage if Biovitel proves as big as its hype."

"Asian market manipulations," Carl said, remembering Jaylin Byrd's offhand comments. "Naomi's friend got called back to work over it."

"So she did. Now I feel bad about not spotting this facet on Thursday. Anyway, financial exchanges can be unpredictable, but when you add in the airline and port closures and Biovitel's R&D facility in Bellevue, it all ties together. The rot outbreaks played right into their hands."

Carl rubbed his aching forehead. Neil went rambling on. "Conditions this week are perfect for limiting the spread of a contagion. I think it was staged for the benefit of a foreign client who wants Biovitel off the field but doesn't want to cripple infrastructure."

Something finally clicked for Carl. "Are you saying these agents of yours are releasing a new chip-rot variant?"

"God, no. They're greedy, not insane." Neil hesitated. "I hope. No, this looks like a savior scam. Sterilization and recycling are cheap enough for people to pitch hardware at the first cry of 'rot' these days. Malware can mimic it. Picture a lot of highly placed people plugging their units into office nets Monday morning and melting it all down by day's end. Someone would draw lines to this party. Fingers would point at Biovitel, with its taboo genetics component."

He waited for Carl's nod before continuing. "Once the blame is solidly pinned on them, someone else provides a miracle solution, steps right into Biovitel's hype, and steals it. Which brings us to the dead phone and to Pete."

After fifty heartbeats Carl said, "Could you please draw a short straight line to the end before I lose my mind?"

"I'm *trying.*" Neil looked down at his lap. "Justin's magic phone died. I dumped the programming onto my own personal analyst and dropped the shell on those boredom-motivated techs with the order to tell me everything. Deecie recognized the kill code, and the techs spotted the trading patterns when they researched the device's history. They traced the financials to accounts with Delta encryptions and passed it all back to me."

He shrugged. "That's as short as I can make several hundred labor hours. The data dump came as a surprise over breakfast, since I didn't recall ordering any of the work. The first random files that I opened contained a specific type of psych outline that I'd seen recently. Yours. Except it wasn't yours."

"It was Pete's," Carl said. "And the people who rewired him are the only people who would have that file other than Rydder. You decided those people were tied to your Bureau rebels. I follow that far. Why the field test?"

"Other communications indicated this venue was a target, but the account profiles and information my techs found could've been fabrications. That's what Deltas *do*. I didn't have time to hunt down proper corroboration. If those were Pete's real triggers, then it was likely we had real intelligence by the tail. Just luck you both were here in Bellevue too. *You* have a knack for *that*. For what it's worth, I apologize for how it went down."

"Keep the rest of the Bureau off my back," Carl said, "and I'll call us even. How long are you here?"

"Until Dan gives up on his forlorn hope. Deltas can be obsessive meddlers, but chances are good that our rats boarded an international cruise ship under assumed names long ago. Even if they are still lurking, his chances of cornering them before they see him are damned slim." Neil leaned back and shut his eyes. "I can wait in Tyler's suite where we left Tom, if you're sick of the sight of me."

Carl considered the offer. Neil wasn't going to ask for help. He was unhappy and disgusted with himself and frustrated beyond belief, but he wasn't even thinking about asking. It made the decision easy.

Carl said, "Promise you'll keep one hand on a phone in case there's a crisis here."

"What?" Neil blinked, frowning.

"I have my own score to settle with your rats," Carl reminded him. "If you'll sit tight and play babysitter here, I'll track down your partner and give him a hand with the search. Maybe we'll get lucky. Can't hurt to try."

The agent pulled himself back into his wheelchair. "I'd argue, but I'm too tired. Go. I'll watch the nursery."

JUSTIN TOOK his weight off his left leg and leaned his aching body against a wall. He was standing near a bank of elevators in a hotel, and he had no idea why he was there.

The marble floors, chandeliers, and gleaming woodwork belonged to a top-tier venue. He wore a tux with a blank keycard in one pocket, he felt as if he'd been hit by a truck, and he was hiding in a corner. It was easy to deduce that he was playing hooky from a high-profile party after a panic attack, but deduction had limits. If his brain didn't cough up details soon, then he would have to play drunk-stupid and ask for help at the desk.

The place was locked up tight. Uniformed CSB personnel were visible all around the lobby, and a cordon of private security officers barred the way to the interior hall where he was standing. Guests were being directed through a set of temporary privacy booths whose curtains were blazoned with CSB logos.

Guests loitered far down the hall near open doorways. Outside, dark skies and street lights were visible past a glittering portico shared with an attached banquet hall.

Justin was pondering Alison's absence when a lean man wearing boots under an all-black suit emerged from one of the booths. A tall woman in a black tunic piped in silver came out with him, clinging to his arm with both hands.

Black hair swung around her face like a veil. The world spun and tilted. *Serena.* Justin pushed off the wall. "Hey. What is going on?"

"Justin!" Serena detached herself from Parker and attached herself to him, and for a few moments he was too busy soothing her to be worried about anything else.

"It's all right," he whispered into her ear. "It's fine."

"It's better," she said at last. Her arms were quivering. "You made me go without you. Don't do that ever again. My head stays quieter when you're close, even when you're crackly. Don't be afraid to cut me. Stay close."

"I'll stay," Justin promised. Serena felt more rational around him, of all people. The universe had a horrible sense of humor.

"This isn't right," Parker said. He had a look on his face now that Justin had seen only a few times before, an oddly distant focus as if he were looking *past* things. "It isn't nerves. Take her outside. Call—"

The elevator chimed. Parker spun to watch several people moved into an arriving empty car and greet its operator. Then he pulled a handset from his jacket and slapped it into Justin's hand. "Get outside now. Call everybody else, after."

Full sentences from Parker were unusual. Snapped as orders they were thoroughly alarming. Adrenaline cranked Justin's pulse up, and terror hit him out of nowhere.

"Wait, Parker." He winced at the force of the glare that came his way, but if there was trouble brewing, then he needed to be twenty floors up, not outside. "Ryan."

Sympathy cut through the anger in Parker's eyes, and he shook his head sharply. "Not him. Not there. Here."

Another elevator car arrived, disgorging a clump of guests. Dan Patterson stepped out of the elevator in their wake. A tug on the lapels of a gray jacket bought the agent a second to read his surroundings.

His hands went still when he saw Justin, and he stood straighter at the sight of Parker. "I should've known," he said to no one in particular.

"*You.*" Parker could load a lot of frustration into a single quiet syllable. "What. The. Fuck?"

"I'm on a rat-catching expedition." Dan glanced at the lobby. "Were you getting heebie-jeebies? That figures. Take it up with my bodyguard when he gets downstairs from the command center. He volunteered."

Serena said, "There's wrong in the party. I thought it was Blue Dog and Gray fighting, but it's real. There's wrong all around in there."

"That's my dancing girl," Dan said. "Sometimes you almost make sense."

Parker was heading for the fire stairs when the door opened. Carl came through it with his head down, shrugging an armor-lined CSB uniform jacket over a black tee shirt and slacks. The door banged shut behind him, and for the first few steps he looked tense and angry. Then his eyes slid past Parker and Justin to Serena and Dan.

He raised an eyebrow. "Grabbing extra comm sets was a waste of time, was it?"

Dan rolled his eyes. "I stand corrected."

GETTING through the crowd took much longer than Naomi expected. Good-byes turned into chit-chat, and chatting led to new introductions. Progress was indirect and slow. By the time they all reached the hall doors, Naomi's head was so full of new names and faces that it was aching.

The security officers at the interior door waved Gina and Tyler past without looking up from their ID screens, but Alison and Naomi were stopped. "You two will need to exit out the front and enter through the lobby," the officer said. "You've been selected for full sensor searches."

Alison stepped back without comment. Naomi stood her ground. "It's the Sub flag, isn't it? We're not civilized like these other nice people? We might've pocketed rolls or a bottle of wine? Maybe I stole a table knife?"

She'd endured all the earnest after-dinner speeches about

closing the gaps in the social safety net without complaint. She'd said nothing while people who'd never gone hungry a day in their lives except by choice discussed the limits faced by those less fortunate. She could not pretend this was anything but an insult and a personal attack.

Her screener had the grace to look embarrassed. The woman's partner said, "They can do it in the lobby or in custody at the police station, ma'am, but they will scan you. There's a random flag. Don't blame us. It's a Bureau thing."

"Random, my ass." Gina's loud, acid voice startled Naomi as much as it did the assorted bystanders who turned to stare. "As if any of us would be sneaking in contraband or plotting terror attacks. Lie to my face again, I dare you."

"If you want, they'll scan you too." Irritation edged the man's tone. "Ma'am."

"Don't you *ma'am* me." Gina raised her chin. "She's right, isn't she? I've been watching. You're flagging guests who are or have been on the Sub rolls. Who's behind that idiot idea? Income-selective searches are illegal in so many ways that I could stand here all night listing them."

"Orders come to our company from the CSB sector captain, who had his from Central Investigations." The woman glanced around nervously. They were collecting an active audience of men and women who looked more outraged than Naomi had expected. "We don't have discretion in this."

Another male/female pair came in from the hall. These two wore basic dark suits and inset earpieces that were Bureau standard for agents. They brought Tyler back into the room. The man flashed a red and gold badge to the male sentry, and the woman said, "Sir, ladies, if you'll all come out the front with us, we can discuss this in the lobby."

"We'll talk here or not at all," Gina said.

She took a position at Naomi's back with an air of solid permanence. Tyler, on the other hand, eased his weight onto his rear foot as if preparing to run. Alison said to the male agent, "We'll start with a good look at the badges. Do you seriously think you can bully us into following you?"

"It was worth a try," the female agent said, which was a startling answer. Before Naomi could process it, the agent put away the handset she'd been consulting and said to her partner, "Plan and backup are both shot. Cut to wrap five."

Without hesitation the man tapped his earpiece, rattled off an alphanumeric sequence, then said sharply, "Confirmed biothreat, zone alpha! Lock it down. Again, I say biothreat lockdown zone alpha! Lock it down, now!"

The hall doors crashed shut an instant later.

CHAPTER TWENTY-FOUR

T HE INTERIOR ENTRANCE TO the banquet room looked understaffed to Carl. Pairs of security guards blocked each of three double doors, but no one was tending the surveillance monitors on the table near the end of the hall. The screens were active, but the chairs stood empty.

Emergency lights strobed to life on the walls, and sound blasted overhead. Parker was fast. He got a hand onto one of the closing doors before one of the hotel security guards stationed there knocked him away. The door slammed shut, and Parker slammed into the sentry.

Carl put himself between his brother and the other guard just in time. Multiple darts punched into the armor over shoulders and ribs as the rest of the team's "shoot first, sort it out later" reflexes kicked into play.

The jacket did its job. A short struggle ended with him holding an unconscious man as a shield and Parker kneeling beside the man's unconscious partner. Dan had his head down and one hand up, flashing his CSB Central ID at everyone in view. His free hand was pressed over his ear, and he was yelling over the alarms at someone. "You did what? On whose authority?"

None of the guards looked happy, but they were laying down their weapons without prompting. Metal rattled and crashed in the distance, which had to be the security curtains over the lobby windows and doors hitting sills and thresholds.

A half dozen CSB tactical personnel in helmets and heavy protection approached through the muddle of people near the elevators. The unit carried stun batons and riot guns with over-sized mob-suppression magazines, and they left a hushed swirl of retreating guests in their wake.

The unit leader stopped a few meters away upon sighting Dan's Bureau ID. Carl eased his hostage to the floor and put his hands in the clear. Parker rose beside him. A creeping sense of dread scratched down Carl's spine.

"Everybody take it nice and easy!" The Tac leader had to shout to be heard over the alarms. "That's a declared biohazard zone, and that makes it CAF jurisdiction. Is there a problem here, sir?"

He directed that to Dan, who raised his other hand and retreated behind Carl's shoulder. "Maybe. How big is this mess? You're not cleared to release the room?"

"No, sir, not until the CAF brings in their white-suit brigade. Floors one through three are under full containment. Shelter-in-place, above that. We hold the primary site and clear everyone else in the lockdown perimeter to shelter zones. Let's all sit tight, all right? Everything's under control. No sudden moves, nobody gets gassed, stunned, or tranked."

His voice rang loud as the alarms stopped. Despite the people still shouting in the lobby, the sudden quiet seemed heavy and echoing.

Inside the sealed room, something crashed against a wall. That noise was immediately followed by a series of barely audible whines. By the time Carl recognized the sound, Parker was shoving him face-first to the floor.

He hit too fast and too hard because all his muscles had turned to jelly, and he bounced on landing. He couldn't move, couldn't inhale, couldn't even cough past a thick obstruction in his throat.

He spat out a wet mouthful onto the beige carpet. The carpet turned red.

Time slowed to a crawl, leaving Carl a relative eternity to reach the conclusion that he'd been shot in the chest from close range. Logic ended there. He was wearing body armor. Crowd control and armor-piercing bullets didn't mix.

His vision went dim and fuzzy around a dark center, and then his hearing started to go. Parker was cursing, and Dan was yelling, but the angry tones faded in and out, as did the frantic apologies someone was babbling.

There was a lot of distress in that other voice, guilt that begged for absolution. Carl was deciding how to respond to it when someone rolled him onto his back. The snowy silence wrapped itself around him and stole him away.

BODIES JOSTLED all around Naomi as guests surged toward the blocked exits. Deafening klaxons screamed, bouncing echoes off the dance floor, and yellow strobes tore bright streaks through the party-dim chandelier lighting. There were too many people moving in the narrow aisles, and only a steel-tight grip on her forearm kept her from being swept underfoot in the crush.

"What the hell is going on?" Tyler hauled Naomi towards a corner as he shouted the question. She didn't bother answering. Tyler forced his way along by using height and muscle to push or kick away everyone in reach. He'd lifted Alison onto his back, where she was clinging with her skirt hiked up, her feet bare, and the strangest-looking smile on her face.

The suits disappeared into the mob.

Naomi stopped looking for them and stared up at the ceiling over their table. She'd noted the ventilation grills on arrival, just as she had spotted out-routes from every door. It was habit. She always looked.

Biohazard warnings meant a full HVAC shutoff. Everyone who lived or worked in a modern high-rise building knew that. The ribbon on the outflow was still fluttering. The doors were locked, but the air was moving.

The alarms stopped, although the lights kept flashing bright. *Out*, whispered a voice in the middle of her skull, *runrunrunrunrun*, and there was a tight knot of hurt in her chest begging *stay*.

A nearby table went over with a crash, and Tyler staggered as people pressed around them. If he went down, they would all be trampled in seconds. Naomi tugged on his sleeve and pointed up.

The message got through. Tyler swung Alison onto the table, then knelt and laced his fingers together. Naomi kicked off her shoes, put a hand on his shoulder, and placed her foot into his hands.

NOT STEADY. *Not safe*. The feelings dragged at Serena's insides like claws on flesh, keeping the whole den riled up. She made herself deaf and blind to them, kept her hand on Justin's arm, and took a deep breath of cool night air that smelled of dead fish and spilled beer.

Outside they went, across the portico, from one set of CAF soldiers, all stiff-faced and disapproving, to the other set, past a rumbling mass of humanity milling behind crowd barriers. Curious eyes poked at her, *whowhowhowho*, while voices hooted *look-look-lookatme-lookatme*.

Justin listed heavily to the left, pulling Serena off-balance and distracting her from the internal struggle. "Dan needs backup, not batshit," he said. "Do you want to do this or not?"

The growing pressure of *threat* howled, but the dark eyes

watching Serena held only pure, buoyant faith. *Do you want?* he asked, without a hint of doubt that she *could*.

"We can do this," she said. "I hold you up, you hold me steady."

Lights flashed. Horns blared. Metal crashed, doors banged, and soldiers brought up weapons. In a heartbeat they were trapped in the open with guns and motion all around, and all Serena could hear or see was *threat* and *threat* and *threat* everywhere. Only Justin's grip on her wrists kept Red Dog and Brown from tearing loose and taking over.

"Look!" he hissed in her ear, and "Listen!" and she did, saw purpose in all the motion and patterns in maneuvers performed with precision and speed. *Wait and watch* took over from *fight now.* She buried her face against Justin's neck and pulled in breath after breath of spice and stillness that purged all the clamor in her head.

"Sneaky woman," Justin whispered. "Keeping me on my toes by falling apart yourself isn't a risk-free strategy."

Once she held calm at her center again, she could feel a deep echo of something worse than threat to self. "Naomi needs me. Needs us. Now, Justin. We need inside now."

Justin slipped one arm around her waist and limped them both towards the corner of the building. Not safe, not secure, but sheltered from the worst of the uproar of moving vehicles and soldiers. "All right," he said. "How?"

The sky crackled with a hazy burst of lightning, and a "whump" of displaced air gusted over them in an ozone-tainted breeze. Night fell over the hotel, deep shadows leaping to life everywhere from ground to penthouse.

Serena peered upward at the black silhouette of the banquet hall roof now starkly outlined against the radiance of the surrounding downtown skyline. That was where Naomi would go, if she could.

"We climb," she said.

ALL HELL BROKE LOOSE when the lights went out.

Naomi whooped with surprise as she was launched upward into the abrupt darkness, but the sound was lost amidst the renewed yelling and screaming. Her mental image of the grill was clear in memory, and her fingers caught the weave without hesitation.

She felt her way to the edge of the frame, yanked the catch, and levered herself into the shaft feet-first. Seams tore across her shoulders. She slid into the main duct parallel to the floor, and the dust made her eyes water. Chilled air drafted past, riffling her hair. *Stay*, whispered at her center. She ignored the inner plea the same way she was ignoring all the aches from muscles that weren't as fit as they'd once been.

Glaring emergency lights blinked to life over the still-sealed exits. The crowd was a chaotic, shadowy mass around pale island blots of tables. The stampede slowed, denied outlet, but the roar of voices was mind-numbing. Naomi shouted, "Come up! Alison! Tyler! *Up!*"

The view was blotted out by a gasping, laughing shadow. Naomi grabbed Alison by the forearms and squirmed backward with her. "Oh, my God," Alison said. "Good thing I hated this dress."

Tyler jumped up from the tabletop to join them, huffing and puffing and banging into everything with his head and elbows. His body blocked most of the noise and all the light. They sat in the dirty pitch-black and caught their breath.

Go, sang along Naomi's nerves again in discordant contradiction to *stay*, and her heart tied itself in knots. She tucked herself through the compressed somersault necessary to begin crawling headfirst and moved out.

Tyler hissed, "Where are you going? What if the contamination's outside the room?"

"Then we're all dead already. The air's still on. This is all wrong. We have to go. We *need* to go."

"Uh-oh," Tyler muttered. "I know that tone of voice. It's never good news."

"Hush, you," Alison said firmly. "Go, Naomi. We're right behind you."

They reached a T intersection, and Naomi stopped between the horns of a dilemma. Helpless tears welled up. She couldn't move. Alison's hand crept up her leg, a steady soothing touch. "Naomi, what is it?"

The words wouldn't come. She banged a hand down on metal. "Parker." Another slap, another unsatisfying clang. "Serena." She swallowed. "I can't."

She could not choose. She had to choose.

Alison understood. "They both need help? Then we split up. You go right, we'll go left. Problem solved. Tyler, I'll follow her a bit so you can get in front of me."

Her tone was brisk, decisive and sympathetic. Her hand moved, pushing, and then patted one last time. "Go," she said.

Naomi wrapped *go* around the ache that cried *stay* and squirmed down the right-side passage.

THERE WERE PROBABLY SNIPERS on the roof.

Serena mentioned the possibility while she was heading for the fire escape, and Justin couldn't tell if she was joking or not. The soldiers in front of the hotel were starting scans with emergency spotlights, but they hadn't gotten to this corner of the building. As a general rule Justin preferred asking forgiveness over permission, but climbing right into someone's rifle barrel seemed imprudent.

"This is a bad idea," he said. "Pick a new plan, crazy woman."

"No. Naomi is *up*." Serena moved in close enough that her lips brushed Justin's cheek. "Why are you buzzing?" she asked. "Why am I buzzing? Oh." She tapped her ear. "Serena. Go ahead."

Carl had given them both tactical communication earbugs. Justin's was in his pocket, because the directions on using it had slid right off his brain.

Serena said quietly, "You're what? Oh. Will you tell the army we're going up the building? Justin doesn't want to get shot. What? Yes, I'll try."

Justin's pocket buzzed again. "Serena, talk to me."

She put a finger on his lips and spoke to the air. "Listen. Naomi's scared and there's *wrong*, so count to fifty and follow Dan's orders. I'm crazy, but I'm right, and you need to be calm. For Naomi. Please."

A few seconds of silence, more fiddling with the earbug, then: "Is he better? Good. Tell the army fast. We need to dance."

Justin's lips were returned to him. Serena said, "Dan says it's a false alert, but it's all FUBAR inside. He's working the Bureau side, but he'll make sure we're okay with the CAF to go up and help. It's wrong up there, I know it is."

The explanation's sincere delivery didn't make it any more coherent. Justin decided to let it go. "Who needed to calm down? Besides you, I mean. Dan?"

"No, he's bleeding." Serena moved along the side of the building. "He and Carl got shot, and Parker can't help Carl, but he could help Dan, so he needed to be calm so we can be *up*. Come on, *come on, come on*."

She stared up unto the dark, hopping from one foot to the other. Justin's whole body shuddered as chill horror washed through him. "Did you say shot?"

Guilt swelled up. His selfish need for company had brought them all here tonight. Muscles started to shake with the need to find an outlet for emotion. "Alive or dead, Serena? I need to know. It's my fault he's even here. Him, and Ryan, and you, and Alison—"

His breath went out of him in a cough when Serena squeezed him tight. "Not dead. Hurt. Baby-you is safe. He's way-way up high in the nest with fierce Neil. I don't know about anyone else. Naomi needs us now. Don't shatter. I need you quiet and solid. Stay with me."

"I'm here." Carl was alive. His son was safe. His friends were all more competent than he was. He could hope. "I'm staying."

A shout from above gave them permission to climb. Serena hit the ladder release and went up as if she had springs in her feet. Justin shucked the ruined jacket and the dress shoes and followed her. By the time he reached the top, he was nursing a calf cramp.

After tripping over the parapet, he sat down on the flat graveled roof to remove his socks. "I should've asked this earlier, but why is Naomi up?"

Serena helped him to his feet. "I don't know."

The soldier covering their side of the building approached. "Hey, white-shirt. I don't know why the hell you two were allowed up here, but stay out of our way. We have the approaches covered. The doors are bio-sealed, the hatches into the air shafts are locked—"

She stopped speaking as the roof vibrated underfoot. A coal-black line appeared on the dark rooftop a few meters away, near her previous position.

"Brea—" Her voice broke off. Rifles barked. Justin dropped flat at the sound, and Serena landed between him and the parapet wall. The lines on the rooftop expanded to a rectangular blotch, and shadows emerged. The soldier beside Justin grunted and then dropped in her tracks.

One of the other guards got off a shot at the figure rising from the hole, but a second ambusher followed, and three seconds later they held the roof. Night-vision lenses glinted, reflecting distant lights. Justin stood up, wondering what kind of ammunition could —noiselessly, bloodlessly—drop someone wearing body armor.

Something splattered against his throat and face. He spat out a foul-tasting droplet that deadened his lips and then lit them on fire. "Wha' the *fuh*?"

"What the fuck is right," one of ambushers said, and they both charged. It wasn't much of a fight. They caught Justin under the arms, then carried him the few necessary steps backward to efficiently toss him off the roof.

The downward trip went a lot faster than the climb up, but he still lost his temper long before he hit the ground.

THE HOLE WAS UNEXPECTED.

Naomi contemplated the sky glowing city-night gray through the open maintenance access. The panel hung down, blocking the duct ahead. A twisted locking mechanism was its only remaining point of attachment.

She listened now before poking her head out. Sirens, voices on wind, the hum of traffic, a distant bell: all those were innocuous. The groans and the scraping of weight over gravel were more worrisome.

A soft alto voice grumbled close by. The sound was followed by a sniff. Serena said, "Naomi, come out. Up is safe, but we need down again fast."

Naomi wobbled to her feet and was hauled out of the duct into a hug. There was nothing like being enveloped in strength and love to make her feel strong too. The inner chill receded, drowned out by the warmth of here and now, and the hug turned into a tooth-rattling shake.

"Too close, Naomi. You almost ran into the rats. If we hadn't been distracting them—Oh!" Serena rubbed her cheek against Naomi's hair. "You need to be safer."

"Where's the fun in safe?" Naomi said. "Wait. Rats?"

Serena moved off, moving around bodies that stirred and moaned. "Rats with awesome guns like Dan's," she said. "I played dead, but Justin didn't, and they threw him off the roof. Now he's shattered and stormy and not listening. Here. These are for you."

A heavy black jacket landed in Naomi's arms. Night vision glasses landed on it. *Go-go-go* was pounding away inside her head, and *stay* was screaming now, and her skull felt too small. She put the jacket down. "No, Serena. No."

Her brain was stuck on "threw him off the roof." If Justin was broken and dead on the sidewalk three stories down, then why was Serena so calm? "I don't understand."

Serena bent close, and her face resolved out of the darkness. The silver piping on her outfit glimmered. She was wearing night-vision glasses, and her jaw was set under the blank lenses. "Don't *doubt* at me," she said in a voice like heartbreak. "Not you. Trust me, Naomi. Please."

The plea yanked Naomi out of the emotional mire. She leaned in to rub noses. "Always."

The other pair of glasses was stuffed onto her face. Scattered objects and bodies leaped into bright monochrome detail. Serena pointed to her left.

"The rats went down that street," she said. "Justin went after them. I had to wait for you to be safe. Are you coming with me to hunt or not? I'm going hunting, Naomi. They killed your mama. They *don't* get away."

Boiling hot anger slammed into Naomi out of nowhere, so overwhelming that for a few frantic seconds she couldn't even breathe. She had no idea what to do with so much rage. All that vicious energy couldn't be hers.

She closed her eyes and quaked. She wanted to put her head on her mother's lap one more time, to feel shaky hands stroking her hair all the way down her back, to hear her mother's thin voice mumbling reprimands and compliments and wondering where she'd gone wrong, that her smart strong daughter always left her all alone.

The anger wanted out because at last she had somewhere to

aim it. She pictured the bland woman from the banquet hall, with the authoritative suit and authoritative scowl, heard the bland voice sneering. She saw the smirk again. She looked up into Serena's determined frown. "No, they do *not* get away. Lead the way."

The dent in the sidewalk at the bottom of the fire escape gave her a case of giggles that lasted for a full block. The crushed outline was a clear spread-eagled body imprint. By the end of the second block, she was feeling puzzled.

"I don't care how hard the man's skin gets, his insides should've been jellied by a twelve-meter fall," she said. "Not to mention his brain. That's physics."

"Ask him about physics later," Serena said. "When he's not all crackly and crazy-angry."

They reached a block with buildings that had power and lights, then had to detour into an alley and wait for a radio call to distract CAF sentries at a security perimeter. Serena tucked their night-vision glasses inside the ballistic jacket she'd stolen from a paralyzed but furious-looking sniper back on the roof of the banquet hall. Naomi used the delay to wrap her feet in the tattered remains of her leggings.

Serena set off again with confidence. Naomi asked, "How do you know where Justin is? When you say 'crackly,' do you mean you can feel him like you feel me?"

"I'm crazy, not special like you. You're the only one I feel. You and Parker, now. No, I saw crackly, when I could see Justin, and he has a comm in his pocket that talks to the one in my ear, so I know where he goes." Serena paused and tipped her head as if listening. "He's stopped. We should hurry."

CHAPTER TWENTY-FIVE

TYLER KICKED OUT THE intake vent and squeezed himself through the opening before the cover hit the floor. The vent cover bounced away, and he lifted his hands to help Alison out of the duct. Alison closed her eyes and slid forward, trusting him to catch her.

She was set gently on the floor of a room with soft seats and mirrors on the walls. They were in the women's bathroom in the lobby. A yellow emergency flasher provided some light. She got no-signal alerts when she tried calling Parker, then Justin, and then the suite.

The time on the handset caught her by surprise. It felt like a million years since the lights had gone out, but the clock insisted that less than ten minutes had gone by. When she reached for Tyler, he put his hands behind his back and shook his head. A squeaky gasp was all that came out when he tried to speak.

"Scrapes," he gasped. "Blood. Don't look."

Alison's heart melted, and she hugged him close. "Oh, you poor man. You must've been squished in there. Are you all right? I won't faint, I promise."

"I'm fine. Better every second." He embraced her so tightly that he squeezed all the air from her lungs. "God, I love you, Allie." Then he froze, not even breathing. "You can ignore that last part."

Alison stepped back and tucked her arm into his. Tyler had offered up his beating heart to her not so long ago. Maybe it was time to accept the offer. She turned him toward the bathroom door. "Too late. You're not getting rid of me that easily."

Bright light flashed across her face. Tyler immediately stepped in front of her, blocking the glare so that Alison could see the soldier under the headlamp in the doorway. The move also put Tyler in front of the soldier's rifle, and Alison knew he'd done it deliberately.

"Hey, guys," he said in a shaky imitation of calm. "What's up?"

The dark-skinned man facing them was in a decontamination suit blazoned with CAF insignia and "Lt. Molina" on the name badge. The suit's seals were open, the hood down and gloves off. The five soldiers behind him were identically dressed.

"Biohazard lockdown, floors one through three. Maybe you didn't hear the alarm." Lieutenant Molina's eyes slid down Alison's body. "Looks comfy in there, but the designated test-and-shelter is on the second floor. We'll take you up."

He evidently thought he'd found guests screwing in the bathroom, not escapees from a quarantine zone. Alison had no intention of disillusioning him. She ducked under Tyler's elbow and got straight to the point.

"How far does it reach? I need to find Justin Wyatt." If she could find him, then Parker wouldn't be far away. "I'm his business manager, Lieutenant. I can't reach anyone. He has family here. They'll be frantic."

She was feeling a little frantic herself. At least Ryan would be safe enough, well up on the twentieth floor with Carl and Pete. Helen must be climbing the walls, though.

The lieutenant was unimpressed. "Everyone's looking for

someone right now, ma'am. Civilian bandwidths are overloaded. I can't help. Our priority is getting you safe upstairs to shelter."

"Dr. Wyatt is my priority. Him and his family. I am not *sheltering* unless you can tell me he's already there."

Molina tried to stare her down. She stared back. "Kick it up the line if you have to. This is not negotiable."

Tyler moved up beside her and turned that guileless smile of his on Molina. "You don't want to push her," he said. "Think of the publicity. Surely you can call someone?"

The lieutenant moved away to key his comm and returned looking happier. "Wyatt is unaccounted for, but the Bureau team says they'll take you off my hands," he said. "This way."

They parted ways at a point in the wide corridor where a CSB tactical squad stood idle. Alison wondered where their weapons were. The screeners had carried stun wands and pistols. This group's holsters and belts were empty, and they looked uncertain where to put their hands. One of them waved Alison and Tyler past.

Emergency lights shone on the closed banquet room doors, and indistinct announcements were audible through the walls. A table sat blocking a dead-end alcove past the last set of doors. Three people in suits and three more in CAF uniforms were arguing with someone behind it When they shifted, the gap revealed a tall dark man reclining in a chair. A burly woman wearing a medic's badge was working on his left arm while he snarled at the others: "—can't issue orders to the CAF, no. I *can* refuse access, and that's exactly what I'm doing until you start cooperating."

It took Alison a moment to recognize Dan. The dry voice was familiar, but the blood-spattered gray tux threw her off, as did the ashy pallor of the man's skin.

He tried to stand up when he spotted her. The medic shoved him down. "Get up again, and I will put you down with my fists before locking you in restraints."

Alison couldn't find her voice. Tyler spoke for both of them. "Dan? What are you doing here?"

"I have been asking myself that question for some time now." Dan wiggled fingers at Alison. "Hi, tiny tyrant. Nice job bullying the poor soldier boys. Stick around and sit on Parker for me, will you? I have my hands full."

The blood on his tux was bad enough. When the medic tossed away wads of stained cloth Alison's stomach heaved. She turned her back just in time to see Parker arrive through the CSB cordon. He had a rifle in one hand and a pistol in the other, and both hands were so coated in blood that he seemed to be wearing dark gloves.

He looked uninjured except for a fresh scrape under one eye, but he was alone, and fear made Alison feel even more light-headed than the blood. She prayed for strength and asked, "Where's Justin? Where's Serena? Did they get upstairs safe? What is going on?"

Parker barely spared her a weary glance as he strode by. Alison followed with Tyler, nearly running to keep up. Parker tossed the weapons onto the table in front of Dan, and the suits and uniforms backed up so he could make his way into the alcove behind them.

Three medics in CAF uniforms knelt around someone lying on a patch of floor tracked with dark footprints. Alison could see only glimpses of the patient between them: black uniform slacks, red hair, and an oxygen mask. One of the medics was sitting on his legs while the others worked over his chest.

Parker fell to his knees and took the injured man's hand. Alison didn't realize she'd whimpered until Tyler took her in his arms and pulled her face against his chest.

"Don't look," he said. "Don't."

The hair shouldn't be red, it should be blond, and Carl didn't look tall enough, lying on the floor, and he shouldn't be there at all. He should be watching over Ryan, not lying on the floor with blood in his hair and Parker rocking beside him.

The room spun and whirled.

Carl had been watching Ryan. Naomi had been worried about Serena too, and Serena had been with Justin. "Oh, God, no. Not them, too. Where's Justin? Serena? Ryan?"

Tyler held her up, and the haze receded. Dan's voice finally registered, saying, "—and the junior version is upstairs with a Delta agent as a babysitter. I need a commando-sitter. Do you hear me, Alison? I need your help."

She nodded. He needed her. Being busy would be better. "I hear you."

She made herself move, one step at a time, until she reached Parker. There wasn't room to sit, so she stood behind him and watched the medics, who were busy but calm. She took some hope from that and touched Parker's shoulder. He leaned into the contact.

The medics stood up and grabbed their kits. One handed a fluid-filled IV bag to Parker. "You said you know the drill," he said. "This is pumping fluids, the lung's inflated, the other holes are plugged. Watch his ABCs, and shout if he crashes or when the bag empties. Nothing else to do until they let in a gurney. There's serious injuries reported in that lockdown. We need to prep."

The trio edged past the group at the table, all of whom were now caught up in a close inspection of the weapons Parker had brought. Tyler stared after them with a frown on his face. "Why the hell are they leaving?"

Parker reached out to tug Carl's shirt over skin stained with blood smears and disinfectant. "They're setting up triage," he said, rising smoothly to his feet. "Can help there. Can't help him. He needs a fucking hospital."

He stood there silent with both hands flexing, staring at the men in front of the table with an intensity that by rights should have burned them to ashes. Dan cast an eloquent look at Alison. The last thing he needed was a violent interruption, and Parker was not looking at all peaceful.

"Parker, sit down." Alison sat first, to set the example. Her knees felt too weak to hold her up anyway. She lifted Carl's head into her lap, smoothed back the sticky hair and adjusted the oxygen mask and cylinder that her actions had unseated. The gas made a bleak hissing sound.

"Sit," she said again, because someone at the table was yelling about responsibilities, and Parker wasn't listening to her. "Everything will be all right," she insisted.

She found herself the object of the man's despairing hazel gaze and stared back. "*Sit.* Waiting is a horribly hard thing to do when people you love are in danger, but I've had tons of practice. Sit down. I'll show you how it's done."

Parker knelt and took Carl's hand. Alison put her hand over his and looked up. Right now she needed someone to tell *her* that everything would be all right.

TYLER FELT PANIC RISING UP. Alison looked tinier than ever, all tucked up against Carl's bulk, and Tyler had no idea how to help. Running felt like a good idea. So did vomiting.

"Yo, Tyler. You can shoot, yes?"

Tyler turned to face Dan with his fears and resigned himself to being mocked. "You coached me through my license refresher, so you know I suck at it. Why?"

Dan jerked his head at the CSB suits and CAF uniforms who were all glaring at him. "I need a demonstration, but they won't even try. I can't trust Parker not to shoot these buffoons, and I can't. Shoot, I mean, Not without aggravating the broken collarbone, or worse, the medic. Help me out." He hefted up the rifle with the arm that wasn't in a sling.

Tyler took the weapon. "Who was throwing bullets? The CAF guys were carrying stun wands and trank rifles."

"Not once Parker finished with them. They're barehanded now.

I collected the rest of that." A wave indicated a collection of pistols and riot guns Tyler hadn't even noticed stacked in the corner past Carl. Dan pointed at the wall above the banquet hall doors. "Aim for the ceiling. Keep the muzzle steady, please. Autofire will run through the magazine in five seconds or so. Waste it all."

"One heavily sedated wall, coming right up." Tyler aimed high. The rifle whined. Darts pinged first, followed by solid impacts that sounded like hammer strikes, and then a chunk of wall disintegrated with a loud bang. Tyler ducked and released the trigger. "Dan, you jackass! What the hell?"

His outrage chilled when he saw nothing but grim faces all around. Dan's hard stare encouraged Tyler to lift the weapon again. Before the clip emptied, he'd blown up another chunk of wall and left a line of bullet holes. He checked the spent launch casings. They all looked normal. "What the hell are these?"

"Sabotage," Dan said. "Custom loads in the housings. The explosive squibs penetrate standard body armor. Our two renegades have been in town since Wednesday running Bureau and CAF unit inspections. Other than twenty short-clip pistols from the hotel extra hires, there isn't a round in the building we can trust."

The uniform on the left said, "Central insisted on those inspections."

"Fake orders, to go with the dummied IDs. Prepped months ago, I'm sure." Dan stood up and flexed his arm. "You've vetted my credentials. You know you can't jump high enough to go over my head. No weapons. No more innocents get mowed down."

He glowered impartially at all of them. "Those damned screenings had put everyone on edge. If we released a mob of angry, frightened civilians into a hall full of touchy, adrenaline-pumped professionals—the only reason we're not already hip-deep in massacred VIPs is lying on the floor over there. You owe him a medal if he lives through this."

"There are over four hundred people in that room," said one of the suits. "Without access to stun weapons we don't have the personnel to control them if they stampede."

The angry uniform said, "If you'll just cede jurisdiction, to us then we could—"

"No," snapped one suit, and the other said, "If you'll detach your people to us, then we could form a decent mob wall to channel them. Or you could declare the false alarm, open all the outer doors, let them spill onto the sidewalk."

"Before even running a sniffer? Are you out of your mind? Besides, surrendering to local command violates at least a dozen federal statutes and safety regs. Stop stonewalling. There are people in there who need medical attention."

People in there. Not Carl out here.

A strange feeling of detachment seeped through Tyler's body like icy water. His numb hand reached for the pistol still on the table, and he watched his fingers flip the safety catch and aim the muzzle upward.

The fourth dart was explosive. Everybody stopped talking. Dust sifted slowly down from the ceiling. Tyler said, "Line the walls with a nice, unarmed gauntlet to slow the flow. CAF jurisdiction on one side, Bureau on the other. Appeal to everybody inside to help their neighbors, and open one set of doors. What is so hard about this? Get it over with, unless you want people to start dying."

Another stray bit of ceiling fell. One of the suits stirred uneasily and started giving orders over a radio. Two of the three uniforms went hurrying away.

Dan removed the pistol from Tyler's hand and popped the magazine. "That's enough demonstrating, I think."

Tyler belatedly realized his last statement had sounded a lot like a threat. Then the rank insignia made an impression. He'd just held two CAF colonels, a CSB sector captain, and their aides at gunpoint.

Five seconds later, he threw up. Dan was holding a waste-basket ready, so Tyler was willing to forgive him for laughing. Later, when the EMTs took Carl out the door still breathing, with Alison smiling through tears as she jogged alongside the gurney—later Tyler even started to feel good about himself.

Mostly he felt tired, too tired to argue with the medics who only allowed Alison to climb into the ambulance with Carl. After the vehicle pulled away, Tyler sat on the edge of a planter near the lobby doors to watch the show.

Once the seriously hurt were evacuated, the walking wounded were released. A bedraggled parade of injured partygoers was escorted to hospital vans by solicitous Bureau personnel. Lights and shouting marked the location of the press line beyond the street barriers. Their ranks were backed by spectators who sounded thrilled to be part of a major news event. Some of the guests decided they were not too tired or too hurt to give interviews.

In time Dan came sauntering out the doors with the sling at a jaunty angle and his other hand in the trouser pocket of the bedraggled tux. He took in the view with a lopsided smile. "Helen Armstrong wanted to bring her son downstairs to wave at people. I left her to Neil's tender mercies, God help them both."

Tyler stifled a yawn. "All hail the conquering heroes."

"Speaking of heroes." Dan squinted at the street. "I don't suppose you know where Parker is? When he and Justin go missing in a crisis, things tend to blow up."

———

JUSTIN KNEW HIS LIMITS. He could only push damaged joints and muscle so far before they gave out. Sprinting was on the wrong side of the line. He could jog if he was careful, but speed invari-ably resulted in disaster. When he was angry, however, he stopped caring about limits. By the time he peeled himself off the sidewalk, he was in a towering fury.

His attackers had built up a healthy lead by then. Either he ran to catch up, or he let them disappear for good. He punched up the power and sprinted after them.

He was still a block behind them when his left heel hit wrong and popped. Sanity returned on a hot rush of alarm as he pitched forward. He tucked into a ball to take the impact on his shoulder and back. Momentum bled off in a bouncing somersault that ended against a stone planter. He lay on his back on cobbles and stared up at leafy tree branches and streetlights until his pulse dropped back to normal.

Some days sucked beyond belief.

His fingers brushed swollen skin when he groped for the ankle cuff, and he powered down fast, before he could talk himself out of it. Naomi and Serena caught up with him while he was lying there cursing through the aftermath.

Serena's black outfit somehow looked stylish with the bulky black jacket over it, but Naomi's silver dress was as thoroughly tattered as Justin's tux. They bent over him from either side, with Naomi's bright eyes peering out from beneath her bangs, and Serena frowning as she shook tangled hair off her face.

Serena said sadly, "He does look a little smooshed, Bao."

"Not twelve meters' worth." Naomi's hands were gentle on Justin's leg. "What did you do to yourself now?"

His nerves were insisting that someone had jammed a hot poker into his calf, but the foot flexed, more or less. He resisted the urge to power up again and take the edge off. He might need the boost later.

"I tripped," he admitted. "Help me up?"

"Why? We've lost them now." Naomi sacrificed a semide-tached sleeve to tightly wrap Justin's ankle. It hurt. He answered the question anyway.

"If they were going to hit the road, they could've stashed a car closer, and the rail station is behind us. They're heading for the waterfront. Ferries are nothing but floating traps, but if I was a criminal who wanted to go to ground fast, I might head for the port. It's only speculation, I know, but it makes sense."

Corporate-owned soil was foreign soil, as far as the Fed was concerned, if the business was based overseas, and cargo remained under the sovereignty of the port of origin until it left a company's yard space. Commercial territory was as inviolable as a country's embassy in most cases. If their quarry had a bolt hole on the international side, then they would think they were safe now.

The bastards were not safe. The port was closed. Justin remembered that, although not who had passed along the news. No ships would be leaving tonight. Some of the yards might be legally sacrosanct, but they weren't inaccessible. Not to him. "I can get us onto the property to search for them if you can get me there."

"We'll get you there," Serena said.

Naomi helped him to his feet. When he didn't fall over, Serena tucked herself under his other arm, and they took another step together.

NAOMI LIKED the office at the top of the marshaling tower. The big room's transparent walls would provide a comprehensive view of the operations during daylight. Now the workstation monitors inside outshone the security lights below. Data from various screens like the ones she was viewing cast ghostly reflections against the glass.

The port was a study in organized chaos. The tower kept watch over a snarled tangle of rail lines and roadways that wended between cargo gantries, loading cradles for overland haulers, tank farms, warehouses, and stacked shipping containers. The schematics alone were a marvel. Naomi assumed that the imagery was kept for investigative use. Real-time surveillance would be pointless when the place was active. The human eye could only watch so much at once. Hunting for two people amidst the idle equipment had been challenge enough for her.

Reviewing camera feeds from specific times and locations was always a tricky exercise. Placing her requests from a comfortable seat at a desk was a nice change. The list of current codes had made matters even easier. If not for all the techs pretending they weren't watching, the job would've been pure pleasure.

Naomi flexed a cramp out of her left hand. She couldn't blame her audience for being intrigued. If a group of shabby, barefoot visitors in tattered formal wear showed up on her doorstep in the middle of the night, then she would be curious too.

The man on duty at the gate where they'd entered hadn't asked a single question. After Justin had introduced himself and verifications were completed, the man had said, "Anything you need, sir, name it," and that was that.

So far, results had included a first-aid kit, cleaning wipes, and eager assistance from the staff up here. Naomi rubbed her hands on the soft gray sweatpants that had also been donated to the cause. She'd rolled up the bottoms to keep from tripping on them.

The gate attendant said they kept spare clothes on hand for everyday disasters like falls from ship decks or spills from broken chemical tanks. He'd even apologized when all of the boots were too big to fit her feet. Naomi wondered where a major diplomatic incident would fall on the disaster scale. She was afraid she might find out soon.

Justin and Serena stood together at the nearest window wall. Justin had replaced the ruined white tuxedo shirt with a red sweatshirt, and he was leaning against Serena. They made a good yin-yang, both of them dark-haired, Serena a little taller, Justin much broader across the shoulders, one all in black, the other in vivid scarlet. They didn't have a gram of common sense or caution between them.

Serena turned, straightening to attention. Her eyes sought Naomi's and narrowed thoughtfully. Then her lips curved up. Teeth showed.

"I have them," Naomi said for Justin's benefit.

He hobbled to the desk with Serena's help and perched on the corner. Naomi beckoned, and he lifted his left leg onto the desktop so that Naomi could check the swelling under the cold wraps. He'd definitely torn muscles in the calf. Not that Justin had asked her for an evaluation, any more than he'd followed instructions to keep the foot up.

His frown was enough to send the room's other occupants hurrying to various tasks that took them out of easy earshot. Naomi asked, "What's your magic, and where do I get some?"

Justin yawned. "Dawnstar's transport companies own a third of the space here, and I used to run Dawnstar, once upon a time. My title is emeritus something or other, and I'm still on some lists." He pointed at the surveillance board. "Show me the bastards."

Naomi hesitated. She did want revenge, and Serena's fulminating anger was still searing through her too, but she wanted survival and freedom even more. Someone had to be practical, and someone had to think about the future.

She gave Justin a long look. "First promise me we won't do anything stupid. Think about Alison and Tyler. Think about your son. Think about your family."

"I am," he said, sounding puzzled. "Why else would I be doing this? No one gets away with hurting me or mine."

A second after he'd turned to leave, Naomi realized that he'd meant he considered her and Serena family. That dizzy sense of dislocation swept over her again. Justin barely knew them.

Serena took her by the hand. "Silly Bao. Everyone with a heart wants to adopt you the instant they meet you. Now hurry up. We don't have all night."

"But—" Naomi swallowed her protests and let Serena drag her into trouble yet again.

Nothing would ever be the same, and tonight might still end in a disaster to end all disasters, but at least she had family again.

CHAPTER TWENTY-SIX

N AOMI BEGAN WORRYING ABOUT the stupid parts of the
plan when Justin and Serena piled into a little yard car that
the yard minions had commandeered. Then she saw the figure
waiting in the shadows a few meters away, and life was suddenly
perfect.

She was standing barefoot in a wet, fishy intersection between
aisles of triple-stacked metal shipping containers, but she couldn't
think of a single place on Earth she would rather be. If she hadn't
been so giddy with happiness, then the sentimentality of the
thought would've disgusted her.

Parker off-loaded a full rucksack into the yard car as soon he
reached it. The little vehicle had two bucket seats in front, but
Serena and Justin were on one of the two benches in back that
doubled as cargo shelves. Justin moved his left leg to accommo-
date the bag. "How's Carl?"

"Hanging on." The duffle settled with a clank. Parker removed
two items, and Serena began handing others to Justin. Naomi
stopped watching them when Parker came around the car. He
lifted a shaking hand to brush her hair off her forehead, and then
he gathered her into a tight embrace, pulling her right off her feet.

She couldn't say she was surprised to see him, not when a murmur of *where* had joined the whisper of *stay* while she was working earlier, not when Justin had coordinated the man's arrival here. She still thought she might dissolve from sheer happiness in that moment.

It wasn't the hug itself that made her melt inside, although it did feel lovely. It wasn't the weaponry Parker had brought, although that might come in handy. It wasn't even relief. It was the shoes Parker held in one hand.

He had brought her a pair of shoes that fit. That one gesture reduced Naomi to a puddle of bliss. Parker set her down and smiled. "Do you want a white picket fence?"

"A what?" She worked her feet into the comfortable slip-ons Alison had purchased for her an eternity of four days ago. "I want a hot bath, a whole lot of what Serena calls body-bumping, and then a month of sleep. After we dish out a little payback. What would I do with a fence?"

"Carl's joke." Parker bent his head to touch his lips to hers. "Ask him later."

There *would* be a later. Resolve tasted like steel against Naomi's teeth, and *stay* was still rippling along under Parker's every breath. Naomi ran her hands down his arms, chasing away pain and fatigue with her fingertips. She caught his wrists and held them, added *please* to his ferocious *stay*. She had no idea whether it would reach Carl, but it couldn't hurt.

Justin said, "The kissing and the hugging do not make the soulful silent staring any less aggravating from my perspective. If you were wondering."

Serena's voice overrode Parker's snort of acknowledgment. "There's only bang ammo in here. Bang ammo shouts, and that makes Red Dog howl, and then I can't keep everyone leashed, and my skin is already itchy. Bad-bad-bad-bad-bad."

"Shit." Justin struggled upright. "Keep your clothes on. Clothes on. Hear me?"

The wildness in Serena's eyes subsided. "I hear you."

Parker took the pistol and shook his head. The weapon was for him, not her. Then he pointed his chin at Justin. "Final rundown. Sneak and snag is optimal, bang and bury as a backup. You on point, Serena on sweep, me on the back door in case they bolt, Naomi on systems. Right?"

Justin stared at him long enough that Naomi wondered if he'd gone blank, but then he said in a dead-soft voice, "Are you sure you want the back door?"

Parker's arms tensed around Naomi's waist. His hands shook. Retribution mattered more than his personal satisfaction. "Barely up for firearms. Can't punch, can't take hits. Your plan, your lead."

Justin nodded.

Naomi bit her lip. Calling his strategy a plan was generous. Their quarry had gone to ground with a Chinese special-market shipper whose inventory included artworks and other expensive commodities. The agents were in a locked warehouse with only two doors, and the warehouse was guarded by two sentries inside a four-meter perimeter fence loaded with alarms and cameras. The company had insurance riders on file stating that their personnel trained with firearms and enjoyed legal immunity.

Sneaking in would have a low probability of success even if they took days to prepare. Justin wanted to walk in the front door and improvise from there. The plan's only redeeming value was that if they died in the attempt, then any affront to a nation whose economy underwrote a substantial chunk of the Fed budget would be minimal.

Parker slung on an armor-lined jacket, strapped the slug pistol into an integrated holster, then added a dart pistol and an ammunition belt from the rucksack. Naomi wondered if he was insane too, and Parker raised an eyebrow at her as if she'd shared that thought aloud. He didn't see Naomi leaving, which any sane person would've done already.

"They don't get away," she said, and he kissed her again.

THEY CROSSED a line on the pavement: hatched red and blue on one side, striped red and gold on the other. Justin said, "Welcome to China, everybody."

It came out hoarse, and cold sweat trickled down his back. Serena nestled closer inside the circle of his left arm. She had his right hand pinned against her chest, and her heart was beating a fast, feathery rhythm against his wrist.

"Now?" she asked. "Done with zeroing?"

When Justin nodded, she ran her other hand down his leg to the power cell and notched up the output. The gesture felt intimate, even though the relief was minimal.

Naomi brushed back wispy black bangs with one hand as she glanced back from the driver's seat. Justin braced himself for the question he knew was coming.

For the fourth time in as many minutes Naomi asked, "What if this doesn't work?"

"It will work. Drunk and famous goes a long way. When I throw a tantrum, people let me into places to shut me up while they call the cops. Look at us. Me looking like three days into a two-day binge, two sexy women, and an expensive bodyguard? We're halfway in already."

He leaned back and smoothed down the Mercury logo on the front of the red sweatshirt. He undoubtedly looked like shit after zeroing out an hour's worth of pain relief. Parker was imposing, with his scowl on his face and his arms crossed to hide his shaking hands. Serena was a fashion-plate soldier with the armor jacket loose over the close-fitting dress.

Naomi frowned, still doubtful, and Justin lost his patience. "If it doesn't work then I'll power up, break in, and beat everyone unconscious with my bare hands—or drive them out and let Parker shoot them dead. Impossible to cover up, possibly fatal for them, and likely to provoke a war, but it will work. I'd rather bring them back alive and in secret if we can."

That silenced the objections, even as it raised inner doubts. If he punched someone to death tonight, it wouldn't be by accident.

Parker turned to catch his eyes. "No hesitation, Justin. No analyzing, no negotiating. Take them down."

Justin glanced at the dried blood beneath Parker's nails. His own anger rose to the challenge, fresh and cold and powerful. "I promise," he said. "One way or the other, they go down."

Parker's jaw worked, and he nodded.

Naomi drove right up to the fence surrounding their destination. Barely five meters separated it from the warehouse, and a tiny, weather-shielded glass guard station stood empty by the locked gate. A security light shone from a pole, illuminating a sign with the company name and a long list of warnings in Chinese and English. Deep shadows skirted both sides of the building, which looked big enough to house a couple of midsized planes or a lot of merchandise. Containers loomed high and close on both sides outside the fence.

Naomi said, "Where are the guards? I could jump to the peak of the roof from outside the fence without breaking a sweat."

"And then you would trip alarms," Serena said. "The board is inside the building, not the gatehouse, yes? You have to get in, to get in."

They continued to discuss irrelevant defenses. Justin checked the remote sensor Parker had brought down from the hotel room for him. He didn't have internal schematics for this building, but he knew the yard routines. There should've been at least four targets on the blank screen: the agents, plus two sentries. He could only place two people inside the space visually occupied by the building.

Parker frowned at the imagery too, then hopped off the car to peer into the gatehouse. He went tense, and Justin felt an uneasy chill watching Serena and Naomi both stiffen at the same time.

Parker reported that the weapons locker was open and empty and the floor was bloody.

The agents had taken out the guards. Either they'd slid so far into paranoia that they dared leave no one at their backs, or the sentries had objected to something and been declared obstacles. Whatever the explanation, the result was that the two people in that building hadn't gone to ground so much as they had bunkered up for a last stand.

Justin considered the way Neil McAllister's mind worked: mission objective above all. "Anyone who walks in there between now and Monday when the next freighter is due is at risk," he said. "Best we can do is take them out. Get us inside the gate, and then you and Serena should leave—in case it goes wrong."

Naomi pulled up the master codes from the file she'd copied in the yard tower and got to work on the gate lock. "Wouldn't you still prefer to avoid a messy international incident?" she said. "The warehouse will be locked. I'll get you inside and follow you in, and see what I can do about covering the retreat."

"It's too dangerous—" Justin stopped when Serena's arms tightened around him.

She said, "I don't care. What if you fall and need us to hold you up. If I stick close they shouldn't see me. I want to help. Naomi is good at this. We hunt together."

"Right." Parker added a rifle from the bag to the pistols in his arsenal, and then he pulled out two heavy vests as well. "We're all backing you, Justin. Deal with it. Now put on the damned protection for once. You aren't invulnerable. Wednesday proved that."

"Not this again. No. Not even if you use all your words. I have enough trouble moving without adding ten extra kilos I'm pretty sure I don't need."

Serena said, "Pretty sure," under her breath, worried.

Parker let it go. He didn't let Naomi get away with objecting. The other vest was dropped at her feet, and he waited, watching her, until she picked it up.

"Only to make you stop worrying at me," she said as she shrugged into it. "If I get killed because it slows me down or gets caught on something, then I will haunt you."

She yanked open the gate. "There. We're in. How much safe time left on the cameras?"

Justin checked the timer. "Under five minutes."

Parker went around the outside of the building. Naomi ran for the lock pad beside the big hangar-style doors. Justin powered up and followed her. The cessation of pain was a rush all its own, and his muscles all but hummed from the burst of energy. Serena kept a hand on his arm the whole time.

Less than a minute remained on the timer before Naomi stepped back and flapped her hands. "Ready?"

Serena petted Justin's arm in jerky little strokes. "Leashes tight. Muscles loose. Spice and quiet in my head. Full of ready."

"I'll take that as a yes," Naomi said. "As soon as you two are in, I'll get to the control interface, shut off remote alerts, and see what else I can do."

She pulled open the wicket door set into the right-hand sliding panel and went to her knees beside it. Nothing happened. No alarms went off, no shots were fired.

The interior was unlit. The high windows let in a minimal glow from the yard lights. The open floor was full of indistinct shapes that vanished into pitch blackness at the far end. Serena pulled IR glasses from inside her jacket, and Naomi produced a pair from a pocket in the sweatpants hidden by the hem of her dress.

Justin looked at his gear bag, a million miles away in the yard car, and sighed. Too late now. He still had the remote sensor for guidance. That would have to be sufficient.

He stepped inside. Interior bins were built along the side walls. Hoists and pulley systems dotted shadowy scaffolding overhead. The air was cool and carried faint odors of wood and herbs and chemicals.

The screen indicated that they would have to travel almost the full length of the building. He was calculating how long that would take when Serena came in through the door low and quick, locating him by touch before dropping to shelter behind him.

Light flashed before she got there.

The first shot hit Justin in the chest like a kick. The sensor unit went flying. The next bullet went humming past his ear before the sound from the first one registered, and the third took him low in the gut and knocked him off his feet, right over Serena's kneeling body.

His left leg slammed into the concrete floor under his full weight. Pain exploded through him and momentarily annihilated consciousness.

He awoke with his cheek against the floor and his breath sobbing in his chest. He managed to silence himself, but he had a newfound sympathy for animals in traps who gnawed off their own limbs. Not even the burns had hurt when he was running under full power like this.

A pale form flashed past in the shadows. Naomi sprinted across the dim warehouse floor, dodging in a zigzag toward a bank of small lights hanging on the far wall. Her right hand was pressed to her hip below the vest. Darkness stained the dress fabric around her fingers.

A flurry of gunshots followed her, immensely loud. She stumbled and fell into the shadows. Serena made a low noise like a howl on mute. She was glued to Justin's back now, hands gripping his shoulders tight.

He hoped that his body was shielding her from the shooters, and he covered one of her hands with one of his, while he evaluated his damages by touch with the other.

There were holes torn in fabric and sore spots beneath, but the only damp spot was on his shoulder, where Serena's fingers were gripped tight. Justin turned to press his lips to her skin and tasted salt: her tears, not his blood.

"Not shot," Justin whispered. "Bulletproof for sure. Did you spot them? Please say you did."

He had seen only brightness, not direction.

Serena's hands trembled. "Sure? Not pretty sure? They saw me and Bao, not you, but it flashed, it was bang ammo, rifle ammo, loudloudloudloud, and Bao's bleeding hurt. I need you whole. Naomi needs us whole."

"Shh." They might be invisible, but experts could target by sound. Justin brought Serena's shaking hand to his lips and breathed against her palm. "Bad guys first, then Naomi. Focus for me. I hurt my leg again. Can you get me to them?"

"Yes." The word was a vicious hiss. Serena planted a kiss on the back of Justin's neck and got him upright, and she stayed right behind him all the way across the warehouse floor. Pride was barely enough to keep him from sobbing out loud with every limping step.

Maybe he could get Carl to knock him out before he powered down this time if he promised he wouldn't throw a fit. If Carl were still alive to accept a promise. If Justin were alive to give a promise. Because if he'd gotten Naomi killed then Parker would cut off his balls with a dull knife and watch him bleed to death.

Too many ifs. Justin stopped adding them up. Serena pressed even closer as they reached the end of the huge room. A hall with a cheerful lit EXIT sign at the end was centered between two large partitioned rooms.

The door to the one on the left was cracked open, and from this close Justin could see the weapons. The muzzles were aimed past them, at the distant shadows.

Serena snickered, a sound she tried to muffle against Justin's neck. Then she began counting almost inaudibly, "Five, four, three, two—"

"What are you doing?" Justin whispered.

The warehouse lights came up bright and full overhead, banishing every shadow. Serena shoved Justin forward with enough force to pitch him sprawling through the doorway. He crashed into the jamb, stumbling headlong, blind with pain. As he rolled past the portal, he hit someone else who was staggering and cursing.

They landed in a tangle, and punches started raining down on Justin. He got one arm around his opponent's throat, locked it place with the other hand, and buried his face against his own shoulder as best he could.

Then he ignored everything else in the universe until long after the other person's heels stopped kicking and the body went limp. He lost a fair amount of hair in the process, but he won the fight, and his adversary was still breathing when it ended.

His opponent also felt female and smelled like strong musky perfume. Justin pushed her away and rolled onto his stomach so he could wipe sweat and hair and blood out of his eyes. His vision wouldn't clear. He couldn't catch his breath.

Something made a horrendous tearing noise nearby. Fear coursed through him. That gave him enough energy to raise himself on his arms. They shook under the strain. There was motion in the red haze. "Serena?"

"Ha. You *are* there. Wait, I'll bring you the tape."

Blinking washed away the blood and sweat for him to see again. Serena stepped over the body of an unconscious man to get a better grip on his ankles, and tore a tape strip off its roll. She glanced over her shoulder in Justin's general direction and smiled. Her eyes glittered. The expression was triumphant and utterly pitiless. "Mine's alive. Yours?"

"Yes," Justin said. "We won. Fantastic. Also confusing. Please tell me what just happened. And tie this one up for me. I'm not feeling coordinated."

The room was set up as an office with lockboxes along one wall and a workstation in the corner. There were also two sets of bunk beds, a kitchenette, and an open door revealing a no-frills bathroom: housing for crew members who didn't want to stay aboard ship but couldn't legally leave the port.

Serena got the other agent tied up, pulled blankets off bunks, and wrapped up both captives. "Bao squeezed the warehouse systems," she said. " 'Lights up, be ready in five,' she said, so we were and they weren't. Clever Naomi." She frowned at the air near Justin's left shoulder. "You sound hurt. You are bulletproof. You *said*."

Justin said carefully, "I am, but Naomi isn't. Bleeding hurt, you said."

"Why would she be bulletproof?" Serena's brows quirked up. "Oh. That. You are bulletproof like a rock. She caught a ricochet coming past us. One gouge. Her vest got the rest. Parker is patching her up so we can go home. After we give Dan his presents, I mean. It's over. Why are you hiding from me? Did I hurt you?"

Justin gave his tired arms a rest and put his head down too. His leg was on fire, his head was throbbing, and his body refused to stop quaking. Queasy shivering couldn't be a good sign, not when he was already running at full power.

Serena raised her chin and scowled. "I am trying, Bao. I can't find him. My head is loud and crowded and I want a hug full of quiet and spice, but he's hiding and won't let me help, and I think maybe I broke him."

One last baffling detail resolved itself in Justin's mind. "Ear-bug. You were talking to Naomi the whole time."

Serena's eyes widened a little, and she stalked two steps closer, setting her feet down as tentatively if she were traversing a minefield. "I'm talking to Bao, yes, and to Parker, and I'm sorry I threw you, only there were two and I couldn't take them both. I knew you could take one, and you did, and now it's all over, and we need to go."

She looked to the side and said, "Bao, help."

Parker and Naomi came into the room leaning heavily against

each other. Naomi kept one hand on her hip, and the bloodstains on her skirt made Justin wince. Parker held her around the waist and looked around the room with a narrow, cold smile.

Naomi said, "Strangest commando team ever," and Parker laughed, a sharp surprised sound.

He got to work hauling the captives elsewhere, and Naomi approached Serena with her face scrunched up in a frown. "Sweetie, how can I help? I can't see him either." She glanced around the room. "Justin, we need to hurry if you want to get away clean. What is your problem?"

"Do you want the full list, or will a summary do?"

"Ha." Serena pounced, landing on her knees next to him. "Found you."

Her fingers touched here and there, and Justin shuddered when she rested her hand on his ankle, near the power switch. He knew Serena couldn't see him, but she seemed to be looking right at his face.

"You aren't scared of me, you're scared of hurting," she said with an air of revelation. "Oh."

"Right. It is going to hurt a lot."

"I promised I would hold you up. I can do it."

"Yes, you can." Justin found the strength to roll onto his side, stretched down to put his hand over Serena's. One last deep breath, because he was going to need it. "But you're wrong about one thing. Nothing's over. We're only getting started."

AFTERMATH

There was a room with green paneled walls, a door at one end and a window over a wide couch at the other. There was a big bed with colored lights on side rails and a recliner lounge nestled beside it. For some unmeasured time it was a place of serene nonexistence. Except for a thin, tiny thread woven of *hold on* and *heal*, he might've let himself sink below tranquility into oblivion, but the anchor held him.

Shredded pieces of *self* slowly drifted together in the void. The world solidified around Carl in quiet darkness. His mind felt unsettled. He let it wander while his eyes watched a lighter rectangle slowly emerge from shadows. That was a window, behind a drawn shade. The sun was coming up.

Someone was holding his hand in a loose grip that tightened when a loud noise warbled nearby. A smooth voice beside him said, "Jesus, Tyler. That took ten years off my life. Isn't that tone for emergencies?"

"Yeah." The warble stopped. A figure rose in silhouette against the window, and screen-glow illuminated boyish features. "Parker's being an idiot." He opened the hall door to a brighter light.

"Hi, Allie. Can't you or Naomi stop him? It's pointless for him to come now. He pulled a double shift yesterday with the exam, and we'll be home in a few hours. Pete and I can handle the exit—"

The door closed. A headache sprang to life when Carl tried to make sense of Tyler's words, and his palms went clammy with sweat. He clung to the stability of touch.

Pete pried his fingers loose. "Yes, I know, all the loud confusion makes you twitchy. Hang on. I'll get you some light and air."

The blinds lifted on a hazy sky, and the window squeaked open, delivering a cool draft of fresh air. Pete turned back. Carl's heart clenched around feelings that he could not put into words. Pete's eyebrows rose. "Hello, sunshine. You recognize me. No wonder Eddie's excited."

Pain fluttered behind Carl's eyes, thoughts settling unevenly into gaps.

"Hey there, take it easy." Pete hurried back to the bed, slid his hands up Carl's arms and squeezed. Pressure communicated concern. "Take it slow. Are you hurting?"

Carl shook his head and let his expression do the talking. Pete gave him a long look from tawny eyes set in healthy bronzed skin, "My face and hands? Healed. Looks like you're oriented to person and events. Nice. If you can ace the full set, I'll give you a cookie."

It was couched as a joke, but Pete was in deadly earnest about wanting to run a mental status drill. Carl considered his own fragile, silent shakiness and pushed himself upright to sit on the edge of the bed. His joints were stiff from inactivity, and he felt as wobbly as a newborn lamb, but he didn't *hurt*.

He'd been shot. He should hurt.

Agony ghosted in memory, and he rubbed his chest under a soft blue tee shirt that had seen better days. His fingers traced tender new divots and lines, and surprise jarred his voice loose at last. "Not even scabbed? How much time am I missing?"

Pete's face went stiff as he sank onto the lounge. "Six weeks.

You're cleared for release from surgical rehab at noon today. Jesus wept. Start at the top. Full name."

Tyler returned near the end of the evaluation. He sat next to Pete and listened with his phone in his hands and his blue eyes as big as saucers. The astonishment radiating from both of them scraped Carl's nerves raw. "What is so amazing about watching me count backwards and recite word groups?"

Pete said, "After watching you shuffle around in a docile, donkey-brained fog of silence for a month and a half? Everything."

"What happened? I know I got shot ..." Carl followed fragments of memory into a moment of chaos. Light stabbed into his eyes, noise shrilled in his ears, pressure squeezed his face and chest, unbearably heavy. He flinched back to the present with the answer. "Allergic reaction?"

Pete nodded. "You crashed before your chart loaded. The emergency staff did the right thing, considering, but getting you onto a ventilator and countering the effects took time."

Oxygen deprivation slaughtered brain cells. Carl unclenched his fists, laid his hands on his knees, and breathed carefully against rising fear. Words wouldn't come. He shook his head.

Pete's voice went soft. "This isn't the first time you've pulled a Lazarus, Carl, and full recall is a great sign. You may hit some bumpy patches with ego integration, but you'll put the pieces back together if anyone can."

The reassurance came wrapped in secondary messages that Carl wasn't up to translating, but desperation eased its grip on his throat. "You come up with the most atrocious mixed metaphors."

Tyler said, "Justin started collecting the worst ones." He broke into a broad smile when Carl scowled at him. "Wow, look at that frown. You are back. Allie will weep. She cries when she's happy. We filed a five-year marriage contract, by the way. In case you don't remember about that either."

Carl's chest started to ache along with his head, and fatigue washed over him. "I imagine I have a lot of catching up to do."

"We talked to you all the time, but you clearly never listened. Not important. No one will mind going over everything again. Captain Chaos will be showing up any time now, so you can start with him. I guess I should call Justin and the Terror Twins so we can throw a real coming-home party too."

Pete said, "Tyler, your idea of conversation is exhausting. Go inflict it on the nurses, please. There's no point in waiting until noon. Finish the paperwork and intercept Eddie. Invoke my name with him if necessary. Use the words *quiet* and *slow*. We'll meet you back at the house."

"You're the pro," Tyler said cheerfully. "Quiet and slow. Catch you later."

Once he was gone, Pete bustled around the room, opening panels and pulling out things that Carl supposed must belong to him. The headache and the other pains melted away, and he was content to rest and observe. There was more silver in Pete's hair than he remembered, but every action affirmed a healing sense of purpose.

Carl said, "What will you do for fun if I'm not taking up all your time?"

His tone earned him a frown. "Don't even joke about relapsing for my sake. It was good to have a reason to get out of bed in the mornings, I won't deny that."

Details started to bother Carl. "'Donkey-brained' doesn't rate full-time monitoring, not in a rehab facility, not if I grasp the meaning. Tyler mentioned shifts."

"Your brain activity skyrocketed when people you knew were nearby. The functional scans are fascinating. Alison set up the buddy rotation to keep Eddie from sitting watch 24-7." Pete grinned. "And you weren't docile with strangers. The nurses stopped objecting to us after the first shower. Speaking of which—"

Carl took the hint and the clean clothes he was handed into a bathroom hidden behind one of the panels. Habitual routines were exhausting. He took his time, avoided the mirror, and ignored the way his muscles protested even minor exertions.

Pete offered him a sympathetic smile as a reward for finishing. "Let's get out of here before you fall over. Eddie and Tyler handled the release forms. You're a free man."

The view outside the rehabilitation center was a shock. A hazy gray sky stretched all the way down to a flat horizon. The institutional huddle of buildings guarded a landscaped area thick with gold flowers. Dry grass moved in a stiff, steady breeze. In the distance dust rose high over fields being harvested. There were no mountains in sight, no evergreens, and precious few trees of any kind.

It was emphatically not Seattle.

Pete got six steps farther along the sidewalk to the transit garage before he noticed that Carl had stopped. His face was twisted with chagrin when he turned back. "Christ Almighty, I forgot that you wouldn't know where—"

Carl stopped him with a gesture. "I know *where*, more or less. You can skip ahead to why, how, and when we got to Middle-of-Nowhere Nebraska."

"Later, I think." Pete squinted at him. "After you have a nap. Come on, Doctor Grumpy. One step at a time."

Carl took a deep breath of air that was ripe and dry and full of life. One step at a time. He could do that.

NAOMI ENJOYED HELPING Alison in the kitchen, even when she felt like she was being steered from task to task by an energetic, dark-haired tugboat. Alison seemed to enjoy her company too, so Naomi felt a stab of worry when she found herself being pushed right out of the kitchen, down the main hall to the front door of the farmhouse.

"Did I do something wrong?" she asked.

"Vacant stare alert," Alison said with a smile. "I'll finish lunch. You sit and concentrate on keeping Captain Chaos calm so that he doesn't scare Tyler to death."

Naomi retreated to the cushioned porch swing Justin had installed the second week of their residence here. She was still getting used to the way everyone took her for granted. Alison regularly came to her to determine if Serena or Parker were in approachable moods. It was odd to be accepted as normal. Then again, they were sharing a roof with a man who turned invisible. It did stretch the definition of "normal" a long way.

That roof sat on a rambling old building big enough to house twice their number. Justin said the bones of it were two centuries old, but it smelled like fresh paint, and Naomi felt guilty about wearing shoes on the shiny floors.

The yard was pretty in an overgrown way. Uneven ranks of trees and untidy evergreen shrubs provided a welcome windbreak around a wide stretch of lawn that was currently blanketed in falling leaves. Past that, fields showed the faded gold of ripe crops.

She let her eyes rest on the scenery and tickled at Parker until he stopped jangling her nerves. The connection between them hummed, growing stronger every day. Every day he filled more of her heart.

Now something else nibbled at the edges of her attention, something fragile and shadowy. "Dark sky," Serena called that, even while she still insisted she didn't *feel* it, she only saw it. Naomi hugged her knees to her chest, setting the swing rocking. "Hello, Carl," she whispered. "I hope you'll like it here. I do."

The ever-present breeze was a cool touch against her face. She wondered, not for the first time, what that wind would feel like when it turned brutal cold in winter.

There was no going back. Some days grief was still a fresh,

sharp pain. Some days she felt lost and empty inside. Most days she was too busy adjusting to the marvels of this strange new life to worry about anything else.

The overnight relocation from Seattle here to Justin's childhood home had been one of the first and biggest surprises. They'd moved as soon as Carl was stable, after a confrontation involving Serena, a reporter, and a hospital chair. Lincoln had a top-notch medical campus, thanks to certain past donations, and three hundred hectares of personal property made an excellent privacy shield.

Every time Naomi checked the news, she was glad to be half a continent away from the west coast. Members of the dissident group claiming responsibility for the Day Two bombing were still being rounded up, and raids of Ghost labs up and down the coast were getting major press coverage. The CSB was also arresting people who had aided and abetted their unsanctioned agents. Those operations were being handled much more quietly.

The situation was a sobering lesson in the way reality could be twisted for corporate and political ends. The CSB's Central unit had shrouded the confusion around the charity ball in a credible narrative that hid unsavory truths. The false biothreat alarm was acknowledged as a cover for a terror conspiracy, but the rest of the story had no resemblance to reality as Naomi knew it. The Chinese government was keeping mum, and the financial repercussions had been minimized, although various stocks were still going up and down like roller coasters.

Official news outlets polished the cover story and gave it a suitably pretentious name, calling it the Restoration Plot. Naomi had signed a strict confidentiality agreement without regrets. History could fend for itself.

Some journalists always suspected cover-ups and conspiracies, and careers were made or broken over this kind of story. Those who enjoyed the bright glare of fame were still cashing in their celebrity points.

Justin had to threaten demanding full custody of Ryan if Helen didn't stop grandstanding. The warning proved remarkably effective. Helen had done an immediate one-eighty, and now she minimized the significance of Justin's presence at every opportunity. They got the occasional intrusive call and trespasser, but the media circus stayed on the coast. By the time Justin's visitation rights went into effect at the end of the year, the world might have forgotten about him and his son. Naomi hoped so. She liked the tranquility here.

Thumping percussion was audible from the back lawn where Serena was dragging Justin through the daily exercises for his healing leg. Naomi delivered an unspoken warning to keep the man on his feet, not his back. Then she mentally poked Parker again because he was getting twitchy. Again.

Within five minutes of Parker's arrival with Tyler, Alison escorted them both to the backyard to join Justin and Serena. Naomi was deemed the only one who understood *quiet* and *slow* well enough to stay behind and greet Carl.

She had to sit on her hands when he unfolded himself from the passenger seat of Pete's car. Doing nothing was difficult when any client was exhausted and hunched in pain, and Carl was more than a client now.

Naomi let him get as far as the top of the stairs on his own. Then she put her foot on the floor to stop the swing's motion and patted the cushion in invitation. One side of Carl's mouth drew up. He raised one hand to comb back his hair. "You aren't as scared of me now. I like that."

There were bruised smudges under his blue eyes and hollows in his cheeks. Naomi patted the seat again. "Respiratory and occupational therapy every other day. Plenty of touching, plenty of time to get comfortable with you. Sit. I won't bite."

Pete came past with luggage in hand. "Naomi, Dan pinged me while I was driving. One of his rats is chewing its own tail again, and he wants a consult. Dr. Grumpy is all yours. He slept on the drive, so there's a good chance he'll retain facts. Can you ease him up to speed before hitting him with the welcome wagon?"

Naomi nodded, smiling when she sensed a flutter of irritation from Carl that didn't make it to his face. Something must've been visible, because Pete said quickly, "Sorry, Carl. I got used to you not listening. Bad habit."

"Horrible habit." The swing sank under Carl's weight. "You're consulting with the Bureau?"

"Did I learn nothing from your example, you mean? I needed distraction, and the CSB needed to defuse and debrief a pair of lunatics with booby-trapped minds. It's a single short-term contract. Call it my therapy."

The porch wasn't silent once he was gone, not with the trees rustling in the wind and the noise from the nearby construction, but it was calm. Carl abandoned the swing after a few minutes and paced to the railing at the far end of the porch, staring at the view once he finally got there.

"It takes me forever to think things," he said in a sour voice. "When Pete said lunatics, he meant the agents Dan and Neil were hunting, didn't he? Who caught them? When? How did we get here? I can't remember anything. Have I asked those questions a hundred times?"

"No. You never spoke at all. I'd forgotten how amazing you sound." Naomi wished she knew if there were topics she should avoid. "Serena said you were hibernating until new feathers grew in, for what that's worth. I can fill in the blanks for you now, if you want."

Carl turned and leaned back on the railing. His eyes warmed, and he crossed his arms over his chest. "Please."

Naomi told him about the aftermath of the party and the cover stories as well. The talking made her mouth dry, and Carl started to droop. She brought him to the kitchen while she explained the strategic retreat to Nebraska and answered questions about his convalescence. By the time he was seated on one of the benches at the big wooden kitchen table, he knew all the news.

Pete's voice drifted down the back stairwell, but otherwise the house was silent. Naomi checked outside. The lawn was empty now, but the door into the restored barn that served as a garage was open, and she identified the inner telltales of Serena's favorite game; they were doing a feral cat count.

Lunch was waiting on the kitchen counter under lids and wrappers: vegetables, sauces, breads, a noodle salad and brown cookies. Fresh coffee sat in a carafe. More importantly, the tea pot was prepped.

Carl smoothed a palm over the tabletop and frowned at the plate of food Naomi placed in front of him. "It doesn't make sense. I can't understand what those maniacs hoped to accomplish at the end."

"Don't try," was the best advice Naomi could offer. The cookies were ginger. She took three and started a pot of tea. "I think they're crazy, not that anyone asked me. They'd made most of the arrangements for the Biovitel frame before they lost their clearances and legal powers. They say they stuck around to finish the job because they needed a success to persuade their clients to extract them, but I think they wanted to see bloodshed. The part where survivors went home and spread malware—they knew that plan was blown, and they started the panic anyway."

She probably wasn't supposed to know most of that information, but her room adjoined Pete's and shared ductwork. Sometimes she couldn't help herself.

Carl's eyes moved past her. "Ignoring basic security measures, or discreetly keeping her curiosity bump from constantly bumping you?"

Pete approached with a sheepish grin and checked on the steeping tea. "I admit nothing. Her assessment is solid. Malice was a driving motivator. So was pride. They're taking credit for anything they can dream up. At this point they're so far off the rails that the trick is figuring out what's fact and what's confabulation. All of it is brain-bending."

Naomi said, "What bends my brain is that I'll never even know their names. Whoever they were, whatever they did, it's all being erased. It gives me chills."

"It should." Carl poked at his noodles with the carrot. "Normally that would be my cue for a rant about institutional abuse of power, but I'm too tired right now."

Silence fell. Pete poured himself a glass of tea and went to the back door. "Politics can wait. The party's here."

Soon the kitchen was full of bodies and noise and energy. Carl fielded hugs from everyone but Parker, who hung back in the doorway.

Alison got everyone else focused on moving dishes and food to the table, and Carl pinned his brother with an exasperated glare. "Really? Guilt? If you make me stand up and hit you right now, then I will beat the crap out of you as soon as I have the strength for it. Get over here."

Naomi closed her eyes, caught between Parker's relief and Carl's affectionate understanding, and the overload welled up as tears. Parker scooped her up on the way to the table, and Naomi ended up tangled in their embrace like a rag doll. Thought became both impossible and unnecessary.

Carl helped her sit down properly between the two of them, and Parker put his face in her hair, sighing against her ear. Joy sang in her heart.

Serena put a pitcher of water and glasses on the table. Then she bent over to sneak a kiss onto Carl's forehead before cuddling up next to him. Naomi laid her cheek against Carl's other shoulder and soaked it all in.

"All right, stop it." Justin sat down across from them, accepting a steadying hand from Pete. "My house, my rules. No long, soulful, silent group hugs or any other exclusionary behavior in the kitchen. It ruins my appetite."

He was too thin, and Naomi suspected that he avoided shaving because stubble minimized the pain-etched lines around his nose and mouth. He actually looked stern until he grinned, and then it was like the sun coming out on his face. "It's good to see all of you together, Carl."

"It's good to be all together," Carl put an arm around Serena. "When are you going back to Seattle?"

Justin leaned back to lift his left leg onto the bench. "To Seattle? Never. Allie misses the city, so Tyler's going to rack up a lot of rail time visiting her, but we'll work it out. Why?"

Alison said, "He's worried about imposing, Justin." She set down beer bottles in front of Justin, Pete, and Parker and backed away. "There. All comfy. You have to learn to survive without me someday. Time to start practicing. Discuss the future among yourselves. We're off to town."

She headed for the back door, capturing Tyler's hand in passing and tugging him outside after her. Naomi barely had a chance to wave before they were gone. Silence fell and quickly grew stifling.

"Future." Carl said the word as if it were a foreign concept. "Justin, what are you up to?"

"Convincing you that you're not imposing." Justin said. "I think. Look, I'm tired of the whole world watching me fade in and out. I'm building a new workshop out here. Parker says he can base anywhere, so I'm putting up bond for a corporate license for him. Stick around and help out."

Serena leaned across the table to steal a cookie off Justin's plate. "Birds need nests," she said solemnly.

"I have a house in Seattle," Carl said, but he didn't sound happy about it. "I don't need charity."

Naomi had the perfect retort for that. She leaned in. "That's a house," she said. "This is a home."

Carl looked down. Muscles trembled in his arm where it

pressed against Naomi, and she felt those feathery emotions soaring inside.

"I like the sound of that," he said.

The End

* * *

ABOUT THE AUTHOR

K. M. Herkes writes and publishes books that dance in the open spaces between science fiction and fantasy, specializing in stories about damaged souls, complicated lives, and triumphs of the spirit.

Professional development started with a Bachelor of Science degree in Biology and now includes experience in classroom teaching, animal training, aquaculture, horticulture, bookselling, and retail operations. Personal development is ongoing. Cats are involved.

When she isn't writing, she works at the Mount Prospect Public Library. She also digs holes in her backyard for fun, enjoys experimental baking, and wrangles butterflies.

Visit dawnrigger.com and check out extras like free short stories, story-inspired artwork, links to the author's media, and blog rants on life, the universe, and writing.

Lastly, subscribe to receive rare Dawnrigger Publishing email alerts and get an exclusive free short story just for signing up.

EXTRA: A BIT OF FUTURE HISTORY

From: "Enduring Legacies: Twenty-first Century Institutions Old & New"

The creation of Restoration Week and related civic holidays may prove to be the most enduring legacy of the New United Senate's first session. Other laws proposed in that historic meeting are endlessly critiqued and questioned, but the national festivals were adopted with enthusiasm and gain in popularity every year.

The meanings assigned to each day of Restoration have drifted from the original definitions over the years, but taken as a whole, the event provides a regular infusion of nationalism. All the national holidays are periodic reminders to this splintered confederation that—despite all our many differences—we are all citizens of the same union, and we do hold crucial beliefs in common.

The importance of this shared experience cannot be overstated. In many ways, Restoration Week's evolution and acceptance emphasizes how much deep, cultural change Restoration itself accomplished.

The visionaries who built the Restored United States government were idealists, but they were also practical. Their new nation was a splintered mess of polities as small as ten acres and as large as three fused "old states." All agreed that continued infighting would lead only to eventual barbarism, but few were willing to give an inch on matters of local doctrine. Rather than leave the idea of the greater good to grow or die at the whim of regional opinion, the New Constitution's writers etched pomp and circumstance into the new document along with stringent requirements for civic education. They deliberately promoted nationalism with the passionate fervor of true believers.

Reading the historical correspondence and memoranda reveals a delicious bit of irony: they never thought it would work. Never in their wildest hopes did they believe their cynical measures would become defining cultural touchstones. The record clearly shows that the nation's commemorative legislation has far outperformed the expectations of its framers.

They had good reason to doubt their ideas would ever gain traction. Traditions glorifying the State seldom outlast the founding generation—even when they are required by governments that wield far more local power than the Restored Republic does. No previous regime in history had successfully established its own rituals of blatant aggrandizement and self-interest.

No one could have predicted that this time, a weary populace traumatized by decades of conflict would embrace any excuse for a party, nor that those adults would agree to their children being indoctrinated in ideologies that might someday lead them to question their own upbringing. And yet, observation of Restoration Week has grown from its original minimal, meditative focus to become an annual economic juggernaut with global impact.

The right ideas came along at the just right time, they were delivered with polish and skill, and all the stars aligned. Restoration Week reigns supreme in these United States, and its social influence shows no signs of fading.

58209543R00207

Made in the USA
Columbia, SC
21 May 2019